For my daddy,
Thanks for taking such good care of us,
Lots of Love
Stuartje

Her Majesty's Yacht, Britannia

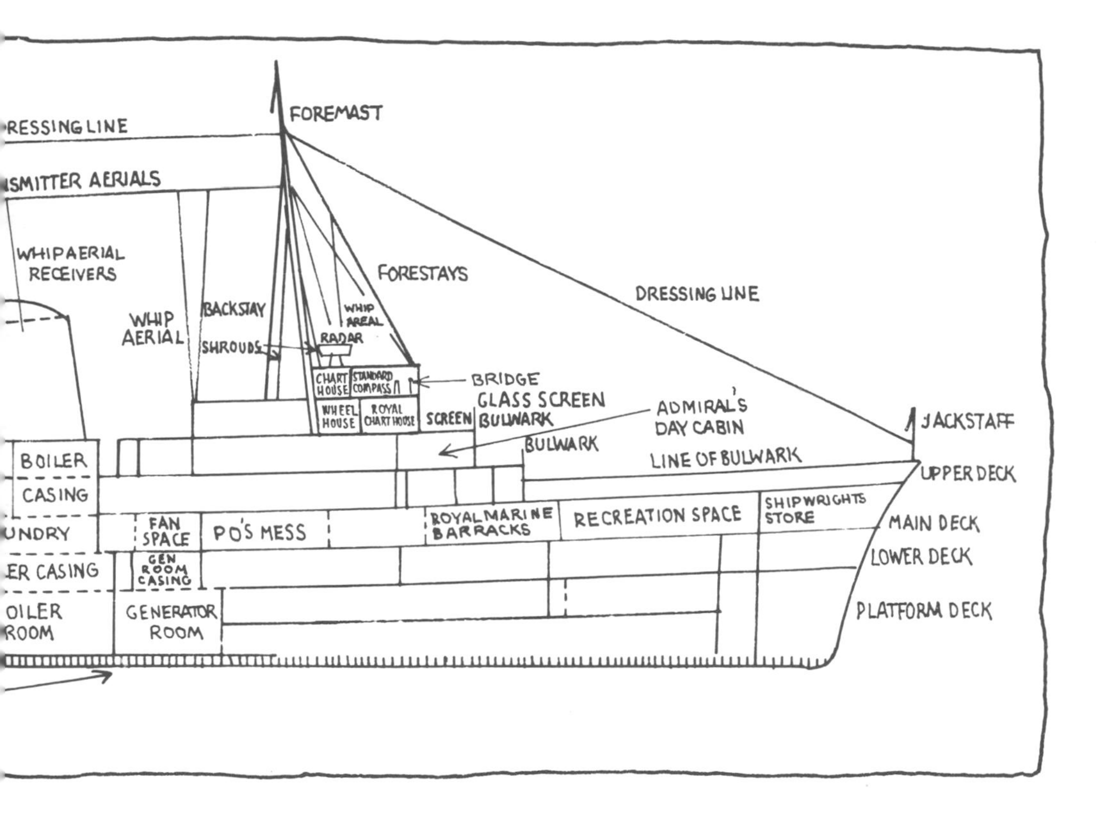

The Britannia Contract

Other books by Paul Mann

Prime Objective
The Beirut Contract
The Traitor's Contract
Season of the Monsoon

THE BRITANNIA CONTRACT

Paul Mann

Carroll & Graf Publishers, Inc.
New York

First Carroll & Graf edition 1993

Carroll & Graf Publishers, Inc.
260 Fifth Avenue
New York, NY 10001

Library of Congress Cataloging-in-Publication Data

Mann, Paul.
The Britannia contract / Paul Mann. — 1st Carroll & Graf ed.
p. cm.
ISBN 0-88184-933-2 : $21.00
1. Hijacking of ships—Middle East—Fiction. 2. Terrorists—Northern Ireland—Fiction. 3. Queens—Great Britain—Fiction. I. Title.
PS3563.A53623B75 1993
813′.54—dc20 93-7978
CIP

Manufactured in the United States of America

For Alexandra, the adventurer

Every subject's duty is the King's—
but every subject's soul is his own.

Henry V

Acknowledgments

The research and preparation for this book would not have been complete, and certainly nowhere near as enjoyable, were it not for the generous support and cooperation of the United States Navy. Special thanks are due to Captain Don Dill of the Department of the Navy, who expedited all queries and official visits with friendly dispatch. To Rear Admiral T. W. Wright and Captain Doyle J. Borchers of the aircraft carrier USS *Carl Vinson* and to all those other officers and men of Battle Group Charlie, not only for their on-board hospitality but for the patience and frankness with which they responded to all requests for information, some of which were undoubtedly impertinent. Their willingness to open doors and respond to questions was an impressive validation of the philosophy that there is strength in candor. I also wish to thank R.A.M. Seeger, MC, MCA, former commander of Britain's Special Boat Squadron; and Ralph Osterhout, founder and chairman of S-Tron and special adviser to the United States Chief of Naval Operations, for their invaluable contributions to my research into weapons and tactics employed by the maritime special forces of both the United Kingdom and the United States.

Contents

	Prologue	13
1.	The Boarding Party	19
2.	Scotch Mist	68
3.	No Place Like Home	106
4.	In the Path of the Winged Pig	147
5.	A Matter of Principle	181
6.	By Appointment to Her Majesty	213
7.	Reptiles Rising	254
8.	The Moving Finger	285
9.	Operation Scepter	335
10.	A Bloodied Crown	372
	Epilogue	439

Prologue

From a distance the house looked abandoned and incomplete. As though the builder had gone broke before he could finish it and it had become the haunt of bums and vandals. Now no one would want it. A gaunt, gray edifice, it stood alone on a scrubby patch of grass, dark and foreboding on a moonless night, like a child's haunted house. No lights burned in its rooms and there was no glass in its window frames. The only door still standing was a slab of raw pine at the front. There was no handle, no lock, and the door was wedged shut from the inside with a wooden post jammed against the dusty cement floor.

Inside, it smelled of dampness and dirt and its gloomy hallways whispered with unseen threats. A couple of rooms were furnished with bits and pieces that might have been scavenged from a dump: a crookback sofa with one arm missing, a Formica-topped kitchen table, a motley assortment of crippled chairs. There was no sink, no stove, no bathtub, no toilet. Only one room was occupied. An upstairs room at the back of the house. It was in this room, behind the only locked door, that the building's sole occupant waited. A tall, bony man in a plain navy-blue track suit. He sat on a cheap chrome-legged kitchen chair with a seat cushion in green marbled vinyl. His hands were tied behind him with plastic cord and his legs were bound to the chair at the ankles and knees. There was no sound. No movement. Only the silent coils of his breath misting in the chill night air. His captors had warned him that if he made any noise at all, he would be killed. He could still see them, black silhouettes crouched around him in the gloom, unnaturally still. Waiting.

He had no sense of time. It might have been only minutes but it felt like hours. The cold had begun to seep through his fleece-lined track suit and he shivered. He wished he had put on a thicker sweater before leaving home. But, he smiled ruefully, that was the nature of these things. They were impossible to predict. He shifted to ease an ache in his lower back. The chair creaked and he stopped. Rescue was coming, he knew. But it could be hours away. He tilted his head to see if he could pick up anything from outside, but there was nothing. Not even the sound of a cricket or a distant passing car. He felt a pang of irritation. He wished they hadn't taken his watch. He wouldn't have been able to see it with his hands tied behind his back, but it was a bit presumptuous all the same. He flexed his toes inside the thickly padded running shoes to keep the blood moving. The cord had not been tied tight enough to hurt. Only enough to stop him going anywhere without taking the chair with him and making a great deal of noise. But he had no intention of going anywhere. He sighed, stifled his annoyance, and looked around the darkened room again, trying to interpret the dark silhouettes. At first, when they had removed his blindfold, he had counted five guards. Now he thought he could see one more. He counted them again. There was one on each side, one behind his left shoulder, and two more on a sofa against the wall. He stared hard at an opposite corner, eyes straining through the gloom. He was right. There was a sixth man, propped awkwardly in the corner. As stiff and as silent as a shop-window dummy. Just like the others. And then he realized that that was exactly what they were. Department-store mannequins dressed in secondhand clothes.

There was a loud crash downstairs as the front door exploded inward. Shards of splintered pine ricocheted around the downstairs hall. The man upstairs froze. He knew exactly what he was supposed to do now. He was supposed to do nothing. Absolutely nothing. His life depended on it. He started to count the seconds down in his head . . . one thousand, two thousand, three . . .

The door to his room burst open and two liquid black shapes spilled inside and disappeared. There was a short, deafening blast as two Browning Hi-Powers opened fire at the same moment and a dozen rapid shots blended into a single percussive roar. The man in the chair flinched, bowed his head to his chest, and clenched his eyes shut. He heard the thwack of the bullets as they hit their targets and fragments of plaster spattered around the room like fine hail.

It stopped as suddenly as it had begun. A few seconds before, there had been nothing but silence. Then a short, terrifying burst of noise and violence. Now there was only silence again. And the ringing of gunfire in his ears.

"Are you all right, sir?"

The room filled with light and His Royal Highness, Prince Philip, Duke of Edinburgh and Consort to the Queen of England, opened his eyes and looked up to see a man from outer space standing over him. The black-suited spaceman reached up, unclipped his night-vision goggles, then pulled off the blastproof balaclava underneath to reveal the concerned face of a captain of the Special Air Service.

"I think I am," the duke answered dryly. "But I'd be much happier if you could help me out of this bloody awful chair now."

John Gault smiled and quickly untied the ropes while his SAS colleague inspected the damage around them. Every mannequin had been hit the same way. Two neat holes in the center of the forehead, some of them so close they might have been on top of each other. The businesslike double tap of the SAS. The second just to make sure.

"Well," the duke asked as he got gratefully to his feet and stretched his long arms and legs, "what was it this time?"

"I made it six point three, sir."

"Six point three?" the duke echoed. "From the moment you entered the building to the moment you cleared the room?"

"Yes, sir."

The duke looked impressed.

"That's very good, isn't it?"

"Yes, sir. Thank you, sir."

"Last year it was eight point something, wasn't it?"

Prince Philip took more than a professional interest in the captain's performance. Gault had just been appointed the duke's personal bodyguard for an upcoming royal visit to the Middle East. The two men would be spending a great deal of time together in the following few months.

Gault opened his mouth to answer but was interrupted by the clatter of footsteps down the hallway.

"Hope you didn't mind us keeping you waiting a little longer this year, sir?"

Colonel Aubrey Quillan, Commanding Officer, 22 Regiment, SAS, Hereford, appeared with his adjutant, both wearing battle fatigues.

The duke waved away the colonel's concern.

"The only change I'd make, Colonel, is that next time I might take you up on the offer of earplugs. My ears are still ringing."

Quillan frowned. It wouldn't do for him to send a member of the royal family back from their annual hostage-rescue exercise with an injury.

"I'm sorry, sir," Quillan apologized. "I should have insisted. My men are using extreme low-velocity rounds. If they were any weaker, they'd have to throw them at the dummies. Even so, the sound level shouldn't have been that high."

"Not your fault, Colonel," the duke reassured him. "I should have taken your advice instead of insisting on a taste of the real thing. Perhaps it was the long lead-up. It seemed like a hellishly long time compared to last year. How long was I waiting all told?"

"Shade under ninety minutes, sir," Quillan answered. "My decision. I thought you should have a sense of the tension that would precede the real thing."

"The boredom, you mean," the duke huffed.

"Precisely, sir."

The duke gave him a thin smile. He knew what Quillan was up to. It was difficult enough to inject the right note of authenticity into these exercises involving members of the royal family. In the early years the SAS had done everything in its power to make the operations quick, safe, and convenient for their royal visitors. Often they had been little more than procedural demonstrations and their royal charges had been off the base after a couple of hours. But confronted by increasingly sophisticated terrorist organizations in general and the proven determination of the IRA in particular, the government, the regiment, and the royal family had agreed that there was a need for greater realism in security exercises involving the royal family. Now, every major royal figure, including the queen, Prince Philip, Prince Charles, and Lady Diana, had to make at least one visit to the killing house at Hereford each year to take part in security exercises. The purpose was not only to familiarize each member of the royal family with SAS procedures and tactics, but to teach them how to behave under fire. The only problem as far as the SAS was concerned was that there were never enough opportunities to run through every possible emergency with every member of the royal family. It was this concern that prompted Quillan's next question.

"I don't suppose you could spare us a little more of your time this evening, could you, sir?"

The duke looked at the colonel through narrowed eyes.

"We'd really like to run through a few moves using stun grenades," the colonel explained. "Working in darkness is one thing, but there may be occasions when we have to lob in a grenade or two. If that happens, it's a good idea if you know what to expect."

"And what should I expect, Colonel?"

Quillan shrugged.

"You'll be blinded and disoriented for at least a minute, perhaps longer. The grenades we use have multiple flashes and explosions. They're like very powerful firecrackers, and once they go off, you really can't wait to get away from the bloody things. The urge to run around like a chicken with its head cut off is very strong and, of course, that's exactly the effect they're meant to have. It's a very difficult reflex to resist, but that's precisely what we want you to do. You should try to freeze, wherever you are, and remain very still. Let everyone else panic and run around . . . and leave it to our chaps to decide between friend and foe."

The duke thought about it for a moment.

"Stun grenades, eh?"

"Yes, sir."

Quillan, Gault, and the others waited. At last the duke nodded.

"You know, gentlemen," he sighed. "I think I'll arrange for my youngest son to come next year. Close exposure to a stun grenade or two might just shake him up a bit."

Colonel Quillan smiled broadly.

"The pleasure would be all mine, sir," he said.

1 The Boarding Party

JIDDA, SAUDI ARABIA. MAY 15, 23.05 HOURS

If the Queen of England had to sit through one more speech, she thought she would scream. Instead, she did what she had done so many times before during her forty-year reign. She smiled inwardly at the very idea. And for one brief, tantalizing moment she played out on the cinema screen of her mind the effect that such an unregal display of hysteria would have on all those around her. Her small, pale face and her canny gray-brown eyes betrayed nothing of these subversive thoughts to those who could not take their eyes off her. Outwardly, Elizabeth Alexandra Mary Windsor, Her Most Excellent Majesty Elizabeth the Second, by the Grace of God of the United Kingdom of Great Britain and Northern Ireland and of Her Other Realms and Territories Queen, Head of the Commonwealth, Defender of the Faith, remained quite serene. Britannia incarnate. An island of grace in a world awash with vulgarity. Delicately, she set her hands on the tabletop and toyed with the diamond solitaire on the third finger of her left hand. Her engagement ring and her wedding ring were the only pieces of personal jewelry she had not changed since her marriage to Prince Philip in 1947. The diamond snared every ray of light in the dining room of the royal yacht and heliographed an urgent semaphore of distress across the wide walnut table to Sarah Joyce-Wittier, lady-in-waiting to the queen.

His Royal Highness, Prince Philip, the Duke of Edinburgh, saw the signal, too, but said nothing. His tanned, angular face retained an expression of intense fascination in the words of the Saudi foreign minister who sat opposite, plodding methodically through a speech of stupefying dullness in praise of the friendly relationship that had always existed between Great Britain and the Kingdom of Saudi Arabia. King Fahd sat to the right of Queen Elizabeth, his dark hawklike face immobile inside his white kaffiyeh. For all the interest he displayed in his surroundings, the Saudi monarch might have perfected the art of sleeping with his eyes open. It was a talent the Queen of England envied.

Lady Sarah cleared her throat and arched a finely drawn eyebrow at Admiral Sir John Marchant, who sat beside her. Admiral Marchant was Flag Officer Royal Yachts and captain of Her Majesty's Yacht, *Britannia.* The admiral leaned his great gray head fractionally closer to Lady Sarah, who whispered into his ear with the speed and efficiency of a spy satellite firing a data burst into a computer bank. The admiral waited a moment, then leaned with equal imperceptibility the other way, toward the Saudi chief of protocol, an Arabic-speaking Englishman called Alderton who had been retained by the Saudi royal household for just such state occasions. Almost all the Saudis present, including the king's brother, Prince Abdullah, had been educated at British or American universities and spoke English very well. But not all. King Fahd could not follow the language when it was spoken quickly, and the queen did not include Arabic among the five languages she spoke fluently. Interpreters were present on both sides, just in case.

A moment later Alderton coughed just loudly enough to attract the foreign minister's attention. The minister paused from his rambling diatribe to glance down the table. The chief of protocol elaborately straightened his shirt cuffs, then folded his hands on the table in front of him. The minister looked wounded, but dutifully he swallowed his pride and brought his speech to a close with a few effusive words of admiration for all things British, especially traditions of democracy and fair play. It was almost exactly the same speech that Alderton had written for an official dinner with the American secretary of state three weeks earlier, except that the word *British* had been substituted for the word *American* and the sporting references were confined to cricket instead of baseball. The queen looked relieved. It was late, almost midnight. The final hours of the final day of a long and exhausting royal tour. Her Majesty gave the minister her most beguiling smile and complimented her Saudi hosts on the hospitality she and her husband had received during their visit. There was an awkward moment's silence and then the soft murmur of general conversation as word passed discreetly around the thirty-two-seat table that it might be time for the Saudi royal party to be going ashore.

Somehow, as though they were both on the same regal wavelength, the queen and King Fahd contrived to get up from the table at precisely the same moment. This was followed by a genteel commotion until the two royal parties could begin their slow procession from the dining room to the drawing room and up the mahogany staircase to the upper deck. Outside on a deck of polished Burma teak, a Royal Marine honor guard in scarlet tunics, snow-white helmets, and gloves stood smartly to attention as the two monarchs emerged into the blaze of light that bathed the royal yacht from stern to bowsprit. The *Britannia,* too, had been dressed for dinner. Its creamy superstructure glowed under the blaze of a thousand dressing lights strung from the ensign staff to the mizzenmast, the mainmast, the foremast, and back down to the jackstaff at the bow. High atop the mainmast the Saudi royal standard fluttered regally alongside the queen's standard in the warm desert breeze.

The two sovereigns made their formal farewells on the afterdeck, then King Fahd led his party down the red-carpeted gangway to the floodlit jetty, where his bulletproof Rolls-Royce waited with a motorcade of a dozen royal cars filled with security men and flanked by police motorcycle outriders. There were no crowds to cheer either monarch. The dock area had been cleared of all unauthorized personnel for half a mile. It had been like that throughout the *Britannia*'s week-long visit. There were three security cordons around the royal yacht manned by the Saudi Army and monitored closely by the British. Every dockworker who needed to get close to the ship had to have an updated security clearance just to get through the first cordon. To get through the second cordon they had to submit to a full search at a Saudi Army checkpoint. All dockworkers who passed through the third cordon, which covered the immediate area around the royal yacht, were accompanied by armed guards. And no one, not even General Mahmoud, who was in charge of all Saudi troops on the waterfront, was allowed on board the *Britannia* without the approval of the queen's chief of security, Inspector Hardacre from Special Branch, who routinely refused everyone everything.

A dour-faced man with a thin mustache and a bad haircut, Hardacre heaved a sigh of relief as he watched King Fahd leave the royal yacht. He and his two assistants, who formed the queen's permanent security staff, had been responsible for the safety of the Saudi monarch, too, while he had been on board. The inspector turned and exchanged a knowing glance with the SAS captain who stood at the portside rail with Prince Philip. Hardacre was one of only a handful of people on board who knew John Gault's real identity. Because the SAS bodyguard was not wearing his correct uniform. Instead of the khaki tunic and sand-colored beret of the SAS, Gault wore the uniform of a junior orderly in Her Majesty's Royal Yacht Service. A minor subterfuge that might make all the difference in the confusion that would accompany an assassination attempt. Gault gave the inspector a brief nod of acknowledgment, then turned his attention back to the dock. It was too soon for him to breathe a sigh of relief but, he had to admit, the Saudis had done a first-class job. They had done everything they had been asked to do and there hadn't been a single breach in security, accidental or otherwise. From his position at the ship's rail, Gault counted a dozen combat-ready troopers from the Royal Saudi Army's special forces patrolling the high chain-mesh security fence that encircled the dock. Every link in the fence was forged from high-tensile steel that would not yield if it were rammed by a truck. On the other side of the fence, half a company of regular soldiers patrolled a maze of darkened alleys created by hundreds of shipping containers stacked three or four deep. At the water's edge a dozen steel-legged cranes cast crooked shadows across the dock. Gault knew that the cabins of the four cranes closest to the royal yacht were occupied by Royal Marine sharpshooters who scrutinized everything that moved on the waterfront. Their orders were not to watch for intruders, as the Saudis had been told. Their eyes were on the Saudis. If any Saudi soldier, policeman, or bodyguard even looked as though he might be making a threatening move toward the British monarch, he would find himself on the receiving end of a sharpshooter's bullet. At the far side of the dock a couple of British-made Saladin armored cars guarded the two main exits to the street.

Two hundred yards away in the harbor basin, on the starboard side of the royal yacht, the *Britannia*'s guard ship, HMS *Hotspur,* stood at anchor, her twin spotlights scything the dark waters of Jidda harbor, searching for water-borne intruders. The *Hotspur* was a front-line missile destroyer with a ship's complement of 373 men that had been assigned to escort the royal yacht for the duration of the royal tour. The tour had begun six weeks earlier in Gibraltar, then proceeded to Valletta, Athens, Istanbul, and Alexandria before concluding in Jidda. Whether the multimillion-pound trade contracts expected to flow from the visit would ever materialize was now a matter of interest only to Her Majesty's Government. Her Majesty had done her best to persuade the Maltese, the Greeks, the Turks, the Egyptians, and the Saudis that British was best. As it had always been. As it would always be. The following afternoon the *Britannia* would slip her moorings with the nineteen musicians of the Royal Marine band on deck playing the "Beating of the Retreat." She would sail north from Jidda, through the Red Sea and the Suez Canal and into the Mediterranean for a much-deserved two-week cruise to her home port of Portsmouth. Then, and perhaps only then, Gault, Hardacre, and all those others on board who had sworn to give up their lives to protect the queen and her consort might be able to relax.

In the meantime, Gault knew, there was still much to be done before dawn. Two men from the twelve-strong Royal Marine commando squad that comprised the *Britannia*'s shipboard defense, would put on their wet suits at least two more times before the sun came up and make underwater sweeps of the hull to insure there had been no unwelcome visitors below the waterline. The blood-red hull of the *Britannia* was coated with a plastic antimagnetic compound that was supposedly resistant to magnetic mines. But ever since a diver from the Royal Navy's elite Special Boat Squadron had attached a deactivated mine to the yacht in Portsmouth harbor just to prove that it could be done, underwater security had been made a priority. As an added security measure, Saudi special forces ran nonstop patrols throughout the harbor in speedboats fitted with Browning heavy machine guns while helicopter gunships from the Royal Saudi Air Force patrolled a strict air perimeter. What it all meant was that there wasn't a bird, a fish, or a snake that could come within a hundred yards of the royal yacht without somebody knowing about it. Still, Gault fretted, it wasn't enough. It was never enough. This was the Middle East. The playground of terrorists. It had been said many times—all it took was one terrorist to get lucky once. The royal family had to be lucky all the time.

The queen's cousin, Earl Mountbatten, hadn't been lucky.

Gault watched as the Saudi monarch stepped into his car and a royal aide closed the door after him. Doors fluttered open and shut the length of the motorcade. Engines started and the police outriders kicked their machines into life. A moment later the royal motorcade pulled away from the dockside and crawled across the dock like a glistening black centipede, the twin lines of police outriders wobbling at the head like antennae. Saudi troops opened the gates to the street and the motorcade headed northward to the Shara Al Malik Khalid Bin highway, past the steel and glass skyscrapers along the waterfront and back to Khuzam Palace.

The queen and the Duke of Edinburgh watched from the afterdeck of the *Britannia* until the last car had gone. When the soldiers had shut the gates once more and the sound of the departing motorcade had faded into the distance, it seemed as though everyone in the royal party heaved the same silent sigh of relief. The last night of the tour was almost over. Gault glanced around and was just in time to catch a quick, private look the queen gave to her husband, a look that was understood by husbands and wives the world over when dinner guests have tarried a shade too long. With the Saudis safely gone, Admiral Marchant took the opportunity to seek his sovereign's permission to return to the bridge. There was work to do for the skipper of the *Britannia,* and it would be at least a couple of hours before he would be free to seek the comfort of his bed. The few remaining members of the household staff lingered long enough to be dismissed for the evening too. Hardacre and his men drifted off down the deck to give the royal couple a little extra breathing space. Only the Marine honor guard and the two royal bodyguards remained on the afterdeck with the queen and Prince Philip. For a moment Gault thought the queen and her husband might want to spend a few moments alone to enjoy the warm night air before they retired for the night. Sentiment told him it was probably okay. Prudence said he couldn't allow it. Gault was worried about the lone sniper, the shoulder-launched missile from some distant skyscraper, the errant bullet from a rogue soldier's rifle . . . anything. He glanced pointedly behind the duke's back to the queen's personal bodyguard, his eyes asking only if it should come from him or from her.

Judy Stone understood and gave him a look that said she would take care of it. A tall, willowy woman with straw-colored hair, she looked older than her twenty-nine years and dressed with the kind of elegant plainness that characterized all Her Majesty's ladies-in-waiting. Few people would have suspected that behind the drab façade were the hard mind and body of a highly trained soldier. Anonymity was Judy Stone's greatest asset. She knew how to play down her looks, to disguise her features with unflattering hairstyles and bland makeup, to mask her shapely figure behind formless dresses that were always a size too large. She had been trained to affect an appearance that would not draw a second glance. Especially from men. At state receptions and around the dinner table she knew how to talk brightly about nothing so that listeners would dismiss her as an engaging dimwit—another daddy's girl from a good family with the right connections to the palace.

"Forgive me, ma'am," she said in a voice quite at odds with her appearance now that the four of them were alone, "but I really do think—"

"We should be going inside now?" the queen finished for her.

Stone hesitated and smiled.

“Yes, ma’am,” she said.

Prince Philip turned to Gault in a way that irritated Judy Stone. It was as though the duke were always looking for a second opinion—from a man.

“I’m afraid so, sir,” Gault said.

Prince Philip frowned and looked as though he were about to say something unpleasant. His wife saw it too, and put her hand gently on his arm. Between any other two people it would have seemed a perfectly ordinary gesture, but when it involved the Queen of England and the prince consort, there was something strikingly intimate about it. Gault was reminded that behind the pomp and circumstance, behind the novelty that attended every little movement, they were just like any other couple who had been married for forty years.

“Tomorrow night we’ll be at sea,” the queen reminded her husband soothingly.

His Royal Highness Baron Greenwich, Earl of Merioneth, and Duke of Edinburgh hesitated a moment, then relaxed.

“Bloody security,” he grumbled. “Bloody bore.” But there was more resignation than resentment in the words, and he allowed himself to be guided toward the drawing room. Gault and Stone swapped brief smiles. It was the first hint of temperament in six weeks. Otherwise the duke had been Prince Charming to everyone, despite his fearsome reputation. Gault thought much of the credit for the duke’s good spirits could be attributed to the ambience of the royal yacht. The *Britannia* was a superbly run vessel and its atmosphere of unhurried elegance belied the below-decks efficiency that kept it that way. For those fortunate enough to be its guests, the royal yacht offered a glimpse of a way of life that existed nowhere else in the world. It wasn’t so much the luxury that impressed Gault. There were bigger, more opulent private yachts in the world. It was the mood of stately calm that pervaded the *Britannia.* An inviolable air of serenity rooted in the continuity of history. A history that was evident everywhere in the portraits and photographs of earlier British monarchs and in the things they had left behind. It was the feeling that this was the way it had always been and this was the way it would always be, no matter what had happened to the rest of the world. And, when the *Britannia* was on the open sea, far from the anxieties of land, it was as though all on board were suspended in a time of grace. Only a few hours more, Gault thought, and they would all feel better.

The queen and her husband were almost at the door to the drawing room when Prince Philip stopped and turned to the two bodyguards who tagged along behind them like a pair of royal corgis.

"Thank you both . . . Captain Gault . . . Lieutenant Stone," he said dryly. "I think we can manage on our own from here."

The queen appeared not to have heard and went into the drawing room, content to let her husband enjoy his moment of authority. Both bodyguards recognized the tone in the duke's voice and knew that the time had come to make a discreet withdrawal. Their orders were clear enough: accompany their royal highnesses everywhere within reason, unless specifically asked not to do so. Even then there were certain situations when security considerations might overrule the royal prerogative. This was not one of them. The duke might feel like a nightcap and a few moments alone with his wife before they both went up to bed. They were entitled to that much.

"Certainly, sir," Gault acknowledged. "Good night, sir."

"Good night, sir," Judy Stone echoed. "Ma'am."

But the queen was already out of earshot. The duke stepped into the drawing room and closed the door behind him, leaving the two bodyguards on deck. Gault sucked in a breath and looked at Judy Stone.

"Ever had the feeling that you're not wanted?" he mumbled.

Judy gave him a faint smile, then turned and walked over to the bulwark. Gault joined her and leaned with one elbow on the ship's rail. It had been a long day. They had both been up since before dawn, and it wasn't over yet. They had to wait until the lights in the drawing room had gone out and the queen and Prince Philip had gone upstairs to their separate apartments on the royal deck. Even then the two bodyguards would have a few final security checks to make before they could retire to their own beds in the guest apartments across the corridor from the royal bedrooms. For a while the two of them stood in silence, enjoying the quiet, taking in the spectacle of the Jidda skyline. A mirror of Manhattan in the Arabian desert and a monument to the foul black sludge beneath the sand that had held the industrialized world hostage for half a century. A light offshore breeze wafted across the waterfront. Gault caught a trace of Judy's perfume. It smelled pungent and flowery. Old-maid's perfume. He shifted slightly and watched her as the mischievous fingers of the wind toyed with her dress and molded it slyly against her body, telling him how she really looked beneath the disguise of her wardrobe. He wondered what clothes she wore when she wasn't working. When she wanted to relax and have fun. Assuming she ever had any fun. He couldn't see her in the matronly navy-blue uniform of a lieutenant in the WRENS, the Women's Royal Navy, where she had served five years before becoming a bodyguard to the queen. But he could see her in black. It was the cut of the clothes that would be different. The skirt would be short and tight with a high tuck at the seat to emphasize the roundness of her thighs. The stockings would be black too. Black and sheer with seams at the back to emphasize the curves of her legs. And the shoes would have two-inch heels to stretch and define her calves.

Gault switched to her face. As always, she looked as though she had put on her makeup with a roller. Her features looked like they'd been stenciled onto a layer of hard white ceramic, giving her face the pallor of a kabuki mask. Her lips were full and well formed, but she had applied her lipstick artfully to make her mouth look thin and uninviting. Her fine nose was perpetually shiny, giving it a pointed look. Her eyebrows had been plucked into extinction and replaced by thin, ugly lines. Her lashes were the same color as her hair and unembellished by mascara so that the whole effect was to give her light brown eyes a blank, staring look. Her straw hair was lacquered into an old-fashioned bob with a ridiculous flip to one side that made her seem flighty and insubstantial. She looked every inch the plain jane who had no idea how to make the best of the little she had. Which was exactly what she wanted. Judy Stone knew exactly what she had going for her. She knew what men looked for. She knew what she had to hide. The fewer people who remembered her, the better she could do her job.

Gault was different. He had to work with her. One day his life might depend on how she reacted under pressure. He had studied her from the beginning, ever since they had been introduced by Hardacre when the *Britannia* was still dockside at Portsmouth. A woman like her intrigued him professionally and personally. So few of them had made it into this highly specialized branch of the armed forces. Equal-opportunity policies might have shown that women could fly planes and operate missile defense systems just as well as men. But very few had ever made it through the kind of training that preceded bodyguard selection by the SAS. Gault had heard of only half a dozen women who had made it in the past ten years. Judy Stone was one of them.

"Think we'll have to run a hard check on Alderton," she announced suddenly, intruding on his thoughts.

Gault remembered the elegant silver-haired Briton in his late fifties who had acted as Saudi chief of protocol.

"You read the report Six did on him?" Gault asked.

Six referred to MI6, Britain's foreign intelligence service.

Judy nodded.

"It was more notable for what it didn't say than what it did say," she answered. "I think he's gay. He could be a security risk."

"Never married, collects antique silverware, bit of a fusspot, and has worked for the Saudis for three years," Gault recalled a few key details from the report. "That makes him gay, does it?"

"Maybe he's been more discreet than most," Judy shrugged.

"I could give you the names of a dozen of our chaps who have gone on to do a bit of dirty work for various Arab governments," Gault said. "Not all of them are married either. Just because they don't enjoy the company of women doesn't make them gay, you know?"

Judy gave him a wry look.

"I don't think you'd know unless he wanted you to know," she said.

Gault stifled a small laugh.

"But you can tell just by looking at him?"

"I think he's a risk," she added stubbornly. "And I don't like risks."

"Okay," Gault conceded. "Say you run a queer check on him. It's inconclusive but Six decides they can't live with the suspicion any more than you can. They tell the Saudis he's persona non grata with our government. His usefulness disappears overnight—there's always some other smarmy ex-government PR type to be picked up cheap off the streets of London—and Alderton gets bounced. His reputation is ruined in the world diplomatic community and he has no idea why . . . that's nice."

"Frightfully sorry," she answered coolly. "But I'm not paid to be nice."

Gault paused. He harbored no particular sympathy for Alderton, but he was willing to play the devil's advocate a little longer if it helped open another window into the mind of Judy Stone.

"I have it on pretty good authority that there's more than one queen at Buckingham Palace," he said. "And it has been said that the occasional limp wrist has pulled at the halyards of the *Britannia.*"

Judy fixed him with a level stare.

"For the record," she said, "I never assume that just because somebody is gay they are automatically a security risk. But they do tend to be more susceptible to blackmail than heterosexuals, especially if they haven't come out of the closet yet. And Alderton is in a high-risk category. He's single, he's getting on in years, he could be lonely, and he's rented himself out to a foreign power. I think he could be turned. Sure, it's instinctive—but sometimes gut instinct is all we've got to go on. And mine has been pretty good so far. Unlike you chaps from the regiment, I'm not entirely comfortable with the sound of gunfire. I regard it as a sign of failure. So, I still think I'll give our Mr. Alderton a little push if you don't mind . . . and we'll see which way he falls."

Gault nodded slowly, his face thoughtful, weighing what she had said.

"You want to know something funny?" he said after a moment. His voice was matter-of-fact but there was an undertone, a hint of hidden meaning. She waited, wondering what he knew that she didn't.

"When you get intense, your eyebrows get so close together"—he held up his thumb and forefinger so they were nearly touching—"they almost meet in the middle."

She stared at him for a moment, then turned away with a dainty snort of disdain. Gault smiled. He couldn't be certain, but he thought he had seen the flicker of a smile in her eyes too, just before she had looked away. Still, he had had his moment of fun and he let it pass. He wasn't frivolous by nature and he knew it would reflect poorly on him if he tried to introduce even a little flirtation into their relationship. Especially with a woman who was so determinedly professional. He leaned back against the rail and watched the molten reflections of the skyline on the water for a while.

"Madge strike you as a little tired tonight?" he asked, easing the conversation back into a neutral zone.

"Madge" was shorthand for "Her Majesty," the nickname Gault had given the queen when he first came on board. It had quickly become an in joke among the household staff.

"Well," Judy answered, "she's no spring chicken anymore. I think she's been feeling the strain—she's just very good at hiding it."

Gault nodded.

"She's not alone there, is she?" he said offhandedly.

Judy sighed and her kabuki mask crinkled into something approaching a smile. Then she did something that surprised him. She stood back from the rail and looked at him in a way that she hadn't looked at him in the weeks they had worked together. For a second he thought he saw real loneliness in her eyes. She opened her mouth to say something, but at the same moment a shadow moved across the curtains in the drawing room and distracted her. She turned to look. The first shadow was joined by another. Their royal highnesses had finished their nightcaps and were going upstairs to bed. Judy followed them with her eyes, watching them until they disappeared.

"Sergeant Ibrahim . . . it is me, Javad. I have the provisions for the ship of the English queen."

Sergeant Ibrahim of the second battalion of the Saudi First Royal Guard looked up at the round, mustached face of the man who had pulled his battered Mercedes truck off Shara Al Amir Fahd highway at the northern gateway to the dock. Ibrahim recognized Javad. After a week of nightly deliveries, the friendly young Jordanian was well known to the soldiers. He had been a truck driver for seven years. He had a clean sheet with the police and had no trouble getting a pass from the Saudi security service while the royal yacht was in port. Every morning around the same time he brought a load of fresh produce to the *Britannia.* Sitting next to Javad was his laborer, a sullen-faced man with acne scars called Youssef. If it had been any other ship, Javad would have driven through the open gate, along the dock road, and unloaded his cartons right at the dockside. But, because this was the *Britannia,* he was permitted to bring the truck only through the first security cordon. Once inside, he and Youssef had to unload the cartons and pull them on trolleys through two more checkpoints before they would be met at the dockside by the catering officer and a couple of galley hands from the royal yacht. And they would be accompanied every step of the way by Saudi troops.

Ibrahim reached up for both men's papers. Youssef yawned, took an old camel-hide pouch from his shirt pocket, and rolled himself a smoke. Javad drummed his fingers idly against the steering wheel and waited. He knew there was nothing to worry about. They had cleared all Saudi security checks and cross-checks with Interpol. More important, they had cleared the files of Special Branch, MI5, and MI6 when the Saudis had sent a list of all Jidda's dockworkers to the British a month before the *Britannia* had sailed from Portsmouth. There was simply no reason why the names of Javad Malik or Youssef Shaheen would trigger an alarm. They were good citizens. Migrant workers with Jordanian passports who held steady jobs and joined their Suni brethren at prayer every Friday at the Al Fallah mosque. They did not belong to any political party and had never been in trouble with the law. They had never even made the drive to the Sultanate of Bahrain to gamble, drink scotch, and enjoy the western whores like so many of their Arab brothers who seemed happy to tempt the wrath of Allah by indulging their vices every night of the week. That alone might have aroused suspicion. Javad and Youssef were simply too good to be true. Their records were as clean as new snow. And no one, not the police, not Saudi intelligence, or any of their Saudi workmates had even an inkling that both of them were Palestinians. That they had been born in the occupied West Bank and were lifetime members of the PFLP-GC, the Popular Front for the Liberation of Palestine-General Command —one of the world's most sinister terrorist organizations. An organization that operated under a Syrian flag of convenience and was not averse to hiring its people out to anyone who could come up with the right amount of hard currency.

Both men had been sent to Saudi Arabia as sleepers for the PFLP-GC. Both of them told to wait twenty years, if necessary, until the right moment came along. Now, with the visit of the *Britannia,* that moment had arrived. The PFLP-GC was poised to become the richest, the most powerful independent force in the Middle East. It was a prospect that made it worthwhile to use up two of its most valuable agents.

Sergeant Ibrahim handed back the passes and identity papers.

"Is my face still the same, then, my brother?" Javad grinned cheekily. Ibrahim did not answer. Instead, he shouldered his rifle and walked around to the back of the truck. The tailgate was bolted shut but the cargo was uncovered and open to inspection. Ibrahim put one foot on the fender, hoisted himself up, and peered inside. There were plastic-mesh bags filled with potatoes, onions, and oranges, and cardboard cartons filled with lettuce, tomatoes, artichokes, and asparagus. The bounty of vast Saudi hothouses nurtured by desalinated seawater and tended by migrant laborers. Ibrahim inhaled deeply. There was something sensual about the smell of fresh ripe fruit. He unsheathed his combat knife, slit open the nearest bag, picked out six of the fattest oranges, and stuffed them inside his shirt. Then he jumped down, strolled back around to the front of the truck, and gestured to his men inside the gate. They slid back the bolt and the truck jerked forward, through the first security cordon.

Javad drove slowly along the dock road, feeling every pair of eyes that watched him from the surrounding industrial maze. The road forked in front of the customs house, and he made a right turn onto the slender spit of land that separated the outer harbor from the inner harbor, where the *Britannia* sat at anchor, safe and snug in her bristling cocoon. He drove another fifty yards, then pulled up at the first in a long line of warehouses and switched off the engine. Just as he had done every night since the *Britannia* had berthed. The doors to the warehouse were padlocked shut, but a couple of trolleys had been left outside and the two men would use them to haul the produce the last few hundred yards to the *Britannia.*

Both men climbed down from the truck and stretched their legs, taking their time, looking around with studied nonchalance, the way they always did. Like everything else in Jidda, the port was a showpiece of industrial modernism. A thousand shining acres of cement and steel and every square inch rendered naked beneath a battery of powerful arc lights. The lights were so powerful and so numerous that a man could not cast a shadow. Every nut and bolt was illuminated to a theatrical intensity so that Javad and Youssef could not help but feel like players on a well-lit stage. Like all bad actors, Javad had to turn and give his audience a wave. Sergeant Ibrahim and his men watched from a couple of hundred yards away, eating their oranges.

"Come, my lazy brother," Javad said. "Let us make a start so we can finish quickly and go home to our beds." He stepped to the nearest trolley and pushed it to the back of the truck. Youssef stuck his cigarette between his lips, slipped the bolt on the tailgate, and dropped it with a loud crash. Then he pulled out the first cartons of produce and began stacking them on the back of the trolley. Javad returned for the second trolley and parked it beside the first, creating a narrow corridor between the two trolleys that reached from the back of the truck to the door of the warehouse. Then, except for the occasional grunt and curse, the two of them worked on in silence, unloading the truck and piling the trolleys high with cartons and plastic-mesh bags. They had both been warned. The British might have directional microphones. They would say and do nothing that might arouse suspicion. Gradually, the load on each trolley climbed higher and higher until they formed walls that were high enough for a man to pass between them without being seen by anyone but the sea gulls that wheeled overhead, waiting for the first spilled morsel of fruit.

The truck was almost two thirds empty. Javad was not as strong as Youssef. He had to take frequent breaks to catch his breath and look around. The night was warm. Sweat streamed from his scalp, glued his hair to his neck in thin, glistening strands, and spread damp patches across his shirt. He leaned against the truck, took out a handkerchief, and dabbed delicately at his face. With his other hand he gave the side of the truck two sharp knocks. He paused, then did it again. Just a few random sounds among many. The sounds of two men working. For a moment nothing happened. Then the remaining wall of cartons inside the truck slid silently back and a dense black shape materialized through the darkness. A man wearing a black combat suit and balaclava, an M-16 ready in his hands. He padded across the floor of the truck, peered warily into the hostile glare of the lights, then jumped down into the space between the trolleys. Another man appeared, carrying a pair of long-handled bolt cutters. They were followed by six more, all dressed the same, all of them carrying heavy backpacks. Javad and Youssef bustled around the outside of the two heavily laden trolleys, pushing and shoving at the topmost cartons, arranging and rearranging them for the benefit of those who were watching. On the other side of the cartons the man with the bolt cutters stepped toward the door of the warehouse and cut through the padlock chain with a loud snap. Javad was ready. At the same moment he pulled down a carton of tomatoes and swore as the box hit the ground. The cardboard sides split open and dozens of fat red tomatoes spilled across the glaring white pavement. The waiting gulls shrieked and swooped. Youssef laughed and Javad swore at him, louder this time. The two men scurried after the tomatoes, swatting away the gulls, pushing the bruised fruit back into the carton, holding the attention of all those who spied on them from afar. The warehouse door slid open with a thin metallic squeal; the intruders filed inside and slid the door shut behind them. It took only seconds.

Javad glanced at his watch. A full minute had ticked past before he and Youssef had gathered up the last of the spilled fruit and put the damaged carton carefully back on the trolley. Both men were sweating and breathing hard. Behind their fake curses their fear was real. But they heard nothing. No fast-approaching jeep, no shouts of alarm. Only the welcome, deafening chorus of the gulls. Javad stood up, mopped his face with his handkerchief again, and gave another reassuring wave to the men at the gate. Two hundred yards away Sergeant Ibrahim put down his binoculars and shrugged.

“Clumsy fools,” he grunted. Then he went back to his stolen orange.

At last they were finished. Javad paused and looked at Youssef one last time. The big man nodded his readiness, walked around to the first trolley, and took hold of the handle. Despite the heavy load, it moved smoothly and easily under his touch. Javad took the handle of the second trolley and maneuvered it behind his companion. Together they began the slow procession back along the dock road toward the second checkpoint.

Behind them, inside the darkened warehouse, the eight intruders worked quietly and efficiently. Four men secured the perimeter of the building while the others worked on their backpacks in the middle of the empty floor. The first pack was the largest and was not a backpack at all but a bale of tough, rubberized material that unrolled across the floor like a length of black carpet. Two men produced a bundle of metal poles from another pack and joined them together to give the carpet a rigid frame. They worked easily in the darkness, a skill developed through months of practice. One of the intruders opened a third pack and produced a yellow canister about the size of a can of Coke. He attached the canister to an inlet valve on one side of the carpet, then attached a second canister to the other side. When he was ready, he flicked a small lever on top of each canister. A thin hiss filled the warehouse as the canisters poured out their twin streams of compressed air and the carpet snapped, rippled, and bulged until it began to assume the shape of a rubber dinghy. The dinghy had not fully inflated before two of the men had unpacked a small seventy-five-horsepower outboard and attached it to the rear of the Zodiac. The motor had been muffled, its casing, rudder, and telescopic prop coated with nonreflective black paint. It had already been primed with enough gas to give them half an hour at ten knots. It was all the fuel they would need to last them the rest of their lives.

The canisters yielded their dying breath into the inflatable, and the men swarmed quickly over it, listening for the thin, telltale hiss of leaks. They found none. They turned to the remaining backpacks and laid out the other tools of their trade. A row of M-16s, clips and spares loaded, satchels filled with slabs of plastic explosive, shoulder harnesses laden with sinister black aerosols. And gas masks.

At last everything was ready. They stood up, looked to their leader, and waited. The next signal had to come from him. The man who was first out of the truck watched from the shadows and smiled approvingly behind his mask. He glanced at his watch. Four minutes twenty-eight seconds. Nearly a full minute better than dress rehearsal. And they weren't even breathing hard. Silently, he crossed the floor and gave each man a reassuring pat on the arm.

"Good lads," he growled softly. "Not long now. Not long at all."

He spoke in English. English with an Irish accent. But it was not the seductive Irish lilt of the south. Not the tourist-brochure brogue that so charmed the tourists in the pubs of Dublin and Donegal. It was the thick, guttural accent of the north. An accent that had been gnarled and burled into something harsh and brutish in the ghettos of Belfast.

Dominic Behan studied his men through the eye slits in his balaclava. Despite the masks and the identical clothes they wore, he could still tell them all apart. He knew them by their height, their build, by the way they moved, even by the way they stood. He had come to know them well during the long months of isolation they had spent in preparation at the old sheep farm on the south coast of County Clare, far from the prying eyes of the British. He had chosen them all himself from the active service ranks of the Provisional IRA. Every man was a specialist. Every man a killer. They were the best. The best team the IRA had ever put into the field against the British. A killer elite on a historic mission that would change the course of history and bring freedom to all Ireland.

"Get her ready," Behan rumbled. The waiting men bent in unison, hoisted the dinghy into the air, and carried it to a pair of cargo doors in the opposite wall, the wall that flanked the inner harbor. On the other side of those doors, they knew, was a wide jetty and a set of concrete steps that led down to the water.

Behan checked his watch again. It was 12:56. He turned and walked to the end of the warehouse, where one of his men kept watch through a slit cut in the aluminum wall.

"They there yet?"

"Another minute," Bobby Devlin whispered back. He stepped aside to let the other man take a look. Behan squinted through the metal fissure and found the two bright yellow trolleys on the other side of the harbor, within a hundred yards of the second checkpoint. Behan stepped back and indulged himself in a small, grim smile of satisfaction. If the Brits only knew. All the IRA's most wanted gunmen on the same job at the same time. And him and Bobby Devlin at the top of the list. Boyhood pals from the Falls Road. Foot soldiers for the Cause since they were old enough to throw a petrol bomb. The lives of seventeen British soldiers to their credit, slaughtered in bomb blasts and ambushes from Belfast to Berlin, from Derry to Dusseldorf. Though it was Behan alone who held the distinction of killing four Royal Marines in a single ambush in Armagh. One of them finished off with a rifle shot as he lay wounded on the ground near his bomb-shattered armored car. An incident that had made Behan a legend in the ghettos and turned him into one of the most feared men in all of Northern Ireland. Even that would pale into insignificance compared to the operation he was about to commence.

"Looks like the buggers are going to go through with it," Devlin whispered.

"You thought I'd let them get this far and then back out?" Behan rumbled.

"They're Arabs, aren't they?" Devlin answered.

Behan smiled coldly behind his mask but said nothing. Instead, he thumbed open a pocket in his combat vest and pulled out a radio transmitter the size of a packet of cigarettes. He pressed a button and watched the luminous green figures flicker across the display panel while he ran through the frequencies locked into its memory. When he was satisfied, he slid the transmit switch into the on position. A red warning light blinked. All he had to do now was press the signal button and the transmitter would run electronically through the preset frequencies. Once activated, it didn't matter what happened to him, the transmitter would keep sending.

A few feet away Devlin shifted and raised one hand in the air. The two yellow trolleys were almost there. Behan's finger hovered over the signal button.

* * *

"Permission to join you on the bridge, sir?"

Gault waited at the door for a response, Judy Stone at his elbow. There were three officers on the bridge. Admiral Marchant, who had been conferring with Commander Berenson about preparations for the yacht's departure in the morning, and Lieutenant Russell, officer of the watch. The two junior officers looked to Marchant and waited.

"Certainly, Cap—" the admiral began. He corrected himself. "Lieutenant Gault."

Gault stood aside to let Judy pass in front of him. She shot him a quick look of disapproval, then went ahead. In other circumstances it might have been good manners; in this context she found it condescending.

"Their royal highnesses retired for the evening?" Marchant asked.

Both bodyguards nodded.

"With your permission, sir," Gault said, "we'd like to sign off with Commander Berenson here and Captain Purcell aboard the *Hotspur* and then we'll turn in."

"Can't say I blame you," Marchant responded affably. "Glad it's all over and done with. I think we'll all be better off for a few quiet days at sea, eh?"

"Give me time to work on my tan," Judy joked. Gault felt slighted. With him she was proper to the point of coolness. With Marchant she was almost coquettish. He had noticed that the closest she came to flirting with anyone was when she was around the courtly gray-haired Marchant. He wondered if she harbored a fondness for older men.

The skipper smiled broadly. The idea of the queen's bodyguard in a bikini on the upper deck of the *Britannia* was an enticing but unlikely piece of whimsy. Still, it was a welcome sign that the tension of the six-week tour might have begun to lift a little. He hoped so. The admiral had seen many changes in the five years he had been skipper of the royal yacht. Most of them bad. With the increase in terrorism and all the sophisticated technology terrorists had at their disposal, royal cruises were no longer the carefree jaunts they had once been. Everyone felt the strain. Everyone was glad when they were over.

An elegant man with a long and distinguished career, Marchant was due to retire soon, in all probability with a knighthood in recognition of his outstanding service to Her Majesty. All he had to do was get through this last cruise without a hitch and then it was a desk job at the Admiralty while he helped choose his successor. John Gault could not be churlish about Judy Stone's affection for the old sailor. He shared it. He would love to spend a few hours with Marchant, to hear some of the stories he could tell about a career that spanned Suez, Korea, and the Falklands, including six years as skipper of an aircraft carrier before he was transferred to the Royal Yacht Service. Gault hadn't said as much, but he planned to look him up after he had retired, pay his respects, and see if he could loosen the old boy's tongue with a bottle of his favorite Pusser's rum.

"We're all quiet here." Commander Berenson interrupted Gault's thoughts. "Stand by and I'll raise *Hotspur* for you."

He punched a button on the display panel and leaned over the microphone.

"Britannia to *Hotspur.* This is *Britannia,* come in please, *Hotspur."*

A moment later the bridge filled with the familiar voice of the commander from the *Hotspur,* which they could all see a few hundred yards away in the middle of the harbor.

"This is *Hotspur,"* the voice said. "Purcell here, what can we do for you, *Britannia?"*

The admiral leaned toward the microphone before Berenson could answer.

"Marchant here. You're up a bit late, aren't you, old chap?"

"With respect, Admiral, I might say the same about you."

Marchant chuckled. He and Purcell went back a long way. To the days when they had first met as officer cadets at Dartmouth. They had received their sea commissions at the same time. They had gone on shore leave together, chased girls together, even married within months of each other. And now they were likely to retire within months of each other. The admiral had been delighted when he heard that the *Hotspur* would be providing escort duty on the cruise, with his old friend Harry Purcell in the captain's chair.

"Let's see if we can get Her Majesty's yacht back out to sea without either of us bumping into anything tomorrow, shall we?" Marchant added.

"We'll see that you don't get into too much trouble, *Britannia,*" Purcell answered.

Marchant smiled and yielded the airwaves back to Berenson.

"Commander Berenson here, Captain. Final security check for this watch. Anything you care to tell us about?"

"All clear this end, Commander. Tell security they can get their beauty rest. *Hotspur* will keep an eye on things for the next watch."

Relieved that they had concluded the last of their official duties, Gault and Stone said their good nights and walked back down to the main deck. On the way they exchanged greetings with a combat ready Royal Marine guard making his rounds. They took one last turn along the deck. There were two gangways leading down to the dock on the port side. One near the stern, which the Saudi royal party had used, and another amidships, where the galley crew would take on supplies before dawn. An armed marine in full battle dress stood on the dock in front of each gangway. Saudi soldiers still patrolled the security fence. At last they came back to the stern and paused for a moment at the gangway that led up to the shelter deck and their cabins.

"Bet I'm asleep before you," Gault said.

"You lose," Judy answered. "I've been sleepwalking for the past five minutes."

Half a mile away, Javad and Youssef brought their heavily laden trolleys to a halt in front of the second checkpoint. A six-wheeled Saladin armored car was parked in front of the gate, its 76mm turret gun and twin 7.62mm machine guns trained on the new arrivals. Javad eased his trolley to a full halt, paused to catch his breath, and wiped the sweat from his eyes. Behind him Youssef did the same. Then Javad raised his hands to show that they were empty and ambled slowly toward the gate. Outwardly, he looked as calm and as relaxed as he always did. Inside, his heart was pounding.

There were three men in the armored car, including the commander, who watched them from the open hatch in the top of the turret. Two more Saudi soldiers stood inside the gate, rifles slung over their shoulders. Javad recognized none of them. He waited for Youssef to slouch up beside him, then gave the commander of the armored car his most ingratiating grin.

"Please, sir," he said. "I am Javad Malik and this is Youssef Shaheen. We bring fresh fruits and vegetables for the *Britannia* every night at this time."

The commander of the armored car nodded but said nothing. He swung his legs out of the hatch, jumped down to the ground, and drew his pistol. Another man appeared in the turret, wiped his sweat-covered face, and sucked at the fresh night air. The inside of the vehicle must have been like an oven, Javad thought.

"Hot in there tonight, my brother?" he asked pleasantly. Secretly, he was pleased. One of the machine guns was now unmanned.

"Take them all down." The commander gestured at the stacked cartons. "Let's see inside."

"But, sir," Javad pleaded, injecting a whining note into his voice as if it were all a bit too much. "We have worked so long today. We are both tired. The other officer—"

"Take them down," the commander interrupted, his voice showing that he could not be swayed.

Javad gave him a pained smile, then shrugged and turned back to do as he was told. Together he and Youssef began unloading the trolleys. The commander strolled around them as they worked, bending occasionally to poke through the neat stacks of fresh fruit. In the warehouse a few hundred yards away, Bobby Devlin dropped his hand sharply.

"Now," he grunted.

Behan thumbed the button on his transmitter. For a moment there was nothing. Then a brilliant flash of flame followed by the loud thump of an explosion as a shipping container blew up and showered the distant dockside with burning debris. Behan set the transmitter down on the floor and he and Devlin hurried away. Behind them the luminous green figures on the display dial counted down the seconds to the next frequency.

The commander of the armored car jerked upright and looked around.

"Mother of God."

The soldiers inside the gate turned and stared at the glare of fire coming from somewhere amid the maze of containers between them and the third security fence. They heard shouts and the sound of a man screaming. Someone had been hurt.

Javad ducked toward the nearest trolley, pulled a Skorpion submachine gun from a carton of lettuce, and fired a short burst at the commander of the armored car. The officer screamed and staggered under the impact of the bullets, his back shredded from shoulder to hip. His legs buckled and he crashed forward onto the open cartons, his blood mingling with the pulp of crushed tomatoes. At the same moment Youssef pulled a Skorpion from the carton nearest him and sprayed the soldiers inside the gates who were still turned toward the sound of the explosion. They went down in a tangle of splintered limbs, their weapons clattering uselessly to the ground. The soldier in the turret of the armored car was just a second too slow. Javad caught him with his second burst. The man spasmed like a hooked fish as the bullets ripped through his chest and throat. Then he slid down inside the car, entangling his comrade in a mess of bloodied limbs. Javad leapt up onto the armored car and fired a long burst through the open turret hatch. There was a short choking cough, and then silence.

Youssef jumped up beside his comrade and together they hauled the two dead Saudis out of the turret and threw them to the ground. Javad was grinning as he climbed inside. It was easier than he had thought. Much easier. Just like they had told him at the training camp in Mashhad. Surprise was everything.

He dropped down into the driver's seat and Youssef wormed in after him, slid into the turret gunner's seat, and pulled the hatch shut. Javad turned on the ignition and the engine rumbled into life. He shifted the gearshift into first and the car leapt forward violently and stalled. Over his head he heard Youssef growl. Javad wiped his hands on his trousers and checked the controls once more. The Saladin was a newer model than the British-made Ferret he had trained on at the camp, but the controls were similar. He restarted the engine and tried again, easing the clutch in gently before shifting gear, as if it were a car he was driving. This time it didn't stall. The heavy armored vehicle rolled forward, crushing the body of a dead soldier. Javad shifted up quickly through second and third, then pointed the car toward the first security gate and stepped on the gas.

Sergeant Ibrahim saw it coming. He and his men had seen the explosion and the hijack of the armored car. They were already on their way, fanned out across the dock in a ragged skirmish line, when the Saladin accelerated toward them. Then, Ibrahim realized his mistake. They were all caught out in the open at the mercy of the car's 7.62-millimeter machine guns. He yelled at his men to take cover any way they could. Then he hurled himself forward onto his belly, aimed his rifle at the driver's hatch, and fired a series of short, rapid bursts. Javad flinched, but the bullets clanged harmlessly off the sixteen-millimeter-thick steel hull and ricocheted into the night. Youssef squinted through his machine-gun sights and squeezed the trigger. A white-hot stream of bullets chain-sawed the length of the dock, ripping up the pavement and filling the air with lethal concrete shards. Ibrahim threw himself to one side and started rolling, fast. The bullets chattered past his shoulder, throwing up a stinging hail of debris. The second burst hit him and butchered him from head to toe, smearing the ground with tattered pieces of his flesh. Youssef turned his attention to the others, rotating the turret through 180 degrees, filling the air with a white-hot scythe of bullets. More men screamed and fell.

Javad jerked the car to a halt and squeezed out of the driver's seat. They had taken out the initial opposition on the ground. They knew what they had to do next. Youssef checked the breech of the seventy-six-millimeter main gun and saw that a HESH round was already loaded; a high explosive shell with a squash head. Ideal for taking out an intruder in an oncoming car or truck. Youssef shut the breech and shut off the safety override. Then he squinted into the computerized aiming system. He locked onto his target, keyed the numbers into the computer, and hit the firing button. Both of them clapped their hands over their ears as the inside of the car reverberated to the roar of the departing round, but still their eardrums screamed with pain. The shell howled high over the harbor and missed. A moment later there was the sound of a distant explosion as it landed in the streets on the southern side of the harbor.

"One more," Javad yelled.

Youssef placed a fresh shell into the smoking breech. His body was slick with sweat but his throat felt dry like sand. He rolled his tongue and tried vainly to moisten his mouth. He struggled to remember everything he had learned on the artillery range at the camp in northern Iran. He thought he had been locked on perfectly, but the round had gone high. A storm of bullets raked the length of the car. He had no more time. He checked the coordinates once more, compensated again for elevation, and punched in the new numbers. Then he hit the firing button, put his hands over his ears, and prayed to almighty God. The car bucked and roared and a second shell howled over the harbor. A moment later the cabin of the crane nearest the *Britannia* disappeared in an orange and white fireball. Fragments of burning metal spumed into the air like comets. The crane groaned, its skinny metal legs buckled, and it started to fall.

Javad cheered and slapped his comrade on the back. Youssef grinned dumbly and mumbled his thanks to Allah. But their exuberance was cut short by a renewed storm of bullets on the hull of the armored car.

"We have done as they asked," Javad shouted above the barrage. "We can go now—and hold up our heads like heroes."

He squirmed back into the driver's seat, revved the engine, and aimed the armored car at the first checkpoint. A moment later they burst through the gates with a screech of tearing metal. Javad kept his foot down hard and steered for the causeway that marked the northern arm of the outer harbor. They were lucky. The dock road was clear. Javad had expected to see more soldiers. To him it seemed as though they had been fighting for an eternity. And yet, only three minutes had passed since they had fired the first shots. The momentum of surprise was still with them. A moment later they bumped off the main road and onto the narrow causeway. The car hummed along the blacktop with the sea glimmering dully on both sides. It took only seconds to reach the point where the causeway elbowed sharply toward the harbor mouth. Javad cut the engine, ground brutally down through the gears, and brought the car to a noisy, juddering halt. Youssef was ready. He threw open the turret hatch and the two of them squirmed outside. Sweating and cursing, they both grabbed a jerrican and began dousing the armored car with gasoline. Javad drenched the outside of the car, then poured the rest of the gas down through the open turret and threw the can in after it. Then he jumped down after Youssef, who was laying a gasoline trail along the causeway. The trail ran for about sixty yards before Youssef ran out of fuel. Javad hurried another thirty yards, then clambered down into the jumble of giant boulders that held back the open sea. Behind him Youssef plucked a cheap plastic lighter from his shirt pocket, thumbed up a flame, and threw it into the glistening wet trail of fuel. The flame leapt along the road like a livid pointing finger. Youssef turned, sprinted a dozen desperate paces, then hurled himself down into the sheltering boulders. The flame touched the fuel-drenched armored car and erupted in a brilliant fountain of fire. Seconds later the remaining forty rounds of high-explosive shells and two thousand rounds of machine-gun shells detonated inside the car. The night sky was ripped apart by a thunderous explosion that rocked the Jidda skyline and echoed among the giant skyscrapers like artillery fire. Windows shattered and crystal waterfalls spilled from the tallest buildings, filling the streets below with a beautiful deadly spray.

Javad and Youssef cowered among the boulders and waited till the last echoes had died away and the last pieces of falling debris had spattered harmlessly into the sea. Then the two of them clambered cautiously into the open and looked back along the causeway. Where the armored car had been, there was now a thirty-foot gap in the road. The causeway's spine had been broken and the open sea was rushing into the fissure, soothing its jagged, burning edges with a hiss of steam.

Youssef looked around and saw Javad beckoning him to follow. The two men clambered down among the boulders again, down to the water's edge. There they stopped and looked at each other. Then they stared anxiously out to sea and waited. Behind them they heard the mournful drone of the first ambulances.

A moment later, they heard something else. The deep mutter of a powerful engine growling through the dark water. The two men crouched back into the shadows and peered expectantly into the night, both of them filled with the same dreadful doubt. Would their new comrades-in-arms prove themselves trustworthy allies? They were about to find out.

Gradually, it came into view. A black powerboat riding low in the water, carrying no lights and impossible to see until it was within a few yards of the shore. Javad picked them out first. Four hooded men in black, silent and still. Javad thought he saw the glint of moonlight on a gun barrel. It was them. It had to be. And there would be only one pass, Javad had been warned. Only one chance to get away.

"Brothers," Javad called out suddenly, making up his mind. "We're here . . . over here!"

The men in the boat turned in unison. The gun barrels came up. Javad hesitated, held his breath, and stepped out into the open. Youssef saw him and followed. Their choice was simple. Die quickly now or risk capture and torture at the hands of the Saudis. The driver of the speedboat throttled up and spun the boat around. The guns remained pointed at the two men on shore the whole time, but did not open fire. The boat idled to within ten feet of the rough-edged boulders.

"Jump, you fools," an Arab voice spat at them from the boat. "Be quick or we will leave you here."

The two Palestinians kicked off their shoes and leapt into the water. It took only a few seconds to swim out to the launch and grasp the outreached hands. Their rescuers pulled them in roughly and threw them onto the deck, where they remained, fearful and confused. They looked around at the hooded faces of their rescuers. The man at the wheel revved the engine, and the boat banked hard as it turned, then gathered speed and headed toward the open sea. The two Palestinians grabbed for handholds as they slewed across the slippery deck. The men in black swore at them in a language they did not understand. Javad and Youssef eyed each other uneasily. They had done everything they had been asked. Why would these men speak to them so harshly now, without gratitude? What kind of allies were they?

Then one of the hooded men stepped forward, steadied himself with one hand on the gunwale, and used the other to pull off his mask. Javad and Youssef watched him warily, fear creeping through their bodies like a chill. Then they recognized the thin, bearded face of Abu Musa, regional commander of the PFLP-GC, and their fear faded.

"Allahu Aqbar," Musa shouted above the roar of the engine as the boat picked up speed and spray whipped inboard, past his long, flowing hair. "My brothers, you have earned thrones of honor in paradise."

Two miles away, Dominic Behan and Bobby Devlin watched from the cover of the warehouse as the last Saudi patrol boat peeled away from the *Britannia* and sped toward the sound of a new and more massive explosion at the outer harbor. Two fires burned on the dock-side, one from the sabotaged container, the other from the shattered loading crane. The harbor front swarmed with Saudi soldiers and the night crackled with gunfire as confused men fired at shadows amid the maze of containers where they believed terrorists had taken refuge. Behan turned to his waiting men.

"Our turn, lads," he grunted. "Let's show 'em some real trouble."

His men slid open the warehouse doors and pushed the inflatable down the wide concrete steps to the sea. Quickly, they climbed in, weapons ready. Devlin started the muffled engine and steered them under the cover of the nearby pier. Then he motored quietly between the pilings, heading for the end of the pier, hugging the shadows, edging closer and closer to the *Britannia.* Behan glanced at his watch. He had memorized the times. The second hand ticked past the hour, and a moment later came the sound of another huge explosion as a second container went up onshore, adding to the mayhem that raged above their heads. There were more to come, Behan knew. A year of meticulous planning was yielding its deadly dividends. The British couldn't begin to imagine the scale of this thing that had been launched so suddenly, so violently against them here in this alien desert port.

* * *

John Gault closed the door of his cabin, sat wearily on the edge of his bed, and fell backward onto the soft covers with his eyes closed. He could fall asleep in an instant, he knew, exactly the way he was. Without opening his eyes he began to loosen the knot in his tie. At the same time he used the toe of his shoe to prise the other from his foot. And then he heard the sound of the first explosion. The weariness evaporated. A jolt of adrenaline surged through his body. His eyes snapped open, he pushed the loosened shoe back onto his foot, and sprang from the bed to the door. His MP5K was out of its holster and in his hand when he stepped into the royal corridor. Judy was already there. She was still wearing her evening dress, but the same stubby Heckler and Koch submachine gun was in her hand too, snatched through a pocket slit in her dress from the holster on her thigh. She hurried to the door of the queen's apartment and rapped loudly.

"Are you all right, ma'am?"

Gault heard a faint reply.

"Please stay where you are until I return," Judy snapped. It was the first time in her life she had given her monarch a direct order.

Gault hammered on the door to the duke's apartment.

"Are you all right, sir?"

There was nothing. Gault tried the handle. The door was locked.

"Sir . . . ?" he began, his voice loud, urgent.

"Yes, yes" came the irritable reply. "What the hell is going on?"

The door opened and the duke appeared, his thin hair ruffled and his dressing gown rumpled as though it had been put on in a hurry.

"I don't know what it is, sir," Gault answered. "But I want you to stay here with the door locked till I get back and give you the all-clear."

He turned to go, but something stopped him and he hesitated just long enough to look back.

"I think you'd better get dressed, sir. As a precaution. And I think Her Royal Highness should do the same."

A look of real concern shadowed the duke's eyes.

"What . . . are you sure, Captain?"

"I'm sorry, sir, but I think it would be wise. I didn't like the sound of that . . . whatever it was. If somebody's having a go at the *Britannia,* we might have to transfer you both to the *Hotspur."*

The duke saw the look in Gault's eyes. He nodded and closed the door without another word. Gault knew this was one time when the duke would do exactly as he had been told. Nor would he attempt to join his wife unless Gault told him it was safe. In the event of a direct assault, the two heads of the royal household would be protected separately, so that if things went wrong, at least one of them would survive. The duke also understood that if this were a genuine emergency, his wife's safety would come before his. Gault broke into a trot along the corridor. Judy Stone was already at the door leading to the shelter deck that overlooked the royal deck. She paused and looked at Gault.

"You tell him to get dressed?"

"I think it's best," Gault answered.

"Me too," Judy said. "Let's just take a quick peep outside and see what's going on, shall we?"

Gault fought the urge to push past her. He had to keep reminding himself. He might be more experienced than she was, but she had seniority on board the *Britannia.* Even if she was a woman. He nodded and prepared to follow her. Then they heard anxious voices in the corridor behind them. They turned to see Lady Sarah and Tony Stevens, the duke's equerry, still in their nightclothes, hurrying down the corridor toward them. They were the only other people on the royal deck and occupied the servants' cabins next door to the pantry.

"Get dressed and stay with their highnesses till we come back," Gault ordered.

Stevens and Lady Sarah looked apprehensively at each other, then turned back to do as they were told.

Judy nodded and opened the door. They hurried past the cane chairs and tables in the darkened sun lounge and out onto the veranda deck, where they could see over much of the harbor front. The scene that confronted them told them that their worst fears were about to come true. The *Britannia* was under attack, and wherever they looked they could see only alarm and confusion. Saudi soldiers were running across the open dock, weapons raised. Gault could see several Saudi officers who seemed to be adding to the chaos by giving contradictory orders. A fire was burning fiercely amid the maze of containers on the adjacent dock, and the soldiers were heading toward it as though it were a magnet.

"Damn," Judy swore. "They shouldn't desert the security area around the yacht."

At that moment Inspector Hardacre, the queen's chief of security, appeared on the deck below. He looked worried and disheveled in a hastily thrown on track suit. He didn't appear to notice Gault and Stone on the deck above as he cupped his hands to his mouth and yelled down to the Royal Marines on the dock. Hardacre must have had the same thought as Judy. He urged the marines to get the Saudi soldiers back around the yacht, but his voice could not be heard above the noise on the dock.

Then they heard the first shots from the northern security perimiter. A short staccato burst, then two more, almost in unison. A pause and then another burst.

"That's a skorpion," Gault muttered. The shots only escalated the uproar on the dock. Saudi soldiers swarmed into the darkened alleys between the stacked containers, hurrying toward the sound of the shooting. One of the Saladin armored cars roared into life and rolled toward the center of the dock, gun turret swiveling nervously from side to side. A second Saladin switched on its engine but held its post near the southern gateway.

"Jesus," Gault mumbled under his breath. The first sign of trouble and discipline among the Saudi troops was breaking down everywhere. Gault leaned over the rail and yelled down to Hardacre.

"Forget the Saudis," he shouted. "Tell Grant to get all his men up here . . . now!"

Hardacre looked around and saw Gault and Stone for the first time. He hesitated a moment, then nodded and disappeared in search of Colonel Grant, commanding officer of the ship's guard. The sound of renewed firing rang along the dock. The sharp, flat crack of the Saudis' M-16s, then something more powerful.

"Shit," Gault swore. Judy looked at him.

"Heavy machine gun," Gault said. "Might be one of the Saladins. Whatever is going on out there . . . it isn't good."

"Let's get the yacht moving," Judy decided. In situations of clear and imminent threat to Their Majesties, they had the power to override all other security levels on board and give orders direct to the captain.

Gault nodded and reached into his jacket for his radio. Again Judy beat him to it.

"Security to bridge," she said calmly into the mouthpiece. "Winter Robin calling. I'm declaring a code red. Repeat . . . code red. Get this vessel moving, please. Clear the harbor and keep her moving. Advise *Hotspur* we're coming over."

"Bridge to security," Berenson's voice came back sharp and clear. "Acknowledge Winter Robin. Acknowledge code red. We're under way."

A moment later the yacht shuddered as the *Britannia*'s 12,000-horsepower diesel turbines grumbled into life and the royal bodyguards felt the reassuring vibration of the ship's engines through the deck. Gault heard crewmen running and shouting loudly to each other as they rushed to cast off. A sure sign of emergency. Ever since the *Britannia* had been launched in 1953, it had been a standing order that whenever members of the royal family were on board, commands were not shouted. Orders on deck were conveyed only by hand signal. Now something dangerously close to pandemonium ruled.

Foam boiled at the stern as the prop churned water. The two gangways that connected the yacht to the dock creaked in protest as the *Britannia* shifted at her berth. The marines onshore glanced apprehensively at each other as they realized they were about to be left behind.

"Look lively, you men." Gault heard the familiar bellow of Colonel Grant below. "Get your arses back on board."

The marines hesitated. The gangways were still in place but the hatches had been secured and locked. There was no way back on board except up the side of the yacht. Colonel Grant read their minds.

"Right bloody now," he roared in a voice that could cut through cannon fire.

The two soldiers hesitated no longer. They shouldered their rifles and sprinted for the stern gangway. It was the ramp that came closest to the ship's rail. The first man to the top of the gangway made a stirrup with his hands and catapulted the second man up the side of the yacht. He grabbed hold of the bottom rail and hauled himself on deck. The moment he was safe he squirmed around and reached back over the side to pull his comrade up after him. The second marine dropped back a few steps, then ran for it and jumped. It wasn't good enough. He missed the outstretched hand by inches, cannoned off the side of the yacht, and fell badly back onto the gangway. For a moment he looked dazed by the fall. The yacht stirred and began to edge away from the dock, dragging the gangways with it. Another two seconds, and the shore end of the stern ramp would fall free of the dock and the whole thing would plunge into the water, taking the dazed marine with it. Everyone on board watched anxiously to see what would happen next. Even Colonel Grant had fallen silent. The man struggled back to his feet, retraced his footsteps on the shifting gangway, then tried once more. He ran, leapt, and clawed desperately upward with both hands. The marine on deck held on to a rail brace, thrust himself out over the side of the yacht . . . and caught his buddy's hand with a loud slap. The soldier's boots cleared the ramp as it scraped free of the dockside. Slowly it twisted and turned beneath him, then snapped free of its bolts, splashed heavily into the water, and disappeared. Half a dozen crewmen rushed to pull the two dangling marines on deck, where they landed in a sprawling heap.

Gault heard Colonel Grant's voice echo along the main deck.

"When you two lovebirds have quite finished buggering around," he bellowed, "we've got a real emergency on our hands!"

Despite the nightmare that seemed to be unfolding all around them, Gault smiled. Then something happened that wiped all trace of the smile from his face. It was the sound of a loud thump from the northern security fence followed by the unmistakable whine of an artillery shell.

"Jesus," Gault swore. "A three-pounder."

He and Judy ducked as the shell screamed overhead. A moment later they saw the flash of the explosion a half mile south of the dockyards, followed a second later by the hollow crack of the explosion.

Gault looked at Judy. Her mask was still intact and he saw no hint of fear in her eyes. She caught him looking at her and raised an eyebrow.

"So much for an early night," she said evenly.

There was another bang from the northern side of the docks, and again they ducked and watched. The second shell came in low and flat, and Gault knew it was going to come close. It ripped into the cabin of a crane eighty-five yards from the royal yacht and exploded in a shower of molten metal. The crane staggered for a moment like a stricken bird on thin metal legs. Then it gave a great metallic groan and toppled sideways across the dock in a shower of spark and flame. The soldiers underneath scattered. The Saladin tried to back away, but it was too late and the wreckage of the falling crane reached out and touched the armored car like the tip of a giant branding iron. Clouds of smoke spurted from the thick rubber tires and they burst into flame, gluing the vehicle to the pavement. The flames billowed upward to engulf the turret. Gault watched grimly as the hatch crashed open and a Saudi soldier tried to escape. The man leapt through the inferno, but his uniform caught fire and he fell to the ground, screaming and writhing, trying to beat out the flames with his hands. A second soldier appeared through the turret. He leapt clear, then turned back to try to rescue his burning comrade on the ground. A third man was halfway out of the hatch when the flames snaked through the car's open vents and touched off the shells inside.

The car and the three soldiers disappeared in a boiling cloud of flame and a terrible blast of heat rippled across the dock. Instinctively, Gault grabbed Judy, threw her across the deck, and dived after her with his hands clamped over his ears to stop the concussion bursting his eardrums. A moment later he felt the shock wave wash over him accompanied by a deafening clap of thunder that rattled every bolt and rivet in the *Britannia.* Gault stayed still, listening to the ping and clatter of falling metal fragments. When it stopped, he opened his eyes and looked cautiously around.

"Gault?"

It was faint and urgent and it was very close. Then he realized. It was Judy Stone, underneath him, and her mouth was next to his ear.

"You all right?" he asked.

"I'm fine," she answered breathlessly. "But would you do something for me, please?"

"What?"

"Get the hell off me."

"Oh," Gault muttered. "Frightfully sorry . . ."

He rolled away, embarrassed by his own protective instinct. Judy got to her feet. She had not been hurt by the fall, and she still had her gun in her hand, though it was unlikely her dress would see any more dinner parties. The slide across the deck had turned it into a shredded rag. Underneath, Gault noticed, she wore a flesh-toned body stocking. Immediately he knew what it was. One of the new Lycra-Gore-Tex body suits. Practical, flexible, indestructible. Able to turn potentially fatal wounds into mere grazes. She had been better equipped to survive the blast than him.

"One of these days, Gault—" She paused to push her hair back from her forehead so she could look him directly in the eye. "Trying to be a gentleman will get you killed."

Gault shrugged awkwardly. He knew she was right.

"One of these days . . ." he murmured.

But she had already turned away to survey the scene on the waterfront. Together they edged warily back to the ship's rail. The dock seemed eerily still after the fury of a few moments earlier. There was no sign of the burning armored car. Only a massive, still-smoldering crater and the glowing fragments of metal from the shattered crane. The rest of the dock was empty except for the broken bodies of a dozen Saudi soldiers, men who had been caught in the open by the full ferocity of the blast. Gault leaned over the rail to look down the length of the ship. The sleek royal-blue hull had been pitted and gouged from bow to stern. A few ugly pieces of shrapnel had become embedded in the side, and there were a couple of dents that might have become holes had the hull not been reinforced at the yacht's last major refit. All these scars were superficial, Gault knew. Scars on a ship could be welded clean and painted over. What mattered most was that the yacht was undamaged and still moving. She was thirty to forty yards away from the dock now and maneuvering for the turn toward HMS *Hotspur.* Gault squinted over the harbor to where the guard ship sat at anchor, alarms howling, spotlights cleaving the water for any sign of intruders. They were close enough for him to pick out darkened figures moving on the warship's bridge and to see steel helmets bobbing along the deck as sailors rushed to their stations. There was another explosion amid the containers and a sudden upsurge of firing from the skittish soldiers who prowled the container alleys.

"Jesus—"

His words were cut off by yet another explosion, though this one was a long way off. Gault saw the flash reflected from the buildings along the waterfront. He guessed that it was a couple of miles away, near the harbor mouth. Then he heard another sound. The sound of boat engines racing at high speed. He looked down as two Saudi patrol boats streaked past in a hiss of foam. They were followed a moment later by a third, filled with Saudi marines. All headed toward the northern arm of the harbor, from where the attack seemed to have been launched.

What was it, Gault wondered. A terrorist attack from the sea? An attempted coup? The beginnings of a new Gulf war?

"You thinking what I'm thinking?" he asked Judy.

"I think we go below and batten down till we're sure this is over," she decided. He nodded his agreement and together they turned back toward the royal apartments. Colonel Grant and his men could secure the ship. The bodyguards would take care of the royal apartments.

At that moment Dominic Behan and his men stood poised a mere hundred yards from the *Britannia,* still undetected in the shadows at the end of the loading pier. Behan took one last look around at his men to make sure they were ready. Then he gave the signal that would begin the final assault.

Everybody but Bobby Devlin at the helm opened fire, their rifles trained on the *Hotspur*'s port side spotlight. The streaming tracers knitted together to form a scarlet ribbon that lanced across the water and smashed the spotlight into a thousand pieces. Instantly, the narrowing stretch of water between the *Hotspur* and the *Britannia* was transformed into a black ravine. Devlin opened the throttle and the dinghy leapt from the shadows like a beast free of its chain. The men held tight and huddled low as the boat hammered across the open water at full speed. For one long, precious minute no one saw them as they hurtled through the blackness. Then, when they were within fifty yards of the *Britannia,* they heard the first shouts of alarm from the *Hotspur.* Seconds later they heard the hum and smack of bullets hitting the water all around them. Behan and his men flinched but hung fast. The dinghy could take a few hits without deflating, but not many. They needed some luck . . . and a few more seconds. That was all. A few more lousy seconds to execute an operation that would alter the course of history.

They were almost there. The gap between them and the royal yacht narrowed to thirty yards. Then twenty. Then ten. Behan's heart pounded. They were going to make it. Bobby Devlin cut the motor. They coasted the last few yards and scraped against the slow-moving hull of the *Britannia.* The shooting from the *Hotspur* melted away. The sailors were afraid of hitting the royal yacht. Still, no one on board the *Britannia* had seen the dinghy. Everyone was on the port side, riveted by the spectacle of the carnage onshore. It was exactly as it had been planned. From the bridge of HMS *Hotspur* Captain Purcell radioed an urgent warning to the bridge of the *Britannia.* Berenson heard it and turned to alert Colonel Grant. But it was already too late.

The first gas canisters arced through the air and onto the upper decks of the *Britannia.* Behan plucked two more cans from his shoulder harness, pulled the rings, and lobbed them high over his head. Misty coils of GBX danced lightly in the breeze on the upper deck, then melded into a rolling gray cloud that swept the length of the ship. It poured through vents and portholes, filling cabins and wardrooms. It snaked down through air-conditioning ducts like cold fog until it permeated the entire yacht, crippling everyone it touched. The gas created a hydrocarbon mist, heavier than air. It clung to everything, formed an oily sheen on clothes and human skin. Those who came in contact with it were stricken instantly. First there were convulsions, spasms so violent they could tear the walls of tightly clenched stomach muscles like tissue paper. Then came the nausea, the vomiting, and diarrhea. And finally the partial paralysis of the limbs, the weakness and loss of control that could last up to four hours.

Behan threw the first grappling hook and felt it latch on to the ship's rail. He tucked his M-16 across his back, grabbed on to the rope with leather-gloved hands, and walked up the side of the *Britannia* as easily as if he were taking a stroll along a country lane. A second hook flashed past him, then a third and a fourth. From the bridge of the *Hotspur,* Captain Purcell watched in horrified silence as terrorists swarmed up the side of his monarch's yacht.

"Gas," he muttered out loud. Then to himself. Why hadn't they been better prepared for a gas attack? He stepped out onto the flying bridge and shouted down to the men who were hurrying to launch the *Hotspur*'s two jolly boats. Lined up on deck were fifty fully armed sailors eager to cross to the *Britannia* and go to their monarch's aid.

"Lieutenant," Purcell shouted down to the first officer. "Send only men with gas masks."

The officer looked up in dismay. More precious minutes lost.

Behan reached the ship's rail first and paused while he snatched a quick look over the side. Immediately, he saw a middle-aged man in a track suit only a few feet away, writhing helplessly on the deck, alone in his agony. Behan also saw the automatic pistol dangling loosely from one hand. Security, Behan realized. Special Branch or SAS. He'd had a few encounters with those bastards in other times and places. He glanced quickly around to make sure there was no other threat, then hauled himself over the rail and landed squarely on deck. Then he took the M-16 from his shoulder, pointed the muzzle at the back of Inspector Hardacre's head, and pulled the trigger. Someone landed on deck behind him. Behan turned to see Bobby Devlin's eyes through the visor of his gas mask. Behan gave him the thumbs-up and the two of them moved through the fog together. They had gone only a few more steps when they found their first marine. He was on his knees, face contorted as he fought the pain and the nausea and struggled to lift his rifle. Behan signaled Devlin with a raised finger. Devlin nodded and fired a burst point-blank into the young marine's chest. Behan smiled. It was a bonus to be able to settle a few old scores while he inflicted on the British their greatest defeat in the hundred-year history of their struggle with the IRA.

Gault smelled it before he saw it. He and Judy were halfway across the veranda deck when he caught a trace of something new and bitter on the night air. Immediately his stomach recoiled. He looked around and saw a billowing cloud of gas rolling down the yacht toward them.

"Gas," he shouted to Judy. "Get inside."

He pushed her roughly through the door to the royal sun lounge and followed. He was almost inside when he heard gunfire close by and he felt compelled to turn back. He threw himself flat across the deck and tried to stay under the encroaching gas. He reached the edge of the deck and peered through the rail at the deck below. For a moment there was nothing, then he saw two black shapes moving through the gas, both wearing hoods and gas masks and carrying M-16s.

"Bastards," he muttered. His stomach spasmed and he held his breath while he leveled his MP5 and squirted a long, wide burst at the terrorists below. The first man gave a muffled scream, staggered backward, hit the guard rail, and slumped forward into a heap, his rifle clattering across the deck. The second man fired back, but Gault had gone. He rolled to the side and peered over the edge of the deck again. This time he saw another black figure about to climb over the rail. Gault aimed and fired. The shape disappeared in a soundless flurry of arms and legs. Then a savage volley of shots ripped up through the deck and Gault was forced back. He took an involuntary breath and gagged. His body was gripped by a terrible pain.

"Gault," Judy shouted behind him. "For Christ's sake . . ."

He struggled to his feet, stumbled back across the deck, and threw himself through the sun lounge door to the safety of the royal corridor. Judy pulled him roughly inside and slammed the door behind him. Gault slid weakly down the wall till he was slumped on the floor, battling the pain and sickness that boiled up inside his gut. Judy ignored him. She bent toward a flat gray panel set in the wall behind the door at floor level. She flicked it open and threw a series of switches. Immediately there was a dull electronic whine as a titanium alloy screen a quarter-inch thick slid out of the bulkhead and sealed the door airtight. At the same moment, other armored screens slid smoothly into position all around the royal apartments, sealing the corridor, the skylights, and the portholes, cutting the royal deck off from the rest of the yacht, turning it into a self-sufficient stronghold. The royal fortress even had its own air-filtration system that kicked in the moment the screens were activated and screened out the worst of the gas.

Then Judy looked at Gault. He had contracted into a fetal crouch on the floor, hands clutched to his stomach, his face white and covered with sweat. His gun lay uselessly by his side. A foul and unmistakable stench drifted up from him and ugly, choking sounds came from his throat as though he were about to vomit.

"How much do you think you got?" she asked sharply.

"Not much," he wheezed. He tried to say more, but his voice dissolved into a harsh, racking cough and he had to clench his eyes against the pain that seared his gut and his bowel.

"More than enough," she decided. She took hold of an arm and shoulder and heaved him roughly to his feet. Gault groaned and looked miserably at her. The bitch was stronger than he expected. Then she half pushed, half dragged him down the corridor to his room, shoved him into the shower fully dressed, and switched on the faucet, hot and hard. She waited while the water washed the worst of the oily toxins from his hair, skin, and clothes, then switched it off.

"Take everything off and wash yourself with soap," she ordered. "I'll be back when I can."

Then she left him. Outwardly she looked calm. Inwardly she was furious. Furious and terrified at the thought of what might have happened if Gault had gotten himself killed and left her to look after the queen and Prince Philip on her own. She recognized the gas too. Gault might be lucky. Perhaps he had gotten only a mild dose, or he would never have made it back inside. The others who had been caught outside hadn't stood a chance. None of them had expected a gas attack. Not here. Not now. It was the one thing that no one predicted.

She stepped back into the corridor and looked around. It was still empty. She sniffed tentatively at the air. Still nothing. If everything else worked as well as the filtration system, they would be safe till help came. The screens that protected them were sandwiched layers of titanium and Kevlar, an added precaution secretly installed during the *Britannia*'s last refit at Devonport. A precaution that would have drawn squeals of protest from the royal family's many critics, if anyone had deigned to tell them. But now these screens would demonstrate their worth. They had to be used only once to demonstrate their true value. She also knew that everyone in the royal apartments was safe as long as they stayed where they were; the queen, Prince Philip, Tony Stevens, Lady Sarah, Gault, and herself. There was water, waste disposal, and provisions enough to get all six of them through a month or more, if necessary. More than enough time for their security forces to neutralize any external threat. She heard the faint sound of firing from outside. The battle was still raging out there. Good men were dying. And the unthinkable had happened. The *Britannia* had been boarded. The Queen of England had been taken hostage on her own yacht.

Judy took a deep breath to compose herself, then walked the few steps down the royal corridor and knocked on Her Majesty's bedroom door.

"It's Lieutenant Stone, ma'am," she said. "May I see you for a moment, please?"

There was a pause, the sound of a lock turning, and then the door opened. Lady Sarah appeared, her face set, eyes tense. She nodded, made a halfhearted attempt at a smile, then stood aside to let Judy in. Judy stepped inside and looked around. She knew the royal bedroom quite well. She had inspected it many times in the absence of its usual occupant. It was a large room for a yacht, even for the cabin of a queen. Much of the furniture was priceless and included antiques from the royal yacht that preceded the *Britannia,* the *Victoria and Albert.* Lady Sarah walked back across the room and joined Tony Stevens, who stood beside a large sofa against the opposite wall. The queen and Prince Philip sat almost in the center of the room, side by side in two large armchairs. Judy frowned but said nothing. Clearly, the duke had decided to disobey the rules and go to his wife's side. Again she cursed Gault for not being there to help her.

She paused for a moment while she took in the whole bizarre scene. In her wildest imaginings she had never expected to see herself in a bedroom with the two heads of the royal household. The double bed, with its heavily brocaded covers, added just the right touch of absurdity, she thought. Then she thought how she must look in her ripped and tattered dress, her MP5 in her hand. There was much about this moment that was eerie and surreal. Then the sound of distant firing intruded again. Unfortunately, it was real. All of it.

The duke had put on a pair of gray slacks and a navy-blue polo shirt. On his feet were a pair of deck shoes. His ankles were bare. The queen had put on slacks and wore a Windbreaker over a cream blouse and a dark brown sweater in anticipation of the switch to HMS *Hotspur.* Her left hand toyed restlessly with the headscarf she had intended to wear outside. The only sign of nervousness. Her right hand was on the arm of the chair with her husband's hand rested reassuringly on top of it. It was touching, Judy thought. A husband comforting his wife in a moment of danger. Despite all the stories of a marriage long gone sour, it was exactly how every other married couple in the world would have behaved in a similar situation. Except that this was no ordinary couple. This was no ordinary situation. This was the Queen of England and her consort. And no one had taken a British monarch hostage in five centuries. No one had dreamed that it could be done.

Suddenly, Judy felt the enormity of the moment weighing down on her slight shoulders, threatening to crush her. She felt a rare surge of panic. They were all looking at her. Judy Stone. Born Reigate, Surrey, March 1963. High school athletics star, honors graduate from Dartmouth Naval College. Career naval officer. Best of the new breed of female special forces. Suddenly, all that high-level SAS training wasn't enough. Her partner was out of action for at least an hour. She was on her own. And they were all looking to her, waiting for her to say something, to do something that might make them feel better. She opened her mouth to speak, but her throat had suddenly gone dry.

Then her royal highness spoke the words Judy had intended to speak.

"Well," she said in that light, delicate voice that was known all over the world. "It looks like we've got ourselves into rather a tricky situation, doesn't it?"

Judy smiled.

"Yes, ma'am," she answered, her nerve steady again. "I'm afraid it looks that way . . . but I dare say we'll all muddle through."

Dominic Behan kicked open the door to the bridge, ducked back, and waited. But there were no answering shots from inside. Only the sound of men groaning. The gas had done most of their work for them. He had used enough GBX to disable every man on board ten times over. It was a calm night and the gas had coated the yacht like paint. They had emptied canisters into every air vent and shaft, sending long, noxious columns of gas probing deep into the ship's interior, where it would linger for hours, disabling anybody who came in contact with it.

Even so, it had been bloody. Behan had lost three of his men, including Bobby Devlin, his strong right arm. Kevin McBride had been shot as he was boarding, by one of those SAS bastards guarding the queen. Though Behan had driven him back fast enough. The third man to go down had been John Kavanagh. Shot by a marine who had swallowed enough gas to sicken a bull but who still managed to get off a killing shot. A shot that cost him his own life.

That left Behan with Patsy Ryan, Jimmy Mulcahey, Billy Deveny, and Michael Kenney. So far, Behan estimated, they had killed or wounded eleven crewmen, including three marines. It was the marines who were left that worried him most. The marines and the SAS. The SAS men would be keeping their heads down with the queen and the Duke of Edinburgh until the gas cleared, Behan knew. And some of the marines would have been stuck ashore. But there were 277 officers and men on board the *Britannia.* More than his small squad could handle when the gas wore off. And still they hadn't taken the bridge.

The engines had slowed to neutral but the yacht was drifting in wide circles across the harbor, and if Behan's men didn't take control soon, they would run aground or ram the dock. The *Hotspur* had launched two boats into the water, filled with armed men. Behan was running out of time. But he didn't want a gunfight on the bridge if he could avoid it. He wanted the bridge and the radio room intact. He took another gas canister from his belt, pulled the ring, and lobbed it inside. The gas billowed thickly in the confined space, and there was a wretched chorus of moans from the already stricken men inside. Behan didn't know how much of the gas might be fatal. Nor did he care.

He braced himself, then dived low through the door and rolled across the floor. He saw two men in naval uniform lying on the deck, both huddled in the fetal position, their bodies racked by spasms, arms and legs twitching like men in their death throes. A fire mask lay uselessly on the deck nearby. The other man had managed to put his mask on, but it had proved useless against GBX. If it couldn't penetrate the lungs, it simply attached itself to any patch of exposed skin, however small, and seeped through the pores.

Two doors led back from the bridge. Behan recalled the deck plans he had studied every day for the last year until they had been engraved on his mind. One door led to the radio room. The other to the charthouse. He scrambled to his feet and beckoned to the men outside. They swarmed onto the bridge and took up positions on each side of the doors. Behan nodded and they lobbed fresh canisters of gas through each door. Almost immediately a crewman stumbled out of the radio room, one hand holding a handkerchief uselessly over his nose and mouth, the other gesturing feebly in submission. Behan grabbed him by the neck and shoved him outside. Jimmy Mulcahey kicked him to the deck and brought his rifle butt down hard on the back of the man's head, splitting his skull.

Behan crept warily into the radio room. It was empty. Next, they stormed the charthouse. It had only one occupant. A distinguished, gray-haired man sprawled beneath an open porthole, his eyes glassy, limbs trembling, fresh vomit staining the front of his crisp white shirt. A shirt that bore the golden insignia of an Admiral of the Fleet. Behan signaled to his men. Marchant was one man he wanted taken alive.

Behan strode back onto the bridge while his men dragged Marchant and the other officers below to be made prisoners in the admiral's day cabin. Then he beckoned to Patsy Ryan to stay with him. Ryan was the man with the master mariner's ticket. The new captain of the *Britannia.* Behan had known for a long time that he wouldn't need an army to seize the yacht. Despite its regal role, the *Britannia* was a ship like any other. All a hijacker had to do was hold the bridge and the engine room and he could take the ship wherever he liked. For a time. They couldn't keep the crew subdued indefinitely. There were too many hiding places on a ship 125 meters long. But then, Behan knew, they didn't have to hold the *Britannia* forever. Just long enough to get what they wanted.

Ryan stepped up to the computerized console and took a moment to study the instruments while Behan walked impatiently backward and forward across the bridge. Patsy Ryan had served as first mate on some of the biggest freighters in the world, smuggling weapons to Ireland from all four corners of the globe under the guise of his regular occupation. There was nothing on the bridge of the *Britannia* that he hadn't seen before. And everything seemed to be working. The prop was still turning and the instruments responding. The gas had been too quick for anyone to have the time to sabotage the controls. But the yacht was nearly a hundred yards out from the dock and still turning. Ryan reached for the ship's telegraph and cranked the handle from slow astern to slow ahead. Then he grabbed the wheel and gave it a spin to bring her around. The *Britannia* was leaving port a few hours ahead of schedule.

The rest of the hijackers returned to the bridge and Behan signaled that it was time for Kenney to go down to the engine room. He sent Mulcahey and Deveny with him in case the gas hadn't knocked out everybody below deck. It wouldn't take them too long now, Behan knew. Kenney was the best bomb maker the IRA had ever trained. He had all he needed in the satchels they had brought and he knew how to place them for maximum effect.

"You got it under control?" Behan asked Ryan, his voice a muffled grunt through his mask. Ryan gave the okay signal, then bent back over the controls. Behan peered outside. The boats from the *Hotspur* were almost alongside.

"Where's the ship-to-ship radio?" he asked.

Ryan quickly scanned the console, then handed the radio handset to Behan. The IRA man held the mouthpiece close to his mask and pushed the transmit button. He knew the *Britannia* would already be locked on to the *Hotspur*'s wavelength.

"This is the new commander of the *Britannia* calling the *Hotspur,*" he said. "I have taken over the *Britannia* in the name of the Irish Republican Army."

Ryan looked at Behan, his eyes shining behind the visor of his mask.

There was no response from the *Hotspur.*

"I know you can hear me," Behan went on. "You can probably see me too, so you know we've taken control of the bridge. Tell your sharpshooters they better hold their fire and tell the men in the boats to stand off. We've got enough Demex on board to blow this ship to kingdom come . . . and your queen and your prince with her. So tell your men to stand off, *Hotspur,* or there won't be a second chance to talk."

Still the radio stayed dead.

Behan put down the handset and stepped outside onto the compass deck to look at the oncoming launches. If they wanted to kill him, this would be their chance. He was in clear view of any sharpshooter on the *Hotspur.* But he was willing to bet his life that they wouldn't. Because they had to know that they had no choice. They had lost the battle. If they mounted an attack now, the *Britannia* would go up and they would all die . . . and with them the British monarch, who cowered below. It was the moment when history hovered over all their heads like a dark and menacing shadow.

Impulsively Behan pulled off his gas mask and tasted the night air through his hood. The GBX had dispersed, the night was clear once more, and there was only the residual bitterness of gas in the air. Behan stepped forward and rested his gloved hands on the rail and stood there for everyone to see: the officers and men on the *Hotspur,* the men in the oncoming boats, the packed ranks of Saudi soldiers on the dock. A burly figure in black, his narrowed eyes staring defiantly into the lenses of their sniper scopes, daring them to shoot.

Then it happened. The oncoming boats throttled back and drifted to a dead stop in the water a few yards from the *Britannia.* The sailors all wore gas masks, helmets, and combat vests. But they were too late. All they could do now was stand back and watch. Behan could feel their eyes on him. He could feel their impotent hatred. He grinned and turned back into the bridge to look at Patsy Ryan.

"We've got her," he said.

2 Scotch Mist

BALLACHULISH, SCOTLAND. MAY 16, 04.52 HOURS

Colin Lynch jolted into wakefulness eight minutes before the alarm was due to go off. Something was wrong. One moment he was deep in an untroubled sleep. The next he was wide awake, eyes and ears straining through the darkness, trying to determine what it was that had woken him. There was no drowsiness, no blur. Just plain animal instinct warning him of some vague and undefined threat. It was an instinct he never ignored.

He reached under the bed and eased the Browning Hi-Power out of the holster he had attached to the underside of the mattress with Velcro. It felt cold and reassuringly heavy in his hand, its fourteen-round magazine fully loaded with nine-millimeter hollow tips. It was an evil gun packed with evil ammunition. But Lynch had never believed that shooting people demanded any kind of professional courtesy. He needed a man stopper. And his customized Hi-Power would stop anybody. A nick from a single bullet was enough to cause an explosion of metal that would take out four or five pounds of flesh and bone. He had seen it done.

He slipped out from under the covers and padded across the hardwood floor without making a sound. He had worn only his underpants to bed. The air inside the cottage was cold and clung damply to his skin. He suppressed a shiver and quickly pulled on a pair of black track pants and a matching T-shirt. Then, still in bare feet, he stepped to the open door of his bedroom, looked around the kitchen, and listened. A gaunt half-moon shone through the window and covered the stone floor with a litter of splintered bones. He heard nothing, saw nothing. He ducked down, opened a cabinet door, and lifted out a black Kevlar helmet with a pair of night-sight goggles attached. The kind of helmet used by special forces troops. He put the helmet on, fastened the chin strap, and pushed the goggles back off his face. Then he padded across the living room at a fast crouch. He knelt down beside a window at the front of the cottage, moved the curtain a fraction, and snatched a quick look outside. There was nothing. Only a small, empty garden, a low stone wall, and a silvery ribbon of track that followed the mountainside down to the bottom of the glen. He leaned back, dropped the goggles over his face, switched on the night-sights, and looked out through the window once more. A tense two-second scan. If there were anyone out there watching him through their own set of night-sights, this would be their best chance to snap off a quick shot. But there was nothing. No sudden flare from a sniper's rifle. No luminescent blob in the half-light to indicate the body heat of an unexpected visitor. Nothing to indicate the cooling engine of a motor vehicle that had stopped halfway up the track.

Quickly and quietly he moved past every window until he had surveyed most of the surrounding mountainside. Still he found nothing to justify his alarm. The cottage stood alone on forty of the most useless acres in all the Scottish Highlands. The unmade track that led to the front door was steep and unwelcoming and threatened to rip the guts out of any soft, city car that might presume to climb it. The road at the bottom of the track was the A82 that reached southward out of Fort William, through Glen Coe to the nearest branch of Loch Linnhe and the village of Ballachulish, where hikers and climbers lodged before catching the ferry from Inchree to Corran. Lynch knew the terrain around his cottage well. There were no sheltering trees, no bushes or ruins where a sniper might conceal himself on this wind-blasted mountainside. Wherever he looked he could see nothing but open country and the distant, friendly glimmer of the loch. If anyone had been out there, Lynch would have seen him. It was one of the reasons he had bought the cottage. He preferred to hide out in the open.

He returned to the front of the house, unlocked the door, opened it a fraction, and listened. A few minutes ago there had been nothing. That had bothered him. Now he heard the reassuring chirrup of crickets. He waited. The soft whoop of an owl drifted eerily across the heather. He slipped outside, hurried across the dew-soaked grass, and crouched behind the dry stone wall in front of the cottage. Still nothing happened. He sniffed at the night air to see if there was anything unusual on the wind. There was nothing. No sulphurous taint of exhaust fumes. No tang of sweat from the bodies of approaching men. Only the saltiness of the inshore breeze as it drifted in from the Mull.

Something flared in the corner of his left eye. Lynch ducked and tensed, but again there was nothing. No overhead hum from a passing bullet. No loud smack of metal on stone. He scurried the length of the wall and snatched another look in the direction of the flash. He saw it again. Unmistakable this time. Body heat. It was moving fast, east to west eighty yards down the hill. A man running at a half crouch, carrying something? A gun? Lynch lifted the Hi-Power, aimed, and squeezed the trigger. Then he caught himself. The pulsing white blob in the night-sight was body heat all right. But it was moving too fast for a man. And it was on four legs. A dog, maybe, or a fox? Too big. A deer? It had to be. He watched it carefully through the goggles. A long, graceful bobbing motion moving diagonally across the mountainside in a path that would take it right past the cottage. Then it stopped. Lynch pushed the night-sights off his face and blinked his eyes to adjust to the natural light. Then he saw it, standing in the moonlight barely twenty yards away. He could just make out the narrow profile of the head as it turned to look in his direction. A young four-pointer. Lynch was still downwind, but the deer knew he was there. Suddenly, it veered sharply away from the cottage and broke into a run again. Faster, more urgent this time. A moment later it vanished across the brow of the hill. A lone highland buck searching for its mate. Lynch relaxed, lowered the Hi-Power, and slumped back against the wall, not minding the cold and damp as it seeped through his thin T-shirt. Then he smiled. Maybe he was getting old. Old and jittery. After all, today was different. It was his thirty-ninth birthday. The last year of youth. And he had something special planned. Something that would test the nerves of any man. Maybe that was what had woken him up before the alarm.

Lynch stepped back into his bedroom to hear Rod Stewart whining "Downtown Train" on the radio for the benefit of any early morning commuters who might be listening. The red digital numbers on the dial said 5:17. He frowned and shut it off. This little scare had robbed him of a good start to the day. Another sign of age maybe? He had noticed that the older he got, the more easily he was irritated by disruptions to his routine. It was ironic in a man who had chosen a life that had never lent itself to routine. He would have to get moving if he wanted to catch up. He stripped off his clothes, stepped into the bathroom, brushed his teeth, and washed his face and hair in cold water. The shower could wait till later, when he was really dirty. He paused to look in the mirror. His thick chestnut hair was cropped short, but here and there he could see telltale strands of silver. Early-warning signs of mortality. If he let his sideburns grow, he knew they would be almost all gray. He wasn't ready for that. He didn't feel like a man on the brink of forty. He didn't think the face that looked back at him was the face of an old man. Despite the reddish-brown stubble around the jaw, it was a fresh, clean-cut face. The women he met still seemed to find it appealing. His hazel eyes were sharp and clear, and there weren't too many lines in the soft skin around the eyes. He could easily pass for early thirties, he thought. He smiled at his own vanity, and a web of creases appeared instantly at the corners of his eyes. The smile dissolved into a sniff of resignation as he remembered why he hardly smiled anymore. The reminders were everywhere, even in the mirror. Life was a deadly affair.

He toweled himself dry, then walked out to the kitchen and opened the refrigerator. What he wanted was on the top shelf. A murky cocktail of soy milk, raw eggs, powdered multivitamins, and chocolate syrup in a clear plastic bottle. He took it out, shook it till it began to foam, then drank it slow and steady in one long swallow. Energy to burn, he hoped. He was going to need it.

He lobbed the empty bottle into the sink, walked back into the bedroom, put on his running shorts, a clean T-shirt, and pulled an Everlast sweatshirt over the top. Next he put on a pair of thick-soled running socks and then a sweatband that had once been snowy white and was now gray. When he was ready he headed for the back door and laced on his mud-stained Nikes. Last, he Velcro-snapped a survival pack around his waist. Inside were a couple of Mars bars, a roll of tropical fruit Life Savers, and a pint of water. All a man needed for a day of mountain running. Everything else he needed he could pick up along the way. He knew several clean streams where he could replenish his flask.

Lynch stepped back out into the clammy darkness, locked the door, and slipped the key under a loose stone halfway down the path. He wasn't too worried about it. If anybody wanted to break into the cottage when he wasn't home, it wasn't hard. It was a possibility he had to live with, and he had taken a few precautions that were likely to discourage the odd youthful housebreaker rather than the knowledgeable professional.

He took a few minutes to go through his warm-up exercises, referring constantly to his watch. Then, as the second hand swept past 5:45, he began an easy jog down the mountainside to the broken gate at the bottom of the track, the gate that said there was nothing up there worth exploring. He skipped over the gate, turned right onto the blacktop, and picked up the pace. There was a certain tightness in his gut and his throat that told him he was still tense, but that was only to be expected. His legs felt strong and he enjoyed the feeling of power in his stride, power that would eat up the first five miles. The easy miles. From his gate to Fort William and the signpost to Ben Nevis it was twelve miles. From the bottom of the mountain it was a climb of 4406 feet to the summit of the highest mountain in the British Isles. A mile and a half straight up but a round trip of seven miles according to the route he took. Seven miles of strength-sapping mountain running in the middle of a marathon. Lynch wanted to make the top before nine and be back home by eleven, before too many hikers could clutter up the mountainside. His best time so far was five hours forty-three minutes. Today he intended to get it under five. What better present could a man give himself on his thirty-ninth birthday?

He found his internal metronome and settled into a steady, fluid pace. The surface of the road was wet with dew and the soles of his shoes made fat slapping sounds that seemed unnaturally loud in the early morning quiet. He looked around him as he ran. The moon was still bright, but the sky had begun to lighten over the darkened hummocks of the Grampian Mountains to his right. Milky strands of mist coiled silently in the hollows like ghostly serpents. Scotch mist, he thought. For some reason, that made him smile. He breathed deeply, his breath pluming the cool air. He felt the tension ease in his gut. He had always found it to be this way. There was nothing like a bit of action to reduce the tension in a man like him. And this was the best time of the day, the time when he felt as though he had the whole world to himself. Lynch was never happier than when he was alone and testing himself. To the limit, as always. And he never saw the dark figure who emerged cautiously from behind the stone wall, a half mile back down the road, across from the broken gate. He never felt the gloating eyes on his back as he rounded the first long curve on the way to Fort William. He never saw the man who crossed the road and started confidently up the track toward the cottage.

JIDDA, SAUDI ARABIA. 01.35 HOURS

"Sir, I'm sorry, but you'll have to get up. All hell has broken loose."

Zachary Clarke, U.S. Consul in Jidda, stirred reluctantly from his slumber and tried to make sense of the two silhouettes at his bedside. The voice was thin and urgent and belonged to his consular aide, Tommy Giotti. The second figure stood in the doorway. He was twice the size of Giotti and seemed to be armed. A marine in full combat gear, Clarke realized. Suddenly, he was fully alert. They hadn't tried to get him on his bedside phone. That could mean only one of few possibilities, all of them bad.

He struggled out of bed and slipped on the robe that Giotti held ready. Clarke's wife stirred and murmured something behind him, but she didn't wake up. Clarke followed his aide from the room and closed the door softly behind him. He blinked in the harsh glare of the light on the second floor landing and tried to smooth back his untidy gray hair. Giotti's hair was a mess too, and from the look of the jeans and the sweatshirt he had on, he'd dressed in a hurry. Then Clarke heard voices downstairs. Loud, worried voices. The sound of people hurrying back and forth, doors being slammed. The whole building was awake. Clarke glanced from Giotti to the marine, a sergeant-at-arms with a face like granite, except for one small nerve working on the left side of his jaw. The consul looked back to Giotti.

"What," he asked, his voice dry and raspy. "Are we at war?"

Giotti shook his head.

"It's the British royal yacht, sir—the *Britannia.*"

Clarke nodded.

"It's been attacked by terrorists."

A sudden coldness flooded the consul's body, as if he'd been cut with a knife and his insides laid bare. The last time he'd felt anything like it was when he had been a young Democrat in the ballroom of the Ambassador Hotel in Los Angeles and he'd just heard that Bobby Kennedy had been shot.

"Jesus," Clarke mumbled, his voice faint and disbelieving. "This is confirmed?"

"The attack is confirmed, yes, sir," Giotti added.

"Are the queen and the duke . . . ?"

"I'm afraid so, sir," Giotti finished for him. "As far as we know, they were both on board at the time of the attack. We don't know yet if either of them has been harmed."

"Christ almighty," Clarke muttered. "When . . . what the hell happened?"

"It started just over an hour ago," Giotti continued. "There were two big explosions on the dock. Sergeant Cusack here sent a couple of guys to check it out. They just got back."

"That's it?" Clarke demanded as though hoping he might still, somehow, prove them wrong.

"Sir, it looks like the explosions were directed at the royal yacht. Our guys say it's a battlefield down there. Fires, explosions, bodies all over the goddamn place. These are reliable eyewitness reports, sir. Consular staff. I just finished talking to them, not five minutes ago."

Clarke slowly shook his head, seemingly unable to absorb what he had just been told.

Giotti paused and spoke his next words carefully and evenly.

"Sir," he said. "It's beginning to look like the *Britannia* has been hijacked—with the queen and Prince Philip on board."

All strength seemed to drain from the consul's body. He sagged against the wall, eyes glazed, jaw slack. The sergeant-at-arms moved to support him, but Clarke waved him away.

"I'm all right," he added, seeing the concern in the young marine's eyes. "I just need a minute to . . ."

He left the sentence hanging. Giotti and the sergeant exchanged glances but did as they were told and waited. The three of them stood quietly for what seemed like an eternity with only the noise from downstairs to remind them that an emergency was under way. For one long, terrifying moment Clarke's mind stayed blank, as though it had shut itself down rather than deal with the reality of such shocking news. Then the pictures came rushing back. He had been at the official Saudi reception for the royal couple at Khuzam Palace only a couple of nights ago. He had spoken personally with the queen and the Duke of Edinburgh. He had shared interests with the two of them. He liked horses and played polo with a four-goal handicap. It had been easy to talk bloodstock and form, subjects the queen, as Britain's biggest private racehorse owner, knew a lot about. She had laughed when Clarke had asked her for a tip, even though he knew it was a joke she must have heard many times before. He shook the image away, took a deep breath, and forced himself back to the ugly present.

"What do the Saudis say?"

"We're talking to them now," Giotti answered. "They don't seem to know what the hell is going on. They had six hundred men down there and it's total chaos. A lot of their people have been killed."

Clarke sighed and pushed himself away from the wall.

"Okay," he decided, his voice a little firmer. "Get my car ready. I have to go down there and take a look for myself."

"Sir, I'll see to your escort, sir," Sergeant Cusack responded, glad to have an order at last. He saluted and strode back down the landing. The consul turned to his assistant and for the first time saw the depth of his own shock mirrored in Giotti's red-rimmed eyes.

"Good God," he mumbled. "Just when you think you've seen it all . . ."

DOWNING STREET. 22.25 HOURS

The Prime Minister was working late in his office when the green phone on his desk chimed softly. He glanced up from a thick pile of parliamentary papers and saw a light flashing on the inside line. He was to recall later that his first reaction was relief. It was neither the hot line to the President of the United States nor to the Kremlin. Therefore, whatever it was, it could not be too serious. He left the handset in the cradle and pushed the conference button.

"Yes?" His tone was pitched just coolly enough to discourage procrastination. His eyes had drifted back to the latest amendments to the immigration bill on his desk. The Downing Street switchboard operator spoke first.

"It's Rear Admiral Bryden calling from Northwood, sir," she said. "He says it's most urgent."

The Prime Minister took off his glasses, rubbed the little white pinch marks on the bridge of his nose, and sighed. Northwood was the Royal Navy's underground headquarters in Middlesex. It was unusual that a call would come to him direct from there and not via the Admiralty, whose offices were only a few minutes walk away up Whitehall. The movements of every ship in the fleet were tracked by satellite from Northwood, and an urgent call at this hour could mean only one thing; something big had gone wrong with a British warship. A nuclear accident of some kind, perhaps, a submarine down, a collision with another warship. The voice that followed was calm but tense.

"Prime Minister?"

"Yes."

"Rear Admiral Bryden, Fleet Intelligence, sir. I'm afraid we have a problem involving Her Majesty on board the *Britannia.*"

All thoughts about the new bill that was intended to determine Britain's immigration policy well into the twenty-first century vanished from the Prime Minister's mind. He looked up and stared at the dull amber light on the phone.

"Yes, Admiral?" He thought his voice sounded eerily distant.

"I've just finished speaking with the commander of the *Britannia*'s escort vessel, HMS *Hotspur,* sir," Bryden went on. "Captain Purcell advises me that the *Britannia* has been attacked in force in Jidda harbor. The attackers have boarded and taken control of the royal yacht. The queen and the Duke of Edinburgh are both still on board. The attackers have spoken by ship's radio to the *Hotspur* . . . and they claim to represent the IRA. They also claim to have planted explosives on board and say they will blow the yacht up if it is approached. Captain Purcell says he has little option but to believe them. He is standing off now, sir, awaiting our instructions."

"My God," the Prime Minister breathed softly. He fell back into his chair and stared at the wall opposite, seeing the intricate weave of the wallpaper in exquisitely detailed close-up. He remembered the mortar bomb attack the IRA had launched on 10 Downing Street only a few years before. The madman who broke into Buckingham Palace and spent half an hour in the queen's bedroom. The pistol attack on Princess Anne by a lone gunman in Pall Mall. The bombing of the Brighton hotel where the Thatcher cabinet had stayed for the annual Conservative Party conference. The assassination of Lord Mountbatten, the queen's uncle, on his motor launch in the Irish Sea. And now it had happened. The nightmare scenario that every British government dreaded.

We have to get lucky only once, the IRA had taunted them through the years. *You have to be lucky all the time.*

"Admiral," the Prime Minister said hesitantly, "you're quite sure this isn't . . . a hoax of some kind?"

"I'm afraid not, sir," Bryden answered, the undertone of dread clear in the disembodied voice. "That's why I called you on the secure line. I have been unable to reach the commander in chief, Fleet, and I have Captain Purcell standing by now, urgently awaiting our instructions."

Then, for a moment, the protocol faltered.

"We have to tell him something, sir," Bryden added.

"My God," the Prime Minister repeated. For one awful moment he felt faint and light-headed as the shock washed over him. He breathed deeply and willed himself to a level of composure he did not feel. He leaned forward, elbows on the desk, fingertips pressed to his forehead, and gazed unseeingly at the papers strewn in front of him.

"You are in direct communication with the captain of the *Hotspur* right at this moment?"

"Yes, sir."

"What is happening on board the royal yacht now? Where is she? What is she doing?"

"At this point there seems to be very little movement aboard the vessel, sir. The hijackers have maneuvered her into the middle of the harbor and they have instructed the *Hotspur* and the Saudi authorities not to interfere while they put out to sea."

"They're taking her out to sea?" the Prime Minister gasped.

"It looks that way, sir. Captain Purcell wants to know what we want him to do. Does he block their exit or does he allow them to pass?"

The Prime Minister hesitated while one horrifying scenario after another spun giddily through his mind. There was a soft click and he looked up as the door to his office opened. His executive assistant, John Traynor, appeared, looking pale. Like the Prime Minister, he was jacketless and unshaven. His white shirt was unbuttoned at the collar. Word must already have spread around the building.

"Admiral," the Prime Minister decided, "I want you to tell Captain Purcell that the *Britannia* is not to be allowed out of Jidda harbor. Tell Purcell he must stall them by whatever means possible . . . short of a direct assault on the ship."

"And if they try to force their way out, sir?"

"Damn," the Prime Minister swore.

"They may have every intention of doing that," Bryden insisted.

The British leader shook his head.

"Yes, all right, Admiral," he conceded. "If that is the case, then Captain Purcell must not do anything that would directly endanger the life of the monarch. If he has to let them pass, then so be it. But he follows them every inch of the way and he keeps us informed on a minute-by-minute basis. You understand?"

"I understand, sir. I'll let him know."

The Prime Minister pushed the hold button and looked up at his executive assistant.

"Do you want me to alert COBRA, sir?" Traynor inquired.

COBRA was the acronym for Cabinet Officer Briefing Room, which consisted of the Home Secretary, the junior defense minister, the junior foreign minister, senior representatives of the police, MI5, and the SAS, and was the government's first planning response to a major act of terrorism.

The Prime Minister shook his head.

"I want you to get me Hereford. I want 22 SAS on the way to Jidda now. And you'd better get me the ambassador in Saudi Arabia. Then I want you to summon the full War Cabinet. Tell them I want them here by midnight."

The Prime Minister leaned back in his chair, his face gray.

"This is not just another act of terror," he said. "This is a strike against the throne of the United Kingdom. This is an act of war."

Air Force One. 19.55 hours

"Sir, we have an urgent call from one of our consuls in Saudi Arabia. A Zachary Clarke. He's calling from Jidda."

The President of the United States looked up from his supper of chicken, mashed potato, and creamed corn as the presidential 747 thundered through the sky en route from Los Angeles to Washington. Tom Farley, chief of the President's security staff, stood in the aisle, holding a black jam-proof telephone that enabled the President to speak to anyone, anywhere in the world, wherever there was a telephone or radio link.

The President picked up his napkin and dabbed a spot of corn from the corner of his mouth. A call directly to the President from a consul was not usual.

"We've verified the call, sir," Farley added, reading the President's mind. "It's coded and it's been routed here via the White House. It's the middle of the night in Jidda and Mr. Clarke says he's still trying to contact the ambassador, but he believes the situation is so urgent you need to be apprised immediately."

The President nodded, swallowed a mouthful of food, and took the phone. Something told him that he wasn't about to hear that the price of oil was coming down.

"Yes, Mr. Clarke, this is the President, how can I help you?"

It was a little after three A.M. in Saudi Arabia, and Zachary Clarke stood in his office, haggard and unshaven. What he had seen at the Jidda docks in the past hour had aged him ten years. He had tried to follow protocol and alert his superior in Riyadh, but the ambassador was traveling in-country and they were having trouble reaching him.

"Mr. President . . . please forgive me for bypassing the usual diplomatic channels on this one," Clarke apologized. "But I'm afraid we have a very bad situation here. You may be aware that the Queen of Great Britain and her husband, Prince Philip, have been on a state visit to Jidda these past few days."

The President didn't but he stayed silent.

"While they've been here they've been staying on board the British royal yacht, sir . . . the *Britannia.*"

Clarke spoke quickly, as though trying to unburden himself of all the fear and sickness that swilled around inside him.

"About two and a half hours ago the yacht was hijacked by terrorists. People claiming to represent the Irish Republican Army. Queen Elizabeth and Prince Philip are still on board. No one can confirm whether they are alive or dead, sir. There's a British warship on the scene, but they haven't done anything to intervene yet. At the moment it looks like some kind of standoff is going on."

"God almighty."

The President seemed to wilt in his seat. He raised a hand to his forehead as though troubled by a sudden pain there.

"What . . . how are the Saudis handling it?" he asked.

"They're not, sir. I don't think they know what the hell to do. What we do know is that they're talking to the British, trying to figure something out. We haven't been approached or advised officially yet. There's still a lot of confusion here about what is going on, sir. What I'm telling you now is all we can confirm."

"I understand, Mr. Clarke." The President could hear the strain in the consul's voice and sought to reassure him. "You were right to call me. What I want you to do now is to convey this same message to Jim Blainey, the secretary of state, in Washington. You liase with him, keep him fully apprised of the situation. I'll see him first thing in the morning and we'll take it from there. But if there are any major new developments, I want to know right away, okay?"

"You can count on it, sir."

The President handed the phone back to his security chief, then looked at his wife, who sat opposite, her own meal forgotten. Like everyone else in the cabin, she knew something dreadful had happened. She waited with grim anticipation, her face pale and tense.

"It's the queen and Prince Philip," the President said haltingly, as though the words he spoke were too incredible to be real. "The royal yacht . . . the *Britannia* . . . has been hijacked . . . with both of them on board. Nobody knows whether they're alive or dead. . . ."

"Oh, no," his wife said faintly. Her eyes locked with his. Each of them knew what the other was thinking. Both came from the same generation. And both were assailed by the same terrible images of the past. The assassinations of John Kennedy . . . Bobby Kennedy . . . Martin Luther King. Those awful moments in time when goodness and reason perished and evil had risen anew in the world. And now, at precisely that moment when people had dared to hope again, evil had returned. This time to consume the world's most enduring symbol of grace. The Queen of England. What made it all the more shocking to the President and his wife was the fact that they knew the queen and Prince Philip personally. They had met on several occasions, formally and informally. At state banquets in the White House, at the British embassy in Washington, at Buckingham Palace, on a quiet weekend at Sandringham . . . and on board the royal yacht. To them the Queen of England and the Duke of Edinburgh were not mere figureheads, abstract and remote. They were people. Flesh and blood people like them, whose lives had been made extraordinary by fate.

The President's mind flooded with memories. Of a small, slight woman who carried her great office with impressive ease. A woman of warmth and intellect and a surprisingly mischievous wit. A woman who had known her share of pain and borne it with courage and humor. And he remembered the last time they had met, in London, when his problems at home and abroad had seemed almost insurmountable and she had fixed him with a wise and knowing smile and said: "One can only do one's best."

And somehow it had all seemed much more bearable after that. If the Queen of England could boil it down into one deceptively simple philosophy, with all that she had seen and with the weight of history resting on her shoulders, then so could he.

"What can we do?" the President's wife interrupted his thoughts.

The President sucked in a breath and looked back at his wife.

"We have to wait until the British approach us directly," he said soberly. "I expect we'll be getting a call pretty soon. Either from the Prime Minister or from the British ambassador in Washington."

"And then?"

The President didn't pause.

"Whatever they want . . ." he added quietly. "They have only to ask."

HMY *Britannia.* 03.17 hours

As Zachary Clarke hung up the phone in his office two miles across town, on board the royal yacht, Petty Officer Timothy

Brash was fighting for his life. A smallish man with thinning, sandy hair, the *Britannia*'s first engineer had been running maintenance checks with two crewmen in the engine room when he heard the distant thump of an explosion on the dock. Seconds later Admiral Marchant's voice had followed on the intercom, ordering Brash to start the engines. He was ready. There had been little shore leave in Jidda for the sixty-three-man engine room crew and the 12,000 horsepower turbines were in mint condition. Brash thumbed the big green starter button and the turbines turned over as smoothly as a sewing machine. A moment later the ship's telegraph signaled slow astern. Brash had paused only to alert the chief engineer and that was what spared him from the first invasion of GBX gas. To use the direct line to the chief's cabin he had to stay on the topmost deck of the engine room. Because the gas was heavier than air, it had poured down the ventilation shaft like water and saturated the lower deck. The only warning was when the second engineer had doubled over with a racking, convulsive cough and dropped to his knees. The other crewman hurried to his aid, but before he could help, he, too, was seized around the throat by an invisible claw. Instinctively he reeled back, fighting for breath, trying to get away. But it was too late. He lost his footing and fell backward, hitting his head heavily against a steel rail and spattering a necklace of bright-red blood across the deck. Brash stared around in bewilderment, wondering what was wrong. Then he caught it, the stink of something alien and threatening.

He tried to call the bridge, but no one answered. That was something that never happened. The bitter smell intensified and Brash caught his breath in his throat. He dropped the phone and stepped toward the engine room door. Before he could turn the handle, he heard shouts of alarm from the other side and the sound of men running . . . and then the muffled rattle of automatic weapons fire. His hand fell from the handle and he backed away, unsure what to do next. His eyes darted nervously around the engine room. And then he saw the gas snaking through an air-conditioning vent in silent, sinister columns. He turned and stumbled across the engine room in the direction of another hatch. He threw the door open, stepped through to the boiler room, then slammed and locked the door behind him. The temperature rose thirty degrees and the air wrapped around him like a moist warm cloak. Still the gas reached after him, seeping through the air vents in the wall, trying to take him in its noxious, oily grasp. His throat narrowed, his eyes filled with tears, and his stomach cramped so hard, he felt he would throw up. He fought the nausea and stumbled along the gantry that ran like a narrow bridge across the upper half of the boiler room. Somebody had stuffed a rag behind a pipe. Normally that would make him angry. This time he grabbed it and held it over his nose and mouth. It was putrid with oil and didn't seem any better than the gas. Then his eyes fell on a battery of dials at the far end of the gantry. The dials were attached to a series of pipe valves that controlled the pressure release to the ship's boiler, and they gave him an idea. He fumbled around the pipes for something that might help him. And then he found it. A steam hose. One of the most dangerous tools on the ship and one usually reserved for the heaviest cleaning chores. He unclipped the hose, aimed the nozzle in the direction of the approaching gas, and opened the valve. With a banshee shriek a scalding jet of steam leapt across the room and scattered the gas like sprites.

"Jesus . . ." Brash sobbed, fearing he had made the situation worse. He held his breath, forced himself to remain calm, and eased back on the valve handle. Carefully, methodically, he began to weave a curtain of steam between himself and the gas, creating a safety bubble in his little corner of the boiler room. After a moment he breathed easier again. He was right. The gas was heavier than the steam and he had pushed it down to the boiler room floor, where it simmered impotently beneath the restraining hand of the boiling vapor. And there it would remain until the boiler ran out of steam . . . however long that might be. He eased back on the release valve and sniffed tentatively at the surrounding air. It was so hot it burnt the hair inside his nose. But it was safe. The bitterness in his throat had gone and the gagging reflex had faded to a manageable queasiness.

He snatched a glance at his wristwatch, but the face had misted over. His clothes were drenched and his body was slick with sweat. He listened for more hostile noises from the other side of the door, but the hiss of the steam hose was too loud. Soon, he knew, he would have to find a way out. He couldn't rely on the steam hose to keep him safe in there indefinitely. Nor would he be able to tolerate the temperature for much longer. Perhaps another half hour before he succumbed to the heat or grew weak through dehydration. He had another thought. When the gas reached the same temperature as the steam, it could start to rise again and there was no guarantee that it would lose any of its potency. Then, he realized, if the steam could hold the gas back for now, it could also act as a propellant. It ought to be possible to flush the gas out of the boiler room the same way it had come in. Through the air vents. Cautiously, he directed the steam jet into the simmering cauldron below and began to ease it back across the boiler room floor toward an air vent he knew was set in the opposite bulkhead. It was like a man washing his car, trying to flush the soapsuds down a drain. Except he was working blind and the drain was halfway up a wall. After a few moments he got the hang of it and he thought he was making headway. The fog had begun to lighten. He could see patches of deck beneath him as he pushed the vaporous cocktail across the boiler room, out through the air vent, and back up the pipes from where it had come. Minutes passed and the boiler room started to clear . . . and Timothy Brash realized that he was going to make it. Then he heard voices from the other side of the door.

He tilted his head and strained to hear them above the noise of the hose, but they had gone. He stood still, waiting for them to start again, praying that the attack was over and they were voices he would recognize. The minutes passed and he heard nothing. Suddenly, there was a loud bang and the door flew toward him with a rush of smoke and flame. He felt himself picked up and thrown backward by the force of the blast, the steam hose torn from his grasp. He landed against the wall and gave an involuntary shout of pain. The steam hose thrashed about on the gangway in front of him, spewing scalding jets of vapor wildly into the air. Brash realized he hadn't been badly hurt. He struggled to his feet and tried to grab hold of the hose without burning himself. Something flashed past the open door. A figure in black. A canister arced into the boiler room, trailing a fresh cloud of GBX. It landed on the gantry near

Brash but was swatted away by the writhing steam hose and spun down to the lower deck, where it rolled across the floor, spewing out a thick gray cloud. Brash knew he had only one chance. He grabbed for the hose, ignored the pain as it spat at his exposed flesh, and held on tight. Then he opened the release valve all the way. The hose leapt in his hands, trying to fight free. He held on tight, took a breath, and charged toward the door, holding the nozzle dead ahead. A long, burning plume of steam poured out ahead of him, as lethal as a flame thrower.

There was a muffled shout of warning as the men on the other side scrambled to get out of the way. Brash almost made it through the door. Then there was the deafening roar of assault rifles opening up at close range. Three streams of burning metal poured back through the open door and filled the boiler room with a murderous torrent of bullets. Brash felt as though he had been pummeled by sledgehammers. His chest shattered beneath the impact of a score of bullets. They lifted him into the air and hurled him contemptuously against the far wall. The room spun crazily around him, the roar of sound faded, and all sensation vanished from his broken body. When it stopped, he found himself looking up at the ceiling. He had landed on his back, he realized. Instinctively, he tried to move. This time nothing would work. There seemed to be no feeling in his arms and legs. No feeling anywhere. A terrible cold reached into him, replacing the warm blood that gushed out of his shattered body. So, this was what death felt like, Brash thought. No pain, no fear, no . . . anything. Just a strange and terrible calm. Resignedly, he let go and all consciousness slipped away in an enfolding wave of darkness.

The hose continued to dance on its own like a giant nightmarish serpent, lashing back and forth on the upper deck, spitting venom at all who threatened Brash's corpse. Outside, Michael Kenney looked at Deveny and Mulcahey and signaled them to wait. He took off his satchel filled with explosives and left it on the deck with his rifle. Then he turned and slid down the gangway rails to the floor of the engine room. He ignored the two wretched men sprawled across deck and scanned the engine room controls. The red handle that operated the cutoff switch stood out like a traffic light. He threw the handle and the ship's turbines slowed immediately to a dull whine and then stopped. Everything went strangely quiet except for the faint moans of the men on the floor and the hiss of steam from the boiler room. In a moment that would stop, too, as pressure dropped and the snake lost the power to dance. Kenney looked up at the men on the top deck and signaled them to go ahead. Jimmy Mulcahey went first. Cautiously, he approached the door that Kenney had blown open a few moments earlier. The snake was still hissing, but it had lost its fire. It seemed to be sagging, growing tired. Mulcahey looked around. The boiler room was filled with a steamy haze, and there were ugly gouges in the bulkheads where bullets had hit. But the boiler was intact, protected by blast shields. The snake died quickly, dropped to the floor and twitched pathetically as the last remnants of steam dribbled from its ugly snout. Mulcahey stepped inside and dropped to a crouch, rifle ready. Deveny followed. Both men looked around the battle-scarred boiler room, but, apart from the body of the man they had killed, there was no one else. Mulcahey smiled behind his mask. They had done it. The last pocket of resistance had fallen. He got up, walked the length of the gantry, and shut off the steam hose. Then he turned, slid the toe of his boot under Brash's bullet-ravaged body, and rolled it over the edge and onto the deck below, where it landed with a messy thud.

Deveny glanced around for a moment, then stepped back out to the engine room and gave Kenney the okay signal. Kenney turned and punched the green starter button. The turbines obediently whined back to life. The *Britannia* was under power again. Kenney had to hand it to the Brits—the engine room of the *Britannia* was superbly maintained. Everything started the first time. Everything worked exactly as it was supposed to. It was so easy, he thought, a kid could sail the *Britannia.*

He hurried back to the upper deck, collected his satchel and his rifle, and followed Deveny and Mulcahey through the broken door to the boiler room. The three men moved confidently, as though they had been on the *Britannia* before. In a way, they had. Like every other step of the operation, they had rehearsed this stage too, using taped outlines of the engine room and the boiler room on the floor of the barn in County Clare. A page they had taken from the SAS operations manual. Deveny and Mulcahey handed their own canvas satchels to Kenney, then took up guard positions inside the boiler room. Deveny on one side of the door, Mulcahey on the other, rifles aimed down the corridor that led forward, past the generator room to the seamen's mess, from which any counterattack would have to come. It was a critical moment and much depended on the coolness of Dominic Behan up on the bridge and his ability to bluff the skipper of the *Hotspur* into holding back his men just a few minutes more. If a determined enough counterattack was launched now, the IRA men knew, it would succeed. The explosives had not been set. They had nothing to bargain with. Nothing to back up their threat of instant destruction. And they would all die for nothing. Just a few minutes more and all that would change.

Kenney knelt down, opened the first satchel, and gently slid three slabs of Demex plastic explosive out onto the deck. Each slab was about as long as a house brick but only half as thick. At one time he had worked only with Semtex, the Czech-made plastic explosive. But the collapse of the Communist regime in Prague and the determination of Western intelligence agencies to account for all outstanding consignments had choked off the IRA's traditional sources of supply in Eastern Europe and the Middle East. Still, Kenney wouldn't complain about Demex. The British-made high explosive packed a bigger punch than Semtex and it was more reliable. He would never have been able to get his hands on it had it not been for the right man in England. The right man and the right combination of bribes and threats to the foreman of a demolitions company in Liverpool. A greedy and uncaring fool who had left behind a grieving family after a callous hit-and-run accident the police had still been unable to solve.

Kenney removed the waxy waterproof wrapping from the first slab and began kneading the pale pink plastique carefully, like bread dough, until it became soft enough for him to stretch out at one end into a kind of tongue. Then he snapped open a side pocket on the first satchel and pulled out a hard plastic container about the size of a Crayola box. Inside were a dozen crayons, all fastened securely in their own plastic sleeves and all colored red. Blasting caps. Kenney took out a cap, pressed it into the extended tongue of Demex, then folded it back into the body of the explosive, leaving one end of the cap visible. Then he set the charge to one side and moved on to the next slab. It took him half an hour to prime nine separate charges from the three satchels, each charge consisting of fifteen pounds of Demex. Each enough on its own to blast a hole the size of a football in the hull of an armored car. Enough to blast a hole the size of a garage door in the unprotected hull of a ship.

When he was finished he stood up and quickly surveyed the line of charges laid out neatly on the deck in front of him. Then he looked around. The royal yacht was different from other naval vessels in many ways, but there was one key difference above all the rest that made it particularly vulnerable to sabotage. A weak point that the knowledgeable saboteur could use to murderous advantage. That weak point was right beneath Kenney's feet. Between the deck plates that supported him and the welded steel plates of the outside hull there was a gap of about two and half feet. Because no good ship designer ever wasted space, the Admiralty architects who designed the *Britannia* had used this space to install a series of watertight compartments. These compartments, sandwiched between the bottommost deck and the hull, stretched the entire 412-foot-three-inch length of the *Britannia.* The compartments at the stern and the bow were filled with fresh water which acted both as ballast and as a reservoir. The compartments amidships, right underneath the engine room and the boiler room, were filled with fuel oil. Thousands of gallons of fuel oil stored in honeycombed compartments that cradled the yacht amidships.

Kenney knew that all he had to do was place his charges in such a way that the blast would cut through the deck plates and into those fuel-oil compartments. All of which would have been filled to the brim for the voyage home. Even on their own, nine big blasts ought to be enough to cut the royal yacht in half and send her to the bottom within minutes. But, by igniting the fuel oil and creating a catastrophic secondary explosion that would engulf the yacht amidships, the combined force of both blasts would cause massive and instantaneous disintegration. The *Britannia,* or what was left of her, would sink in seconds. There would be no time for anyone to escape, and no one could survive such a blast. No one.

He molded the first three charges into the corner crevices where the deck plates joined the inside hull along the starboard side of the yacht, each charge about twenty feet apart. He laid a matching three charges along the port side. This meant the force of the explosions would be directed downward, through the deck plates, and outward through the hull. The last three charges were a little harder. He had to get down on his belly and worm his way between the boiler mountings to place all three charges in a six-foot circle underneath the boiler. Even if somebody got to the other six charges, Kenney knew that the blast from these last charges would blow the boiler and ignite the fuel tanks below.

He got back to his feet, plucked a hand reel from the last satchel with 200 feet of firing wire, and set about connecting the blasting caps in all nine charges. When he had finished, he knitted all the charge wires to a single firing wire, then climbed back up to the top deck, playing the hand reel out behind him. It was a slow, awkward process, but he had advised Behan long ago that an electrical firing would be far more secure than a radio firing. He knew how much radio traffic there would be around the royal yacht after the hijacking, and nobody wanted to risk an accidental detonation. Wire had its drawbacks, not the least of which was that it could be cut. But when things got messy, an electrical firing was the most reliable. And Kenney had his own ideas about how to safeguard the exposed wire.

He laid the wire along the upper deck for ten feet, then stopped, put the reel down, and looked long and hard at the ceiling. Deveny and Mulcahey watched him, fascinated, aware that they were observing a master at work. Kenney was looking at a cluster of tubes and pipes that ran for the width of the boiler room. One of the pipes would carry water, another would carry communications cables, another would carry electrical circuits. All he had to do now was to isolate the right pipe, cut into it, identify those wires that ran from the boiler room up to the bridge, and splice the firing wire into one of them. Then the charges could be fired from the bridge without a chance of interception. The weakest link would be the exposed length of firing wire in the boiler room. But it was unlikely anyone would find that either, once he had disguised it.

The veteran bomb maker smiled to himself. He wasn't sure why he smiled. He could well be planning his own funeral. But of one thing he was certain. The light from his funeral pyre would be seen around the world.

When Judy Stone pulled the shower curtain shut on Gault, the first thing he did was to empty his stomach and his bowels. It didn't help. His limbs still felt weak and watery, his vision was blurred, his balance was off, and he couldn't curb the spasms that continually racked his body. For a long time he squatted miserably in a corner and tried to regain his strength while warm water played over him. It was like a hangover he'd had once, after drinking something called Wild Turkey all night with a bunch of guys from Delta Force following a successful joint exercise. He'd spent a long time in the shower after that too. Somehow, as long as the water kept running he felt he might live. But this was a thousand times worse. And he couldn't afford to waste water. Their supply was not inexhaustible. After a while he struggled to his feet, peeled off his clothes, and sluiced the evidence of his wretchedness down the drain. Then, too weak to dry himself, he crawled into the bedroom, climbed wet and naked between the sheets, and lay there, shaking, while the filthy toxins leeched out of his body. He passed two miserable hours like that before he noticed any improvement. Judy had looked in on him once to ask how he was doing. All he had managed in response was a feeble grin and an even feebler wave. Gradually, the nausea had ebbed away and he felt a little stronger. Impatiently, he ignored the gut aches that followed hours of dry retching and forced himself to get out of bed.

He shuffled unsteadily across the carpet into the bathroom and washed his face in cold water. Next he drank half a dozen glasses of water to counter the dehydrating effects of the gas. Then he combed his short black hair straight back from his forehead and looked at himself in the mirror. He was surprised by the face that looked back. It seemed almost healthy. His eyes were just slightly bloodshot and there was only a suggestion of pallor beneath the olive tones of his skin. He had expected that at the very least he would look as bad as he felt. And he felt like death.

He stepped back into the cabin, opened his closet, and picked out the clothes he needed. Navy sneakers with ridged soles to grip fast on slippery decks, black combat pants, and a navy-blue crewneck sweater. Clothes that would help him blend into the shadows when he went outside to reconnoiter, which he intended to do the moment he was fully recovered. It took him twenty minutes to get dressed, cursing under his breath when the tremors came back and his fingers wouldn't do what he wanted. At last he was ready. He walked back to the closet and pulled out a black suitcase that looked like a photographer's equipment case. He carried it back to his unmade bed and opened it. Inside was a P7K3 nine-millimeter pistol with ankle holster and spare clips with two hundred rounds of ammunition. The pistol bore the stamp of the German arms manufacturer, Heckler and Koch, preferred supplier to the SAS. He took the pistol out of the case and loaded it with an oversize thirteen-round magazine. Even when fully loaded the pistol was surprisingly light and compact. He strapped the holster to the inside of his left ankle and clipped in the pistol. Then he put on his shoulder harness and retrieved his submachine gun from the dresser. The harness left both hands free but held the gun snugly in the small of his back, where it could be retrieved in a moment.

At last he was ready. He swept aside all the lingering aches and pains, turned out the light, opened the door, and looked outside into the royal corridor. He was pleased to see that Judy had dimmed the lights and the corridor was in semidarkness. He stepped onto the soft cream carpet that matched the rich cream-painted walls and closed the door behind him without making a sound.

The first person Gault saw was the duke's equerry, Tony Stevens. He had dressed in a gray V-neck sweater and slacks and he stood outside the queen's bedroom, talking to Judy Stone. Judy was dressed like Gault, all in black, combat-ready.

"So." She greeted him with an ironic smile. "How's my big brave boy, then?"

Gault looked discomfited. Tony Stevens turned to look at him, concern mingled with relief on his face.

"Better," Gault answered. "Wouldn't say I'm ready for the decathlon though."

Judy shook her head.

"Had to try and stop them at the drawbridge single-handed, didn't you?"

"Had to try," Gault shrugged. The note in his voice said she shouldn't push her point too far.

"Madge all right?" he asked, nodding toward the closed door.

"I suggested they both try and get some rest," Judy answered. "Sleep might be out of the question. They know they have to be ready in case we have to move them in a hurry."

"They're both in there?"

There was a new note of concern in Gault's voice. Procedure said the queen and the Duke of Edinburgh should be separated at a time like this.

"For the past few hours we've had only one bodyguard," Stevens said coolly.

Judy spoke quickly before Gault could react to Stevens.

"Under the circumstances," she said, "I felt they should spend this time together. Quite frankly, I think they need it."

Gault nodded but said nothing. From the expression on his face it was plain he didn't approve. But he also knew he had undermined his own authority with a rash display of heroics that could have left Judy on her own to deal with the emergency. He would have to proceed carefully for a while to win back their confidence.

"What about Lady Sarah," Gault asked. "Where's she?"

"In her cabin," Stevens said. "She's okay. She's sleeping, believe it or not."

"Lucky girl," Gault said. "Sleep is going to be a precious commodity around here if this drags on for a while."

"We can't let it go on for too long," Stevens said nervously. "We can't . . ."

Judy and Gault looked at each other but said nothing. Stevens seemed skittish enough already.

"You spoken to the *Hotspur?*" Gault asked Judy.

Both of them had radio phones with a secure link to the *Hotspur* for a radius of 120 nautical miles.

"The hijackers have taken control of the bridge," she answered. "They claim they're IRA."

"Jesus . . ." Gault let out a sharp exhalation of breath. "I wouldn't have thought . . . I mean, this isn't their style. This is too big. Too dumb . . ."

"They seem to have done all right so far," Judy responded.

Gault nodded slowly and considered this unwelcome piece of intelligence.

"If it's the Provos," he said, "it's a suicide job. And they must know that."

Tony Stevens's face seemed to blanch in the half light.

"Whom did you speak to?" Gault added.

"They patched me direct to Purcell," she said. "I told him we were all secure."

"You tell him I was down?"

"Didn't see any point in adding to their anxieties," she answered.

"Thanks," Gault said.

Judy shrugged.

"What else?"

"He told me to stick with Royal Raven."

Gault nodded. Royal Raven were the code words for the contingency plan that had been drawn up to deal with what had once been unthinkable: the hijacking of the *Britannia* with members of the royal family held hostage on board. Both Gault and Judy knew what role they were expected to play. Basically they were to keep their royal charges safe inside this floating bunker until help arrived from outside—or they received direct orders to do otherwise.

"What did he say about a rescue?"

"Referred to London."

"That means the ship's wired."

"They've threatened to blow us up if anybody comes close," Judy confirmed.

There was no certainty that the ship had been wired with explosives, but the fact that the threat had been made meant the *Hotspur*'s skipper had no alternative but to hold any counterattack while London decided what the next move should be. Gault knew how the chain of command would kick in. *Hotspur* would alert the Admiralty, the Admiralty would alert the Prime Minister's office . . . and a couple of squads from 22 SAS would already be airborne. Maybe the whole bloody regiment, considering what was at stake.

"So," he decided, "we do nothing and sit tight for a while?"

"It rather looks that way, doesn't it?" Judy answered.

Tony Stevens looked wretched but stayed silent.

Gault paused for a moment, then looked around and listened. He heard nothing. It was the bunker's greatest drawback as well as its greatest asset. Once the armored screens had been activated, everybody on the inside was cut off from the rest of the yacht, the rest of the outside world. Nothing could penetrate. Not gas, not light . . . and nothing but the loudest sounds. It was impossible for him to tell if the *Britannia*'s engines were running. He knelt down, put an ear to the carpeted floor, and listened carefully, but he heard nothing. He touched the floor and the bulkheads with his fingertips and still felt nothing. Not even a slight vibration to tell him they were under way. He stood up and looked back at Judy. The *Britannia* was fitted with stabilizers too, and unless they were in an open sea with a big swell running, it was impossible to know whether they were moving at all. Their radio link to the *Hotspur* was their only connection to the outside world. Their only way of knowing where they were headed and what was going on around them. Without that link, they were deaf, dumb, and blind. Gault didn't like it.

"We're moving?" he guessed.

"According to the *Hotspur,* we left inner harbor twenty minutes ago," Judy said. "We're running at about five knots. We should be leaving the outer harbor soon. Whoever is in charge up there seems to know what he's doing. They're taking it nice and easy. Obviously they want us out in open water in one piece. After that, I expect they'll start dealing."

"So, they haven't issued any demands?"

"Not yet."

Gault nodded. It was a good sign. It meant the hijackers still weren't properly organized. They could be bluffing about the explosives. They could be vulnerable.

"We should take them out," he decided abruptly. "Now."

"No . . ." Tony Stevens began, a panicky edge to his voice.

"Shut up," Gault snapped. "You're not in command around here, Tony."

"Neither are you," Judy reminded him, her voice soft but firm. "We don't know what's going on outside. We make one wrong move and we could be responsible for the death of the Queen of England. I don't know anybody but you who is in such a hurry to take that responsibility upon themselves, Gault. So, I think we'll do what we've been ordered to do. *Hotspur* will be in touch with Downing Street by now. We'll let the Prime Minister decide what happens next. It's what he's paid to do. I for one am glad it's not me who has to make this decision . . . and so should you."

"Dammit," Gault muttered. He turned and walked a few paces down the corridor toward the security door. But there was nowhere to go. He stopped, took a breath, and leaned forward against a bulkhead with the palms of both hands, his fingers drumming the wall in frustration. Judy Stone was right. But so was he. He knew every secret nook and cranny of the *Britannia* and the hijackers didn't. They were still vulnerable. He could take them out quickly and methodically. Hit them before they knew what was happening. It was what he was trained to do. What he did best. Close combat in dark and confined spaces. Something inside him told him there was still time. Time to turn things around. Time to stop this thing while it was still in its infancy. But he knew what Judy and Stevens were thinking. He knew that the weight of opinion was against him. He had already been hurt trying to stop the hijack and he hadn't been successful then. Who was to say he would be any more successful on a second attempt? And his orders were clear, even if instinct told him that a golden opportunity was slipping away.

"Dammit," he mumbled under his breath again.

Stevens eyed Judy Stone warily but said nothing. Judy waited a moment, then walked over to Gault's side and looked at him.

"Tell you what," she said softly. "I bet a nice cup of tea would make you feel a whole lot better."

BALLACHULISH, SCOTLAND. 10.57 HOURS

Lynch came around the last bend in the highway and onto the downhill straight that led past his cottage and into town. His Everlast shirt was sodden with sweat. It poured down his torso in rivulets, sprayed from his hair like a misty halo, and left fat splash marks in the mud that caked his calves. His breath came in deep, rasping gulps. His chest burned, his gut ached, and the soles of his feet felt like they'd been flayed with barbed wire. He ran like an automaton, oblivious of the passing traffic, eyes fixed on some indeterminate spot in the road ahead. An occasional passing car had to pull wide to overtake him, and some drivers cursed him. Lynch seemed not to notice. He snatched another glance at his watch.

"Shit," he swore to himself. He had cut twenty-two minutes from his best time. But it wasn't enough. He had five hundred yards to go before he reached the broken gate at the bottom of the track and only three minutes left on the clock. He wouldn't make it. He had used up everything in the backbreaking run up Ben Nevis and now he had nothing left.

His mind slid back to his early days with the Special Boat Squadron, the Royal Navy's elite sabotage and reconnaissance unit. Commando training was tough and Lynch had begun his career as a Royal Marine commando. But for every twenty commandos who thought they were good enough for the SBS, only one would make it through the selection process. The entire complement of the SBS was between two and three hundred men. They were the most effective fighting force in the world. Their preferred method of operation was in two-man teams, though they could expand to eight-man teams when they had to, and they could operate alone. What made them so deadly was that their enemies never saw them. Never even knew they were there. Until it was too late. When they started taking casualties. When men died mysteriously in the night. When officers disappeared without trace. When missile batteries and radar installations were destroyed by unseen hands. When soldiers began to lose their nerve because they couldn't fight an invisible foe.

SBS men were the best of the best—superior even to the fabled SAS—though none of them would dream of saying so publicly. They didn't have to. The word in the military was that if you weren't good enough for the SBS, you could always find a place in the SAS.

When the United States Navy decided to set up its own elite sea, air, and land special forces unit, they turned to the SBS to show them how. The result was the SEALs. The philosophy behind SBS training was the antithesis of all military lore. Standard military practice was to build men up, to toughen them, boost their morale, show them what they could do under pressure, teach them to rely on each other. Standard training in the SBS was to seek out every man's weak spot, then use it against him to break him down. Lynch had never forgotten what they had put him through. The marathon underwater swims through winter-fouled seas in the dead of night when there was nobody to rescue him if he got into trouble. The brutal cross-country dashes on starvation rations after days without sleep. The hellish exercises in the storm-scoured islands of the Outer Hebrides when he had to find his way across impossible distances, through frozen lakes and treacherous, fast-flowing rivers, over sheer-sided mountains and deep, deadly bogs, past pitiless instructors whose job it was to urge him to fail. Many of the tests were designed to be so demanding that they couldn't be completed in the times allotted. Over the years there had been men who had died in the attempt. Young men who had thought themselves invincible. Their strong hearts burst into pieces by exertions beyond the comprehension of ordinary men. Others had died in the icy deeps of the North Atlantic, lost to their own stubborn refusal to admit that these were challenges that were beyond them. And others quietly surrendered when they understood that what they were up against were their own inner limits.

The men who made it through usually fell into one of two categories. There were the naturals, those fortunate few possessed of such extraordinary athletic ability that they seemed only to thrive under duress. And there were the others. Those whom the inexpert eye would have assumed least likely to survive. Those men of such apparent ordinariness, it would appear that the only explanation for their success could be a confluence of errors. They were not big or powerfully built men. They did not fit the stereotyped image of the super warrior. There was nothing about them that would cause them to stand out in a crowd. They were of average height and appearance. If anything, they were underweight, their sinewy bodies stringy to the point of scrawniness. And that was the secret of their strength. That was what gave them their stamina, their staying power. They had the kind of build that enabled them to put up with anything. To move fast and light, to endure weeks of hardship on bad water and scraps. And they were possessed of such bedrock toughness, such resilience of mind, that once they had started something they would die before they would quit. These were the men who could survive anything. And Lynch was one of them. He had never forgotten what his early days in the SBS had taught him. No matter how sick, bloodied, starved, dirty, or dog-tired he might be, there was always something left. If only he had the will to find it.

Somehow he forced himself into a sprint.

The air seared his gullet as he sucked more oxygen deep into his lungs to revive the tired blood that pulsed through his veins. His legs were slow to respond. They felt slack and wooden at the same time. Like the disconnected limbs of a puppet. One bad footfall now, he knew, and he would hit the road hard. Break an ankle, a knee . . . a leg. Give them an excuse to invalid him out of the squadron. He forced himself through the pain and the nagging, weakling fears of an old man, willed himself to run faster. He picked up speed. He could feel it. The seconds ticked past and the gate drew closer. Four hundred yards, three hundred, two . . .

And then the pain seemed to melt away. The woodenness in his legs evaporated and was replaced by an exhilarating surge of power as his brain responded to the need and released a fresh spurt of endorphins into the bloodstream, those mystic analgesics that enable the body to blot out pain and achieve extraordinary feats of strength and endurance. His heart seemed to expand in his chest as it pumped new strength into tired, mutinous muscles. His stride lengthened and his legs accelerated to a blur. Suddenly he was not a marathon runner anymore. He was a sprinter. An Olympian. A superman in a hundred-yard dash that had to be covered in ten seconds. And he knew he could do it.

His feet flew across the pavement. The lopsided gate at the bottom of the hill rushed toward him like the banner of the finishing line. Suddenly he was past it, a tortured cry of triumph on his lips. He dropped his pace, wiped the sweat from his eyes, and looked at his watch. It was eleven o'clock sharp . . . but the second hand showed four seconds past the hour.

Fast. But not fast enough.

The cry of triumph was replaced by an anguished groan. He slowed to a jog, then a shuffling, dispirited walk, his breath coming in long, shuddering gulps. For several minutes the momentum of the run refused to leave him and he felt as though he were still rushing headlong down the road. Gradually, it faded. Drained and defeated, he turned and walked slowly back to the gate. Eager to add humiliation to defeat, his brain cut off the supply of endorphins to his bloodstream, the anesthesia faded, and the aches and pains of the ages flooded back into his body.

"God . . . damn," he swore. He could scarcely believe it. So close and so far. Somehow it was all too obvious. An inevitable consequence of the advancing years. No matter how hard he tried, he would never do better than this. Maybe never do as well again. This was it. His best time ever. He stopped at the gate, slumped against the wall, and resignedly let his head loll forward to his chest while his labored breathing slowly returned to normal. It seemed to take forever. His clothes were sweat-sodden rags. Steam plumed off him as though he were a stricken beast, an aging racehorse back from the steeplechase, unable to regain his championship form, destined for the slaughterer.

Lynch smiled at the unflattering image he had conjured of himself. His mind, not his body, had always been his greatest enemy. He'd done okay . . . for an old guy. Next time maybe he'd try a different route up the mountain, make one less water stop. He'd find a way to shave a few seconds off. The motto of the SBS came back to him: Not by strength, by guile.

He wiped his streaming face, tried to shrug off the mood of defeat, and started up the hill toward his cottage. Right now what he wanted most in all the world was a long, restful soak in a hot bath.

The cottage was just as he'd left it. The key in the same position under the stone. The strands of thread he'd left on the doors and window sashes were unmoved. There had been no visitors. He opened the door, shuffled inside, and took off his Nikes and his belt pack. Then he shambled tiredly into the laundry room, stripped off his sodden clothes, and shoved them into the laundry tub. He paused for a moment and looked down at his naked body. His feet throbbed and the arteries in his legs stood out like cables. But his belly was flat and ridged with muscle and his skin was smooth and firm. There wasn't a gram of fat on him anywhere. It wasn't the body of an old man.

He walked back out to the kitchen, took a carton of orange juice from the refrigerator, and drank it all in a series of long, delicious swallows. Then he padded gingerly into the bathroom, put the plug in the bathtub, and turned on the hot water faucet. But there was something else he had to attend to before he got into the tub. A heavy workout in the morning had a way of loosening a man's bowels. He flipped back the lid on the toilet seat and sat down. It was the first time he had taken the weight off his legs all morning, and they blessed him for it. Wearily, he leaned forward and put his elbows on his knees, rested his face in his hands, and waited for his bowels to perform. And then the grenade that had been taped beneath the rim of the toilet bowl exploded.

The compression in such a confined space was devastating. A wave of raw pain seared across his unprotected flesh. The white-hot tip of a spear lanced up into his innards. The force of the blast lifted him into the air and hurled him toward the open door. He hit the stone floor hard, the sound of the explosion ringing in his ears. Behind him, fire and steam leapt from the toilet bowl with the fury of a volcanic eruption. The water in the bowl evaporated in a hiss of scalding steam and merged with the smell of burnt flesh to fill the room with a disgusting stench.

Lynch scrabbled across the floor to the bedroom, barely able to grasp that he was still alive. Shock must have robbed his body of all sensation, because he could move and yet, he knew, his injuries had to be ghastly. Then he came up hard against the legs of his assassin, who stood contemptuously in front of him. He froze. He had been right after all when he had woken up early that morning. There had been someone out there in the dark. But he had been sloppy. He hadn't looked properly. He had been in a hurry to start his run. And now it was too late. He was about to pay with his life. He lay still and waited for the bullet to the back of the head that he knew was only a moment away.

The seconds ticked past and nothing happened. Then the man spoke to him. A deep American voice with an amused undertone.

"Man," it said. "I swear to God I saw lightning shootin' outta both o' your ears."

Lynch's head swam. He knew the voice. Knew it well. And it dawned on him what had happened. Then the tension melted from his body and his limbs turned to water. He sagged to the cold stone floor and moaned, a long-drawn-out moan of relief . . . and resignation. At last he found the strength to lift his head and look into the face of his tormentor.

"Red Bonner," he whispered hoarsely.

The big red face of Lieutenant Commander Tom Bonner, US Navy SEALs, grinned maliciously back down at him.

"You ain't hurt so bad," Bonner added reassuringly. "You just got your ass burned from a little old flash grenade is all. Kinda like the one you put in the crapper back in Norfolk. The one that lit up my pecker like a highway flare, remember? I told you I'd get even with you for that, you limey son of a bitch."

Lynch lowered his head and shook it tiredly from side to side.

"What in the name of God have you done to me, you mad bastard?" he muttered.

"Hell," Bonner responded in his distinctive Texan drawl. "I cut the magnesium by seventy percent just so as it wouldn't blow your crapper apart. 'Course, you'll be shitting charcoal for a day or two . . . but that's a small price to pay for a bit of fun between friends, ain't it, ol' buddy?"

He reached down and offered Lynch his hand. Lynch looked at it to make sure it concealed no more ugly surprises, then took it and got shakily to his feet, trying not to wince as the pain flared anew across his rump.

"Jesus Christ," he mumbled. "I thought you'd blown my arse off."

"Ask me, you got plenty to spare," Bonner grunted.

Then he gave Lynch a friendly slap on the back and turned toward the kitchen.

"Don't suppose you'd have any glasses hereabouts, would you?" he bellowed in his usual amiable fashion as he pulled a bottle of Macallan's malt whisky from an inside jacket pocket. "It's my guess you could use a shot of good whisky about now, huh? Maybe even two?"

Lynch watched him as he poked through the cupboards in the kitchen, a big man with a weather-glazed face and a bullet-shaped head with the flame-red hair that gave him his nickname. His clothes were simple enough, the kind of baggy, off-the-rack outdoor jacket that many visitors wore to this part of the world, a brown-checked shirt with a button-down collar, expensive tan corduroys, and new hiking shoes. But he couldn't have been mistaken for anything other than an American. Not that he ever tried to disguise his nationality. Wherever he went he wore it like badge to be proud of. Most people who met him assumed he was a cop, a retired football player, or some kind of military man. If people asked him outright, as they sometimes did, he said he was navy. If they pressed him further, he would tell them he was an executive officer in the Seabees. He knew enough about construction to satisfy the most inquisitive strangers. That was not because he was an expert at putting things up. Rather, he was an expert at blowing things up. Bridges, buildings, highways, power lines, docks, locks, dams, railroad tracks, trains and boats and planes. He knew how they were made, he knew all their strong points and their weak points, and he knew where to put his explosives so they would do the most damage. Red Bonner was the best demolitions man in the US Navy. And, at forty-two, he was the oldest and most experienced commander in the SEALs. He and Lynch had known each other for twelve years. Ever since their first joint exercise together when Lynch had been with an SBS squad that had worked with the SEALs on exit and entry techniques from the new generation of Trident nuclear submarines at the joint US and British naval base at Holy Loch.

Like men-at-arms everywhere, they had formed an easy camaraderie based on shared hardship, mutual respect, and a taste for the kind of rough humor that was a special-forces trademark. Like flash grenades in toilet bowls. Over the years they had worked together often under the Anglo-American joint intelligence treaty which required the armed forces of both countries to share new weapons and techniques with each other. And each of them had risen within their respective units to command rank: Lynch to squad commander and Bonner to be chief of the SEALs weapons-testing unit at Norfolk, Virginia. That was where Lynch had seen Bonner last, when he had spent six months in Norfolk, participating in the sea trials of a revolutionary new minisub. As always, he hadn't known quite where or when he would run into his American friend again. He hadn't expected to find Bonner lying in wait for him at his highland retreat.

"Bonner?" Lynch tried to inject a note of authority into his voice despite the fact that he was standing naked in a doorway with his rump scalded to the color of beetroot. "Would it be too much to ask what the hell you're doing here in Scotland?"

"You gotta have glasses here someplace," Bonner muttered, ignoring Lynch's question. "Don't tell me you don't have any decent goddamn whisky glasses here?"

"Bonner?" Lynch repeated.

The big man paused to look at him.

"Came to help you celebrate your birthday," he said. "Can't let a guy turn forty without some kind of party."

"I'm thirty-nine, not forty," Lynch corrected him.

"Whatever." Bonner shrugged and turned his attention back to the cupboards.

"Top right," Lynch added.

"Thank you," Bonner said. He opened the top right cupboard door where Lynch kept his whisky glasses, pulled a couple down, and set them on the table. Then he opened the bottle of good malt whisky and filled each glass to the brim.

"Tell you the truth," he added reflectively, "I couldn't give a flying fuck about your birthday."

Lynch nodded.

"Thanks for the present anyway," he said.

"You're welcome," Bonner sniffed. Then he picked up a glass, held it to his lips, took a slow, appreciative sip, and swallowed. "Man," he breathed approvingly, "that is fine whisky."

Lynch watched from the doorway.

"Well?" Bonner shot him an accusing look. "You going to have a drink with me or you plan to stand there feeling sorry for yourself with your asshole glowin' in the dark?"

Lynch hesitated. Revenge would come later. What he wanted to do now was to soak his rear end in a bucket of ice water, then smother it in zinc and vitamin E cream. In the meantime, he decided, a shot of whisky wouldn't do him any harm and might do him a lot of good. He reached forward, picked up the remaining glass, downed half of it in one gulp, paused a moment, then finished it. The whisky scorched down his gullet and into his stomach. A minute or two, and he would start to feel better as the anesthetic effect of the alcohol reached his backside.

Bonner picked up the bottle and moved to refill the glass. Lynch shook his head and stepped back. He wanted to leave, but he was reluctant to turn around and give Bonner the satisfaction of seeing the damage he'd done. Bonner studied him, smirking.

"Tell you the truth," he added, "I've come here on the auspicious occasion of your birthday to make you an offer that will make you a rich man."

"Oh." Lynch's eyebrows arched. "You've got an offer I can't refuse?"

"Yep." Bonner went on without missing a beat. "Got a business proposition that only a blind fool would turn down."

"What kind of proposition?" Lynch asked.

Bonner pulled out a chair, sat down, and leaned it back on two legs, cradling his drink on his lap in his big red hands.

"I'd be happy to tell you if you can bear to sit your ass down on one o' these chairs for a minute," he said. "But first I think you better get some clothes on . . . 'cos you're startin' to make me horny."

3 No Place Like Home

London, May 16. 00.05 hours

The hastily assembled members of the British War Cabinet fell silent as the Prime Minister strode into the Cabinet room. He had shaved, showered, and changed into a freshly pressed suit, but his face was drawn and his posture rigid with tension. In his right hand he held a buff-colored folder stamped Most Secret.

"Gentlemen." He nodded a general greeting to everyone in the room and took his seat, midway down the long oval table with its green leather inlay. His executive assistant, John Traynor, shut the heavy double doors and glided, silent as a ghost, to his own chair set against the wall, directly behind the PM. There were pitchers of ice water on the table and on a side table there was a coffee urn with neatly arranged rows of china cups engraved with the Number 10 logo. At the opposite end of the room Traynor had set up an easel with a large color map of the Middle East.

The Prime Minister waited until everyone was seated, then glanced around the table at this urgent gathering of the most powerful men in Britain. He had already been advised that everyone would be present except for the foreign secretary, who was on an official visit to Rome but was expected back in London by morning.

"For those of you who haven't already heard," the Prime Minister began without preamble, "I can now confirm that Her Majesty's Yacht, *Britannia,* has been hijacked in Jidda by persons claiming to represent the IRA and that their royal highnesses, the queen and the Duke of Edinburgh, are both held hostage on board."

There was no one at the table who did not already know about the hijack. Even so, the formal announcement by the Prime Minister injected a dreadful feeling of foreboding into the room. As though everyone shared the same belief that a terrible chain of events had begun which were destined to inflict the most fearful wounds upon the nation and from which there would be no escape for any of them.

The Prime Minister opened his folder and glanced through the notes that Traynor had completed only moments earlier.

"HMS *Hotspur* is at the scene, and I have spoken to Captain Purcell," he said. "So far he has received one message from the hijackers. They claim to have two hundred pounds of high explosives on board, which they say they will detonate if anyone tries to board the yacht or to interfere with its progress. At this moment the yacht is under way and in the process of leaving Jidda harbor. Captain Purcell has also spoken by secure radio link with the queen's bodyguard on board the *Britannia* and he has been assured that both their highnesses are safe and unharmed in a secure section of the yacht. I have ordered Captain Purcell not to interfere with the passage of the yacht but to follow it closely until he is ordered by me to do otherwise."

He looked up from the folder.

"The first information on the crisis came in to me two and a half hours ago. I took the immediate step of calling 22 SAS, Hereford, and ordered the CRW team to Jidda."

CRW stood for Counter Revolutionary Warfare and was the SAS cadre trained especially to deal with hostage situations involving terrorists.

"I have also spoken personally with King Fahd, although it is still very early morning in Saudi Arabia. The king gave his approval for the SAS to operate from Saudi territory and promised his government's full cooperation. I have also spoken to the king's brother, the defense minister"—he paused to check the name on the sheet of paper in front of him—"Prince Sultan ibn Abdul Aziz. The prince has assumed direct responsibility for arrangements with the SAS when they arrive. I can assure you, gentlemen, the Saudis are as rattled by this as we are."

He paused for a moment and looked at the pinched white faces around the table. No one uttered a word.

"And now," the Prime Minister added, "we have some hard decisions to make."

He nodded first to a small, wiry man in his mid-forties who still looked like a soldier despite the plain gray suit he wore.

"Colonel Quillan, commanding officer of 22 SAS, is here to assist us."

Quillan nodded formally but said nothing. His face remained blank, his dark eyes fathomless. The only clue to his temperament was the way he sat forward in his chair, shoulders tense, hands curled on the table in front of him, like a wrestler in a crouch, ready for a fight.

The PM continued: "The other gentleman with us today, whom some of you may not know, is Colonel Quillan's predecessor at the SAS, Sir Malcolm Porter, now chief controlling officer with Counter Terrorism Command."

A tight-jawed man with crinkly gray hair and hard blue eyes, Sir Malcolm looked like a Whitehall warrior who had once dodged real bullets. It was an accurate assessment of one of the shrewdest men ever to swap a swagger stick for a rolled umbrella. Counter Terrorism Command, or CTC, was his creation. A shadowy government department that operated out of the Ministry of Defence, it was responsible for coordinating the armed response to terrorist attacks against British interests anywhere in the world. His powers were such that he could call on the resources of any branch of the armed forces, including the SAS and the SBS, to neutralize any terrorist threat. He was nominally answerable to the Minister of Defence, but in practice he was answerable only to the Prime Minister. And, because CTC's work relied heavily on interception and prevention, it operated its own intelligence division, which worked closely with MI5, Britain's internal intelligence service and MI6, Britain's foreign intelligence service.

Sir Malcolm was a long-time chum of the tweedy Arthur Leamus, director of MI6, who sat next to him and who looked so uncomfortable because his agency had not picked up a single solitary whisper of a plot to hijack the *Britannia.* If it was the IRA, as the hijackers claimed, they had been uncharacteristically efficient in keeping it secret. Next to him, MI5's director, Byron Blair, sat a little more comfortably. This was an offshore disaster, thank God, and he was reasonably sure that his department would not be tainted by the unholy political row that would ensue when everybody scrambled to blame everybody else for not seeing it coming.

The Prime Minister continued around the table until he had included Nigel Shepherd, the home secretary, Teddy Lawson, the minister of defence, Fleet Commander Sir Bernard Harriman, Rear Admiral Bryden, the Admiralty's director of intelligence who had first alerted the PM to the hijacking, and Commandant General Aubrey Sharpe, commanding officer of the Royal Marines. Like Colonel Quillan, all the senior officers had worn civilian clothes to come quickly and anonymously to Downing Street in the dead of night.

"Gentlemen," the Prime Minister resumed. "We are confronted by the gravest act of terrorism ever to have been committed against the Crown. There is no precedent for what has happened in Jidda. It is a crisis unique in this nation's history. It is incumbent upon us, therefore, to make sure that our response is the correct one. As everyone at this table is aware, it is the declared policy of this government not to make deals with terrorists. On this occasion we may be forced to improvise policy to accommodate the situation. As I have already indicated, I stand ready to impose a military solution. However, the military option may or may not be appropriate. I am sure that all of us gathered here tonight, at this terrible moment in our nation's history, understand perfectly well that we must do everything in our power to preserve the lives of her majesty the queen and Prince Philip.

"I have spoken by telephone with all immediate members of the royal family to advise them personally of the situation: Prince

Charles, Lady Diana, Princess Anne, Prince Andrew, Prince Edward, Princess Margaret and the Queen Mother. Prince Charles is returning to London from Scotland at this moment and I shall be meeting with him later today. I have ordered increased security for all members of the royal family. Owing to the extraordinary nature of the crisis, I have also advised that their highnesses cancel all public engagements until further notice. I further advised that I think it best if they were to remain in London for the duration of the crisis, where their security can be guaranteed and where they can be kept abreast of the situation on a moment-to-moment basis. Despite their marital situation, Prince Charles and the Princess of Wales will both relocate to Buckingham Palace. Their sons, Prince William and Prince Harry, will join them there. Prince Andrew and Prince Edward will also be taken to the palace later today. We understand that Prince Andrew's daughters, the princesses Beatrice and Eugenie, are in New York with their mother, Sarah Ferguson. We have commandeered a Concorde flight to bring them back to London and they, too, will be at the palace by morning. Princess Margaret will be joined by Princess Anne at Kensington Palace and the Queen Mother will remain at Clarence House. Security has already been increased at all these locations. Naturally, I have assured them all that this government will do everything in its power—and I do mean everything—to preserve the lives of the queen and Prince Philip. If that means that we must endure the humiliation of a negotiated agreement with terrorists, then that is what we shall have to consider."

He hesitated and looked around the circle of solemn faces.

"If that scenario should seem unacceptable, I would simply ask you this: is there anyone here today who is prepared to go down in history as the man responsible for the death of the Queen of England?"

The small conference chamber in the heart of the British capital, where so many historic decisions had been made, filled with an aching silence. The Prime Minister's question found no takers.

"The decision, therefore, is mine," he said finally. "If I have to, I shall treat with the terrorists until their royal highnesses are safe, and then I shall resign. The violent death of the monarch cannot be considered an acceptable outcome of this crisis.

"Now, gentlemen"—he took a deep breath and leaned back in his chair—"I am ready for your suggestions . . . and let us proceed in the sober knowledge that the fate of the monarch rests in our hands."

Sir Malcolm Porter was the first to venture into the void.

"How secure are their highnesses at this moment . . . and how long can they be expected to remain secure where they are?" he asked.

The Prime Minister looked to Admiral Sir Bernard Harriman for an answer. The royal yacht was not the property of the royal family. The *Britannia* was owned and operated by the Royal Navy on behalf of the royal family. It had been built to an Admiralty design, based on the old Daring class destroyer, with modifications for the royal apartments aft of the mainmast. Its annual running cost of six million dollars came out of the defense budget. In time of war the yacht could be converted to a hospital ship and had been used many times to rescue injured and stranded Britons from trouble spots around the world. Harriman was very familiar with the secret modifications carried out on the yacht during her costly 1987 refit.

"If they remain in the secure section on the royal deck, they are safe," he said. "The system we installed is very sound. The armored screens are virtually impregnable. They have their own filtered ventilation system. They have food and water to last a month. When the system was installed, of course, it was never envisaged that it would have to be utilized for anything like that length of time. It was intended purely as a safe area on board the yacht to protect members of the royal family in the event of attack from air or sea. When the danger had passed, the system could be deactivated. I'm bound to say that the likelihood of the *Britannia* being boarded and held for any length of time was never considered a likely scenario."

It sounded like a veiled criticism of the Royal Marines, who were responsible for the *Britannia*'s shipboard defense. Harriman still felt guilty because he had been unavailable when the crisis had broken a couple hours earlier and Bryden had been forced to go direct to Downing Street. The admiral had been on his way home from a convivial dinner with old friends and had ordered his driver to take the car phone off the hook so that he could doze undisturbed in the backseat. Across the table, General Sharpe remained impassive. He was too old and wise a bird to worry about positioning for advantage this early in the crisis. He was content to let others show their hands. He knew that if his men had been unable to thwart a boarding of the *Britannia,* there had to be a reason. He knew that what had happened so far could only have happened over their dead bodies.

"These armored screens are . . . impregnable?" Sir Malcolm queried.

"Well," Harriman hedged. "Nothing is impregnable. The screens can be breached . . . but only by the application of a level of violence that would also involve the destruction of considerable sections of the superstructure."

"You mean the kind of violence that would most likely result in the death of the occupants?" Sir Malcolm said.

"Yes," the admiral sighed ominously. "I'm afraid we would have to consider that a likely outcome."

A chilly current passed through the room as the awful image came to everyone's mind.

"Presumably"—Defence Minister Teddy Lawson spoke for the first time—"that would defeat the purpose of taking them hostage in the first place?"

"The hijackers have already threatened to sink the ship," Sir Malcolm reminded him. "That would have a fatal effect on the occupants too."

"Yes," Lawson drawled, a note of irritation in his voice. "But we all know that kind of threat is standard procedure in these situations. Based on what we already know about the psychology of terrorists, we also must assume that they don't want to die either—if we can offer them an incentive not to. They have hijacked the *Britannia* for a reason. They have taken the queen and Prince Philip hostage for a reason. They want something. And, in order to maintain some kind of bargaining position, they have to keep the hostages alive. If they carry out their threat to kill the hostages, then they lose their protection. The moment they kill the queen and Prince Philip, their own lives become worthless."

"There are two hundred seventy-two officers and men on board the *Britannia* too," Rear Admiral Bryden added.

"Quite so," the Prime Minister intervened. "And we must weigh the lives of every one of those sailors with the same concern that we weigh their majesty's lives.

"However," he paused, "we must not lose sight of the fact that we have been placed in the abhorrent position where the lives of some hostages must take priority over the lives of others. As callous as that may sound, we cannot delude ourselves that it is any other way. The life of the monarch takes precedence over the life of the foot soldier. Thus it has always been and thus it will ever be . . . as long as Britain chooses to remain a constitutional monarchy. Soldiers, sailors, and airmen pledge their lives to the preservation of the Crown. The queen is the embodiment of the Crown. I am sure every man aboard the *Britannia* understands that."

An awkward silence settled. Every man at the table knew that the Prime Minister had just put into practice something that had hitherto only been a subject for speculation. Even though they were supposedly at the apex of the egalitarian age, the life of the sovereign was worth more than the life of the common man. If only because of how much she symbolized. Queen Elizabeth the Second was not just a woman. She was the Crown. The living symbol of British sovereignty. If she was killed by terrorists, it would be a blow against the sovereignty of Great Britain. If the lives of the officers and men aboard the *Britannia* had to be sacrificed to save the life of the sovereign—then so be it.

"I wonder," Home Secretary Nigel Shepherd mused out loud, "how long that principle would hold up if it were a Labour Cabinet sitting around this table."

"Fortunately," the Prime Minister responded quickly, "this government believes in the sanctity of the monarchy. We shall learn soon enough about the true loyalties of Her Majesty's Loyal Opposition . . . when we go into Parliament."

"The defence secretary is quite right," Sir Malcolm interjected, steering the meeting back on course. "The hijackers want something for their trouble, and they know that the only way they're going to get it is by keeping the queen and Prince Philip alive. Therefore, it is in our interests and theirs not to sink the royal yacht. But only for a while. Until they have issued their demands and they have had a chance to determine whether those demands are going to be met."

The Prime Minister shook his head.

"They haven't made any demands yet," he said.

"They will," Sir Malcolm answered. "At the moment they are still consolidating their hold. And if they are clever enough to take the royal yacht, they are clever enough to know that they can control the situation for only a short period of time. We can expect that they will make their demands known soon and that those demands will be accompanied by a very tight deadline. That means we shall have a very short time in which to act."

"How short?" the Prime Minister asked.

"Days, I suspect. Not weeks," Sir Malcolm said. "They know that we'll have our very best antiterrorist people all over them within a few hours; navy, air force, intelligence, SAS . . . the lot. They know they can control the situation for only a short time before we take it away from them. Either by killing them or by preventing them from blowing up the ship. Therefore, the only way they can possibly win is by getting what they want fast. By giving us no time to maneuver, so we have no alternative but to meet their demands. And if they don't get what they want by a certain time, they carry out their threat."

"You mean a suicide job?" Lawson asked.

"I think they've made that decision, yes," Sir Malcolm said. "I certainly don't think they would put themselves in the position they are in now unless it was an all-or-nothing venture. They have decided that we are going to give them what they want or they are going to blow themselves up and take the queen, Prince Philip, and two hundred seventy-two officers and men of the Royal Navy with them."

"A death-or-glory job?" MI6 chief Arthur Leamus murmured sceptically. "It's not the IRA's style. They'd rather take hostages and send them off to die with bombs. The only time they blow themselves up is by accident. Besides, they haven't got so much talent that they can afford to squander it on a single suicide mission, however spectacular."

"It's a suicide mission only if it fails," Sir Malcolm remarked.

"They've taken a calculated risk that we'll concede rather than risk the monarch's life . . . and they're right. Nor, may I add, do we know for certain that it really is the IRA we're dealing with here."

"The hijacker who spoke to Purcell claimed it was the IRA," Leamus added.

"Officials or Provos?" Porter asked.

"They didn't say," the Prime Minister answered.

"That's unusual," Leamus conceded.

"He had a lot on his mind when he made the call," Shepherd observed dryly.

"If it is the IRA," Porter continued, "they're operating a long way from home. They've operated in Europe and the United States before, but never the Middle East."

"A considerable number of them have trained in the Middle East," Leamus said. "The Provos and the INLA have close ties to the PLO and half a dozen PLO splinter groups, including the Abu Nidal and the Abu Musa groups. We also know of at least a dozen IRA men who trained at camps operated by Hezbollah in Iran. If they wanted to use the Middle East as a launch pad, the infrastructure is all there."

"You mean a collaborative effort between terror groups?" the Prime Minister asked.

"It's been done before," Leamus said. "This is the first time they've attempted anything on this scale, of course, but there's a first time for everything."

An ominous and apprehensive silence settled around the table.

"Your people are working that angle now?" the PM asked Leamus.

"We're working every angle, Prime Minister," the MI6 chief answered. "We're squeezing every asset in Europe and the Middle East to find out who's behind this."

"Byron?" The Prime Minister looked at Byron Blair, head of MI5. "You have any theories?"

"Could be the Provos or a rogue IRA cell," Blair responded. "The hard men are always quarreling with each other about which tactics have the most impact. They know that terrorist attacks against British civilians only seem to work against them. Killing British soldiers is all very well, but soldiers are paid to take that risk. On the other hand, the Mountbatten murder shook the country to the core. So, a stroke like this may be desperate, but it is very effective. Either they get what they want, and we know they're going to want something big, or they kill the queen. If that happens, it could provoke such a wave of revulsion that the nation would want to be rid of the Ulster problem once and for all. There comes a point in the psyche of any nation where the principle is no longer worth the sacrifice. And a lot of people are sick to death of Northern Ireland. They wish it would just go away. And that would be playing right into the IRA's hands.

"However." He paused to make one small point. "I don't know how much more help my department can be. We deactivated our assets in Northern Ireland a while ago—on the instructions of your predecessor."

Everyone at the table knew of the long and bitter feud that had raged between MI5 and MI6 during the Thatcher era about who should run intelligence operations in Northern Ireland. For a while both departments had run their own agents inside the embattled province, often getting in each other's way, intentionally and unintentionally sabotaging each other's operations. It had ended with an exasperated iron lady siding with MI6 on a technicality. Even though Ulster was a province of the United Kingdom, it was outside the mainland and therefore outside MI5's traditional realm of influence.

"Byron . . ." The Prime Minister looked soberly at Blair. "This is hardly the time to be fighting old battles."

Porter smiled inwardly as he watched the exchange. He and Leamus and the Prime Minister knew damn well that Blair would not have deactivated all his agents inside Northern Ireland, despite a direct order from Number 10. That would simply have gone too much against the grain.

"Okay," Blair gave a noncommittal shrug. "I'll see what I can do."

"In the meantime," Porter stepped in, "we have to proceed on the assumption that military intervention is inevitable—it's only a matter of when."

"Sir Malcolm." The Prime Minister turned his attention back to the chief of CTC. "A moment ago you said that, ultimately, we would take control of the situation away from the hijackers. Either by killing them or preventing them from blowing up the ship. Can we stop them from blowing up the ship? Can we kill them before they can harm the queen and Prince Philip?"

"That would depend on whether we could locate and neutralize the explosives without the hijackers knowing about it until it was too late," Porter answered.

"Can we do that?"

Sir Malcolm hesitated.

"There are a couple of ways it might be possible," he said. "The most difficult part would be putting a man on board the *Britannia* without the terrorists' knowledge. The *Britannia* is equipped with state-of-the-art electronics. Correct, Sir Bernard?"

"Correct," Harriman confirmed.

"That means the hijackers can watch what we're doing," Porter continued. "They can eavesdrop on our communications. They can pick up any approaching vessel or aircraft on their radar. They can use sonar to see if we're trying to sneak up on them by submarine. We could jam the *Britannia*'s electronics, of course, make them deaf, dumb, and blind for a few minutes while we put someone on board. But if they're clever enough, they'd know that we were trying something and things might get a little . . . intense."

Porter paused a moment to let his words sink in. Then he said: "There's something else."

"I was wondering when you'd come to that, old chap," Leamus murmured.

"Electronically jamming the *Britannia* might trigger an explosion," Porter said. "Assuming one or more of the charges on board is radio activated. Presumably the hijackers know this . . . and they know that we know. That means we have no choice but to leave them with their eyes and ears in full working order. Otherwise, the moment we begin jamming, we not only risk an explosion, we tip off the hijackers that an attack is under way. And, if their charges are not radio activated, they still have time to blow the ship manually. Either way, they've got us bluffed into leaving them alone. My money says they're using wires as their primary firing method. That way, they don't lose control of the situation. If it is a suicide job, they probably have a man sitting on top of their biggest bomb, ready to throw the switch."

"Good God," the Prime Minister sighed. He rested his face in his hands and stared bleakly at the tabletop for a moment. Still, from the corner of his eye, he saw a few anxious glances exchanged around the table. He knew what they were thinking. Some men grew in stature when confronted by a crisis of this magnitude. Others were diminished and ultimately destroyed by it. He felt as though he were shriveling before their eyes.

"Unfortunately," Porter went on, adding to the Prime Minister's wretchedness, "I don't see any other way. We have to get a man on board the *Britannia* to locate and neutralize the explosives without the hijackers knowing about it. Then and only then can we undertake a full-scale boarding operation."

"Yes . . ." The Prime Minister nodded and looked up at Porter. "But can we do that without putting the life of her royal highness in further jeopardy?"

Porter didn't answer directly. Instead, he turned his gaze, and with it the attention of all others at the table, to Colonel Quillan of the SAS.

If Quillan felt discomfited by the sudden shifting of the heat toward him, it didn't show on his face.

"It's possible," he answered evenly. "We already have a man on the *Britannia* who is capable of carrying out that task."

The Cabinet Room filled with an expectant silence.

"Captain Gault was the assigned bodyguard to his royal highness for this tour. I haven't spoken to him yet, but, to the best of my knowledge, he is free and mobile in the secured area of the ship. He's one of the regiment's most experienced officers. Seen service in Northern Ireland as well as the Middle East. Speaks fluent Arabic—which is why he was assigned this tour—and he's very familiar with the *Britannia.* He should be able to find any explosives they've got hidden away. Communication is secure. He could give us important information about the hijackers too. How many there are, strength, and disposition. All useful stuff when we plan our attack."

Porter gave a barely perceptible nod of approval to his successor at 22 Regiment. He already knew about John Gault. He had borrowed him for several successful operations of his own. But Porter had deferred to Quillan because he didn't want to be perceived to be taking over the show.

"Yes," the PM agreed. "But if he gets unlucky, he could panic the hijackers into blowing the yacht up anyway. And if they kill him, it accomplishes nothing and leaves their royal highnesses with the protection of only one bodyguard."

"There's no such thing as a risk-free military operation, sir," Quillan answered.

Coming from a politician, it might have sounded like insolence or sarcasm. Coming from Quillan, it was merely a statement of fact.

The Prime Minister nodded.

"I understand what you're saying, Colonel. If anybody can pull this off, it's the SAS. But I'm afraid I have to take another view. Unless an operation of this kind is as close to one hundred percent risk-free as we can possibly get, then I simply can't take the chance. Ultimately, Captain Gault would be acting on my orders. And, if he failed, it is I who would be responsible for the death of Her Majesty."

Quillan nodded, his face expressionless.

"With respect, sir," Teddy Lawson interjected, "the SAS has rather a good record at this sort of thing. You yourself ordered CRW into the air. It would seem logical to explore every opportunity for using them."

"And we will, Teddy," the PM answered shortly. "But if I do elect for the military option, I suspect there will be only one chance to get it right. Which is why we need to proceed swiftly but prudently. The hijackers appear to be in the process of taking the *Britannia* out to sea. We have no idea what they are going to do when they get there. Whether they will turn north toward Suez or south toward Aden. Whether they will attempt to seek safe haven in another country or whether they will sail around in circles till they tell us what they want. It would seem to me that our first priority should be to establish an operations base in the area, preferably one that is exclusively under British control."

Porter nodded in silent agreement. The Saudis might have offered willing cooperation but, if there was a Middle Eastern connection to the hijacking, the last thing they needed was the chance of a leak about British intentions from a Saudi-controlled base.

"That means an aircraft carrier," Lawson added.

"And that is why I have asked Admiral Bryden to report on all our warships in the area," the PM countered, seeking to regain control of the discussion.

Bryden took his cue.

"We have eight warships in the region," he said, glancing at his notes. "The antisubmarine frigate *Avenger* and the destroyer *Claymore* are in the eastern Mediterranean, and both could be in the hijack area within thirty-six hours. The minesweepers *Bristol* and *Newcastle* are in the south Persian Gulf with the frigates *Ardent* and *Adder* and the Royal Fleet Auxliary *Renown.* They could be off Aden in thirty-six hours and in the hijack area twenty-four hours after that. The only other ship we have within reasonable striking distance is the destroyer *Courageous* at Gibraltar, but she would take seventy-two hours to reach Suez and another twenty-four hours to reach the hijack area."

The minister of defence looked balefully at Bryden.

"No carriers in the region at all?"

"*Invincible* is at Portsmouth undergoing a refit," Harriman interrupted on Wickham's behalf. "*Hermes* is taking part in a NATO exercise off Norway."

"Good God," Lawson grumbled. "If ever there was a time . . ."

Teddy Lawson was the most hawkish defence minister to serve in the cabinet in twenty years. Perversely, the Prime Minister had appointed him because he could think of no one better suited to sell the idea of defense cuts to the military. It hadn't worked out quite as well as the PM had hoped. Lawson had become a willing hostage to the British military-industrial lobby and bleated incessantly about the need for budget increases instead of cuts. Lawson wanted Britannia to rule the waves once more, and if he had his way, he would have abolished the National Health Service and used the money to buy a dozen nuclear-powered aircraft carriers.

"Teddy," the PM cut him short. "It would be a grave miscalculation on your part to use this crisis as an opportunity to lobby for an increase in defense spending."

Lawson's cheeks jiggled with indignation, but he shut up and fumed in silence. He could bide his time. Unless he was mistaken, this was one prime minister who would not be lodging at 10 Downing Street for too much longer.

"What's your recommendation, Admiral?" The PM looked across the table at Harriman.

"If the hijackers are taking the *Britannia* out of port and if we are to have any hope of controlling the situation at all, we shall have to isolate her at sea," Harriman answered crisply. After an inauspicious beginning he knew it was time for him to demonstrate why he still deserved to hold the rank of most senior officer in the Royal Navy.

"I would recommend that, first, we set up a total exclusion zone around the *Britannia.* The zone would exist within a tightly controlled security cordon similar to the one we put in place at the Falklands. No vessel or aircraft would be permitted to enter this exclusion zone. This would not only give us a clear sphere of operation, it would stop any other nation offering relief or refuge to the hijackers."

The admiral pushed his chair back and walked over to the easel at the end of the room.

"There are seven countries bordering the Red Sea," he said, gesturing at the map of the Middle East. "Jordan, Saudi Arabia, and the Republic of Yemen on the Arabian peninsula side. Egypt, Sudan, Ethiopia, and Djibouti on the African side. Of these countries we can assume the People's Republic of Yemen, with its hard-line Marxist regime and its long and distinguished history of offering aid and comfort to terrorists, would be the most likely refuge for the hijackers. Ethiopia and Sudan would have to be considered suspect, if only because both countries are in a perpetual state of chaos and both have long, underpopulated coastlines that offer many points of escape for the hijackers. Still, we can expect that given an appropriate warning, neither of these countries would be eager to play an active role in assisting the hijackers. The only real threat from the outside would be posed by Yemen. We know that the Yemeni Navy would be largely ineffective against a sophisticated force such as ours. Their fleet consists mainly of lightly armed coastal patrol craft. Even if they wanted to, they couldn't do much more than make a nuisance of themselves. However, many of those patrol craft are German built. They're fast—top speeds of fifty knots in some cases. They could get a patrol craft in and out in time to take off the hijackers . . . if we offered them a big enough loophole. We have to make sure we don't. We have to make our security cordon tight enough to discourage any possible intrusion."

The admiral paused while he took his chair back at the table.

"Therefore," he added, "it is my recommendation that we order HMS *Avenger* and HMS *Claymore* to the area immediately, to assist *Hotspur* in setting up a total exclusion zone around *Britannia.* We should declare the exclusion zone in effect from midnight tomorrow. We should also order HMS *Bristol* and HMS *Newcastle* and the frigates *Ardent* and *Adder* to make all speed to the area. That would put seven warships in the Red Sea within seventy-two hours. Enough to discourage anyone from sticking their noses in where they're not wanted. And enough to give us a secure floating-operations base in international waters to provide a springboard for military action."

"Thank you, Bernard." The PM nodded his approval. "I'm inclined to agree. If the hijackers are taking the *Britannia* out to sea, we need a secure floating base before we can even contemplate a military strike."

"Assuming the hijackers give us seventy-two hours to put it together," Quillan added soberly.

"If they do not," the PM responded coolly, "we shall have no alternative but to give them what they want."

The Prime Minister put his hands palms-down on the table and leaned back in his chair, his signal that the meeting had come to a close.

"Give the orders to the fleet, Bernard," he said. "I'll speak to the foreign secretary about the declaration of a total exclusion zone. Colonel Quillan, let me know when CRW has arrived in Jidda, will you? Thank you for coming, gentlemen, and I shall see all of you here again in"—he paused, looked at his watch, and gave a wan smile—"in about eight hours."

He stood up to leave, and everyone else got up to follow. Everyone except Teddy Lawson.

"We should have a carrier there," Lawson grumbled loudly to the emptying room.

"We can manage very well with what we've got, sir," Admiral Harriman responded coolly, not bothering to hide his annoyance at Lawson's persistent bad form.

"I'm sorry," Lawson continued stubbornly to his dwindling audience. "But I warned against this kind of thing years ago. This is a situation that cries out for a carrier, and we haven't bloody well got one."

The Prime Minister was almost at the door when he stopped and turned back to look at his mutinous defence minister.

"Teddy?" he said in a voice so soft that it stilled everyone in the room.

"Yes, Prime Minister?"

"Be a good chap and stop whining, will you?"

Everyone, including Lawson, heard the barely controlled anger beneath the softness. This time the defence minister had the good sense to remain silent. He pushed back his chair and got up from the table to follow the others. The Prime Minister might be under siege. He might be intent on pursuing a policy that would bring lasting shame and humiliation down on them all. But he was still not a man to be angered lightly. It was, nonetheless, an unsettling exchange at a War Cabinet meeting. An environment where tradition demanded that political differences be set aside while everyone pulled together for the good of the nation. Sir Malcolm Porter had watched it with concern. He and Blair, the director of MI5, were the last two men to get up from the table. Porter looked at Blair and saw the same concern reflected in his eyes. He knew then that both of them were wondering exactly the same thing. What the hell did Teddy Lawson think he was playing at?

JIDDA, SAUDI ARABIA. 03.55 HOURS

Mulcahey grabbed hold of the dead marine's legs and Deveny took his head and shoulders. Together they carried him to the rail and hefted him over the side. He hit the water with a heavy splash, then bobbed to the surface a few feet away, his body turning clumsily in the *Britannia*'s wake, arms flopping brokenly back and forth in a grotesque semaphore of death. A Saudi patrol boat peeled away from the escorting armada to investigate.

"Garbage scow," Mulcahey chuckled. Then they picked up the second marine and heaved him over the side too. The third body was a man wearing a blue track suit with a head wound. Hardacre, the queen's chief of security. When the two IRA men picked him up, he groaned.

"Shit." Deveny let the bloodied body slump back to the deck. "This one's still alive, Jimmy."

"So what?" Mulcahey shrugged. "You heard the boss. The wounded go over the side too. If he makes it, he's better off anyway."

Deveny sucked in a breath and did as he was told. They swung the wounded policeman over the side and watched him splash into the black water and disappear.

"Not bad," Mulcahey grunted. "Full pike with a half twist."

Deveny shook his head.

"You're a hard man, Jimmy."

"Fuck 'em," the IRA man growled. "They'd do the same to us."

They walked back across the fantail, careful to avoid the sticky puddles of blood that soiled the beautiful teak deck. There were other bodies, eight in all, littered along the upper deck. They identified one more marine, two officers, and five crewmen who had fought the gas and tried to repel the *Britannia*'s boarders, only to pay with their lives. The two IRA men dumped them all over the side. Deveny thought that at least two more might still have been alive. He didn't like the idea of throwing helpless and unconscious men into the water, but Behan and Mulcahey were probably right. The wounded would only get in the way.

Two more Saudi patrol boats and a launch from the *Hotspur* had fallen back to pick up the jettisoned bodies. They milled around in the *Britannia*'s wake like giant panicky gulls plucking one lifeless figure after another from the water. Three army helicopters wheeled overhead, and one of them hovered in low to train his spotlight on the dismal scene in the water. Deveny and Mulcahey watched impassively from the stern rail. They could hear men shouting angrily, despairingly, to each other through the thud of the rotors. Some of them dived from the boats and swam furiously to each new body that appeared, knowing that seconds could make a difference.

Deveny felt the deck rise and fall beneath his feet. They had run into heavier swells. He turned and looked forward to see where they were. For the first time he noticed that the concrete arms of the outer harbor seemed to swoop dangerously close to the *Britannia* on each side, like a pair of pincers trying to seize the royal yacht to grab her and stop her getting away.

"Jesus . . ." he hissed through his black balaclava.

Mulcahey heard him and dragged his eyes from the water to follow Deveny's gaze. Then the two of them stared in unison at the spectacle that surrounded them. The harbor walls on both sides were thickly lined with soldiers. Thousands and thousands of them. Their eyes and rifles trained on the passing yacht in a gauntlet of impotent rage. They were so close, the IRA men could make out the details of their faces . . . until they blurred into one continuous mass. So close that some of them might have been able to jump aboard if they had been given the chance. But they had not. Their orders were clear. Do as the British requested. Let the *Britannia* pass.

Deveny heard a snort of contempt behind him and he turned just as Mulcahey raised his fist and pumped the air in a gesture of defiance.

"Christ, Jimmy . . ." Deveny began. He stopped when he saw the manic glitter in Mulcahey's eyes. Mulcahey was higher than any junkie, Deveny realized. He had what he wanted. What he'd always craved throughout his short, violent life. He had his place in history. This was his moment. The moment when it felt as if the whole world was watching him and him alone. Deveny suppressed a shudder and looked back at the silent ranks of soldiers as they slid silently by. Unlike Mulcahey, he was unsettled by it. He found the silence threatening. It was the silence of the grave that waited for them all.

Then the harbor walls came to an end, the silent ranks of soldiers fell away, followed by the flashing lights of the harbor exit—and they were clear. The *Britannia* nosed sluggishly into open water. Half a mile ahead of her, HMS *Hotspur* began the slow loop back to pick up her launches and to follow the *Britannia* wherever she might go.

Deveny turned to Mulcahey and yanked his upraised arm down hard.

"For Christ's sake, Jimmy," he urged. "We've a ways to go yet, y'know."

Mulcahey pulled his arm free and glared at Deveny. Then he caught himself. Deveny was right. There was still plenty of work to do before they could start claiming victory. They had to look for stragglers, round up the rest of the crew, and lock them below decks. Then, maybe then, they might be able to have a little fun.

The two of them picked up their rifles, pulled on their masks in case of lingering pockets of gas, then looked up and down the deserted deck. The choice was made easy for them. The double doors to the royal drawing room were already open. They swung back and forth on their hinges, beckoning to the two gunmen, inviting them inside, to a world where they did not belong.

Deveny went first, followed by Mulcahey. Someone had dimmed the lights, but Deveny only had to turn them up to see that the drawing room was empty and carried no hidden threat. The room was just as it had been when the queen and Prince Philip had gone upstairs to the royal apartments that were now their prison. Just as it had been when the maids from the household staff had finished tidying it before they, too, had gone to their beds.

Emboldened by the same tawdry thrill of the burglar, the two IRA gunmen walked into the middle of the room and looked around. It was bigger than they had expected. A wide, high-ceilinged room that used all fifty-five feet of beam. The sense of space was enhanced by the all-white decor and satinwood paneled walls. In the middle of the sternside wall was a large marble fireplace and above it a painting. Deveny looked closer and saw that it was a painting of the *Britannia*'s launching at John Brown's Clydeside shipyards in 1954. Mulcahey wandered off on his own, eyeing the priceless antique furniture: desks, side tables, chairs, and book cabinets that had come from the *Victoria and Albert.* He didn't seem to notice that his boots had left stains on the thick blue-gray carpet. Bloodstains in the shape of footprints.

Deveny wandered over to a white baby-grand piano. He lifted the lid and trailed a gloved hand over the keys. A descending cascade of notes chimed eerily through the room. Mulcahey heard it and looked around. Then he spotted a couch covered in intricate pink and cream chintz. He walked across to it and sat down heavily in the thick, enveloping cushions, his rifle still in his hand. There was a small oval coffee table in front of the couch, and he swung his feet onto it with a heavy crash. Deveny looked at him. Mulcahey grinned back. There was a vase with a flower arrangement on the table. Mulcahey looked at it for a moment, then prodded it with the toe of his boot until it fell to the floor with a thud, spilling the flowers and water across the carpet. But it didn't break.

Disappointed, Mulcahey got up, lifted the vase high in the air, then let it drop back onto the table, where it broke apart with a loud crack and tumbled to the floor in pieces. Behind his mask Mulcahey's eyes glowed with pleasure. They had taken the royal yacht—it was theirs now to do with as they liked.

"So." Mulcahey's muffled voice echoed across the room. "This is how it feels to be the fucking King of England."

Deveny snickered and looked around for a place to leave his own mark. He saw an elegant rosewood escritoire in a corner. He had no way of knowing its value. All he knew was that it looked expensive. Expensive and useless. He walked over to it, raised his rifle, and drove the butt into the delicately inlaid doors. Instead of shattering them as he expected, he only chipped them. They were sturdier than they looked. The old craftsmen really knew how to build things right, he thought. He drove the rifle butt into the doors again. Harder this time. Then again and again until at last they splintered and shattered, spilling slender glossy fragments across the floor.

He heard a whoop of excitement from across the room. Mulcahey lifted his Armalite and sprayed a burst of bullets around the walls. Deveny dropped into a squat and watched, enthralled, as the bullets shattered fine paintings and ripped huge holes in the wood-paneled walls. Then Mulcahey turned his attention to the furniture, smashing and splintering the fine antiques, destroying priceless vases and ornaments, shredding the plush couches and chairs. The noise was deafening and when it stopped, Deveny's ears creaked with pain. He stood up, pointed a finger at his head, and drew circles in the air to show that he thought Mulcahey was off his rocker. It was typical, Deveny thought. Bloody Mulcahey always had to go one better.

Mulcahey grinned back and beckoned him to follow him through the door to the queen's anteroom. It was a much smaller room, half the width of the yacht and furnished like a sitting room in a stately home. There was a small two-seater couch, side tables, and a glass-fronted bookcase filled with leather-bound books. On one shelf, instead of books, there was a beautiful glass tray engraved with crabs, sea horses, and shells. An inscription said the tray had been presented to Her Majesty by the yacht's builders. Set on the tray were a half dozen exquisite glass goblets, each engraved with a picture of the six royal residences. The case was locked to prevent the contents spilling out in rough weather.

Mulcahey lifted his rifle and methodically smashed every glass panel. When he had finished he reached inside, plucked out a goblet engraved with a picture of Balmoral, and turned it lightly in his hand. Then he tossed it to Deveny. Deveny stepped back, swung his rifle around like a club, and hit the goblet hard. It exploded like a light bulb. Mulcahey chuckled and threw another. Holyrood this time. Then another and another, Windsor, Sandringham, and Buckingham Palace all in quick succession. Quicker than Deveny could hit them. At last all six goblets had been reduced to powder on the rug.

Next, Mulcahey turned his attention to the books. He pulled out a volume at random and looked at the embossed gold lettering on the spine. It was a volume from the Navy List dating back to 1836. He threw it contemptuously over his shoulder. He pulled out another book, flipped it open, and looked at the silky, finely printed pages. Listed there were the names and specifications of some of the most famous ships in the history of the Royal Navy. They meant nothing to him. He grinned at Deveny, ripped out a handful of pages, crumpled them in his fist, and pretended to wipe his behind. Bored, he threw the book and the torn pages to the floor. Then he stuck the barrel of his rifle into the space between the books and raked it the length of the shelf, spilling all the remaining books onto the floor in a mangled heap. He looked at them for a moment, then gave them a cursory kick and stepped over them to examine a new door that might lead to more exciting discoveries.

The door opened onto a small vestibule flanked by an array of closed doors and dominated by a narrow mahogany staircase. One flight of stairs led upward to the royal deck and the armored apartments that protected the queen and her husband. Mulcahey approached the stairs cautiously, watched by Deveny. He crept up the first few steps and peered warily around the first corner. He already knew what to expect, and he wasn't surprised. The top of the stairs was blocked by a gray metal screen that reached from staircase to ceiling. Mulcahey looked around for a camera lens but saw none. He approached the screen warily and tapped it with the butt of his rifle. It made only a soft thud. Behan had told them there would be something like this. Some fancy metal compound that would be impervious to bullets or explosives. Mulcahey sniffed. It didn't matter. They didn't intend to waste any energy trying to breach it. They didn't have to. The queen, the duke, and their bodyguards, and anybody else who was in there could go down with the ship, locked inside their big armor-plated coffin, if that was what they wanted.

Mulcahey turned back down the stairs. For a moment he thought about following the staircase down to the deck below, to the cabins where members of the household staff slept, but Deveny shook his head. They had to finish their check of the state apartments first.

The walls of the vestibule were punctuated by four doors. Two of them led to the royal sitting rooms, a third led to the state dining room, and the fourth opened to reveal an elevator. Deveny cocked his rifle and stood ready while Mulcahey cautiously opened the elevator door. Behind the door was another armored screen exactly like the one at the top of the stairs. Mulcahey swore. He didn't like it. The elevator served three decks. The royal deck, the state deck where they were now, and the household staff deck. If the elevator shaft was sealed shut behind these screens, it offered a convenient means of exit and entry to the rest of the ship for those in the royal apartments. Mulcahey turned to Deveny and gave him the cut-throat signal. Deveny knew what it meant. They'd get Michael Kenney to wire all the elevator doors with one of his booby traps, just in case.

Deveny decided it was time for him to take the lead again. He picked out one of the closed vestibule doors and kicked it open. It opened into the Duke of Edinburgh's sitting room and it was empty. Deveny stepped inside and looked around. It was furnished exactly as he might have expected, like a gentleman's study. The walls were paneled with dark English oak and the carpet was smoky gray. There was a rust-colored leather sofa against one wall, a matching swivel chair, and a big desk with russet leather inlay. The desk was empty except for what looked like a heavy leather-bound diary. Obviously the duke was an orderly man. The only other embellishments were seascapes on the walls and a set of photographs on the desk. Photographs of his children and his grandchildren. Except these children had the most recognizable faces in all the world.

"Come on," Mulcahey grumbled impatiently behind him.

There was another room on the opposite side of the vestibule. The door was already open and it revealed what could only be the queen's sitting room. Its walls were creamy white and the carpet a deep moss green. A two-seater couch and matching chairs were decorated in rosebud chintz. There was a built-in kneehole desk and chair in matching silver ash. The leather inlay on the desk was the same color as the carpet. Deveny watched as Mulcahey tried to open the desk drawers. They were locked and neither of them was going to bother looking for a key. Mulcahey brought his rifle butt down hard, splintering the edge of the desk and smashing open the drawers. Their contents spilled onto the carpet.

"Jesus." Mulcahey gave a triumphant gasp and stooped to pick up the contents of a broken jewelry box. There were several strings of pearls, diamond-studded earrings, and brooches.

"Look at this, will ye," he hissed at Deveny, brandishing the glittering jewelry in his black-gloved hand. "How much more of this do you think there is?"

"Millions of quids worth," Deveny answered. "Billions mebbe, who knows? Now, get a bloody move on or Behan will be cuttin' our balls off."

"Aye," Mulcahey grunted as he stuffed the jewels into his pocket.

"But he didn't say we couldn't help oursel's to a few bits an' pieces along the way."

When he was sure he'd taken the best stones, he got up and brushed past Deveny at the door. Deveny was about to follow when he noticed a few scattered gems left on the carpet. He leaned down, scooped them up in his fist, and shoved them into a pocket. Grinning smugly to himself, he went after Mulcahey.

The dining room was the biggest and the most sparsely furnished of all the state apartments. Like the royal drawing room, it stretched from one side of the ship to the other, though it was at least another twenty feet deeper, which was the reason for the white-painted steel pillars that supported the deck above. The room was dominated by a massive oval-shaped banquet table of dark walnut encircled by thirty-two chairs. Against the walls were a couple of serving tables and a sideboard. The walls themselves were hung with a number of portraits, members of the royal family stretching back to the time of William the Fourth, whose love of yachting earned him the title of England's sailor king. His other great love was represented in the portrait that hung beside him. Mulcahey approached the painting curiously. It was a portrait of a woman whose plainness was relieved by a pleasant smile, an amused expression in her eyes, and a low-cut gown that revealed an extraordinary cleavage.

"Jesus Christ," he muttered, "if it wasn't for the head, I'd swear it was Dolly Parton I was lookin' at."

Deveny joined him in front of the picture.

"Now, that's what I'd call a right royal set." He nodded. "Who is she?"

Mulcahey peered at a small brass plate at the bottom of the frame.

"Adelaide," he said. "Queen Adelaide."

"Never heard of her." Deveny shrugged and wandered off in search of more material rewards. "Probably just some royal whore."

Mulcahey pulled himself reluctantly away from the painting. It wasn't easy. The picture had stirred something in him. Something strange and unexpected. He was surprised that a painting like that could have such an effect on him. It wasn't as if it were like the pictures in the magazines he usually liked to read. But just looking at it had done something to him. There was something about those breasts, the creamy white skin, the sly, imperious smile . . . all drawn from life.

"Fuckin' bitch," he swore, and spat at the painting. He had been about to rip it into pieces. Instead, he watched his spittle trickle down her painted face and it made him feel better.

"Here, Jimmy," Deveny interrupted his thoughts. "What do you suppose they've got hidden away in here?"

Mulcahey turned to see what Deveny wanted. He was standing in front of the heavy walnut sideboard, prodding a locked door with the toe of his boot. Mulcahey walked over to him, swung his rifle, and stoved in the door with a single vicious blow from his rifle butt. The door burst open and a pile of solid gold dinner plates cascaded at their feet.

"Holy Mary, mother of God," Deveny breathed. He bent down and picked up one of the plates. It was thick and solid and so heavy he guessed it must weigh at least a couple of pounds.

"It's the real thing, Jimmy," he said, looking up. "It's gold."

Mulcahey slammed his rifle butt into a locked drawer, then hauled it out. It was so heavy it twisted out of his grasp and fell to the floor in a thunderous shower of gold. Knives, forks, and spoons, all bearing the royal crest. Mulcahey's eyes glittered with greed. He bent down and grabbed a half dozen pieces of cutlery. Then he felt Deveny's restraining hand on his arm.

"We can't," Deveny said warningly. "We can't carry it around with us, Jimmy. We'll have to leave it, mebbe come back for it later."

"No . . ." Mulcahey grunted and pulled his arm free. "I know who'll get it if we leave it here."

"Behan will kill us, Jimmy."

Mulcahey heard the undertone of desperation in Deveny's voice.

"He warned us about this," Deveny went on. "And he told us what would happen if we took any of it. We've got to keep our heads, Jimmy. He warned us what he'd do if we ignored his orders and started chasin' the money."

Mulcahey hesitated. Then he let the cutlery slide from his fingers and fall heavily back to the floor.

"Come on, Jimmy." Deveny turned back toward the door.

"There's nobody up here. We know what we've got to do. We better get on with it."

Mulcahey took a series of quick breaths to calm himself. Then he nodded and got back to his feet. Deveny was right. Treasure like this could get him killed. But they could all die anyway before this thing was over . . . and he meant to get some pleasure out of it before it was too late.

They took the stairs down to the household deck and found the first three members of the household staff sprawled in the corridor. A middle-aged man and two younger women. All of them with dressing gowns they had pulled hurriedly over their nightclothes as they had tried to escape the gas. They were still conscious but unable to do much more than moan and crawl. When they heard Deveny and Mulcahey coming, they looked up in hope, only to fall back in despair as the two IRA men barked at them to start moving down the corridor toward the front of the ship.

While Deveny pushed, pulled, and prodded their first captives into movement, Mulcahey strode the length of the corridor, throwing open doors and dragging stricken men and women outside to join the others. Any doors that were locked he smashed open with his rifle butt. After a few minutes there were a dozen wretched people in the corridor, all of them too weak to stand. The IRA men were growing impatient. There were at least another two hundred hostages to be rounded up and locked in the forward cabins before the incapacitating effects of the gas wore off.

Deveny yelled at the royal servants to move. The corridor filled with a chorus of moans and whimpers. He felt his temper rise. He reached down, grabbed a woman by the arm, and dragged her roughly along the corridor. Mulcahey kicked and screamed at the middle-aged man nearest him. The man tried to get up on all fours so he could crawl, but his limbs were too weak to support him. Mulcahey grabbed hold of his robe and hurled him viciously down the corridor. Then he turned to the women.

"Crawl or die, you fuckin' bitches," he screamed through his mask.

The women tried to crawl. Some managed a few feet. Others

could barely drag themselves a few inches. Some began to retch again.

"Jesus fuckin' Christ," Mulcahey raged.

He grabbed the arm of an older woman whose nightdress had been torn open, exposing her pale, slack breasts. She struggled pathetically to pull her clothes around her and cover herself up, and Mulcahey grinned.

"Never mind coverin' up your titties, darlin," he mocked her. "You've got nothin' a real man would want."

He dragged her roughly down a series of corridors, past a dozen bulkhead doors, to the crew's forward quarters. Deveny dragged another two captives behind him. Together they herded the queen's servants into the petty officer's mess that was to become their prison, and then they went back for more. This time Mulcahey held back. He waited until Deveny had selected two more hostages and disappeared into the forward section of the ship. Then he looked at the remaining captives. Not all of them were old and withered. Some of the women were young and pretty. Maids and ladies-in-waiting to Her Majesty. To look at them reminded him of the painting he had seen upstairs. They made him feel anger and excitement at the same time. He knew their type. Soft. Spoiled. Plummy accents. Fancy manners and expensive educations. Stuck-up English bitches, every one of them. Handed the good life on a silver platter just because they happened to be born into the right families. They looked down on men like him. Thought they were too good for him. Except as a bit of fun, mebbe. A bit of rough on the side. Yet, here they were now, helpless. At his mercy. He could do anything he wanted with them. Anything.

He noticed a girl with long brown hair that hung down around her shoulders in thickly tangled waves, hiding her face. He stepped over to her, grabbed a handful of hair, and jerked her head up so he could see her face. She yelped in pain and looked at him dimly through fright-glazed eyes. She was beautiful, with a white gamine face and a rash of freckles across the bridge of her nose. He yanked her to her feet so he could see what kind of body she had. Her dressing gown fell open, revealing a long white nightdress. He ran his hand the length of her body, feeling her breasts and legs. Her breasts felt heavy and firm. Her belly was flat but her buttocks and thighs seemed shapely and well rounded. She would do, he decided. He started along the corridor, dragging her after him. He came to the first bulkhead, hesitated, and looked around. There was still no sign of Deveny. Then, instead of going on, he kicked open the nearest cabin door and pushed the girl inside. She staggered and fell to the floor with a soft cry of pain. Mulcahey stepped after her and lifted her onto the bed. Then he grinned.

"You bide here awhile, darlin,' " he told her. "Be a good lass and do as you're told and I'll see you come through this all right."

He didn't know whether she had heard him or not, but he didn't have time to wait. He stepped back into the corridor and slammed the door shut behind him. Quickly he looked around and spotted a fire ax beside the bulkhead hatch. He grabbed it and wedged it between the door handle and the wall. Now it was impossible for her to get out. She was no longer just an ordinary prisoner. She was his prisoner.

Mulcahey grinned, picked out two more hostages, and started toward the front of the ship. He felt better. Maybe he would end up a dead hero before it was all over. In the meantime he'd got what he wanted. One last sweet wish to be fulfilled.

When they had moved all their hostages from the aft section to the cabins in the bow, the two gunmen started their sweep through the officers' and crew's quarters. Behan's orders were to lock everybody forward of the laundry room, which included the petty officer's mess, the marine barracks, canteen, and recreation space. It was a prison big enough for 250 captives. There were toilets, wash basins, and enough food and drink to last a few days. Which meant the hijackers didn't have to worry about feeding or watering their hostages. Or clearing out the Marine barracks, where a couple of diehards might be waiting. All they had to do was seal the section forward of the laundry and forget about them. Perfect no-fuss hostages.

Finally the two gunmen turned to the few remaining officers. Behan wanted all the VIP hostages in the admiral's day cabin. Right under the bridge, where he could get at them easily. They found the Royal Marine colonel with four of his men in a stairwell leading to the upper deck. They had been laying an ambush when they had been overwhelmed by the gas. Deveny and Mulcahey hauled the marines below decks and threw them in with the other hostages. Then they dragged Colonel Grant up to the admiral's day cabin, where they tied his feet to a water pipe with a length of nylon rope, along with the other officers.

At last they were finished. It had taken damn near the whole night, but it was done. The *Britannia* and her hostages were secure, 261 in all. Two hundred and forty-three in the forward cabins, eighteen officers in the admiral's day cabin, including the captain of the royal yacht, Admiral Marchant. Deveny looked at his watch. It was almost five-thirty. Dawn was only an hour away. The two of them climbed tiredly back up to the bridge to tell Behan they were done. If they were expecting praise, they were disappointed. They were just in time to hear Dominic Behan order the *Britannia* to a dead stop.

Patsy Ryan cranked the ship's telegraph. In the engine room, Michael Kenney obediently cut the engines. Mulcahey and Deveny looked around. Every light on the ship seemed to be switched on. The *Britannia* was lit up like a football stadium for a night game. There was no point in switching the lights off and trying to hide. Just the opposite. Behan wanted the whole world to know where the royal yacht was and what they were doing with it. It also meant that nobody could set foot on the *Britannia* without being seen from the bridge. The bridge was the only pool of darkness above the waterline. It was suffused by a dull red glow that made the instruments easy to read but kept its occupants invisible to the outside world.

It took the two gunmen a minute or two before their eyes had become accustomed to the eerie gloom. They realized they were the only two still wearing gas masks. Gratefully, they pulled theirs off and threw them into a corner, leaving them like the others, disguised only by their black balaclavas. They waited in silence, like ugly crepuscular insects hovering in the twilight.

"I heard shooting," Behan said abruptly as he looked up from the radar screen.

Mulcahey glanced slyly at Deveny.

"Just gave the queen's parlor a bit of that lived-in look," he explained. "You know . . . the Belfast look."

Behan grunted. It could have meant anything.

"You get everybody where they're supposed to be?" he asked.

"We did, Nick." Deveny answered this time. "And they're all going to be sick a while longer, I'd say. That gas must be awful powerful stuff."

"Wouldn't have got this far without it," Behan muttered. Then he stepped away from the screen and walked over to where he could see the two men a little more clearly. He stopped in front of them and looked into their eyes.

"Find anything interesting?"

The two men tensed.

"There's plenty of stuff down there, Nick," Deveny answered.

Mulcahey cursed his comrade silently. Deveny was petrified of Behan. You could hear it in his voice. He would give both of them away.

"What kind of stuff, Billy?" Behan asked.

Deveny shrugged. He knew what Behan wanted and he knew the folly of trying to deceive him.

"Pictures, gold plates," he answered. "Bit of jewelry."

Mulcahey groaned inwardly.

"Jewelry?" Behan repeated. "What kind of jewelry, Billy?"

Everyone on the bridge could sense Deveny sweating beneath his black balaclava.

"Small stuff," Deveny added. "She kept a bit of small stuff in her sitting room. Few necklaces, pearl necklaces, mebbe a few diamond settings."

"Diamonds?" Behan echoed. "You found a few diamonds down there?"

"Just a few, Nick. Bits an' pieces, that's all."

Behan nodded.

"What did you do with them, Billy?"

"We left it there, Nick, honest. We left the gold plates and stuff . . . just like you said."

"What about the diamonds, Billy?" Behan stepped closer to Deveny so that their faces were only inches apart. "Did you take any of the diamonds?"

A small moan escaped Deveny's lips. He fumbled in his vest

pocket and pulled out the half dozen loose gems he'd found on the floor where they had fallen when Mulcahey had looted the queen's jewelry drawer. Then he dropped them into Behan's upturned hand. Behan never even looked at them. Instead, he stepped across to the flying bridge and flung them far into the night. There was a sharp intake of breath among the men on the bridge. Mulcahey swallowed. He felt the sweat trickle down his back, into the hollow of his spine. Behan turned and walked back to look at Deveny.

"It's not the money that's important, Billy," he said quietly. "There's plenty of money on board this ship. What's important is that you've stolen from the treasury of the new, united Ireland. Because that's where all the gold and jewels on board this ship are headed, Billy. Are you following me?"

"Nick . . ." Deveny started to speak, but his voice faded to a croak and he had to try again. "It was only a few stones that broke off one necklace. I didn't think . . ."

"I told you what would happen to any man I caught looting this ship, didn't I?" Behan interrupted.

"Jesus . . . Nick . . ."

But Behan had turned his attention to Mulcahey.

"Did you take anything, Jimmy?"

Mulcahey hesitated.

"I never touched nothin'," he said.

An ominous silence settled on the bridge.

"You sure about that?" Behan added. "Because if either one of you was going to steal from the treasury of Ireland, I'd say it would be you first, Jimmy."

Mulcahey stood his ground.

"I never touched nothin', Nick," he said.

Behan stood silently for a moment. Then he slowly nodded his head.

"I need the two of you in one piece," he said in a voice that was terrifying both in its softness and in its certainty. "But before we get off this boat you better give back everything you've taken for yoursel's. And that's the only chance I'm going to give you."

Then he turned and walked back into the gloom.

Deveny's legs went slack with relief, and for a moment he thought he might stumble. He put a hand on the window ledge to steady himself and took a series of deep, shaky breaths. Then he looked at Mulcahey. He could see Mulcahey's eyes shining behind his eye slits. Deveny could tell he was grinning behind the safety of his mask and he knew. It was no longer just a bad joke. Mulcahey was insane.

"Two hundred yards dead ahead," Ryan announced suddenly, cutting through everyone's private thoughts. Behan stepped forward and peered at the circular screen of the radar scanner with its ghostly sweeping arm and an array of vivid, multicolored dots and dashes that showed all the vessels that shared the sea with them that night. Most of them were cargo freighters or ferries carrying the faithful to and from Mecca. One of them was a British warship, the *Hotspur.* That was easy to find. A menacing silver needle one mile astern. Then he picked out the one small white dash that glowed brighter than all the rest each time the radar arm swept over it. The dash was almost exactly at the center point of the screen. Where the *Britannia* was.

"Keep him on the starboard side," Behan grunted.

"Get your rifles and come with me," he said, turning back to Deveny and Mulcahey. Then he picked up his own M-16 and stepped outside. Newly apprehensive, Deveny followed. As far as he knew, a rendezvous at sea had never been part of the plan. He wondered if Behan was playing with them. If this was how he intended to kill them. Then it would be their turn to be hurled contemptuously over the side into the cold, black water. Mulcahey fell in behind Deveny, all fear absent from his mind. Mulcahey had never been a man to be unduly troubled by fear. He had always taken it as a sign of natural courage.

They hurried down to the main deck in single file in the direction of the amidships lifeboat station. The only sounds they heard were the grumble of the sea and the rush of the wind in the mainstays. Outside the brilliant halo of light that bathed the *Britannia* there was only darkness. It felt as if they were alone in the middle of the Atlantic. But they weren't. They were trapped in a thin sliver of water that separated two continents. And a British warship was out there, somewhere close by, watching and listening. Recording every move. Waiting for the moment to strike back.

"Put a ladder down," Behan ordered.

The two gunmen hunted around and found a rope ladder in a locker. They threw it over the side, then joined Behan at the rail and waited. The glare from the ship's lights spilled out over the dark water, but they saw nothing. Suddenly, there was a brief flicker of light. It vanished, then came back again. Several times it winked out the same short code. Someone was signaling them with a flashlight. A moment later a small powerboat slid into view.

"You boys spread out and keep a sharp watch, just in case," Behan ordered. Mulcahey and Deveny did as they were told and sidled out along the deck, rifles ready. Deveny felt better. Behan had been telling the truth. He needed them. And when the time came when Behan would search them both to make sure they were hiding no more gems, Deveny knew that he would be clean. He thought nothing of fighting the British, but he would never dare cross Dominic Behan again. And Jimmy Mulcahey could take his own chances.

The man at the wheel of the powerboat brought his craft carefully up to the ladder that swung from the yacht's side. Deveny craned his neck to see who was in the boat. He counted six men. Three of them were Arabs. Two of them he recognized immediately. They had trained together in the camp at Mashhad in northern Iran. They were the two Palestinians who had staged the diversion in Jidda harbor. The third Arab was someone he had never seen before. The other three men were dressed in black and wore balaclavas like the hijackers. Who were they, Deveny wondered. What the hell was going on? And how much more was Behan keeping to himself?

The first man on to the ladder climbed awkwardly and uncertainly, as though he were unsure of himself. When he reached the top, Behan grabbed his arm and hauled him over the side as if he weighed nothing. Abu Musa landed awkwardly, recovered, and looked warily around. The PFLP-GC regional commander was nervous. He had never felt so exposed. He was a planner, not a fighter. He had never taken part in a live action before. He preferred to pull the levers behind the scenes. But this was different. This was worth the risk. This was a joint operation between two of the most deadly and determined terror groups in the world. It was unprecedented in scale and scope. And it was the operation that would take him to the top of the PFLP-GC and make him the most influential power broker in the Middle East.

Next up the ladder was Youssef and then Javad. Their eyes were bright with excitement. Once on deck, they gave thanks to Allah and then embraced each other with delight. Mulcahey and Deveny watched them, bemused. The last three men climbed quickly and easily up the ship's side and soon all were on deck, leaving the powerboat to drift away, useless now and unwanted. The last man up the ladder turned and looked around.

"Would someone be so kind as to let me have a gun for a moment?" he asked.

Deveny's eyes widened in shock.

"Jesus Christ," Mulcahey swore, and reflexively aimed his gun at the man who had spoken. "He's a bloody Brit."

Mulcahey was right. The man's voice was English. The kind of English he had never heard on the streets of Belfast—unless it was from an officer in the British Army.

Behan stepped forward, grabbed Mulcahey's rifle by the barrel, yanked it from his startled grasp, and handed it to the newcomer. The man took it confidently, checked it, then slapped it to his shoulder and fired. A red hot stream of bullets lanced down from the *Britannia* and raked the drifting powerboat from bow to stern at the waterline. He kept firing until all but the last few rounds had gone. He pumped those into the fuel tank. The boat instantly erupted into flames. The man turned and tossed the rifle lightly back to Mulcahey. The IRA man was so stunned he almost forgot to catch it. Then the newcomer turned to Behan.

"Congratulations, Dominic," he said cheerfully. "A superb job all round, I'd say. And now I think we might all go inside for a little chat, don't you?"

"I do." Behan grunted his agreement. Without another word he turned and led them along the deck and back up to the bridge. Deveny and Mulcahey tagged along at the rear, both of them shocked into silence. Behind them the blazing powerboat began to hiss and sink lower in the water.

Behan led the way across the bridge, pausing only to tell Patsy Ryan to take the yacht up to half speed. Ryan hardly bothered to look up from his instruments. If he had any questions about the new arrivals, he kept them to himself. Far below, the engines grew in power and the *Britannia* continued its northward course. Behan paused just long enough to reassure himself that everything was as it should be, then signaled to the others to follow him.

"In here," he said gruffly, and stepped through to the chart house. Once inside, he perched on a corner of the chart table, folded his arms, and waited while everybody filed in after him.

"Shut the door, boys," he said once they were all settled. It was a small room lined with old-fashioned chart racks and a computer that was used to summon up digitalized images of every port, every harbor, every mile of coastline, and every patch of ocean on the earth's surface. Mulcahey turned and pushed the door shut. Then he tried to find a space to lean against. With nine men in the chart house, it felt uncomfortably close and crowded. Behan switched on the chart-table light and the center of the room lit up. There were no windows in the charthouse, and so they were safe from any outside gaze. Behan reached up and pulled off his hood with a rare sigh of relief. The effect in that indirect lighting was to make his face look ghoulish and forbidding. It was the same kind of effect that kids used to frighten each other by holding a flashlight under their chins. In Behan's case it was an unnecessary piece of theater. There was a moment's hesitation while Deveny and Mulcahey followed suit and then the newcomers. But only two of them.

"Jesus, Murphy . . ." Mulcahey breathed out loud, an expression of utter stupefaction written across his face. "What are you blokes doin' here? I didn't know you blokes was in on this. I thought you was still in Belfast."

One of the newcomers was Declan Brady. The other a man named O'Brien. Both were longtime gunmen for the IRA and were well known to everyone in the room but the three Palestinians. Like Mulcahey, Deveny, too, could scarcely believe his eyes. Brady and O'Brien had done their bit for the Cause. They were supposed to have retired from active service years ago. It was Brady who spoke first.

"Some of us can keep our mouths shut without being locked up for a year, Jimmy," he said.

Mulcahey looked to Behan for an explanation, then to the only man in the room who still wore his hood, then back to Behan.

"For God's sake, Nick," he pleaded. "Will somebody tell us what's goin' on here."

Behan looked at Mulcahey, and for a moment it looked as if he might smile. Instead, he scratched roughly at the itches that irritated his scalp and face, then smoothed back his greasy black hair. The silence in the room lengthened. At last Behan gave a small nod of his head.

"I couldn't let you in on it until now, boys," he answered brusquely, knowing that they had no choice but to accept whatever he told them. "I couldn't take the chance."

Mulcahey and Deveny exchanged nervous glances, wondering just how much they had been played for suckers.

"Perhaps"—the man with the British accent intervened—"I might be able to help."

Behan shrugged and deferred to the only man in the room whose face remained hidden. The newcomer stepped forward to stand alongside Dominic Behan and quickly removed his hood. Everyone in the room fell silent.

The face that looked back at them was a perfect match for the accent. It was a strong, fresh-complexioned face with an imperious cast, light sandy hair, and dark brown eyes that stared intimidatingly back at them all. It was the face of a man who was used to being obeyed. The face of a British officer.

"For those of you who don't know me," he said in his soft English accent. "My name is Doyle. Edward Doyle. Formerly Lieutenant Doyle of Her Majesty's Royal Marines. As of this moment I am taking charge of this operation."

LONDON. 09.15 HOURS

"If we are to have any chance at all of taking the initiative away from the hijackers," Sir Malcolm Porter was saying, "we have to locate and defuse those explosives. Otherwise we may as well ask them what they want and where they want it delivered."

"I've already given you my position on that," the Prime Minister answered. "I will not approve any operation that would carry an unacceptable level of risk to her royal highness."

"Sir," Porter persisted, "I believe I can put a man on the *Britannia* who can work with Captain Gault to neutralize the terrorist threat most effectively, perhaps in a matter of minutes."

The Prime Minister looked skeptical.

"By all means, Malcolm," he hedged. "Draw up your plan and I'll look at it. But you'll have to have it ready to go in seventy-two hours, when all our warships are in position."

"I understand, sir."

The War Cabinet had begun to live up to its name, though much of the warring appeared to be between its participants. Admiral Harriman had come to the new meeting with the information that Her Majesty's warships in the eastern Mediterranean and the Persian Gulf were on their way to the Red Sea. The mood had changed from shock to resolution. All of the men gathered around the table were men who preferred to act, not react. And, in the absence of an ultimatum from the hijackers, most of the discussion had focused on the military options available rather than the political.

"Do we have any idea who will be handling negotiations once they're under way?" the home secretary asked.

"We have a very good chap at Cambridge," Byron Blair, director of MI5 volunteered.

"Yes," Arthur Leamus from MI6 interrupted, "I think I know the chap you mean but I think I'd prefer someone in-department."

"I rather thought Naval Intelligence would handle this . . . unless there is a good reason to believe that someone else could do it better," Admiral Bryden interjected.

The Prime Minister sighed. The last thing he needed was a territorial fight between security departments.

"Sir?"

It was a new voice to the discussion, and everyone looked to its source.

Commandant General Sharpe, commanding officer of the Royal

Marines, waited until he was sure he had the Prime Minister's attention.

"I have only one request to make."

"Yes, General?"

"If you do opt for military intervention, I want Royal to be part of it . . . for obvious reasons."

The whole table fell silent, but the Prime Minister did not hesitate.

"Of course, General," he said quietly. "Do you have any particular unit in mind?"

"Comacchio Group, sir."

The PM nodded. He was familiar with Comacchio. They were one of the most highly specialized units in the Royal Marines, trained exclusively in close-combat operations on oil rigs and aboard ships at sea.

"I don't have any objection to Comacchio performing the backup role, assuming Colonel Quillan is comfortable with that."

"SAS would be proud to have them alongside, sir," Quillan answered promptly.

"Good." The PM looked down the table at Sharpe. "I suggest you liase with Admiral Harriman after this meeting to decide on the best way to get them out there."

There was a discreet knock at the double doors to the Cabinet Room. John Traynor jumped up and glided across the polished parquet floor. He slipped briefly outside and reappeared a moment later, holding a note in his hand. His hand was steady, but his face was filled with foreboding and presaged even more bad news. He crossed to the Prime Minister, whispered briefly in his ear, and handed him the note while everyone watched in silence. The PM unfolded the note. It was a sheet of telex paper bearing half a dozen lines. He read it, then put it down in front of him and looked around the table.

"It's a new message from Captain Purcell aboard the *Hotspur,"* the PM said, his voice clearly strained. "The hijackers took *Britannia* out of Jidda harbor three hours ago. Captain Purcell apologizes for the delay in communication. However, it seems they have been rather busy . . . picking up bodies. As they left the harbor the hijackers dumped overboard the bodies of eleven crew members."

He paused to take a breath and to keep his voice steady.

"The hijackers took *Britannia* north by northwest for twenty-seven nautical miles. Half an hour ago they stopped and picked up a group of men from a small craft. It seems to have been a planned rendezvous. In accordance with my orders, the *Hotspur* did not intervene. Six individuals transferred from the smaller craft to *Britannia.* The royal yacht then resumed its course. A few moments ago the hijackers delivered their demands."

Again he paused, this time to correct himself.

"Only one demand really." His voice faltered momentarily. "They want all British troops out of Northern Ireland in seven days. The countdown begins at noon today, Greenwich Mean Time. Or . . . they intend to blow up *Britannia* and all those on board."

4 In the Path of the Winged Pig

BALLACHULISH, MAY 17. 09.37 HOURS

Before he opened his eyes, Bonner knew he was going to feel bad. But first he had to pry his eyelids apart. For a moment it occurred to him that Lynch might have stuck them together with Super Glue to avenge himself for the flash grenade in the can. Anything was possible. And Bonner wouldn't have noticed. They had drunk whisky long and late into the night, and the big man had no recollection of where or when he had finally passed out.

Slowly, his left eye unglued itself and opened to the world, as lovely as a Venus's-flytrap. He would worry about the right eye later. The right side of his face was jammed against something cold and hard, and he found it difficult to turn his head.

Then he realized what was wrong.

He was stuck to the ceiling.

Somehow in the night, the foul, boiling gases in his gut had expanded until they had reached critical mass and lifted him up to the ceiling, where he had become stuck, like a blimp inside the Superdome. He braced his hands against the flat surface and tried to push himself away, but the forces that held him there were too powerful. He fell back, jolting his other eye open. Blood rushed to his head like the tide surging into a sea cave, booming and pummeling him with waves of nausea and pain. For a moment he thought he would throw up. Or down. He couldn't be sure. He gritted his teeth until it passed. Then he forced his head back off the ceiling and looked around, trying to get his bearings. He blinked. All the furniture was upside down on the ceiling too, just like a capsized ship. And then it dawned on him. He knew what had happened. A landslide. The mountainside had shifted in the night, turning the cottage on its roof, throwing everything upside down. He was lucky to be alive.

"Are you planning to stay there all day?" an unsympathetic voice asked.

Bonner looked around, expecting to see Lynch's curious, upturned face. Instead, he saw Lynch's bare feet standing next to him. The big man flinched, blinked again, and muttered to himself. Lynch was walking around on the ceiling like a goddamn fly.

So that was it, Bonner realized. It was a dream. A nightmare. A sad and stupid nightmare as the alcohol seeped slowly from his tortured brain. It was the only explanation. The room began to rotate slowly, as though in confirmation. Any moment, Bonner knew, it would fade to black and then, he hoped, he would wake up. Safe. In bed. He shut his eyes tight, feeling himself sinking and spinning faster and faster into the vortex. He gagged and tasted the foul bile of stale whisky at the back of his throat. But there was nothing in his stomach to bring up. The spinning stopped, he opened his eyes again, and Lynch's bare feet were still beside him, still stuck to the ceiling.

"Get me down," Bonner groaned pitifully. "I don't care how you did it. We're even. Just get me down from here, for Christ's sake."

"You silly bugger," Lynch said. "You're on the floor, where you passed out. You're too bloody big to move, so I threw a couple of blankets over you and left you here."

Bonner grunted, braced himself, and rolled carefully onto his side. The whole room rotated. He groaned and waited till a fresh wave of nausea had passed. Then he opened his eyes again. Lynch was right.

He was on the floor. Everything was in perspective. Everything was where it should be.

"You might feel better if you got up and soaked that stinking carcass of yours in the tub for a while," Lynch added.

Bonner squinted up at Lynch. He was already dressed in a gray crewneck sweater and jeans and his hair was still damp from the shower. He looked fresh and clean and healthy. Bonner hated him for it. He mumbled and struggled to get up, but it was too much and he fell back with a grunt of resignation.

"Can't . . ." he croaked. "Can't move. Leave me here to die. I take back everything I said last night."

"What . . . about the job?"

"No," Bonner rasped. "About drinking you under the table."

"You did drink me under the table," Lynch answered. "I just decided I wasn't going to get down there with you."

Bonner glared balefully at his tormentor. He knew what Lynch was doing. He hated him now for enjoying himself.

"How much did I drink last night?"

Lynch glanced at the table. The bottle of Macallan's was empty. His own bottle of Glenmorangie stood beside it, half empty.

"I had maybe a quarter of a bottle," he said. "You took care of the rest."

"Oh, shit," Bonner wheezed. "Honest to God, I don't understand how that stuff works. When you're drinking it, it tastes like angels pissing on your tongue. The next morning your mouth tastes like an anchovy's cunt."

"Stop feeling sorry for yourself and get up," Lynch added, and prodded him gently with his foot. "Go get in the tub while I make us some coffee."

Reluctantly, Bonner propped himself up on both elbows and looked around. The blankets had fallen off him during the night. He could see his hiking jacket on the back of a chair, and his shoes were someplace else, but he was still wearing his shirt and pants. They looked exactly the way he expected them to look. He rubbed a hand roughly over his face, feeling the bristles on his jaw. He had to stop doing this to himself, he decided. One day . . . when he grew up.

"All right," he conceded. "I'll have the coffee. You can go shit in the tub. You know what them old Viking warriors used to say. Too much bathing weakens a man. Robs his body of essential emollients."

"From the way you smell this morning," Lynch said as he reached down to help the big man to his feet, "you have no shortage of emollients."

Bonner's head reeled and he almost fell. Lynch grabbed him firmly by the arm and half carried, half shoved him toward the bathroom. For a moment Bonner didn't understand what Lynch had in mind. By the time he realized, it was too late. The door to the bathroom was open and his momentum was too great. Bonner's mouth opened and a deep, heartfelt rumble of protest poured out of him and escalated quickly into a roar of rage and fear. Lynch ducked out from under the big man's arm, and gave him a slight turn and a final hefty shove. It was just enough to put a spin on him and send him crashing backward into the tub.

The tub was filled with cold water and Bonner screamed as he went under. It was a terrible scream. The scream of a man going to his death on the rack. A huge wave washed over the sides of the tub, splashed against the walls, and flooded the floor. Bonner struggled to break free of his freezing coffin, but the tub was slippery and he fell back, bellowing with rage. His words, when they came, were punctuated by desperate gasps for air.

"You limey bastard . . . this time . . . your nuts . . . are coming right off. . . ."

Lynch lunged forward, shoved Bonner's head under the water, and held it there. The big man thrashed and his hands slashed the air, reaching for Lynch's throat. Lynch stepped easily out of reach. Bonner broke the surface like Poseidon. Water streamed from every crevice of his big, granite head, his clothes clung to him like garlands of seaweed, and murder blazed in his bloodshot eyes.

Lynch threw a towel in his face.

"See," he grinned, "isn't it great to be alive?"

Bonner swatted the towel aside, stumbled out of the tub, and went for his pal. Lynch knew exactly what he had to do. He turned and he ran. He darted through the cottage, threw open the front door, skirted the side of the house, and sprinted up the heather-clad mountainside in his bare feet. Bonner followed, cursing.

Lynch was a fit man. In the winter he ran every day, rain, snow, or shine. In the summer he ran down to the loch each morning at dawn and swam half a mile before breakfast. Bonner was fit too, but he wasn't a runner like Lynch. He did four or five miles of roadwork three times a week to maintain fitness. He didn't run up mountains. Lynch knew he could outrun Bonner. Still, the big man surprised him. Fueled by pain and rage, Bonner stayed with Lynch all the way up the mountainside, at one point narrowing the distance between them to a few yards. Every time Lynch looked back, Bonner was there, scrambling, grunting and cursing, his red eyes fixed steadfastly on his quarry. Lynch led him across the steep-sided shoulder of the mountain for more than a mile, and still Bonner clung to his heels. Lynch changed tactics. He turned upward. The mountainside grew steeper. The bracken yielded to sheer-faced crags. Lynch had to be careful not to gash his feet on the rocks. He knew the terrain. Bonner didn't. He hoped the big man wasn't so angry that he would injure himself. He glanced back and saw that his tactic had worked. Bonner was losing ground, picking his way carefully over the rough-edged rocks. Lynch ran for another few minutes until he found what he was looking for. A narrow fissure that snaked up a looming rock face. He leapt for it, grabbed at the familiar handholds, and wormed his way quickly upward for thirty feet. Then he stopped and looked down. As he hoped, Bonner was still at the bottom, shoulders heaving, his flushed face turned upward. Lynch turned and settled himself on a small ledge.

"Need a ladder?" he called down.

Bonner opened his mouth to speak, but he had no breath for words. He lowered his head and took a moment to examine his feet while he caught his breath. His socks were in tatters and blood oozed from a fretwork of grazes on the soles of his feet. He looked back up at Lynch.

"Get your ass down here, you damn pussy," he yelled. "Or I'll burn your goddamn house down."

Lynch grinned. He was having more fun than he expected.

"What's the problem?" he yelled back. "Can't take a little joke?"

Bonner growled and stepped away from the rock face, muttering. Good, Lynch thought. The big man wasn't stupid enough to try climbing with a hangover. He couldn't be that mad.

"You nearly stopped my goddamn heart . . ." Bonner complained.

"Guess that makes us about even," Lynch answered.

The big man muttered to himself a little more, then turned and gave Lynch a conciliatory shrug.

"All right," he conceded. "I ain't about to stand around here all day, arguing about it. You can get your sneaky limey ass down here."

Lynch smiled and worked his way quickly back down the rock face. When he was about ten feet from the bottom he jumped and landed nimbly on his feet. Then he stood up straight and looked at Bonner.

"Tell me something," he said. "Exactly what did you think you were going to do if you caught me?"

Bonner sniffed and thought about it. It was an awkward moment. He had never lost his temper to that degree before. He had shocked himself. There was an unwritten rule between men like them, a sort of code that said whatever happened between them, they would make sure that it never brought them to blows. He looked embarrassed for a moment when he realized how close he had come. Not that he was afraid of Lynch. Nor was Lynch afraid of him. It was simply unthinkable that two men with their deadly skills should ever be so imprudent as to take out their frustrations on each other . . . even if it had started in fun.

"I don't rightly know," he admitted ruefully. "Considering the shape your ass is in, maybe stick you on a pole at some intersection and use you for a stoplight."

The two of them traversed their way back down the mountainside much more sedately than they had gone up. When they reached the cottage they were shocked to discover that most of the morning had slipped away. By the time Bonner had cleaned himself up and Lynch had scrambled some eggs and made some toast and coffee, it was early afternoon. It was a little after three when Lynch suggested they climb into his battered green Land Rover and take a drive into town.

Because it was still early in the year, Ballachulish was not too crowded with tourists. It was a fresh spring day and the old highland town looked a spruce and inviting place to spend an afternoon with its quaint stone buildings and rough-hewn charm. Lynch suggested a walk, but after a few minutes circumnavigating the town center, Bonner began to grow restless. He was not a good tourist. His travels needed a purpose to make them worthwhile. For Lynch it was different. The highlands were his backyard. He had been born and raised in Inverness on the east coast, but the west coast was his spiritual home and that was why he had bought the cottage there. Little more than a ruin when he moved in, he spent a small fortune restoring it, rebuilding the walls, putting on a new roof, new plumbing. There was still much left to do, and part of him knew it would always be incomplete, but working on it was a kind of therapy. The Special Boat Squadron was based in Poole in Dorset, at the other end of the country, and most of his colleagues had bought houses there, unable or unwilling to pry themselves away from the powerful camaraderie that enveloped every man who served in the SBS. Lynch maintained a room in the officers' quarters on the base and escaped to the cottage whenever he needed to recharge his batteries with a dose of highland solitude. But, now, he realized, Bonner expected some kind of response to his business proposition from the night before. Lynch steered his friend back to the Land Rover.

A few moments later they pulled up outside Lynch's favorite pub on the southern outskirts of town. Lynch preferred The White Hart because it was grubby and unfashionable. It was a free house, which meant it had not yet been taken over by one of the big brewery chains and so it sold the ales and beers its customers demanded. More important, it had not been renovated into a kitsch parody of itself by some limp-wristed interior decorator from London. It smelled of smoke and sweat and ale, the way a pub was supposed to smell. And, because it was hard to find, it was patronized mostly by locals, sheep farmers and fishermen, instead of the loud German hikers with big thighs and bigger wallets who cluttered up the other pubs in town. Lynch was known to most of the The White Hart's regulars, though they had only a vague notion of what it was that he did. They knew he was navy but assumed he held an administrative position because, whenever anyone asked, he complained about the boredom of a shore-based job.

Lynch and Bonner climbed out of the Land Rover, tramped up the worn stone steps to the door, and stepped into the welcoming murk. It was still early for serious drinkers, and the pub was quiet. The only drinkers were a couple of old men in flat caps who sat at a window table playing dominoes in the dusty sunlight. Lynch gave them both a nod and received a simple aye in response. Then they went back to their black and white tiles, slapping them down loudly on the tabletop, baiting each other with stony-faced delight. The only other source of animation in the bar was a TV set on a shelf high in a corner. Some sort of quiz show was playing, but thankfully the volume was turned down. There was no sign of McLaughlin, the licensee, or Jackie, the barmaid.

Lynch leaned over the bar and looked around. There was no one in sight.

"Any danger of a man getting a drink around here?" he called caustically into the back of the pub. His voice echoed down the whitewashed walls of the hallway that led to the publican's private quarters. A moment later they heard the light skip of a woman's shoes on the flagstones.

"Aye, all right," Jackie grumbled good-naturedly as she came into view. "Suppose we're dyin' o' thirst, are we?"

The barmaid turned out to be an attractive brunette in her early thirties with lively brown eyes and a sly mouth that curved upward at one corner when she smiled. She wore a white Aran sweater that hid a nicely rounded figure, and tight riding breeches that hid nothing. There were leather patches on the insides of the legs that looked like a pair of gloved hands squeezing her thighs.

"My God!" She smiled mischievously as her eyes shifted from Lynch to his hulking, long-faced friend. "This is no' Tom Cruise ye've brought wi' ye, is it, 'hen?"

Bonner knew she had made some kind of joke at his expense, but because of her thick Highland accent he had no idea what it was. He looked at Lynch.

"What'd she say?"

"She says you remind her of Tom Cruise."

"There's a part of me looks like Tom Cruise," Bonner agreed. "Specially when you get up real close."

"Or the Loch Ness monster," Lynch mumbled.

"Away wi' ye both," Jackie laughed. "You'll be gettin' me a bad name. Now, what can I get ye to drink?"

"Two pints of heavy," Lynch ordered before Bonner could speak.

The big man shot him a disapproving glance.

"It's the local brew," Lynch explained. "You're in the Highlands, you have to try it."

Jackie pulled a straight-sided pint glass from under the bar, turned to a row of fat wooden barrels behind her, and stooped toward a small brass tap. Both men watched as the leather patches on her riding breeches tightened, gripping her thighs harder. When she had filled two glasses to the brim, she set them carefully on the bar. Their soapy heads wobbled precariously but did not spill. Bonner studied the dark cloudy liquid underneath. His eyes shifted warily from Lynch to the barmaid and back to the beer again. It wasn't like any beer he had seen before. It was the color of strong tea and had pieces of leaf floating in it. Most of the pubs Bonner visited when he was in Britain sold the kind of clear, cold lager beers he preferred, as well as a range of familiar European and American beers. Here he was on unfamiliar ground.

"Are you kidding me?" he asked, looking at Lynch.

"Don't think about it," Lynch answered. "Just drink it."

"Oh?" Bonner's eyebrows lifted. "Trust you, huh?"

Lynch was about to say something, but the big man picked up the glass, leaned over the bar, and went to pour it down the drain.

"No . . ." Lynch grabbed his arm. "It's old-style ale, real ale. That's what it's called . . . real ale. They brew it in the wood like they did two, three hundred years ago."

"That how old it is?"

"You might at least try it before you throw it down the goddamn drain," Lynch argued.

Bonner hesitated, then nodded at his glass. "What are those things floating in it?"

"Yeast and hops," said Lynch, a note of exasperation creeping into his voice. "Natural stuff. That's what real beer looks like, okay?

You've never seen it before. This stuff is like liquid protein. You could live off it. A couple of pints of this and you could run up Ben Nevis."

"Ben who?"

Lynch gave up in despair. He turned to his own drink, lifted the brimming pint glass to his lips, and took a long, deep swallow. When he put it down, it was a third empty. He sighed appreciatively and wiped the foam from his lips. Then he looked at Jackie.

"Canny drop," he reassured her.

Bonner hesitated, his face skeptical. He grunted, shuffled, picked up his drink, looked at it, and sniffed it. Then he steeled himself and took a small, tentative sip. He swilled it over his palate, tasted its alien, thick-textured bitterness, thought about it for a moment, then spat it over the bar and into the drain like a long, dark jet of tobacco juice.

"I've tasted swamp water that was better than that," he scowled. Then he looked at the barmaid.

"Got any American beer, honey?"

"We've got Schlitz, Miller, and Budweiser," she answered.

"Don't suppose you've got any Shiner?"

"Never heard of it."

"A Bud will do just fine."

Jackie walked down the bar, plucked a long-necked bottle of Budweiser from a shelf, and went to pour it into a glass.

"I'll take it just the way it comes," Bonner stopped her.

She shrugged and handed him the bottle. He put it to his lips and drained it in a series of rapid gulps, as though he couldn't wait to get the taste of the Scottish ale out of his mouth.

"Goddamn," he grunted his approval. "Now, that's real beer . . . American beer. Give me another one, will you, honey."

Jackie opened another bottle and handed it to him. He took it, pulled up a barstool, and settled himself, the Budweiser cradled between his big red fists. For the first time that day he looked comfortable. Lynch sighed, paid for the drinks, and pulled up the stool next to Bonner. Jackie gave Lynch a knowing look and turned to go.

"Y'all come back now," she chirped brightly as she clicked her way back down the hallway.

Bonner watched her go, then looked at Lynch.

"She trying to be funny?"

"Are you?" Lynch murmured.

Bonner chuckled, lifted his bottle, and took a fresh sip.

"All right," he conceded. "You stick with your ethnically pure hillbilly swamp water or whatever the hell it is, and I'll stick with the king of beers here and never the twain shall meet. You ask me, I know who's getting the better of the deal. And . . ." He looked inquiringly at his Scottish friend. "Speaking of deals, are we going to jerk each other around like this all day, or are you going to give me an answer to that offer I made last night?"

"I'd be surprised if you remembered anything you said last night," Lynch stalled.

"You'd be surprised what I can remember," Bonner added. "Us southern boys can hold our liquor."

Lynch gave a small snort of derision but said nothing.

"Well . . . ?" the big man persisted.

"Well what?"

"Are you going to give me a goddamn answer or not?"

"I can't give you an answer right away." Lynch shrugged. "I need to know a helluva lot more than you told me last night when you were smashed. And even then I'd want to think on it for a while."

"Hell," Bonner rumbled, "what is there to think about? It can't be the money, because I know I'm offering more than you're getting now. And, like I said, if you come in on the ground floor and help me get it started, I'll cut you in for five percent of the business, just like I've done with the other guys."

"It isn't the money," Lynch said.

"Okay," Bonner acknowledged. "What is it?"

"I don't think I'm ready to leave the squadron right now," Lynch said. "I'd planned on at least three more years. After that, we'll see. But what worries me most about your offer is that you're moving into an overcrowded field. Everybody who leaves special forces has the same idea. They all go into private security work. There are offices all over London run by guys who used to be SAS and SBS and I know it's the same in the States. They're all cutting each other's throats trying to land that big security contract and there isn't enough to go around. Most of them don't last a couple of years. They have to take on bodyguard work or turn mercenary to pay the rent. That doesn't appeal to me."

"Listen," Bonner added. "I've already set up a deal with a cruise line operating out of Miami and it's worth a lot of money. I've got a couple of guys on the West Coast working the Mexican and Alaskan cruise lines. . . ."

"I'm not interested in being a cop on a floating trough full of drunks," Lynch said flatly.

"The big money isn't in cruise lines," Bonner added quickly. "The growth will be in merchant shipping. Do you have any idea the kind of shit that's being moved around the world at the moment?"

Lynch knew what Bonner was driving at, but he sipped his beer and waited.

"You've got countries buying and selling plutonium," the big man went on. "Nuclear waste, medical waste, you name it. And all that stuff is moved by private shipping lines. They've got environmental concerns to worry about, political liabilities. There's the continued threat of terrorism, piracy, and hijack. Somebody has to guarantee the security for these high-risk cargoes or the insurance premiums go through the roof. That's where we step into the equation. We bring down the premiums and cream off a piece of the difference. The way I figure it, I can carry an office in London for at least a year, and that's if it doesn't make a cent. I'm not talking about some penny-ante security operation here, pal. I want to build the world's biggest private maritime security agency. And we'll supply everything—advice, technology, manpower."

Bonner leaned closer to Lynch, his voice growing more insistent as he warmed to his topic.

"Think about it for a minute. Wouldn't you feel a helluva lot better if you were running a major shipping line and you had to move a load of enriched uranium from Hamburg to Osaka and you look around to see what's available and there's this company that can put a team of ex-SEALs on your ship to guarantee its safety? That's why I need somebody in London, Colin. I've got to have somebody to run the European end of things for me. You know that London is the world center for maritime insurance. If we can get an endorsement from somebody like Lloyds, we're laughing. And who better to run my London office that a former commander of the SBS?"

Lynch looked uncomfortable.

"I can't . . ." he mumbled. "I haven't had time . . . and besides, what's the rush? Why does everything have to be decided now?"

"Because," Bonner answered simply, "I resigned from the navy two months ago. There's nothing left for me to do at Norfolk. I'm just serving out my time."

Lynch looked shocked.

"What about the Mark 12?" he asked.

The Mark 12 was the name of the revolutionary new minisub Bonner had been testing for the SEALs when Lynch had been posted to Norfolk the year before to observe its sea trials on behalf of the Royal Navy.

"Mothballed, I guess." Bonner shrugged. "You know about all the cutbacks we've had this past year. Word came down a few months back that special forces were next. The Mark 12 is one of those highly specialized, high-cost special-weapons projects the brass figure we can do without. That means the writing is on the wall for the entire test program. I figured it was a good time to make a move. A lot of the guys agreed with me. As soon as I got the signature on that cruise-line contract, I turned in my resignation. Half my unit followed suit. I have to have my office set up in Miami before the end of the year."

"Damn," Lynch swore. He wasn't sure what shocked him more, the resignation of his friend, or the cancellation of the most important minisub program in twenty years.

"And," Bonner went on. "If I ain't very much mistaken, you're going to be seeing the same kind of thing over here before long. Now that the cold war is over, the politicians just can't wait to get their hands on all that defense budget cash. And you're right. This is an overcrowded field. That's why we have to get moving now, get a foothold in the marketplace before everybody else does the same thing."

"Maybe," Lynch responded coolly. "There's still a lot about this that bothers me. I've never really liked the way that some people milk the name of the service for their own personal gain. I know a lot of guys who've done it over the years, but I never really approved of it—and people know that. I don't think I could do it and feel good about it. And that's apart from what a phony, hypocritical bastard I would be if I changed my tune after all these years the minute a few dollars were dangled in front of my face."

Bonner sighed and leaned away.

"So," he added flatly. "You put in your time. You're going to be what . . . forty-two, forty-three when you retire? What the hell do you plan to do with yourself then?"

Lynch finished his beer and slid the empty glass across the bar.

"Can't say I've thought it out that far," he admitted. "I'd probably move up here permanently. I like the peace and quiet. I know the cottage doesn't look like much, but it's paid for. It's mine. I get a service pension. I've got a little put away. It's enough."

"Sure," Bonner sniffed scornfully. "But what are you going to do with your time?"

Lynch smiled self-consciously.

"Go fishing, open a dive school . . ."

"Shit," Bonner swore, and drained his Budweiser. "Open your eyes for a minute and look around. This place is swarming with tourists now. What's it going to be like in five years? They'll be all over the goddamn place then. That mountain of yours will be covered with condos and golf courses with Japanese on 'em in them cute little knickerbockers. What's going to happen to your peace and quiet then?"

Lynch shrugged.

"That's all the more reason for hanging on to my place. Keep it the way it is. Stop the developers from spoiling it all. Hell, I kind of thought I might be buried up there."

The big man looked at him uncertainly, then realized he was serious.

"Look," Bonner added, dropping his tone a level. "Let's get real, shall we? The only way you're going to safeguard your future is to make enough money to buy a big hunk of real estate where you can keep all the assholes on the outside. It's the way of the world, my friend. Think about it."

Bonner decided he wanted another beer and summoned Jackie to bring them two more. The two men sat quietly for a while, each lost in his own thoughts. A few more people came into the pub. Finally Lynch found a way to say what was on his mind.

"You're right," he began. "You're right about a lot of things. And it's a good offer. There's a lot about it that appeals to me."

A faint glimmer of hope crept into Bonner's eyes.

"But," Lynch added, "if you want an answer right away, then my answer has to be no."

The light in the big man's eyes died.

"It's a gut thing more than anything else," Lynch explained quietly, deliberately. "I've had a good life in the navy, a great life. I can feel proud of what I've done because I've done it for my country. Call it what you will, a sense of duty, a noble cause, the simple honor of the man-at-arms. It all comes down to the same thing, however corny it might sound. I took an oath. I pledged my service to Queen and country. And I've killed men in the fulfillment of that oath. And my conscience remains clear. My soul remains my own. If I went into private service, I know it wouldn't be like that. How could it be? I'd be selling myself for money. Everything I did would have the stink of the mercenary about it. And I couldn't live with that."

Bonner leaned forward on the bar and heaved a sigh of deep resignation.

"God almighty," he breathed. "I have to tell you, Lynch. I didn't plan for this. I've done a lot of figuring in the past few months and I—"

"Shhh," Lynch stopped him. "Just hang on a minute, would you?"

Bonner looked at him puzzled, then followed his gaze to the TV set in the corner. The sound was still off, but a news flash had interrupted the regular program. Ordinarily, Lynch might not have noticed, but this interruption was followed by a photograph of the royal yacht, and when the news reader appeared, he looked uncharacteristically alarmed for a BBC news reader. Lynch got up from his barstool, walked over to the set, and turned up the volume. The urgent tone of the news reader's voice filled the bar and grabbed everyone's attention.

". . . the hijacking appears to have taken place shortly after midnight in Jidda," the man was saying. "Early reports indicate that it was a well-planned attack, carried out on a large scale and that there has been considerable loss of life on board the *Britannia.* So far Downing Street has refused to confirm or deny that the queen or Prince Philip were on board at the time of the hijack, but most reports indicate that they were and that both are still on board. Information is still coming in about what is happening in Jidda. We will bring you more news as it comes in."

The screen went blank, but instead of returning to the regular program, it stayed blank for a long time. Then the BBC news logo returned with a subtitle advising viewers to stay tuned for an update. It meant regular broadcasting had ceased and the national broadcaster was preparing to run live with the breaking story.

"Jesus," Lynch breathed. "John Gault is on board that ship."

Bonner turned to look at Lynch.

"Who . . . ?" he began.

But Lynch was already on his way across the room.

"I have to get to a phone," he said tersely.

THE WHITE HOUSE. 18.15 HOURS

The President of the United States sat behind his desk in the oval office and watched the crisis unfold on CNN. With him were his national security adviser, Bob Pike, Secretary of State Jim Blainey, and White House chief of staff, Ed Holland. It was the President's second meeting of the day on the hijacking, and it had overshadowed all other business. Now he had a moment to watch the rest of the world catch up.

The President tapped continually at the remote, skipping back and forth between channels. All the networks had led with it. Peter Jennings on ABC was still running with it, juggling live crosses to correspondents in London and Jidda. So were Dan Rather on CBS and Tom Brokaw on NBC. Fifteen minutes into prime time and there was only one story on the evening news. It didn't matter that tornadoes in Kansas had killed seventeen people, that the second biggest bank in Texas had gone bust, owing $5.7 billion, and that there had been a bloody coup attempt in Manila. The hijacking of the *Britannia,* with the queen and Prince Philip on board, had grabbed the attention of the world. There may as well have been no other news.

The screen flashed to video footage of three cars driving at high speed through the gates of Buckingham Palace earlier that afternoon. Two police cars with a black Range Rover in the middle. The Range Rover had tinted windows and was believed to be carrying Prince Charles. The camera followed the cars between the high black railings in front of the palace, across the parade ground, and through the northern portico until they passed from sight. The TV cut back to a reporter delivering her report live from St. James's Park in front of the palace. It was after eleven at night in London and a fine, drizzling rain was falling. It suited the mood of the crowd. Unlike other crowds that had gathered in front of the palace at times of national celebration, this crowd was somber and subdued. Faces glimpsed in passing showed only numbness and shock. British commentators said there had not been such a mass display of public despair since the death of King George VI in 1952.

The men in the oval office watched in silence. More than anything else that they had seen or heard so far, the image of this shocked and silent crowd conveyed the full and dreadful impact of the hijacking on the British people.

"It is believed that all members of the royal family have now arrived at the palace," the reporter said. "They were joined two hours ago by the Prime Minister, who has yet to make any public statement about the hijacking. Indeed, the British government has been strangely silent so far in this crisis. An indication, perhaps, of the tremendous shock this event has had on the entire nation."

The President hit the mute button and looked at the secretary of state.

"If something happens to the queen," he asked, "would Prince Charles assume the throne immediately?"

"If you'd asked me that question last year, I could have answered with some certainty," Blainey answered cautiously. "Since the separation of Prince Charles and Lady Diana, there's been widespread speculation in Britain that Charles should step aside in favor of his son, Prince William, so that the line of succession would not be tainted by scandal. However, that would still require an act of Parliament. Apart from which, Prince William is obviously too young to sit on the throne. So Prince Charles remains the rightful heir. He would become king at the moment of his mother's death. It's automatic. A coronation would be held at a future date to confirm his succession to the throne and, if there were any doubts about his suitability, they would have to be settled before then. I've asked Ambassador Lewis to send us his thoughts on the political implications but, from what I understand, they would be minimal. Speaking in a purely political sense, the British monarch is only a figurehead. The business of government goes on with or without her. Of course, there's no telling what the psychological effect would be on the British people if the queen were to be killed. Despite all the woes of the royal family over the past few years, the queen has remained largely undiminished by scandal. She retains the affection of the nation and we could assume that the effect on the British people would be profound."

"I'll say," the President murmured softly to himself, recalling his own years at school in England and the precious sense of continuity he knew the monarchy gave to the British people. It was obvious to him, from the images he had seen on television, that this terrible calamity had already served to unite the people in sorrow around the queen, who had served them loyally for almost half a century.

He clicked the sound back on and for half an hour they watched the melancholy spectacle on all the networks with an increasing sense of despair. All three of the President's advisers were acutely aware of how deeply shocked he was by the news of the hijack. All three of them knew how angry and how impotent he felt. And all three knew how much he wanted to help. Britain was America's closest ally. For a hundred years the people of both nations had stood shoulder to shoulder against the worst tyrannies the world had ever known. They shared a language and a culture. They shared the same ideals. They had fought and died for the same democratic beliefs. In a treacherous and inconstant world the special relationship between Britain and America had been the cornerstone of civilization in the war against the forces of anarchy. Now the living symbol of British nationhood was in peril. And the protocols were clear.

With all the power he had at his command, the President of the United States could do nothing to help . . . unless the British asked him.

The crowd stirred behind the CNN reporter on TV. The camera jiggled, then zoomed into a close-up on the gates of Buckingham Palace. The President leaned forward in his chair.

"It appears that a car is leaving the palace now," the reporter was saying. "I think, yes, it looks to me like it's the Prime Minister's car. The British Prime Minister appears to have concluded his meeting with the other members of the royal family and is leaving the palace now."

The President turned to the secretary of state.

"Still no word?" he asked tersely.

"Sir Joslyn called me at the State Department this afternoon to confirm what we already knew," Blainey answered.

Sir Joslyn Clewes was the British ambassador in Washington.

"He told me the Prime Minister would call you personally tonight, but he couldn't give me anything more definite than that. This has really shaken them up. Our intercepts show that their first response was to send several units from their Special Air Service to Saudi Arabia. The Saudis have offered full cooperation for the duration of the crisis. Incidentally, the Saudis haven't told us anything officially yet either."

He paused to grab a sheet of paper from a file on the President's desk and scanned it quickly.

"The Royal Navy's Fleet Command at Northwood ordered six warships to the Red Sea a little after one o'clock this morning, London time. Two of those warships are in the eastern Mediterranean and expected to be there by, oh, I'd say, this time tomorrow night. The remaining four have to sail from the Persian Gulf and won't be there for . . . probably a couple of days, maybe more. The Admiralty said orders will follow once the ships are in theater, but my guess is they're planning some kind of quarantine for the *Britannia* while they figure out what they're going to do. That was followed about two hours later by the despatch of something called Comacchio Group, Royal Marines, to Jidda. I'm still waiting for an

INTEL update on exactly what Comacchio is, but we assume it's one of the Royal Navy's special forces units."

The President nodded, then turned to Pike.

"Bob, what have we got over there if we have to get involved?"

"Nearest army combat units are back in Europe, sir," Pike answered. "However, we do have two carrier battle groups in the region. The *Saratoga* and the *America* are in the Persian Gulf, but they're keeping an eye on the Iraqi situation. The *Carl Vinson* has just docked at Diego Garcia in the Indian Ocean for resupply. She was due to head home from there, but she could be diverted to the Red Sea. She could be there in forty-eight hours."

The President nodded and thought for a moment.

"I don't think it would hurt to get them started in that direction," he decided. "Could you see to that tonight, Bob?"

"Yes, sir." Pike scribbled on a notepad and got up to make the calls. He was gone about twenty minutes. When he returned, he was about to open his mouth to report his progress when the President held up a hand to silence him. Pike looked at the TV screen and saw why. CNN anchorman Bernie Shaw was announcing that they had the first footage of the hijacked royal yacht. The secretary of state froze right where he stood.

The screen cut to bumpy video footage of the *Britannia,* taken through the open door of a helicopter. It started with the yacht visible only as a shining sliver of white metal on a gray sea. The sun was still low on the horizon, indicating that the film had been shot soon after dawn. The helicopter banked and turned, the horizon swung crazily, then settled back in its proper place. The *Britannia* reappeared and started to get bigger as the chopper homed in.

"We regret there is no sound with these pictures," the anchorman's voice said. "We are showing them to you now, unedited, as we received them, only minutes ago by satellite from Cairo. They were taken by CNN cameraman Marty Jantzen, who was the first newsman to locate the *Britannia* after she was hijacked in Jidda harbor soon after midnight last night by terrorists claiming to represent the IRA. Jantzen took off from Jidda in a chartered helicopter at dawn and searched for an hour before locating the hijacked ship. These pictures were taken in international waters about twenty miles off the Saudi coast. Jantzen tells us he was warned off by warplanes of the Royal Saudi Air Force—but not before he took these amazing pictures . . . exclusive to CNN. Jantzen also tells us he was afraid the Saudis would confiscate his film if he returned to Jidda, so he persuaded the pilot to air-hop north to Egypt, where he was allowed to land and from where we received this footage only a few seconds ago. We'll be switching to Marty Jantzen live in just a moment, but first we want you to see these pictures in their entirety as they . . ."

"Goddamn," the President swore.

The *Britannia* was less than half a mile away in the camera's eye and details of her white superstructure were clearly visible. She appeared to be turning, but the camera angle and the position of the helicopter made it difficult to be sure. There was a sudden blur, the camera jolted, and the *Britannia* was replaced by a shot of a cartwheeling horizon.

"We think that was a Saudi jet," Shaw explained. "Jantzen tells us the Saudi Air Force buzzed him several times as he approached the *Britannia* and then threatened to shoot his helicopter down if he did not leave the area. However, we emphasize to you that these pictures were taken in international air space."

The *Britannia* jerked back into focus, closer now. Her bridge, decks, and masts were clearly visible. She was only a couple of hundred yards away and closing. The chopper slowed dramatically, hovering, but still narrowing the gap yard by yard. After a minute it looked as though the helicopter was no more than a hundred feet from the hijacked ship. The camera swept back and forth the length of the royal yacht, but there seemed to be no sign of life.

Suddenly a figure appeared on the deck adjacent to the bridge, a hooded figure dressed all in black.

"Jesus Christ," Bob Pike whispered.

The figure was holding an automatic rifle, and as they watched, he put it to his shoulder and aimed directly at the camera. The camera jiggled again then zoomed in close until the screen was filled with the image of the hooded man with the rifle. The man held his position for about half a minute. Then he brought the rifle down, raised his left arm in a clenched-fist salute, and disappeared back inside the bridge.

The men in the Oval Office all exhaled at the same time.

"These incredible first pictures of the hijacked royal yacht show one of the hijackers appearing to threaten our cameraman," Shaw went on. "Truly incredible. CNN cameraman Marty Jantzen and a Saudi helicopter pilot whose name we still do not know risked their lives to bring these pictures to you."

The camera jolted again, and then there was nothing but sky as the chopper wheeled away from the hijacked yacht. Then the film ended and Bernie Shaw appeared back onscreen trying to keep his composure but looking like a cat that had just swallowed a very plump canary.

"It was at that point, Jantzen says, he was warned away from the *Britannia* under peril of being shot down by the Saudi Air Force. We will show that incredible footage to you again later, but right now we're crossing live to Cairo, where . . ."

The red phone on the President's desk rang. Pike snapped out of his trance, stepped forward, and picked it up. The President hit the mute button on the TV again and waited.

"It's Downing Street, sir," Pike said. "The Prime Minister would like to speak with you."

The President nodded, but instead of taking the handset, he hit the conference button. He realized that the Prime Minister must have decided to call the White House immediately on his return to Downing Street. Relief tinged with apprehension coursed through him. With all his heart and soul he wanted to help. Now, if he was asked, he hoped to hell that he could help. There were a series of clicks as switchboard operators in the White House and Downing Street cleared the line and put the Prime Minister through to the Oval Office.

"Mr. President?" the familiar, soft voice of the British Prime Minister came clearly into the room.

"I'm here, Prime Minister," the President responded. His tone was calm and composed, but the concern in his voice was unmistakable. "I can't tell you how shocked we were when we got the news. Everyone here is appalled by what has happened. If there is anything we can do to help . . . anything . . . ?"

"I . . . thank you . . ." the Prime Minister faltered for a moment, then recovered and went on. "I would have called you earlier, but I've been . . . rather busy."

No one smiled at this particular piece of British understatement.

"We're watching the news broadcasts right now," the President added. "I saw you leaving Buckingham Palace a little while back."

"Yes," the Prime Minister added. "I've just spent two very tense hours with the royal family."

"Please don't think me tasteless to ask," the President said, "but how in God's name are they holding up under this?"

"With some difficulty," the PM responded honestly. "There's a distinct air of unreality about the whole thing. Unfortunately it is only too real."

"Please pass on my heartfelt sympathy and the sympathy of my wife to all members of the royal family," the President added. "Please assure them that we . . . all the American people . . . feel deeply for them at this terrible, terrible time."

The President paused. Under other circumstances they would both have been glad to have the opportunity to talk to each other and might have roamed over a whole range of subjects from the price of oil to the President's golf handicap. But the President was all too aware that small talk at a time like this, however well intended, would only add to the Prime Minister's burden.

"Tell me," he added quickly. "Is there anything we can do to help?"

"Actually, that's the reason I'm calling," the PM responded. "I've asked our ambassador to the United Nations to call an emergency meeting of the Security Council for midnight your time. We're going to proclaim a total exclusion zone around the *Britannia.* It will have a radius of ten nautical miles and it will be enforced by Royal Navy warships, effective from midnight tonight. We'd like your support."

"I'll instruct our ambassador to the UN personally," the President answered. "I can't imagine you'd have any trouble with the other members of the Security Council. What else we can do?"

"To be perfectly frank with you"—the PM hesitated—"I don't know."

The President gave a wan smile and looked up at his advisers. Under any other circumstances it might have been funny.

"Intelligence, logistics, material, anything?" the President offered. "You name it, we'll do our darnedest to oblige."

"I'll know more when our military people have had a little more time to assess the situation," the PM answered. "Presumably they will be able to give me a better idea of our shortcomings in any areas. In which case I may well be coming back to you with a plea for help."

"Ambassador Lewis in London will be standing by to help you in any way possible," the President added. "I'm meeting right now with my security people. I want to know what warships we've got in the area so that we're at least in a position to render assistance upon request. We've also got our own joint facilities in Saudi Arabia that we can put at your disposal. If you don't mind my making the suggestion, Prime Minister, it might not be a bad idea if you were to appoint one of your military people to liase with our chairman of the joint chiefs of staff, General Coburg, until this thing is over. We want to help you any way we can with this. It's an outrage, Prime Minister, an outrage against the civilized world. We cannot allow the people responsible for this to succeed. We won't allow them to succeed."

"Thank you, Mr. President," the Prime Minister said. "I'm heartened . . . and I'm touched to hear you say that. It's nice to know who our friends are at a moment such as this."

The Prime Minister sounded exhausted. The President had no way of knowing that his British counterpart had not slept in almost two days and still had many more hours of crisis meetings ahead of him before he could seek the solace of his bed.

"We are your friends," the President added quietly but emphatically. "And we will move heaven and earth to help you."

"Thank you, Mr. President," the PM added. "Good-bye for now."

"Good-bye, Prime Minister. And God be with you."

Then the line went dead.

The President looked up and slowly shook his head.

"Gentlemen," he said. "I want everyone back here in the morning at seven. Ed, I want General Coburg, the secretary of defense, and the director of the CIA here too."

"I understand, sir," Pike answered.

"Good," the President said. "Because once we've decided what we're going to do to help our British friends, there's something else we have to consider."

"Sir?"

"Well." The President slumped tiredly back in his chair. "We've got thirty million people of Irish descent in the United States. Quite a few of them are supporters of the Irish Republican Army. You don't suppose they're all going to sit back and watch this unfold on their TV screens, do you?"

BELFAST. 23.27 HOURS

The Winged Pig turned into Andersontown Road and confronted its first barricade. Halfway down the street, a bus, an ice cream van, and a car had been jammed tight from sidewalk to sidewalk. In front of the barricade, in the naked glare of the streetlights, scores of youths could be seen, milling restlessly back and forth. When the British armored personnel carrier appeared at the top of the street, a loud cheer went up. The cheer dissolved quickly into a chorus of taunts and jeers. Almost immediately the air was filled with a volley of rocks, bottles, nail-studded golf balls, and other homemade missiles. Most of them fell short and spattered harmlessly on the road in front of the armored car. Sitting in the commander's seat, Lieutenant Christopher Hodges ordered the driver to bring the Pig to a stop.

"Time to get out and catch a breath of fresh night air, chaps," he said, turning to the seven combat-ready soldiers in the back. The troops threw open the rear doors and trotted quickly out into the street, rifles and Perspex shields held ready. Hodges climbed out after them and ordered two men to deploy the vehicle's side-mounted shields that gave added protection and accounted for its unflattering nickname: The Winged Pig.

Two armored Land Rovers were already parked nearby, surrounded by a dozen men from the Royal Ulster Constabulary, carrying rifles and wearing bulletproof vests. One of the RUC men, a sergeant, crossed the road toward the soldiers.

"Sergeant O'Connor," he introduced himself to Hodges. "I'm the man who called in."

Hodges nodded.

"They were still putting it up when we got here," O'Connor added. "God knows where they hijacked the ice cream van."

"Probably felt like a bit of refreshment," Hodges answered dryly. "It's going to be a long, hot night."

"They've siphoned out the petrol to make Molotov cocktails," the RUC man went on. "We saw them splashing some around the bus and the car. It'll go up like a torch when they light it."

"They'll burn down a few of their own houses, then," Hodges responded. "Because I'm not letting the fire brigade anywhere near it till the street's cleared."

"You think this is enough men?" O'Connor asked, nodding at the troops, who had fanned out in a defensive formation. The rocks and bottles were crashing closer to them now as some of the youths edged farther up the road, playing their dangerous game.

"It's all we can spare for the moment," Hodges answered breezily. "Ballymurphy has been going strong for about an hour. There are riots on the Falls Road, at Divis Flats, Clonard, and Ardoyne, and shots have been fired at Unity Flats. Every unit in Belfast is out tonight. And we're stretched pretty thin, I'm afraid."

"Jesus." O'Connor looked worried. "This business with the *Britannia*'s really stirred them up."

"They love it." Hodges smiled thinly. "Anything that's a disaster for us is a triumph for them. They're having a party."

"What are you going to do?"

"Think we might give them a taste of some gas to push them back a bit," Hodges decided. "The best we can do is contain them for a while until we get a few more troops here."

O'Connor nodded and walked back to his men to tell them to put on their gas masks.

"All right, men." Hodges turned to his troops. "Let's give them a little CS, shall we? See how that goes down."

Two soldiers ducked into the back of the Pig and reappeared with gas grenade launchers. When everyone had their masks on, they took a few paces down the street toward the mob and fired. There were two hollow pops in quick succession, and the tear gas canisters hissed down the street and exploded in the midst of the milling youths. Twin plumes of gas billowed out into the street and the youths scattered back behind the barricade. Then one small figure darted through the stinging mist, a handkerchief clutched to his face. He picked up a canister and lobbed it back toward the soldiers.

"Looks like they want to play," Hodges murmured. "Better give them a couple more."

Two miles away, on the other side of the barricade, deep inside the red brick maze of streets and council-owned apartment buildings that made up the Catholic ghetto of Andersontown, Matthew Byrne stopped his car outside a ten-story building of naked concrete that housed two hundred poky apartments. He climbed out of his two-year-old Toyota Corolla, leaving the doors unlocked despite the pile of suitcases, duffel bags, and battered cardboard boxes inside. Nobody would touch the car of an IRA man in Andersontown.

He hurried into the building, where most of the lights still burned despite the lateness of the hour. The news about the *Britannia* had sparked spontaneous demonstrations of support for the IRA throughout Belfast. Everyone knew that something momentous had happened and that it was only the beginning of something bigger. Some were elated. Others were fearful and hid in their homes, watching it all on television.

The elevator was out of order and Byrne was sweating by the time he got to the sixth floor. On the way he must have passed a dozen kids—pulling on their clothes, laughing, yelling, hurrying to join their pals at the riot.

Byrne walked to the end of the corridor, then knocked sharply on a door marked 609.

"It's me . . . Byrne," he said.

There was a pause, then the door opened and he stepped inside. Sean McDermott shut the door and ushered his pal down the tiny hallway. McDermott was the same age as Byrne but looked and dressed much younger. Both men were in their early thirties, but Byrne was overweight and drank too much. He wore a rumpled dark suit, a black shirt buttoned at the collar, and his greasy brown hair was long and untidy. McDermott was leaner and fitter. He wore blue jeans and a white T-shirt and thought he looked like James Dean. It had taken him years to learn how to knit his eyebrows together to get that authentic, brooding rebel look.

"Have you seen it?" Byrne whispered.

"Yeah, I've seen it," McDermott grinned. "There's nothin' else to watch. They won't put a decent bloody movie on or anythin'."

The two men filed into a tiny, cluttered living room. The whole apartment was a basic one-bedroom that McDermott shared with his girlfriend, Jilly. There were a couple of motorbike posters on the walls, and McDermott's helmet and leathers rested on an old armchair in a corner. Neither McDermott nor his girlfriend were fussy housekeepers, and the place looked like a rubbish dump. McDermott's pride and joy was his Honda 650 motorbike which he kept in a garage downstairs. The bike was much cleaner than his apartment. Byrne lit a cigarette to blot out the smell.

"Evenin', Jilly. How ye doin', sweetheart?"

Jilly sat on the floor, her back propped against a sofa littered with discarded clothes, fast food cartons, empty potato chip bags, an ashtray, and dozens of old magazines. A slatternly peroxide blonde, she wore jeans and a T-shirt like her boyfriend. She was smoking too, and there was a half glass of what looked like water on the floor beside her. Byrne knew it was vodka. Not Stolichnaya though. Jilly didn't have enough class to appreciate the good stuff.

"Hi, Matty," she answered without looking at him. She didn't bother to move or to offer him a drink. She was watching CNN on a portable TV in the corner. Once again the combination of crisis and CNN had turned everybody in the world into news junkies. And once again CNN was showing its exclusive footage of the hooded hijacker brandishing his M-16 on the bridge of the *Britannia.*

"Think it's him?" McDermott nodded at the TV.

"Fuckin' unbelievable, isn't it?" Byrne answered, looking around for a place to sit. There was a table and three chairs in the corner nearest the kitchen, but the table looked as if it hadn't been cleared in days and the chairs were covered with dishes and dirty laundry. He decided that McDermott and Jilly must have given up using chairs and gone over to living entirely off the floor as the detritus of their slovenly lives encroached on their shrinking oasis of living space.

"Yeah," McDermott sniffed, oblivious of Byrne's distaste. "Behan said all along if anybody could do it, Doyle could. And I never believed him. When they went, I thought that was it. That was the last we'd see of any of them. But Doyle really must've had the goods over there, eh? And now he's done it. He's fuckin' well gone and done it."

"That's why I'm here," Byrne said urgently. "We've got to get a move on, Sean. Tonight."

He glanced helplessly around the room.

"Can we sit down for a minute and talk in private?" he asked.

McDermott shrugged, then stepped over Jilly's legs and switched off the television.

"Hey . . ." Jilly started to protest.

"Go and wash your hair," McDermott snapped at her. "Now."

Jilly flashed him a sullen look, but she had felt the back of McDermott's hand too often to risk angering him now. Huffily, she grabbed her glass, got up, and bustled past the two of them, pausing only to snatch the ghetto blaster on her way past the kitchen table. She disappeared into the bathroom and slammed the door so hard, the walls shook. A moment later they heard water running and then the muffled thump of loud music. McDermott transferred some of the mess from the kitchen chairs onto the sofa, then cleared a space for them both at the table.

"Drink?"

"A beer would do fine."

McDermott stepped into the kitchen and returned a moment later with two cans of Harp lager. He threw one to Byrne, sat down at the table, opened his can, and took a sip. Byrne took a long pull at his lager, then leaned closer.

"Keegan and the rest of the army council will be shittin' themselves now," he said.

Joe Keegan was commanding officer of the Provisional IRA's Belfast brigades. The idea to storm the *Britannia* and take the queen and Prince Philip hostage had not been his. He and the army council had been opposed to it, seeing it as an unnecessary waste of their best men on an endeavor that was doomed to failure. But Dominic Behan had fought for it, hard. Sick of the never-ending war of attrition with the British, he had always been in favor of the big, spectacular strike. He told them he was going ahead with it anyway. Him and his stooge, Doyle, a renegade British soldier, whom nobody trusted. For a while it looked like there would be a split in the army council that would lead to another bloody feud. In the end, Keegan had grudgingly given his consent and a split had been avoided. But Byrne and McDermott were Behan's men. Byrne had been quartermaster for the Andersontown brigade and McDermott his enforcer. To preserve security they had kept themselves quarantined from the other brigades for a year. Now their patience and their loyalty was about to be rewarded.

"If Nick pulls this off," Byrne continued, "Keegan and his Commie pals on the army council will be finished. The Provo rank and file will think Nick Behan is God al-bloody-mighty."

"Jesus." McDermott's brows narrowed. "You really think the Brits will do it? You think they'll pull out?"

"After tonight, Sean, anything is possible. Just look at what that man has done. He's snatched the Queen of England aboard her own bloody yacht, for God's sake. They'll have to listen to him. The whole world will listen to him now."

"They haven't said anything about a withdrawal or a deadline on the news," McDermott said.

Byrne leaned forward and gripped McDermott's arm.

"It's just starting, Sean. The city's rising now. There's fires and shooting all over Belfast. Everybody knows that this is different. This is really going to hurt the Brits. Remember what Nick told us before he left? He told us to be ready. He told us that when it started, things would happen fast. He said we'd have seven days from the day of the hijacking. He said we couldn't believe anything the Brits said or anything we heard on the TV or saw in the papers. We've got to get up to Larne tonight, before Keegan does something stupid or the Brits come lookin' for us. We've got to be Nick's second voice, Sean. The voice of liberty."

"Jesus." McDermott shook his head. "I still don't believe it. I know it's happening . . . but I don't bloody believe it."

Byrne fixed him with an intense stare.

"Believe it, Sean. Dominic Behan has made it real. That man could be the father of a united Ireland. And we have to keep our end up, like we promised. I'm leaving now. You'd best get your things and follow me tonight. You don't want to be the one man who let Nick down, now, do ye?"

McDermott bridled at the implied threat, but it had its effect. Nobody had ever crossed Nick Behan without paying a price.

"I gave the man my word, Matty. If I said I'm in, I'm in."

Byrne nodded, took another sip of lager, then got up to go.

"What about her?" he asked, nodding toward the bathroom door.

"She knows nothin'."

"You sure?"

"She's a bimbo. She's got a great little body on her, but all she cares about is gettin' fed and fucked. She knows what happens to her when she asks too many questions."

"You can't leave her here," Byrne said. "If Keegan or the Brits get hold of her, they'll squeeze somethin' out of her. You'll have to bring her with you."

"What if she doesn't want to come?"

Byrne sighed. He looked away for a moment and then he gave McDermott a look whose meaning was unmistakable. McDermott looked uncomfortably at the ceiling. The only sound in the small flat was the thump of Jilly's ghetto blaster in the bathroom.

"Okay," McDermott shrugged. "She'll come."

Minutes later Byrne hurried back across the scrubby wasteland to his car. He had just put the key in the lock when the eastern horizon blossomed with a lurid orange flash. A moment later the thump of a heavy explosion echoed between the buildings. Byrne smiled to himself. It was all just like Behan had said it would be.

On Andersontown Road, Lieutenant Hodges and his men watched the barricade burn like a bonfire, filling the street with a harsh yellow glare. Suddenly, they heard a series of flat pops, the unmistakable sound of small-arms fire. Somebody was shooting at them through the flames. Hodges and his men ducked behind the protective screens of the Winged Pig. The RUC men clustered behind their Land Rovers and readied their automatic rifles.

"Don't return fire unless I give the order," Hodges called out, a note of anxiety creeping into his voice. Then he ducked through the rear doors of the Pig and reached for the radio to GHQ. A moment later the duty communications officer came on. He sounded harassed. Hodges identified himself and gave his position.

"It's starting to look a little boisterous down here," he said. "The gas didn't work, they've set fire to the barricade, and we've just come under small-arms fire. I think we're going to need some extra men."

"You and everybody else," the reply came back. "The whole bloody city's on fire. Stand by and I'll see what I can do for you."

Hodges put the microphone down and sighed. It was all starting to unravel a little bit faster than anyone had expected.

HMY *Britannia.* 24.00 hours

"I think it's time we sent a message," Doyle announced to the men on the bridge in his unsettling British accent.

"The *Hotspur?"* Patsy Ryan queried.

Doyle nodded. It was time to make his presence known. Time to unsettle the British further with a new voice. A voice that would add a whole new dimension to the hijacking. He took the ship-to-ship handset from its cradle and held it to his masked face. Behan and Abu Musa were the only other men on the bridge. Mulcahey, Deveny, and the rest were below decks, taking turns watching the hostages and getting some rest. It was nearly twenty-four hours since the hijacking, and everyone was exhausted. Everyone but Doyle.

"It's on the right wave band now," Ryan said.

Doyle thumbed the transmitter.

"This is the commander of the *Britannia* calling the *Hotspur."*

He waited, but there was no answer.

"They can hear you, all right," Ryan added. "They just don't want to talk to us."

The *Hotspur* had failed to acknowledge both previous messages from the hijackers, the first telling them the ship was wired with explosives and the second giving them the deadline to get their troops out of Northern Ireland. But the British warship was still out there. They could see her on the *Britannia*'s radar, the biggest blip on the screen, one nautical mile due astern. There were half a dozen smaller craft too, Saudi naval patrol boats, scattered around the *Britannia,* and every now and again they heard the thump of a distant helicopter.

"Good," Doyle said. "It means they're not ready to open negotiations because they still don't know what to do. The initiative is still ours, boys. Let's show them we run a tight ship."

He thumbed the transmit button again.

"*Hotspur*—you ignored our instructions by allowing that media chopper to come in close today. Keep a watch astern and you'll see what happens when you break the rules. You can put this one on your conscience, Captain."

He hung up the mike and gestured to Behan to get his rifle and follow him below to the admiral's day cabin.

On the bridge of the *Hotspur* Captain Purcell looked uneasily at his communications officer, Lieutenant Drewe.

"Put the night vision scope on the *Britannia*'s stern, Lieutenant," he ordered.

Lieutenant Drewe nodded and bent over the scope to adjust the sighting.

"Got her, sir," he said.

"Get some goggles up here too, would you, Lieutenant."

"Sir." Drewe passed on the order to a petty officer, and the man quickly produced two sets of night vision goggles.

"Give everybody a pair, would you?" Purcell ordered. "I want as many witnesses as possible."

The petty officer did as he was told, and soon everyone on the *Hotspur*'s bridge was equipped with a pair of night sights. Captain Purcell stepped up to the main scope and peered through the lens. It took him a moment to adjust to the gray-and-white shadings of the optically enhanced image, but then he found he could make out the stern rail of the royal yacht quite clearly, rising and falling on the gentle swell as it moved steadily northward. He could even make out the details of the royal crest painted in gold lettering just below the stern rail. Nothing happened for a few minutes, and they began to get restless. Then Purcell saw someone move. Then someone else. There were three figures in all, clearly defined and just like photographic negatives. Purcell recognized the hooded profiles of two of the men. Both hijackers. The third man was impossible to identify but appeared to be a member of the crew. His uniform was all white.

Drewe gasped.

"From the markings of the uniform, sir, I'd say it's Admiral Marchant."

Purcell strained to see the figure in the middle. It was a tall, slender man, and his hair seemed to be blowing untidily in the wind. Admiral Marchant had thick white hair. Then he saw what Drewe meant. The occasional flash of gold braid on the collar and epaulettes of the man's jacket. The flash of color on his left breast where he would have worn his decorations for the state dinner with King Fahd. It was the captain of the *Britannia.* The close friend and fellow officer that Purcell had known for thirty years. The man he had first met at Dartmouth and whose career path had crossed his own so many times in the intervening years. The man who was due to retire following this, the final voyage of his final command.

One of the hooded figures disappeared, and there were only two men standing at the stern.

"No." The word came out of Purcell's lips as a hoarse whisper. "In the name of God . . ."

The man in the hood raised a pistol to the admiral's head and fired. There was a spurt of brilliant white on the screen, and Admiral Marchant toppled forward, over the rail, and into the sea.

5 A Matter of Principle

London, May 17. 08.49 hours

A soaking rain was falling as CTC Chief Sir Malcolm Porter walked the five hundred yards that separated his office at the Ministry of Defence from the Prime Minister's office in Downing Street. But not a single drop of rain touched his crinkly gray hair. Nor was he seen by the hundreds of spectators and jostling photographers who greeted each new arrival at Number Ten with a blizzard of flashbulbs. This was because Sir Malcolm had taken one of the security tunnels that criss-crossed the ground beneath Whitehall's busy sidewalks. Just one section of the labyrinth that connected the Prime Minister's residence with the Ministry of Defence, the Admiralty, the Treasury, the Foreign Office, the Home Office, and all of them with each other. He was met at Number Ten by a man from Special Branch who escorted him up to John Traynor's office. The corridor on the second floor was filled with powerful people—cabinet ministers, department heads, the highest-ranking military officers in the land, all of them murmuring soberly to one another while secretaries, messengers, and ministerial aides bustled backward and forward, adding to the air of urgency. Porter knew them all and exchanged nods of recognition as he moved to the head of the line.

"I'm afraid we're running a bit late this morning," Traynor greeted Porter as he arrived. "We woke him up half an hour ago. He got to bed around five and he really needed the rest. He's had about eight hours sleep in the last three days. I don't know how much longer he can keep going like this. I'm going to try to punch a hole in his schedule this afternoon, give him another couple of hours. Otherwise, he's not going to hold up."

Sir Malcolm nodded. It was difficult for anyone to sleep at such a time, but exhausted men exercised faulty judgment and the Prime Minister could afford to make few mistakes.

"Sneak him a sleeping pill and tie him to a bloody chair if you have to," the chief of CTC said.

Traynor smiled faintly. His color had turned from its usual blotting-paper white to a cadaverous gray. If anything, he had slept fewer hours than his boss.

"He'll only be another few minutes," Traynor added. "You're second on the list. Charles Ingham is up first. Do you mind, terribly, waiting with him? We're starting to get a bit pushed for space."

"Not if he doesn't mind," Porter answered. Space had always been a problem at Downing Street, especially in times of crisis when so many VIPs had to be shuffled through quickly. Besides, Sir Malcolm knew Charles Ingham well. He was the secretary of state for Northern Ireland. They had collaborated often in the past in the planning and execution of security operations inside the province.

One of Traynor's aides showed Sir Malcolm to a waiting room. Inside, an untidy gray-haired man with a heavy mustache looked up from the briefcase on his lap without any show of surprise.

" 'Morning, Malcolm," Ingham greeted Porter affably. "Might have known I'd bump into you sooner rather than later."

The two men shook hands. Porter took a chair opposite Ingham and sat down, setting his own briefcase on the floor next to his feet. An aide offered Porter a choice of tea or coffee.

"Have the coffee," Ingham interrupted in his blunt North Yorkshire accent. "The tea is bloody awful here since they went over to tea bags."

Porter opted for the tea anyway. Ingham declined a second cup of coffee and the aide disappeared.

"Mad business, eh, Malcolm?"

"There has never been a shortage of madness in the world, Charles," Porter answered.

Ingham heaved a deep and heartfelt sigh. It was the sigh of a man who had wrestled with the most vexatious portfolio in the cabinet and who had come to the conclusion that a rational solution could not be imposed upon irrational people. He went back to poking around inside his briefcase for a moment, then snapped it shut and put it down on the floor too.

"When did you last see him?" he asked, nodding in the direction of the Prime Minister's office.

Porter had to think about it; so much had happened in the past thirty-six hours.

"Early yesterday," he said. "War Cabinet meeting. Started at midnight. Think it was about three-thirty when we were finished."

"How did he look to you?"

"All right . . . considering." Porter kept his voice noncommittal.

Ingham nodded.

"I was summoned after the ultimatum came in," he said. "He looked buggered then. They tell me he hasn't slept much since I saw him."

Before Porter could respond, there was a knock at the door and one of Number 10's legendary tea ladies appeared. She handed Porter his tea in a china cup and saucer. Ingham waited till she had gone and the two of them were alone again. Then he leaned toward Porter and lowered his voice to a conspiratorial whisper.

"This will finish him, you know. One way or another."

There was no malice in Ingham's words. Just a bald statement of fact from a man used to calculating the political fallout from disasters such as this. Though this crisis was in a class all its own and destined to claim many casualties before it had run its course.

"I think you'll find that he's well aware of the risks involved,"

Porter answered coolly. He took a sip of his tea. Ingham was right. It was awful.

"Oh?" Ingham responded wryly. He had known the CTC chief a little too long to buy such a disingenuous reply. "You're quite certain of that?"

Porter studied Ingham carefully.

"All right, Charles," he said. "What are you driving at?"

"Have you seen anything overnight from Belfast? Intelligence, TV . . . anything?"

Porter hated to admit that he had not seen copies of the latest intelligence from GHQ Belfast. He had been too busy preparing his operational briefing for the PM.

"I'm aware there have been some . . . disturbances," he bluffed.

"Belfast and Londonderry are on fire," Ingham said flatly.

Porter hesitated, unsure of how much Ingham might be exaggerating.

"A few lively demonstrations of support for the IRA are only to be expected following something like this," he said.

"Lively?" Ingham echoed. "At this moment, every one of our thirty thousand combat troops in Northern Ireland is on the streets," he said. "We have no reinforcements. The RUC is calling up all its reserves. Riots are still under way in the Creggan, Ballymurphy, Andersontown, and Ardoyne. Eighteen RUC officers and eleven British soldiers have been injured so far. Three soldiers wounded by gunfire. It's only a fluke that nobody's been killed yet . . . it's just a matter of time. We should be pouring troops into Northern Ireland, not talking of pulling them out."

He stopped and patted his briefcase.

"I've got the latest army intel in here," he said. "I spoke to General Richards an hour ago. He was supposed to be here with me this morning to brief the PM. The situation is so bad he's afraid to leave Belfast."

Porter set down his cup and took a moment to absorb what he had just been told. General Richards was the commanding officer of all British forces in Northern Ireland, a tough, no-nonsense soldier who had taken a hard line on civil disturbances, always crushing them quickly and firmly before they could escalate into something worse.

If violence had reached a level where Richards could not leave his post, then the situation was critical.

"The hijackers' demands aren't known publicly yet, are they?" Ingham queried.

"There's a blanket suppression for the moment," Porter answered.

Ingham shook his head.

"Won't last long," he said. "Just wait till word leaks out. Wait until they find out that the hijackers want all our troops out in what . . . six days now?"

Porter fell silent.

"For the moment," Ingham added, "the Republicans are just having a party. They think the IRA has pulled off a bit of a coup because this is the best shot they've had at a British monarch since 1921."

Porter understood Ingham's reference to historic precedent. King George V had made a state visit to Northern Ireland in 1921 and the IRA had planted a bomb on the track where his train would pass. The explosives went off prematurely and wrecked the wrong train . . . but it had been close.

"So," Ingham went on, "they're rubbing our noses in it. They think some kind of deal is on the way. They can hardly contain themselves. They're all trying to show what great patriots they are. And the stupid buggers have no idea of the real trouble they're in. They don't seem to care anymore that we're all that stands between them and a bloody massacre."

He paused and jerked his head in the direction of the Prime Minister's office.

"He can't afford to let the truth leak out. If it does, we haven't got enough troops in Northern Ireland to keep the Protestants away from the Catholics. We've got reports of a general call to arms by the UDA, the UDF, and the UDR. You do know that the Ulster Defence Association has fifty thousand armed men at its command, don't you? The other two have at least twenty thousand more between them."

Porter nodded grimly. He knew the figures. Protestants and Ulster loyalists outnumbered Catholics and Republicans twenty to one in

Northern Ireland. At best, the Provisional and the Official IRA could muster two thousand fighting men between them. It had always been that way. The image and myth of the IRA were much bigger than the reality, especially in the United States, where it had been romanticized to a level that bore no relation to fact. The IRA had never represented the popular will of the Catholic minority in Northern Ireland. Which was why it had always been forced to rely on guerrilla warfare. The IRA had neither the numbers nor the support of the people to enable it to fight a pitched battle or mount a general offensive.

"If the loyalists think there is half a chance we're going to abandon them," Ingham added, "you know what will happen, don't you?"

Porter knew. Intelligence reports had long since indicated that in the event of a British withdrawal, the Protestant militias planned to destroy every Republican stronghold in the north and then march on Dublin. The only thing that stood between the genocidal will of the Protestant majority and the annihilation of the Catholic minority was the British Army. And its troops were shot at and spat upon by Catholic and Protestant alike, conspicuous and convenient scapegoats for the propagandists of both sides. With the British out of the way, the Protestants could swat the IRA battalions in the north aside as though they were flies. Then they planned an invasion of the Irish Republic to occupy Dublin and force the recognition of a Protestant Free State in the north. After that those Catholics in the north who had survived the initial onslaught would be driven from their homes and sent to the south as refugees. Fantastic as this scenario seemed, it was all too plausible. The army of the Irish Free State numbered only twelve thousand men with twenty thousand reserves. The loyalists could muster more than twice that. The result would be an all-out war between the Protestant-loyalist militias and the army of the Irish Republic, a bloodbath to rival the breakup of Yugoslavia and the nightmare that had haunted every British government since the partition of Ireland in 1921.

"So," Ingham concluded, "if the PM does order the troops out, Ireland goes up in flames and thousands die. If he orders more troops in, a British monarch dies. If he does nothing at all, the queen and Prince Philip still die . . . and thirty thousand British troops get caught in a meat grinder. Because, Malcolm, you don't think all those Ulster loyalists are going to stand idly by and do nothing while the IRA murders the Queen of England, do you?"

Porter considered Ingham's bleak scenario, then nodded his reluctant agreement.

"What's your recommendation, Charles?" he asked.

Ingham leaned back in his chair, wondering how much he could afford to take Porter into his confidence.

"It's a question of realities, Malcolm. The army cannot comply with a seven-day timetable for withdrawal even if the PM gives the order. It's not physically possible. Oh, we could airlift all the men out in seven days—if they left all their equipment behind. But that's not likely to happen. You see, Malcolm, the hijackers have made a demand that cannot be met. I believe they intend to kill the queen whatever happens. This is terrorism dressed up as politics. The political solution will come later, once they've softened us up by proving they can kill the sovereign."

"Perhaps," Porter mused, "commencement of withdrawal within seven days might be enough."

"Perhaps," Ingham echoed. "But we don't know that. To the best of my knowledge, we haven't opened negotiations with the hijackers yet, and the clock is ticking faster all the time."

Porter sighed and fixed Ingham with a solemn look.

"You do know what you're saying, don't you, Charles?"

"Yes," Ingham answered soberly. "I am saying we may have to accept that the deaths of the queen and Prince Philip are inevitable."

Porter grimaced. There was something ugly and obscene about the way the words had been laid out so coldly in this small room at the heart of the British government.

"As a member of Cabinet," Porter added, "you have sworn an oath of loyalty to the Crown. To the best of my knowledge, every member of the Cabinet has agreed to abide by the PM's decision to negotiate with the terrorists if it will preserve the life of the monarch."

"Yes," Ingham conceded, "but you know very well, Malcolm, that what people say in an open forum like Cabinet is one thing, and how they feel in private is often quite different. We all know that this is not a conventional hijacking and this is not a conventional hostage. We all believe that an extraordinary situation demands extraordinary sacrifice. But in the end, it does come down to one basic question, doesn't it? The lives of the few versus the lives of the many. Or perhaps I should say the lives of the privileged few versus the lives of the underprivileged many. You see, Malcolm, I don't think that anyone—including the PM—fully understands how awful the consequences will be if we proceed with this policy of saving the monarch at all cost. Not everyone understands how high that cost will be. Some ministers may think they can live with the shame and humiliation of a surrender to terrorists and the loss of Northern Ireland—but will they be able to live with the slaughter of those thousands of innocent men, women, and children that will follow that surrender? Because, if the PM does go ahead with this policy, we are looking at a potential act of genocide—right on Britain's doorstep."

He paused for a moment, then added: "Once I have put this new information to the Prime Minister, I think he may see things differently. It is one thing for him to make a deal with terrorists and then resign. But when that same deal will condemn thousands of people to violent death—"

"People who openly despise us and who now riot against our soldiers in the ghettoes of Belfast," Porter interrupted.

"Precisely." Ingham gave him a wry smile. "That is the tragedy and the irony of the situation, Malcolm. And that is why we cannot abandon these people to their fate. Otherwise, how would we look in the eyes of the world? How would we look, Malcolm, if we abandon these people to their fate merely because they rail against us in desperation and ignorance? What is the world to make of a country that shows itself willing to sacrifice the lives of thousands for the sake of one person who happens to occupy the throne of England?

"Of course," he added slyly, "the Britain of old would not have hesitated at the idea of making a dishonorable deal that would result in the death of a few thousand ignorant Irish men and women. And God knows there are plenty of voices in the country who believe that Northern Ireland is not worth the life of a single British soldier, much less the life of the monarch. There are those who will embrace this as a golden opportunity to do what we should have done years ago—to pull out and let the bastards go for each other's throats. Sort it out among themselves.

"So"—he paused to give his words added emphasis—"we have to make a decision, Malcolm. We have to decide what we are. What we really are. The brave new Britain of courage and principle and justice for all? Or are we really the same bad old Britain underneath? Ready to do deals with terrorists because the only people to suffer will be a few thousand nobodies who hate us anyway. Whatever we decide, the whole world is going to know us for what we are . . . for what we really are."

Porter sighed wearily.

"Charles," he said, a warning note creeping into his voice. "You sound to me like a man in too much of a hurry to sell out Queen and country."

Ingham shrugged but did not look uncomfortable.

"On the basis of the facts that have been put before me, I will recommend to the Prime Minister that we double our troop presence in Northern Ireland immediately . . . and we keep those extra troops there until the crisis has passed."

"So," Porter added, "you're the man who is willing to sacrifice the Queen of England?"

"I'm the man who sees the realities of the situation," Ingham answered. "Not the man who will allow himself to be swept away by the kind of emotional hysteria that seems to have clouded everyone else's judgment."

"And what if he doesn't accept your recommendation?"

"My honest opinion?"

"As always," Porter said without a hint of guile.

Ingham smiled.

"I think he could be outvoted in Cabinet. Assuming Cabinet gets to see copies of my reports."

Porter stared at him, unsure if he had heard correctly.

"You think he might suppress your intelligence reports because he would be afraid Cabinet would go against him if they saw what was in them?"

"Wouldn't be the first time it had happened, would it, old chap?"

Porter looked away. Now he understood. Ingham was lobbying for allies to help him undermine the Prime Minister and to ram his own response to the crisis through Cabinet—even if it meant the death of the queen.

"And if Cabinet does see them and still sides with the PM?" Porter asked.

Ingham shrugged again.

"It's a national crisis, Malcolm. It should go to a conscience vote in the Commons. Then we'll see if the PM has the backing he needs."

For the moment Porter decided to overlook Ingham's implied threat to breach the security of the War Cabinet and leak secret documents to the House of Commons.

"The Opposition might vote to give up Northern Ireland," Porter said.

"Not at the cost of Protestants slaughtering Catholics on the nightly news, they won't."

"And if the PM won't put it to a vote in the House?"

"No-confidence motion," Ingham answered abruptly. "If the PM is faced with a choice of changing his mind or seeing the government brought down, I think I know what he'll choose."

Porter remained impassive despite the turmoil that churned inside him. He was shocked by Ingham's scenario. The secretary might be right in his assessment of the dire consequences of the PM's chosen course of action, but Porter was appalled that Ingham was so fueled by his own ego that he was willing to destabilize the government in the midst of such a crisis just to get his own way. It gave the papers in Porter's briefcase a whole new urgency.

"You're taking a hell of a risk, Charles," he said. "What makes you think I won't tell all this to the Prime Minister?"

"Because I'm going to tell him myself in a few minutes," Ingham answered smugly. "And I'll have copies of my reports on your desk before five o'clock today. Because I think you should see them too."

"And what if I don't happen to agree with you?"

"I'm not worried about that, Malcolm." He smiled. "You'll do what's right for the country. Not what is right for the PM. I know you well enough to bet my career on it."

Porter was about to reply, when the door opened and John Traynor appeared.

"The Prime Minister will see you now, sir," he said, and looked at Ingham.

The secretary for Northern Ireland got up from his chair with a grunt and gave Porter a wry look.

"See you at the next Cabinet meeting," he said. Then he followed Traynor from the room, clutching his briefcase packed with political dynamite, destined for a Prime Minister already buckling under the strain.

NEW YORK. 09.22 HOURS

"The slimy, pox-rotten, shit-eating son of a bitch."

Pete Dunbarry threw his long, bony legs onto a chair and lit his twelfth cigarette of the morning.

"He was shitting horseshoes when he pulled that one off, the sly little prick."

Sitting two chairs away, a tough, thin-faced woman called Sheila Scutter shot him a look of mild skepticism that barely masked the contempt she felt underneath.

"Wouldn't have anything to do with the fact that he's a gutsy little guy who left us for CNN because we wouldn't give him a lousy two hundred a week more—and now he's scooped the lot of us, would it, Pete?"

"Fuck off, Sheila," Dunbarry growled.

Half a dozen people lounged around the conference table, watching a rerun of Marty Jantzen's footage of the hooded hijacker on the bridge of the *Britannia.* The footage that every TV news show in America coveted. The footage they all had to beat if they wanted their own piece of the story of the century. Something that wouldn't be easy since the announcement by the British War Office of a ten-mile total exclusion zone around the *Britannia.*

"The little swine just sneaked in under the door," Dunbarry huffed. "There's got to be another angle into this story that everybody else has missed. There's got to be a way that we can make everybody else eat shit."

Dunbarry was not a man who had ever allowed himself to be constrained by the iron shackles of good taste. Which was how he had become the front man for the most notorious tabloid TV news show in America. A show called *Flash,* whose toxic formula of sex, scandal, and violent death had proved that the lowest common denominator was much lower than anyone else had dared imagine. Cannibals, necrophiliacs, serial killers, child molesters—no one was so vile that he or she could not find a ready ear in Dunbarry while he pushed his show's ratings ever higher. Dunbarry had been the first man to show a snuff movie on TV. The first to screen an autopsy of a murdered rock star. The first to show a sex-change operation live. Dunbarry was not only prepared to crawl through the gutter for a story, he would take his audience on a tour through the sewer in a glass-bottomed boat. Now the story of the century had broken. A story that had it all: royalty, terror, violent death, and exotic location. And Dunbarry had been left at the starter's gate.

"If one of those bastards would rape the queen," he had declared at the start of the daily conference, "this story would have everything."

A tall, rakish-looking man his early fifties, with lank salt and pepper hair and a face polished by a lifetime's exposure to harsh sunlight and expensive whiskey, Dunbarry was a New York legend. A graduate of Australia's cutthroat school of tabloid newspapers, he had followed his boss to America to make a name for himself as the man who embarrassed the *National Enquirer.* In the media watering holes of Manhattan it was rumored that, to save space, Webster's dictionary had put a picture of Dunbarry beside the word *sleaze.* To dispute his image, Dunbarry always dressed like a gentleman. Every day he came to work dressed like a Wall Street broker and reeking of expensive aftershave. Or, as one of his staffers put it, "smelling like the shithouse at the Ritz."

Yet he shattered the façade every time he opened his mouth. His speech was a raw blend of back-street Australia and blue collar America, punctuated by the vulgarisms of both.

"All right, girls," he said, turning his attention from the tape back to the daily production meeting. "What have we got to beat that?"

Sheila Scutter, Dunbarry's producer, glanced down her story list while the rest of the crew waited apprehensively for Dunbarry's reaction.

"Well," she began, "we've got the sex-change body-building ex-nun from Pittsburgh who's been refused entry to the Mr. Universe contest."

"Yeah?" Dunbarry groaned. "But what's the fucking angle? I mean, what have we got that nobody else has got? If I've said it once, I've said it a million fucking times, where's the flash? The difference that lifts it out of the ordinary and makes it a *Flash* item?

Sheila looked across the table to the nervous young production assistant who had first dredged up the story, convinced she had a program topper.

"She, sorry, he . . . is going to sue the organizers of the contest for discrimination," the young woman volunteered. "And he'll pose nude if we pay him a few bucks. He's been taking steroids and he looks really, ah . . . great."

"Is he still a nun?" Dunbarry asked.

"Technically," the assistant said, "but he's been disowned by his, ah, her order."

"See if you can get the Mother Superior to say it's demonic possession. Satanism sells. Next?"

"We've got two women who killed and ate their husbands. Or, rather, parts of their husbands."

"Which parts?"

Sheila switched her gaze to another assistant, a woman with short hair and glasses called Heidi.

"I don't know," Heidi admitted, squirming. "I thought any parts would do. You just told me you wanted cannibal brides. It was pretty hard finding these two."

"Bullshit," Dunbarry sneered. "Cannibals are a dime a dozen in this city. If I walked out of this office, I could find you half a dozen in an hour. I bet there's hundreds of the bastards on Wall Street.

Look, I want you to find out if these women ate their husband's dicks. 'I ate my dead husband's weiner, cannibal bride confesses.' That's the angle, okay?"

Heidi flinched but nodded and made a note.

Sheila Scutter continued down the list until she had covered a dozen story possibilities, each more gruesome than the last.

"Bullshit," Dunbarry scoffed, lighting another cigarette. "They're all my ideas. Doesn't anybody have an original idea of their own? If it wasn't for me, this fucking program would be nowhere. What about the hijacking? Nobody gives a shit about anything else while that's going on? Doesn't anybody have any ideas about what we can do on the hijacking? What's Prince Charles doing? Is this going to send him over the edge? What about Princess Di? Has she gone out to buy a new dress? What about the Queen Mum? How's her ticker holding out? Are these guys going to knock off two queens for the price of one? Can we find somebody who knows about the *Britannia?* What about former captains? Former crew members? Some of those homos that got fired from the crew a few years back? Come on, let's dig a few of them up. . . ."

He stopped abruptly in mid-rant, his jaw slack, eyes shining. The room fell silent. The women around the table watched, perturbed and enthralled at the same time. They had seen it before. Pete Dunbarry was having one of his periodic attacks of inspiration. They waited, ready to deliver the appropriate measures of worship and sweat that would be required once he had given voice to his brilliance.

"I'm going to phone the *Britannia* and speak to the fucking hijackers," he said.

The women glanced apprehensively at each other.

"We can phone any ship we like, anywhere in the world," he went on. "It's easy. Satellite communications, ship-to-shore radio, all that bullshit. All we have to do is find the right number or the right radio frequency for the *Britannia,* and we can talk to them."

He looked feverishly around the room and settled on Sheila Scutter.

"Sheila, we're going to have to do this quickly and quietly before anybody else thinks of it."

"Won't this be a breach of security or something . . ." she began.

"Whose security?" Dunbarry snapped. "The Brits say we can't fly over their bloody royal yacht, but there's nothing in the rules about phone calls."

"Getting the number might be hard," Sheila added. "It's got to be high security, or every lunatic in the world would be phoning up."

"Maybe." Dunbarry pursed his lips. "Maybe not. Anybody can ring up Buckingham Palace. All that happens is you get a palace switchboard operator, and if they don't like the sound of you, they piss you off. If the *Britannia* operates the same way—then it's the hijackers who are running the switchboard now. And that's who I want to speak to."

"But . . ."

"No buts on this one, Sheila. Not another fucking word. I want everybody working on it. We'll start with a few telecommunications experts first. Christ, we're part of a major television network. Maybe our people can tell us how it's done. Get our London office on it. See if they can dig up anybody who served on the *Britannia,* particularly ex–radio operators. Tell them we'll pay ten grand for the right number, twenty if we have to. I've got a few old pals I can talk to in London myself. Let's hustle, girls—there's a fucking principle to uphold here."

Dunbarry turned back to the TV monitor. The sound was turned off and the tape had been frozen at a shot of the hooded hijacker aiming his rifle right down the eye of the camera.

"I don't know who you are, my friend," Dunbarry said, straightening his elegant shirt cuffs. "But you and I are going to be having a little chat soon. And then I'll show those fucking dilettantes at CNN how it's really done."

HMY *Britannia.* 10.10 hours

"The queen would like to have a word with you."

Gault looked around to see the small, solemn face of Lady Sarah behind him. He interrupted his inventory of their food supply, stepped back into the servery, and closed the pantry door. In normal times the pantry was used to serve light meals, breakfasts, and late suppers to the occupants of the royal apartments. It was always kept fully stocked and in addition to the usual luxury items there were emergency supplies in half a dozen sealed drums. There was no danger of the hostages on the royal deck starving to death in the near future.

"How is she?" Gault asked.

"Rather well, actually," Lady Sarah answered.

"And how about you?"

"A little bored." She shrugged. "You wouldn't think it possible unless you're actually caught up in one of these things, but the boredom is the worst part. I think I hate them for that most of all."

Gault smiled. Anyone who thought these people were weak could not have been more mistaken. Privileged, certainly. Pampered, undoubtedly. Soft, perhaps. But not weak. In the tense first hours of the hijacking, he had not heard a single murmur of complaint or a word of reproach from the queen, the duke, Lady Sarah, or Tony Stevens. Indeed, it was almost as though they enjoyed the opportunity to show what they were made of. Their stiff upper lips may have been out of practice, but they still functioned pretty well in an emergency. Gault had spoken to the duke several times, but he had seen little of the queen since that first desperate night of the hijacking. He had glimpsed her briefly the previous afternoon, stretching her legs in the royal corridor, arm in arm with her husband. He had retreated quickly into his room to allow them both a little privacy. The rest of the time Her Majesty had remained in her bedroom or in a temporary sitting room Lady Sarah and Tony had improvised in one of the guest apartments.

According to Lady Sarah, the queen had given up watching television for the moment. All the bedrooms had television sets and VCRs, and because the *Britannia*'s satellite communications were intact, the reception was perfect. Gault thought he knew how she must feel. Every channel was consumed by coverage of the hijacking. Every network had its experts and analysts, displaying maps of the region, diagrams of the *Britannia,* pointing out where the royal hostages would be, where the hijackers would be, explaining how the hijacking had taken place, and offering all manner of solutions, military and diplomatic, most of them wrong or reckless. News flashes crossed continually from Buckingham Palace to Downing Street to the White House to the UN and to Jidda with the arrival and departure of every new VIP. Overshadowing it all were two ominous images. The ongoing riots in Northern Ireland and the hooded man on the bridge of the *Britannia.* Gault had seen the CNN footage of the man on the bridge, only a hundred feet from where they were held hostage. And so had the queen. Which was why she may have preferred to leave the television switched off.

"All right." Gault smiled at Lady Sarah. "Better not keep her royal highness waiting."

He followed the queen's lady-in-waiting back down the royal corridor. Judy Stone was on duty, as always, outside the queen's door. She gave him an odd look.

"I've already spoken to her," she said cryptically. "We'll talk about it later."

Gault nodded, puzzled. Lady Sarah knocked on the door and waited for the familiar voice to invite them both in. A moment later Gault found himself sitting in a chintz-covered armchair, taking morning tea with the Queen of England.

"You're sure you've fully recovered from all that gas you inhaled?" she asked solicitously.

"Absolutely, ma'am," Gault answered. "Thank you."

"Are you quite sure you wouldn't feel more comfortable calling me Madge?" she asked.

It took Gault completely off guard, and he almost spilled his tea. Sitting in a chair to one side, Lady Sarah had to look away to keep from laughing.

"Ah . . . just an abbreviation, ma'am," Gault blustered. "A sort of . . . code. An expression of—"

"It's quite all right, Captain," the queen reassured him, her face and voice calm. "It isn't the worst name I've been called over the years. And it's really rather quaint . . . in its way."

In its way. The words burned through Gault's brain like a branding iron. He'd heard that the queen missed nothing. He promised himself never to be quite so smug again.

"Yes, ma'am," he added, feeling like a chastened schoolboy. "Thank you, ma'am."

He thought he saw just a trace of an upward curve at the corners of her mouth, the barest hint of a smile, but it passed so quickly he could have been mistaken. Then, he realized, she was teasing him, making a small point about manners and enjoying herself in the process. Gault sipped his tea in silence, resolved not to speak again until he was spoken to. He glanced up at the queen and smiled apologetically again. There was something terribly disquieting about sitting in this small room, having tea and talking person-to-person with the woman whose likeness appeared on every bank note, on every coin and stamp in the realm. A woman whose features were engraved on the public consciousness but whose true personality would always be a mystery.

"There's something I'd like to ask you," the queen intruded on his thoughts.

"Yes, ma'am?"

"My husband and I . . ." She hesitated and smiled at herself. "Why is it I always feel as though I'm delivering a speech when I say those words," she reflected out loud. "Never mind. Philip and I would like to know if it would be possible to speak to our children by telephone or radio . . . in private?"

Gault hesitated. He was surprised, but when he thought about it, he realized that it wasn't an unreasonable request, given the circumstances.

"It's certainly possible, ma'am," he answered. "I wouldn't advise using the ship's telephone, of course, because you could be overheard by the . . . people on the bridge. But you can use my radio to speak to the *Hotspur* and they can relay you anywhere in the world. The wave band we're using now is already on an encrypter, so it will be safe as far as the *Hotspur.* From there they can give you a secure relay to London and, of course, Naval Intelligence would ensure there was no eavesdropping."

"Good." The queen nodded her head, satisfied. Then she turned the conversation in a new direction.

"You have already spoken to my husband about our situation, I believe?"

"Yes, ma'am."

The Duke of Edinburgh had made it clear that so far as he was concerned, there ought to be no compromise with the hijackers. However, Gault had reminded him, the ultimate decision was not in their hands. This was not just another hostage. The queen was the titular head of government. She had a constitutional duty to the state first and a private duty to her family second. Her life had never been her own. And now, neither would her death.

"I believe the hijackers have demanded the withdrawal of all British troops from Northern Ireland by noon next Thursday. Otherwise, they say, they will blow us all up. Is that correct?"

"Yes, ma'am."

"That ultimatum has not been made public yet, has it?"

"Not to my knowledge, ma'am."

"But, given the nature of the media, it is probably only a matter of time?"

"Yes, ma'am," Gault answered candidly. "I suspect it is."

"Then I think it imperative that I make my views on the situation known," she said. "I wonder if you and Lieutenant Stone would mind arranging for Philip and me to speak with our children at six o'clock this evening?"

"Certainly, ma'am." Gault nodded. "We'll do our best."

"And after that . . ."

"Ma'am?"

"I shall want to speak to the Prime Minister."

"Yes, ma'am." At this bit of news Gault could not keep the concern from his face. He saw no reason to dispute the sovereign's right to speak to her family or her Prime Minister, but he was worried that a conversation with Downing Street could impose a new and unwelcome political twist on the situation. Some unforeseen complication that the hijackers might not like and that had the capacity to make the situation worse.

"I can understand your concern, Captain," she said, reading his eyes. "There are, however, certain affairs of state that must be discussed with my eldest son and the Prime Minister. You should also know that I will be making my position known about our situation here. My husband and I both feel it would be morally indefensible to negotiate with terrorists on our behalf. The government must know this before the demands of the hijackers become known publicly. Otherwise, there will be catastrophe in Northern Ireland. The Crown cannot allow that to happen."

Gault took a breath. He knew when he had been offered this assignment that, inevitably, he would become privy to certain facts about royal life. Most of them, he anticipated, would fall into the category of fascinating trivia. Never in his wildest dreams had he expected to become a party to such momentous affairs of state as those that were unfolding before him now.

"However," the queen continued in a voice so calm that it seemed impossible she could be talking about matters of such historic import, "I am bound to say that it is not only the avoidance of catastrophe in Northern Ireland that concerns me. I should feel the same if these people had no other motive but the destruction of the Crown. We must not bow to terror. That is my conviction and that is my belief. It is the position I take personally and it is the position I must take as sovereign.

"You see, Captain . . ." She paused for a moment and gave him a small smile. "When all the pomp and circumstance have been stripped away, what my position really comes down to is . . . duty. Duty by example. For me, it has always been this way. It is what I was taught when I was a little girl and it is what I have always believed is right. And now I would be forsaking my duty as sovereign if I permitted the government to negotiate with terrorists on my behalf. Britannia, the symbol of our nationhood, cannot kneel to terror. And she will not. And all the people of the world will see . . . Britannia will not kneel."

London. 10.05 hours

The Prime Minister looked worse than Porter had expected. He looked old and bowed, as though the crisis had already beaten him.

"Come in, Malcolm," he greeted the chief of CTC tiredly. "You wouldn't have the solution to all my problems there in your briefcase, would you?"

Porter smiled thinly and sat down across the desk from the PM. Outside, the sun was trying to break through the rain clouds, but a palpable cloud of gloom still hung over the capital. From the corner of his eye Porter could see a photograph of Winston Churchill glowering contemptuously down at them both, as though he knew the solution to their problem. If only they were wise enough and strong enough to see it.

"I'm sure you've been told this already," Porter began, injecting a subtle but unmistakable note of warning into his voice, "but if you don't make some time to get some sleep soon, you're going to fall over. And then you'll be no damn good to anybody."

"I know, I know," the PM concurred. "John Traynor has been telling me the same thing. I think there's an unspoken contest between the two of us to see who drops dead first."

Porter opened his mouth to speak again, but the Prime Minister raised his hand.

"For me, everything stops at six o'clock this evening," he said. "I've promised Traynor that I'll go to bed, bolt the door, take the phone off the hook, and I won't be disturbed until after midnight, even if they do blow the bloody yacht up."

Porter gave him a small, grim smile. The PM had to be tired. He wasn't usually inclined toward graveyard humor.

"Charles Ingham thinks this will be the end of me, you know," the PM added. "What do you think?"

"I think Charles is a little too concerned with political gamesmanship at a time when it doesn't really matter who wins or loses as long as we get out of this with the queen, the Duke of Edinburgh and, we hope, Northern Ireland intact."

"He doesn't think that's possible."

"I know."

"He's already talked to you?"

"Next door, while we waited."

"I suspect he's right." The PM sighed resignedly. "It will be one or the other. Either we lose the queen or we lose Northern Ireland. And I simply cannot reconcile myself to forfeiting the life of the sovereign . . . whatever the cost. My enemies in Parliament could not have devised a more cruel trap if they had set out deliberately to destroy me, Malcolm. Charles says he's going to push for a vote in Cabinet."

"Don't invite him to the next Cabinet meeting," Porter said. "We didn't need him at the last one."

The PM smiled faintly.

"He'll only leak it to the press or the Opposition."

"So, what have you decided?"

"Oh"—he shrugged—"I've made my position clear and I'll stick to it. If they want to throw my policy out, they'll have to throw me out with it. And, if they do that, quite frankly it would come as a relief. I'm perfectly happy for someone else to make the decision to abandon the Queen of England to her assassins."

"No, you're not," Porter responded sharply. "You wouldn't be able to live with yourself. I'm afraid history has chosen you, old chap, and you're stuck with it."

"Afraid?" The PM singled out Porter's unconscious choice of words. "Are you really afraid that history has chosen me and not someone else, Malcolm?"

Porter looked into the Prime Minister's blood-rimmed eyes and wondered if Ingham was right. He wondered if the PM was cracking under the strain.

"What I'm afraid of," Porter answered quickly, "is the mood of inevitable disaster that seems to have overtaken some people. We can save this situation, sir. I'm sure of it. The first step is to reject any notion of inevitability."

He paused and nodded to the portrait of Churchill on the wall.

"As Winnie said in the summer of 1940, the situation is hopeless only when we admit it is hopeless. We already know everything that can go wrong. It's time to concentrate on what can go right. We have to take control of the situation away from the hijackers, reverse the momentum—and then their defeat becomes inevitable."

"Can we save the life of the sovereign without giving these bastards what they want?" the Prime Minister asked flatly.

"Yes, sir," Porter answered with equal certainty. "I think we can."

He rummaged in his briefcase and pulled out two sheets of

printout paper. It had taken him all the previous day to map out his proposal and boil it down to a sequence of short, easily digested paragraphs. He slid the papers across the desk and waited. As tired as the Prime Minister was, it took him only a minute to read them. When he had finished he looked up at Porter with an expression of weary foreboding on his face.

"What you are suggesting is the application of an extraordinary amount of violence, Malcolm. With the queen and the Duke of Edinburgh in the thick of it."

"The maximum amount of violence in the minimum amount of time," Porter agreed soberly. "That is the only way we can succeed, Prime Minister. While Her Majesty may be indispensable, the royal yacht isn't. As long as we don't sink the *Britannia,* at least until after we have rescued the queen and Prince Philip, what happens to the yacht isn't really that important, is it, sir?"

"No," the PM acknowledged. "Under the circumstances, I'd have to say that's true."

"The only way we can remove the immediate threat to Their Majesties is by disabling the hijackers and their explosives within a matter of seconds," Porter went on. "That means we have to identify and locate every hijacker on the ship, target each one individually, and take out every one of them simultaneously. If we do that, we may not have to worry about the explosives. No hijackers means no one to fire a switch."

"Yes, I know," the PM answered. "But can we do that? What guarantees—"

"Let's concentrate on the positive side of things first, shall we, sir," Porter interrupted. "The answer to your question is yes. We can use satellite image processors from space and thermal image enhancers on the surface to identify and locate the hijackers above and below decks. We already know the location of the queen, Prince Philip, their two personal assistants, and their SAS bodyguards. We have a good idea where the other hostages are being held, and we'll get more on that as we go along. It all helps. We'll have to make use of at least one of our SAS people on board to assist us in confirming the location of hijackers and other crew members who may be in hiding below decks."

The PM glanced down at the printout on his desk.

"Presumably you mean Captain Gault?" he said. "We can't leave Her Majesty without protection."

"Captain Gault is not only the obvious choice, he is the best choice, sir. He knows the *Britannia* and he is highly experienced at this kind of thing. He can move around the yacht undetected and provide us with invaluable supplementary intelligence. I would also want him to try to locate and disable the explosives, which would give us added insurance once the assault gets under way. At the very least I would want him to get the word out to all the hostages that they must lie low when the assault begins. Because, once the action begins, the damage will be quite substantial."

"Quite"—the Prime Minister hesitated—"substantial?"

"Yes, sir," Porter added. "Their Majesties will be safe where they are, but we have to proceed on the assumption that everything around them will go."

"What do you mean, exactly, by . . . everything?" the PM asked, a note of apprehension creeping into his voice.

"The only way to guarantee that the hijackers cannot do anything harmful to Her Majesty is to wipe out every single one of them in a split second," Porter said. "Before they have time to think or act. And the only way we can do that is to roll a wave of violence over the superstructure of the royal yacht in such a way that every living thing beneath it is annihilated."

"Good God," the PM breathed. "What . . . do you mean, a missile of some kind?"

"No, sir," Porter answered flatly. "Something a little more precise than that. Once we identify and locate the hijackers, we need to take out every one of them with pinpoint accuracy. However, most of them will not be so thoughtful as to put themselves out in the open for us. Those who are above deck will conceal themselves about the superstructure, behind bulkheads and hatches, wherever they feel safe. That means we must use a weapon, or, rather, a number of weapons, that will penetrate thick metal plate and destroy the man hidden on the other side instantly. In the case of the men on the bridge, our weapon must have the capacity to wipe out everything on the bridge with a single shot. Unfortunately that means most of the bridge and the surrounding superstructure will have to go. We can't take the chance that someone might survive long enough to throw a switch while we get off a second shot."

"What kind of weapon can do all that?" the PM asked doubtfully. "You're talking about some kind of armor-piercing shell, the type of thing a tank or a ship's gun might fire. I'm aware we have to expect some damage but, good God almighty, man, you can't unload a barrage of heavy artillery shells onto the royal yacht."

"Quite so." Porter smiled thinly. "Fortunately there is a weapon that will give us the results we want without filling the *Britannia* full of unacceptably large holes. A weapon with the range and precision of a sniper's rifle and the ability to deliver a small but extremely powerful shell with a high-penetration capacity that will obliterate a highly specific area and anyone unfortunate enough to be standing in the immediate vicinity."

"What, some kind of super gun?"

"Only in terms of performance, sir," Porter added. "The weapon itself is only slightly larger than a conventional sniper's rifle, and the shell is not much larger than a shotgun casing."

"Good Lord," the PM muttered. "And it can do all you claim it can do?"

"It is extremely accurate up to a distance of three miles. It can penetrate two inches of armored steel, hit a target the size of a man's eye, and destroy an area the size of a truck. Our SAS people used them behind the lines in Iraq to blow up Scuds from a considerable distance."

The PM took off his glasses and tried to rub some life back into his tired face.

"All right, Malcolm," he said. "Assuming your . . . super gun, or whatever it is, can do the job, that takes care of the hijackers on the upper deck. It doesn't account for those who might still be hiding below decks. And it doesn't guarantee the disablement of the explosives. We can't just assume our Captain Gault will be successful in locating and disabling all or any of them, for that matter."

"No, sir," Porter agreed. "That is why we must have men standing by to board the yacht the instant those shells go in."

"Standing by, Malcolm?" The PM looked over the top of his glasses at Porter. "In the water?"

"Yes, sir. As my plan indicates, prior to the positioning of the forces that will take out the hijackers on the upper deck, we will move several SBS units into position alongside the *Britannia.* The entire operation will be coordinated by radio from an AWAC circling overhead. The moment the first shells go in, these SBS units will board the royal yacht and move quickly through the vessel, neutralizing all opposition and insuring the disablement of all explosive charges. Captain Gault will be waiting to expedite their progress. Also, at the very same moment SAS units will take off by helicopter from our warships and fly to the *Britannia* to take off Their Majesties. Comacchio will be standing by on the water, and they will follow the SBS onto the royal yacht. Assuming it all works according to my plan, all meaningful opposition on board the *Britannia* will be wiped out in less than one minute. The SAS will have Their Majesties in the air two minutes after the first shells go in. Comacchio will take care of the mopping-up. Even if the worst-case scenario does happen and some charges are detonated, the royal yacht will not go down in under two minutes. We can make it work, sir . . . and luck has nothing to do with it."

The PM gave him a wan smile.

"I don't know, Malcolm," he said faintly. "I really don't know. We have only a few days. Are you absolutely certain you can have all this in place in that time? You said yourself in Cabinet, the hijackers obviously aren't fools and they'll be using the *Britannia*'s own equipment to detect any kind of approach or unusual activity in the air or the water. How can you be so sure you can coordinate all of this and move all these men and equipment into position without the hijackers getting even an inkling of what is going on?"

"Our men are up to the job, sir. All we need is the equipment."

"Oh." The PM looked surprised. "Is there a problem with that?"

"Somewhat," Porter added wryly. "As I have indicated, some of the equipment is highly specialized, highly sophisticated . . . and we haven't got it."

"Oh, and who does?"

"The Americans."

"Who else?" the PM breathed resignedly. He recalled the offer he'd had from the President of the United States only hours earlier. "I suppose this means we have to go back to the Americans cap in hand and ask them if they'd mind helping us out . . . again."

"I don't want to keep paraphrasing Churchill," Porter replied. "But I'd make a pact with the devil himself if it would help us get the job done. And we could do much worse than have the Americans as our allies."

"You're quite right, Malcolm, of course," the PM acknowledged. "It's only wounded national pride, I suppose. Have we become so poor a nation we can't even protect our own head of state?"

"Hardly the point at this stage of the game, sir," Porter murmured.

The PM nodded but said nothing. Instead, he leaned forward on the desk, cupped his hands in front of his mouth to stifle an exhausted yawn, and closed his eyes for what seemed like a long time. Porter waited. The only sound in the room was the sonorous tick of a grandfather clock in a corner, relentlessly counting down their options. At last the PM put both hands back down on the desk and looked up.

"I don't know that you will ever get an opportunity to put your plan into action, Malcolm," he said. "But it would be negligent of me not to let you get it ready—just in case."

Porter nodded. His face remained impassive, but inside he was delighted. For a few dreadful moments he had feared the Prime Minister had been about to balk.

"As it happens," the PM added, "I spoke to the President last night. He made a very generous offer of assistance. It looks like we'll need to take him up on it. So, I want you to be the official liaison between Downing Street and the White House for the duration of the crisis. The President has already cleared the way for us to communicate directly with the chairman of the joint chiefs about whatever we may need in terms of equipment and expertise to insure a successful outcome."

He paused for a moment and looked at Porter with a focus the CTC chief had not seen when he first came into the room.

"It's a good plan, Malcolm," the PM said quietly. "Perhaps under other circumstances I would not hesitate to use it. But you understand my position. I will not authorize the use of force to resolve the situation unless all else fails."

"I want clear authority over all special forces units," Porter added quickly, eager to get out of the PM's office before he changed his mind. "I'll need access to all intelligence reports—and I must have a floating operations base on the scene."

"John Traynor will make sure you see everything that I've seen," the PM said. "I'll see that you get everything else you need. Admiral Harriman has been running naval operations from Northwood since the War Cabinet meeting yesterday. Colonel Quillan flew out to Saudi Arabia yesterday afternoon. He took the negotiator with him. We settled on MI5's man. Chap called Pryne. Professor of psychology from Cambridge, I believe."

"What are his instructions?" Porter asked.

"To tell the hijackers we're ready to deal. He'll tell them that it is not possible to comply with their demands in such a short span of time, of course. He'll try to buy us more time."

Porter nodded. The negotiator could offer the hijackers the world if it would buy more time. Something told him it wouldn't.

"I'm worried about our ships," he said abruptly.

"*Bristol, Newcastle, Ardent,* and *Adder* will be there sometime tomorrow," the PM said.

"It's not the number of ships," Porter explained. "It's the type of ships. They can enforce the security cordon effectively enough, but they're not really suited to the type of thing I have in mind. This operation will involve a hell of a lot of helicopter activity, and we can't take chances with warships that can handle only one or two helicopters at a time. I'm afraid your old nemesis Teddy Lawson was right. We need an aircraft carrier or a helicopter carrier out there."

"I'm afraid we just haven't got one," the PM said dully.

"The Americans have carriers in the region," Porter added.

"Indeed they do," the Prime Minister recalled. He paused to look through the intelligence reports in front of him. "Here it is, the USS *Carl Vinson.* The biggest carrier in the U.S. Navy, I believe. It left Diego Garcia twenty-four hours ago. Should be in the Gulf of Aden tomorrow morning. That do you?"

"Very nicely," Porter answered. "There is something else I'll need from you too."

The Prime Minister waited.

"We have the navy, SAS, and Comacchio out there," Porter said. "All in different places, all with different chains of command. Coordination is the key to the success of this operation. That means someone has to coordinate all of them. That someone has to be me."

"That someone is me," the Prime Minister replied firmly. "I will listen to all advice from all my military commanders. Then I and I alone will make the final decision on whether we use force."

"Understood, sir," Porter responded. "But, with respect, we need an operational commander to coordinate all these assets on the scene. What you have done so far is to respond to the crisis by sending our best troops to the area. Ultimately we must decide how to use them. And that will have to be decided quickly . . . at the scene."

The Prime Minister shook his head.

"I trust your judgment in military matters, Malcolm. I trust you personally. I know you will serve me well. But I do not want this plan to acquire an irreversible momentum of its own."

"It won't, sir." Porter sought to reassure him. "No one will take a single step inside that military exclusion zone without your order. But should you decide to give that order, we must be ready. All our units must be in place and all must know exactly what part they will play."

The PM nodded.

"I'll tell Admiral Harriman and Colonel Quillan that you're in charge of overall planning of the rescue operation and that they are to cooperate fully with you. I will also instruct them that you have no power to launch this operation. That power will rest solely with me . . . and the Cabinet."

"Understood, sir," Porter acknowledged. He closed his briefcase and moved to get up.

"When do you expect to leave, Malcolm?"

"I'll need another day or two to prepare things here. I assume this negotiator chap, Pryne, can get by without me for another day. Perhaps tomorrow night?"

"I'll order the RAF to have a plane ready. Call me before you leave?"

"Not if you're in bed, sir."

The Prime Minister smiled and stood up to shake Porter's hand.

"Good luck, Malcolm," he said. "And I hope you're right about your people. At a time like this we need supermen."

Porter smiled faintly. But there was something in the Prime Minister's tone that gave him pause, something that made him stop with his hand still on the door handle.

"Prime Minister," he began awkwardly. "This might seem like a strange thing to say, but I'm curious. Yesterday you indicated that a military option was all but out of the question. You said you would find a negotiated settlement, no matter how humiliating. What changed your mind?"

A shadow passed across the Prime Minister's face as though Porter had touched an inflamed nerve.

"Yesterday," the PM said, "logic told me we could save lives by giving these people what they want. Sadly, it seems, they are not operating according to any logic that we understand. They may, in fact, already have decided to kill the queen."

"What makes you so certain of that now?" Porter asked.

"At midnight last night, Jidda time," the PM answered, "the hijackers murdered Admiral Marchant in full view of the officers and men on board HMS *Hotspur.* If I had any hopes of finding a rational solution to this crisis, Malcolm, I'm afraid they may have died at that moment."

HMY *Britannia.* 18.10 hours

"The call go through okay?" Judy Stone asked.

"Crystal-clear." Gault nodded. "I suspect they're going to be a while."

He had just stepped out of the queen's sitting room after setting up the three-way link between the *Britannia, Hotspur,* and Buckingham Palace. Judy waited with her own radio clipped to her belt, just in case. Lady Sarah and Tony Stevens stood nearby, drinking coffee, waiting in case they, too, were needed. All four of them understood the importance of the conversation that was under way on the other side of the wall. That it would probably be the one and only time the queen and Prince Philip would be able to communicate with the other members of their family before the crisis had run its course. Sarah and Tony had been promised their own calls later that evening, and their families were standing by at Northwood.

Gault glanced around, then leaned down close to Judy.

"Come with me for a moment, would you?" he whispered. "I need to talk to you."

She hesitated briefly, then followed him along the corridor toward the elevator shaft. The door to the shaft was blocked by an armored screen, just like all the others that kept them sealed tightly inside their floating bunker.

"I've heard from Quillan," Gault said, referring to the commanding officer of 22 SAS.

"He's here?"

"On the *Hotspur.* He called while you were with Madge. He's got two teams with him."

"That's reassuring." Judy gave a sigh of controlled relief.

"He's had word from London. Seems they agree with me. They want me to go outside and have a sniff around."

"Damn," Judy muttered. Then she took a breath and composed herself. "Okay," she added. "I don't agree with it, but . . . if that's what they want . . ."

"I can bypass the master switch easily enough," Gault added. "Then I can move the screen by hand. Once inside the lift, there's a hatch in the floor and I can climb down into the lift shaft."

Judy listened, but the expression on her face showed that she wasn't happy. Gault coaxed her around the corner, out of sight of the two royal servants in the corridor. The elevator alcove was small, and with the two of them squeezed in, there wasn't much space between them. Judy looked tired, Gault thought. She wore no makeup and there were shadows under her eyes, but her eyes themselves were clear and alert. Her hair was pulled straight back and knotted tightly at the nape of her neck.

"Are you wearing perfume?" Gault asked suddenly.

"What?"

He shrugged and gave her an awkward smile.

"No," she answered. "Why do you ask?"

"Just curious," Gault added. "Everything else in here smells stale. You smell . . . different. You smell like you just got out of the bath."

"Meaning what?"

"Meaning . . ." His words trailed away and he started to look embarrassed. "Meaning you smell nice, that's all."

"Want me to sweat a bit more so I smell like you?"

"I don't—" he hesitated. "Do I?"

Judy smiled.

"So when do you plan to go?" she asked.

"You'll be okay here on your own?"

"I've done it before," she answered.

He smiled and slowly shook his head.

"Are you ever going to give me a break?" he asked.

"Are you ever going to give *me* a break?" she answered.

"I'll go sometime after midnight," he decided. "Give myself as much time as I can. God knows what they've got rigged up out there."

"Okay," she answered. "I'll keep the home fires burning. Have a pot of tea and your slippers ready for you when you get back."

Then she turned and walked back down the corridor. Gault watched her go, watched the way she walked, the way her body moved, lithe and confident. Not a sign that she was the slightest bit aware of the way she affected him.

6 By Appointment to Her Majesty

THE WHITE HOUSE, MAY 18. 10.22 HOURS

"Sir?" The President's national security adviser, Bob Pike, stepped discreetly into the Oval Office to interrupt his boss's meeting with General Kurt Coburg, chairman of the joint chiefs of staff. "You wanted me to let you know as soon as the director got here?"

The President looked at Coburg.

"Is there anything more you need from me, Kurt? Anything more I can do to kick things along?"

The general, a burly, leather-skinned man with iron-gray hair, shook his head and reached down for his briefcase.

"I can take it from here, sir. I've alerted my staff to expect a call from Sir Malcolm Porter's office at any time. We're ready when he is."

"That's excellent, Kurt," the President nodded. Then he motioned the general to stay seated. "I think it might be a good idea for you to sit in on this too. I've asked the director of the FBI to give us a report on the reaction of the Irish community to all of this. Obviously much of that will depend on what happens, militarily, in Northern Ireland and the Middle East, and I'd be grateful for any insights you might be able to offer."

"Whatever I can do, sir," Coburg acknowledged, and leaned back in his chair.

Pike stepped out of the office and reappeared a moment later with Charles Guthrie, director of the FBI. Guthrie was a tall man with stooped shoulders who looked older than his thirty-seven years because he was almost completely bald except for a narrow horseshoe of hair that was so blond it was almost invisible. He was also the youngest director of the FBI since the lurid J. Edgar Hoover, a distinction he had earned following a meteoric career as a federal prosecutor in Chicago. He exchanged greetings with the President and General Coburg, then took a seat alongside the chairman of the joint chiefs. It felt cool in the Oval Office, but Guthrie noticed that he and Coburg were the only two wearing jackets. The President leaned back in his high-backed swivel chair, put one leg across the other, and absently tapped an expensive gold pen against the heel of his shoe. Guthrie thought he looked cool and composed in his pristine white shirt and his preppie red and blue striped tie. The FBI director smiled to himself. He was about to change all of that, he knew. He snapped open his briefcase, pulled out a file, set in on his lap, and proceeded to deliver his report in a precise and portentous monotone that would have been numbing were it not for the compelling nature of the subject.

"Our first step was to call in surveillance updates on all Irish-American organizations and personnel with links to the Irish Republican Army," he began. "The largest and most active of these are the Irish National Caucus and the Irish Northern Aid Committee, better known as Noraid. Since 1973 we have successfully rotated a number of undercover agents through both organizations with the result that, directly and indirectly, we have influenced the way both those organizations conduct their affairs. The Irish National Caucus in particular has distanced itself from illegal arms buying and concerns itself instead with raising money for social programs within Northern Ireland. Undoubtedly, some of that money is skimmed when it reaches Northern Ireland, but the British are aware of this and have their own methods of tracking it once it gets there. Noraid, however, remains actively committed to the Provisional IRA and continues to raise money on its behalf through 109 chapters across the United States and through an extensive network of contacts inside the trade union movement, predominantly the longshoremen's unions which have a high Irish-American membership and have provided safe haven for many IRA fugitives, most of them hit men, since the early 1970s."

Guthrie was about to continue, when the President leaned forward in his chair.

"Do we have any idea how many IRA killers the longshoremen's unions have sheltered?" he asked, a note of incredulity in his voice.

"Eleven that we know of, Mr. President," the FBI director answered. "There may be more. There's no way of knowing how many more unless they run afoul of the law. They're usually smuggled in on cargo ships from the Irish Republic and protected by the union once they get here."

"I presume the Justice Department knows about this?" the President added.

"Oh, yes, sir," Guthrie added. "But so far we've extradited only one known IRA hit man into the hands of the British authorities. It's always been a very sensitive issue politically and much depends on the demeanor of the courts at the time . . . I'll be coming to that in a moment."

The President nodded dourly and leaned back in his chair.

"At its peak, from 1980 to 1982, Noraid raised nearly a million dollars a year," Guthrie went on. "Most of this went on weapons. Since then the amount has dropped to around $300,000 per year, though the organization has found other ways of obtaining arms. This is largely a result of the bureau's activities. In the early 1970s the bureau orchestrated a series of sting operations intended to relieve Noraid of both cash and arms intended for the IRA. These operations were successful in some respects but unsuccessful in others and led to unforeseen consequences. The bureau was able to disrupt the flow of arms but was singularly unsuccessful in obtaining convictions against the individuals involved in the procurement of those arms. For every ten individuals charged, the bureau was lucky to get one conviction. This was due in large part to the reluctance of juries to convict and the willingness of judges to show leniency to individuals accused of supporting the cause of Irish unity."

Guthrie paused and looked up from his notes.

"This is a problem that endures to the present day, Mr. President. I am sorry to say that there is a great deal of willful ignorance in the United States when it comes to the situation in Northern Ireland. The common perception is of a struggle between the forces of freedom, represented by the IRA, and the forces of oppression, represented by the British. This simplistic scenario has found a willing constituency of belief in the United States. Because of our country's past, no doubt, Americans are highly susceptible to the notion of the British as evil oppressors and the IRA as brave patriots. Let us not forget, many Irish migrants to the United States brought their anti-British sentiments with them and propagated those sentiments successfully through several generations so that today ideas that are often nothing more than prejudices are widely taken as truths. Noraid has been extremely skillful in the way it has exploited this ready reservoir of American sympathy. In many respects, Mr. President, American popular opinion is the IRA's greatest propaganda victory. Noraid's fund-raising events tend to be emotional and manipulative in the extreme. Organizers know how to push all the right emotional buttons. They create an atmosphere of Irish folksiness with songs and ballads and they focus on historic events like the Easter Uprising. They also like to enlist the aid of celebrities to help them loosen the public's purse strings. There seems to be no shortage of gullible individuals from the worlds of music, film, and politics to promote the cause of Irish unity. The former governor of New York, Mr. Hugh Carey, former House Speaker Tip O'Neill, Senator Daniel Moynihan, and Senator Edward Kennedy have all been happy to act as mouthpieces for the IRA at one time or another. In most cases these individuals have withdrawn their support once the true character of the IRA has been revealed to them, sometimes by bureau personnel. However, many Americans still do not understand that the IRA today bears no relation to the IRA of fifty years ago. Noraid is very careful to conceal any mention of the IRA's Marxist agenda and its connections to other Socialist terrorist organizations around the world. Noraid exploits Irish-Catholic communities throughout North America but makes no mention of the fact that the Catholic Church condemns the IRA as a sacriligeous organization. And there is never any mention of the IRA's terror-bombing of innocent men, women, and children."

Guthrie paused to take a sip from a glass of water offered to him by Bob Pike. The only sound in the room was the faint rumble of traffic on Pennsylvania Avenue.

"Due to the success of its propaganda campaigns in the United States, many of Noraid's organizers remain free to continue their illegal activities in support of the IRA," he continued. "The major difference today is that they conduct those activities in small, independent cells outside the Noraid organization. This has made them more difficult to infiltrate. Instead of buying and stealing weapons themselves, they have established contacts with a number of criminal organizations which will do it for them and then they take care of the shipping end of things. The bureau brought its biggest case against Noraid in 1980, when it charged a number of individuals involved in the shipment of large quantities of M-60s, M-16s, M-79 grenade launchers, twenty-mm cannons, and more than a million rounds of ammunition to the IRA. This was an entire network of people connected to Noraid, the illegal arms racket, and the Mob. When the case went to trial, they claimed the whole thing was a CIA frame-up. The jury bought it and they all walked. Subsequently, a number of those weapons were traced to the killings of British soldiers and police officers in Northern Ireland and on the British mainland."

Guthrie let his last sentence hang in the air like an accusation. It wasn't often he got an opportunity to tell the President of the United States what a farce his country's handling of the IRA had been over the years, and he wanted to make the most of it. The President shifted uneasily in his chair, and Guthrie moved to press home his main point.

"It has to be said that due to the consistently poor conviction rate that has resulted from the cases brought to trial—despite overwhelming evidence of guilt—and due to the absence of any firm commitment by successive administrations in addressing the activities of the IRA inside the United States, the FBI has had no alternative but to downgrade its policy toward Noraid. At this point I'd have to say that the bureau plays no more than a harassing role in relation to Noraid's activities. They know we're watching them and they know we've infiltrated them and so they've become more careful. But the fact is that Noraid continues to ship large quantities of American arms to the conflict in Northern Ireland. Indeed, the Armalite remains the principal assault weapon of the IRA."

"All right, Charles, I take your point," the President interjected testily. "Though I hardly think it fair to bring down the sins of previous administrations on my head. What I need to know is what we can expect from the current situation."

"We can expect a number of developments from the current situation, Mr. President," Guthrie answered, unfazed. "As unfair as it may seem, the bill has come due for the failures and inadequacies of the past twenty years and that bill will have to be paid by us."

A new and ominous silence stole into the room.

"The first consequence we have to address is that some of the weapons used in the hijacking of the British royal yacht may well have originated here in the United States."

"Jesus . . ." the President mumbled.

Even General Coburg's impassive face registered a brief flicker of shock.

"What do you want from me, Charles?" the President asked.

"If we can establish a link between Noraid and the hijacking of the *Britannia,* this would be our best chance yet to cripple the organization in the United States. It's long overdue and it has to be done. I would like to focus the resources of the bureau on those individuals we know have been involved in arms shipments to Ireland so that we can bring charges that will stick. To this end I think it would be useful if you, Mr. President, could make some kind of public statement condemning this latest act of terrorism in which you make it very clear to the American people exactly what kind of an organization the IRA really is. That might put a crack in the bedrock of support for the IRA in this country and give us a better chance of winning convictions when these cases come to trial."

The President nodded thoughtfully but said nothing.

"Such a statement might also be effective in containing political turmoil here at home."

"You're expecting some?" the President asked sharply.

For the first time since he had sat down, Guthrie smiled, though it was not a smile calculated to inspire confidence in any of the men gathered in that room.

"Oh." The FBI director paused, relishing the moment. "I think I can guarantee it."

"What do you know for sure, Charles?" Bob Pike interjected.

Guthrie picked up his files, took out half a dozen sheets of printout paper, and slid them across the desk toward the President.

"That is a list of all those Noraid chapters that are in the process of organizing demonstrations across the United States in support of the IRA and in favor of a British withdrawal from Northern Ireland."

The President took the papers and scanned them quickly, his face lengthening perceptibly as he did so.

"As you will see, sir," Guthrie went on for the benefit of Pike and Coburg. "Major demonstrations are planned for the next few days in Washington, Baltimore, Buffalo, Detroit, New York, Boston, Philadelphia, Pittsburgh, Chicago, San Francisco, and a dozen other places in between. My list includes names of the organizers and those public figures who have been invited to speak at those demonstrations."

The President looked up bleakly.

"I might have guessed Callaghan's name would be here," he said.

Democratic Senator Pat Callaghan from Massachusetts was Noraid's most prominent apologist in the United States. An Irish-American and former chief of the longshoreman's union whose support came mainly from the blue-collar unions of the Boston waterfront, Callaghan had delivered some of the most inflammatory speeches ever heard in the United States in support of an unconditional British withdrawal from Northern Ireland.

"Callaghan will speak at the Boston rally on Friday morning," Guthrie added.

The President nodded. Friday was only two days away.

"I have something to add on that point, Mr. President."

It was Bob Pike.

"I got word from the Hill about an hour ago that Callaghan is expected to table a motion in the Senate sometime today, calling for the British to withdraw."

"That's just what we need," the President breathed.

"He really knows how to do it," Pike concurred.

"All the more reason for you to make a strong statement in support of the forces of reason, Mr. President," Guthrie added quickly.

The President sighed and slowly nodded his head.

"I plan to make a statement," he said. "I have no difficulty condemning such an outrageous act of terrorism as this. But I'll have to consider your other recommendation carefully, Charles. The last thing I want to do is to make the situation worse. These rallies are provocative enough under the circumstances, and I don't want to create a situation that would see them escalate into full-scale riots. Perhaps it would be more circumspect if we let them just burn off a little steam first. We can consider the merits of an expanded statement on the political situation in Northern Ireland a little later . . . when we've seen how things unfold in the next few days."

"With respect, Mr. President," Guthrie persisted. "What you say now could have a direct bearing on what does unfold in the next few days."

The President looked at Guthrie beneath darkening brows.

"Most of the thirty million Irish-Americans in the United States live in the Northeast and Great Lakes regions," Guthrie added. "Only about one third of them are Catholic, those who constitute Noraid's primary support base. The remaining two thirds are Protestant. Historically they have not been as volatile as Catholic Irish-Americans. Something like this might change their disposition. The potential for violence is there now, Mr. President. If the situation deteriorates in Northern Ireland to the point of civil war, as well it might, then we'd have to expect a reflection of that here in the United States."

The President looked to General Coburg, who had remained as still and as silent as a statue through all that had been said so far.

"General Coburg?" the President said. "What do you think of the prognosis for civil war in Northern Ireland?"

Coburg shifted heavily in his seat and thought about it.

"I don't want to duck the issue, Mr. President," he began. "But that's a political question. I wouldn't like to predict how both sides might react in the event of a British withdrawal. And we don't know yet that the British do plan to withdraw despite what has happened to the queen."

"Okay"—the President nodded—"let's treat it as a military hypothetical. Suppose the British do pull their troops out. On the basis of what you know about the military capabilities of the civil militias on both sides of the conflict in Northern Ireland, what would you expect to be the immediate outcome?"

Coburg looked uncomfortable for a moment, then gave a resigned shrug.

"I would expect a situation very similar to what we saw in Yugoslavia," he said bluntly.

The President winced. He had a sneaking suspicion that Guthrie's bleak scenario was not as farfetched as it might sound. And the image of a Balkan-style mess in Ireland, just 2,800 miles away on the other side of the Atlantic, with the potential for a parallel ethnic conflict in the United States, was too awful to contemplate.

"Why such a grim forecast, Kurt?" the President asked. "You really think the situation over there could unravel that fast?"

"In terms of arms and numbers, it is my understanding that the Protestant militias have considerable superiority over the Catholics in Northern Ireland," Coburg answered. "At the moment they are held in check by thirty thousand British troops. If those troops were to be pulled out of Northern Ireland in such a short span of time, the logical reaction for the Protestants would be to move with equal swiftness to fill the vacuum. In that event, we could expect several days of violent conflict between Catholics and Protestants that I expect would be resolved very quickly in favor of the Protestants. Also, the Protestants have made no secret of the fact that they would like to carry out their own version of ethnic cleansing inside Northern Ireland. If they follow through with that plan—and there is no reason to believe that they would not—we could expect to see thousands of Catholic families driven from their homes in a scenario similar to what we saw in Bosnia. The result would be long columns of Catholic refugees flooding across the border into the Irish Republic. It seems unlikely to me that the Irish government would sit by idly and do nothing. In terms of immediate options, they have two choices. One, they mobilize their military and their reserves to handle the flow of refugees and contain the situation inside Northern Ireland by securing the border. Two, they intervene militarily in Northern Ireland to protect their fellow Catholics."

"And if that is the case . . . ?" the President asked.

"According to my information, the Protestant militias and the armed forces of the Republic of Ireland are fairly evenly matched. The Irish have a navy and an air force, which the Protestants do not have, but it is doubtful how effective they would be under the circumstances."

"How so?"

"Most of the action would be on the ground, which automatically precludes the navy from taking part except in a limited shore-based sense. In the case of air strikes, the Protestant militias probably have some shoulder-launched missiles that would limit the operational capabilities of the Irish Air Force. The probable outcome would be an early stalemate on the ground with both sides positioning themselves for territorial and political advantage over the long haul."

"Civil war?" the President said.

"In effect, sir, yes."

There was a sudden pause. Charles Guthrie used it to make one final point.

"In that event, Mr. President," he said, "I don't think it would be long before the government of Ireland and the governments of other nations would be calling for United Nations intervention. Given the fact that the UN is already stretched tight, given our nation's expanded role in peacekeeping operations and bearing in mind the kind of pressures we could expect at home, it is possible that American troops would be called upon to stabilize the situation in Northern Ireland, albeit under the banner of the United Nations."

"Wait a minute." The President leaned back in his chair and looked from one man to the other. "Let me get this straight in my mind here. If what you are telling me is right, if the situation falls apart as rapidly as you suggest, what you are saying is that we could have American troops taking the place of British troops in Northern Ireland?"

"I can't imagine any other nation coming under more pressure than the United States," Guthrie added. "I can't see any other nation that would be considered more effective in the role. Certainly, once the British have pulled out, I don't see them being in a hurry to rush back in. Not after this. Not after they've been whipping boys for both sides over the past twenty years. To me the whole thing has the hallmark of a perfect trap for the United States."

The President looked to Coburg, hoping the general would tell him otherwise.

"It's possible, sir," Coburg agreed. "But it would be a political decision first."

"And," Guthrie added, "there is no reason to expect that American troops would be any more popular or successful over there than the British. Don't forget, British soldiers were welcomed as saviors by the Catholics when they first went into Northern Ireland twenty years ago. And you have only to look at the fate of UN troops in Sarajevo to have some idea of what happens to peacekeeping forces when they get involved in a civil war."

The President leaned forward, rested his elbows on the desk, and tiredly massaged his eyes with the fingers of both hands.

"Well, gentlemen." He heaved a deeply ironic sigh. "This is all very encouraging, I must say. None of the scenarios you've outlined for me today looks particularly inspiring. I guess what it all comes down to is that it doesn't take a tactical genius to know that the interests of the United States would best be served in this situation by doing all that we can to insure that the British stay right where they are. And"—he looked meaningfully at Charles Guthrie—"it probably wouldn't hurt if a few more Americans were to understand that."

HMY *Britannia.* 16.40 hours

"It's getting crowded out there," Doyle murmured, looking at the knife-blade outlines on the radar scanner. "That's seven ships they've got escorting us now."

"And the rest," Patsy Ryan mumbled, standing nearby at the wheel. He had returned to the bridge after catching a few hours sleep in the chart house. His hair was tousled and greasy, his chin wore a three-day growth of beard, and his breath stank. He called up the coordinates he had fed into the yacht's autopilot before turning in. Everything checked. They were heading due south now. They had turned south after Doyle shot Marchant and dumped him overboard.

"Few Saudi patrol boats," Doyle answered, eyeing the smaller dashes outside the circle of British warships. "Doesn't matter. It won't change anything. Where are we now?"

Ryan took his eyes off the radar and looked at the Satnav display.

"Half a degree east of longtitude thirty-eight, two degrees south of latitude nineteen," he said.

"That tells me nothing," Doyle snapped.

"Right here." Ryan stabbed a finger at a screen that showed the glimmering green shoreline of Saudi Arabia on the left and the Sudan on the right. "About 150 nautical miles south of Jidda, slap-dab in the middle of the Red Sea."

"How long before we get to Yemen?"

"At this speed," Ryan calculated, "another twenty-four hours."

"Still too soon," Doyle said. "Bring her down to eight knots. We'll save some fuel. It's time we did a few more zigzags anyway. Keep it up for an hour, then we'll double back at midnight. That'll keep the bastards guessing."

Ryan nodded and cranked the ship's telegraph down to eight knots. Doyle sensed someone else on the bridge and turned around to see Abu Musa. Javad and Youssef waited outside, hooded and armed. Doyle knew where the others were. His men, Brady and

O'Brien, were taking a turn in the engine room. Behan was watching the hostages in the admiral's day cabin. Deveny and Mulcahey were patrolling the main hostage deck, and Michael Kenney had just turned in after laying the last of his booby traps.

Doyle remembered suddenly why Musa was there, and he smiled.

"All right, gentlemen," he said softly. "Let's go shopping, shall we? By appointment to Her Majesty."

He waited while Musa put on his balaclava. Doyle rarely removed his and insisted that all his men take the same precaution. Somebody somewhere would be taking pictures, and he wasn't about to make it easy for them. Which was why he had been so angry with Jimmy Mulcahey for his antics outside the bridge, aiming his rifle at the news chopper when it came in, then giving the clenched-fist salute to the camera. Mulcahey was a clown. It was one of the hazards of working with the IRA. No discipline. Still, they served their purpose. All of them. He shrugged off his irritation, picked up his M-16, and led the way down to the main deck.

At that moment, 170 miles over their heads, an American KH-11 spy satellite in stationary orbit watched them through its unblinking electronic eye and bounced the pictures instantaneously to the USS *Carl Vinson,* 300 miles to the south in the Gulf of Aden.

"We got movement on the *Britannia,* sir," Lieutenant Norton Hale called out from his hunched position over the satellite monitor in the intelligence center. Lieutenant Commander Harper, the *Carl Vinson*'s chief intelligence officer, hurried across and looked over his shoulder at the flickering black and white images as they streamed in.

"Alert the E-2C on station over *Britannia* now," Barrie ordered his communications officer nearby. "Tell them I want close-ups of these bastards. Pictures their mothers would recognize."

"Sir," the communications officer responded, and called up the Hawkeye circling over the *Britannia* at ten thousand feet, its high-resolution cameras, precision radar, and thermal imagers focused on the tiny blue needle in the ocean far below.

"They're on it, sir," he confirmed a moment later.

It took Doyle and his three Arab companions two minutes to cover the distance from the bridge to the queen's drawing room before they disappeared from view again. In that time the KH-11 and the Hawkeye transmitted 324 separate images of the hijackers to the receivers on board the *Carl Vinson.*

"They're wearing hoods, sir," Lieutenant Hale said on board the *Carl Vinson.*

"I see them," Harper answered. "Blow them up anyway. Let's see what a little DIP can do."

DIP stood for digital image processing, a visual enhancement process in which vaguely defined or blurred lines and shapes could be analyzed by a computer that differentiated between true definition lines and false. Even though the hijackers wore masks, their cheekbones, noses, lips, and other facial features still created shapes and impressions in the material. The computer could discard false features and sharpen those that were true. The thermal imaging cameras fleshed out the spaces in between. The combination of DIP and thermal imaging enabled the computer to see through disguises, hoods, and makeup and to build an accurate picture of the face underneath. The intelligence crew aboard the *Carl Vinson* hurried to sift the best images from the satellite and the Hawkeye and then began transferring them to the DIP computer.

"Let's see if we can come up with something good," Harper added. "See if we can't turn up a few terrorist IDs for our British guests when they arrive. Show them just what we do for our money around here."

Back on the *Britannia,* secure in their belief that they were invisible behind their black balaclavas, Doyle and his Arab comrades surveyed the damage that had been done to the queen's drawing room.

"Fucking cowboys," Doyle muttered as he looked over the shattered furniture and ruined paintings. "I told them not to damage anything important."

Musa carefully removed his mask and smoothed back his long hair.

"It does not matter," he said in perfect English. "Some of the paintings were valuable, but they would have been no good to us. We could never have sold them."

Doyle shrugged.

"Take a good look around," he said. "I want you to take anything and everything that's of value. I don't care how much there is. We've got plenty of boats to carry it."

There were four small craft on board the *Britannia* and Doyle knew the carrying capacity of all of them. The royal barge was stowed on the starboard side of the top deck. It was the biggest of the four boats and was used to ferry the queen and large parties of VIPs to and from the royal yacht. There were also two motor launches, each the size of a cabin cruiser, and a sea boat the size of a large lifeboat. Any one of them could have carried two or three tons of royal plunder.

Doyle watched as Musa strolled around the room, delicately fingering his beard, studying those vases and precious ornaments that hadn't been destroyed. He opened drawers in desks and sideboards and poked through the contents, looking for anything of value. He found nothing. He shook his head and walked through to the anteroom but again found nothing worth taking. Next he walked into the queen's sitting room. Doyle waited in the vestibule, watching the stairs. Javad and Youssef looked around, thrilled and fearful at the same time. Despite the destruction, they had never been inside a room so grand. They felt like a couple of children who knew they were doing something wrong and who expected the whole world to come crashing down on them at any moment.

Musa looked disdainfully at the smashed desk, the few scattered pieces of jewelry that had been left on the carpet. These men were barbarians, he thought. Unable to control their passions. Able only to satisfy their most primitive instincts. He stepped back out into the vestibule and walked through the swinging double doors into the dining room. The big table was bare and a couple of the blue leather-covered chairs had fallen over backward, adding to the feeling that they were trespassing in a deserted mansion. Musa crossed directly to the huge oak sideboard with its broken drawers and looked at the solid gold cutlery spilled across the floor. He picked up a dinner knife and balanced it in his hand. It was gratifyingly heavy. An antique, he knew. Two hundred years old. He stroked it and held it up to the light. The embossed crown on the handle glowed dully.

"Come here," he ordered Javad and Youssef. "Take everything

out of the drawers. The gold will still be valuable when we melt it down."

Doyle appeared from the servery, holding a large silver model of an early eighteenth-century battleship in his hand. It was inscribed with a single name: Thunderer.

Musa stared at it, ran his fingers over its exquisitely detailed lines, and peered at the metal.

"Only silver," he pronounced. "Not worth the trouble."

Doyle let the beautiful silver model fall to the floor with a heavy thud. Fragments of silver from the delicate rigging broke off and rolled across the floor like teardrops.

"Okay," Doyle said. "Let's not waste too much time in here, shall we? We know where the real goodies are kept."

Musa smiled.

"I heard that King Fahd gave the queen a solid gold camel two feet high with branches of dates on its back made from rubies," he said. "It is reputed to be worth ten million pounds."

"She's been picking up baubles everywhere she stopped," Doyle sniffed. "That's apart from the jewels she carries with her for all the state occasions. It's exactly as I told you, Musa. There's enough here for both of us. You can bet you're life on that."

"I have bet my life on it," Musa murmured.

Doyle led the way across the vestibule and down the mahogany stairs to the household deck. They had to work their way down three decks, along eerily deserted corridors, past the empty household cabins and staff cabins, their open doors swinging and banging as though on a ghost ship, past the staff mess and the linen room until at last they found the door to the royal baggage room. They were now on the bottommost deck of the royal yacht. Below them were only freshwater holding tanks and the hull. The engine room was two bulkheads away, and the only sound was the rhythmic pulse of the turbines that seemed to envelop them with a numbing, sinister hum. Javad and Youssef looked at each other. The deeper down into the yacht they had gone, the more uneasy they had become. They eyed each other nervously. They could not help but imagine their enemies, vengeful and merciless, waiting for them around every corner.

The door to the royal baggage room was locked. Doyle motioned them to take cover. He unclipped a grenade from his belt, hung it on the door handle, and pulled out the pin. Then, with maddening nonchalance, he strolled back along the corridor and stepped behind a bulkhead hatch. There was a short, deafening crack, a rush of smoke, and the sound of metal pinging around the walls. When they looked again, there was a charred gash where the lock had been and the baggage room door was swinging loosely on one hinge.

Doyle walked through the clearing smoke and stepped inside. He found himself in a long, surprisingly wide room with shelves on each side, reaching from floor to ceiling. He found the light switch and turned it on. The shelves were divided into irregular shapes and sizes to accommodate an array of trunks, suitcases, and hat boxes, all bearing the royal coat of arms.

The others stepped in after him. Doyle watched as Musa went to the first in a row of dresser trunks. It stood on end in its own nook to stop it from moving, and when he sprang the locks, it opened ingeniously outward like a small wardrobe. Inside were two floor-length dresses, both apparently for state occasions. Both were made of silk. One was a deep and gorgeous blue with a silver bodice inlaid with diamonds and pearls. In any other wardrobe the stones might have been fake. These were not. The second dress was a rich burgundy with a blue and white sash. Musa pulled out the first dress and beckoned to Javad.

"Cut out the stones," he ordered.

Obediently, Javad took out a small knife and started hacking at the beautiful fabric.

Musa moved to the next trunk. Inside were half a dozen white uniforms decorated with gold braid. Some of the duke's naval uniforms. Musa clicked his tongue impatiently, closed the trunk, and moved on. The remaining trunks held nothing of interest. He rifled through them quickly, pulling them out, checking for valuables, throwing some of the dresses carelessly to the floor. It was the same with the hat boxes. They held nothing of real value. No jewel-encrusted hats or diamond-studded tiaras. Only silly, worthless concoctions of assorted fabrics and feathers designed to shield the monarch's pale skin from the sun on her royal walkabouts.

"Rubbish," he grumbled aloud. "There's nothing of any value here."

Doyle appeared suddenly from the back of the baggage room, a glimmer of triumph in his eyes.

"Go and bring Michael Kenney down here," he ordered Youssef. "Tell him to bring his bag of tricks. We need him to open a safe."

Musa turned and looked at Doyle, a smile of anticipation forming on his lips.

When Kenney appeared, he was bleary-eyed and disheveled but he knew better than to complain to Doyle about interrupted sleep. From his shoulder dangled a heavy satchel.

"In the back," Doyle explained, and he nodded in the direction of the narrow corridor between the shelves. Kenney trampled over the discarded clothing and disappeared into the gloom at the rear of the baggage room. He emerged a moment later, a note of pleasure in his voice.

"You know what I like about this one, Eddie?" he said. "I don't have to worry about how much bloody noise I make."

He put his satchel down on the floor and pulled out a slab of Demex. Carefully, he took about a third of the slab, then a blasting cap and a short length of fuse. When he was ready he handed the satchel to Doyle.

"Better get these blokes upstairs," he said. "It's not a safe door I'm blowin'. It's a strong room. One of those old walk-in jobs. And it's welded to the deck. It'll take some power to shift it. There's going to be a bit of a bang."

"Just don't blow a hole in the ship yet," Doyle muttered. He took the satchel and stepped back outside with the others. They did as Kenney advised, walked back along the corridor, and took the stairs to the deck above. Ten minutes later Kenney appeared.

"Didn't take long," Doyle observed suspiciously. He was wary of Kenney, the same way he was wary of all the other bomb makers he had encountered in the IRA. They were not known for their subtlety or their safety standards, and the attrition rate from accidental detonations was atrocious. Very few of them lived to see thirty. Kenney was an old hand. He was thirty-one.

Kenney looked at his wristwatch and started counting the seconds.

When half a minute had passed, he lifted one hand in the air and silently counted off the last five seconds. There were two fingers left to go when a ferocious blast echoed along the corridor below. All but Doyle jumped as the deck beneath their feet shuddered and the bulkhead gave a deep metallic groan as though the yacht were in pain. Doyle shot Kenney an angry glance and hurried back downstairs. Halfway along the corridor he encountered thick black smoke and behind it he saw the crimson flicker of flames. It was just as he had feared. Kenney had started a fire in the baggage room.

"Jesus Christ," he swore, and unfastened the gas mask that still dangled from his belt. He threw his rifle to Kenney and snatched the nearest fire extinguisher from the wall. Then he hurried through the smoke at a crouch and aimed the fire extinguisher into the flames. Musa and the others hung back, fearful of what a fire would do to their plans.

The clothing on the floor was burning furiously, and some of the trunks nearest the strong room were ablaze. Doyle recalled that silks and satins were highly flammable. But the fires were not serious. They had not had time to take hold properly, and the foam quickly choked off the flames, filling the air with boiling black clouds of smoke. Somewhere behind him Doyle heard alarms ringing. The ship's fire alarm system.

"Christ almighty," he cursed inside his gas mask. When the last fire was out, he hurried back along the corridor until he was out of the smoke and it was safe to take off his mask. The alarms still clattered all through the ship. He put his shortwave radio to his mouth and yelled to Patsy Ryan up above on the bridge.

"Shut the alarm system off, Patsy," he ordered. "Before we panic the neighbors into doing something stupid."

A moment later the bells stopped clanging and an eerie silence settled over the ship once more. Doyle glared contemptuously at Kenney.

"Jesus, Eddie, I'm sorry," Kenney stuttered. "I had to get the door in one hit so it wouldn't buckle. Or I might have to use more on the second try. I—I forgot about the clothes and the bags and things. Is everything okay?"

"It is now," Doyle growled. He threw the empty fire extinguisher to the floor and snatched his rifle back.

The others watched, fearful, afraid to say anything that might anger him more. After a few minutes the worst of the smoke had cleared and they ventured back down to the ruined baggage room.

"Shit," Kenney chuckled, trying to calm Doyle's temper. "You'd think a bloody bomb had gone off."

The cases and trunks nearest the strong room had been blasted to shreds. Clotted lumps of trunk casing stuck to the walls and the floor, smoldering. Charred strips of clothing hung from the shelves. Some of the shelves had been buckled from the blast. But the strong-room door was open. Or what was left of it. The door had not been opened by the blast. It had been ripped asunder, torn from its steel frame like a piece of cardboard shredded by giant hands. Behind the door there was only darkness. No hint of the priceless secrets that might lie inside.

Musa muttered beneath his breath. Then, clutching a handkerchief delicately to his face, he stepped around Doyle and peered into the strong room. His eyes burned from the smoke that lingered and several minutes passed before his eyes had adjusted to the gloom. Then the room began to acquire some dimension through the murk. It was a big vault. Its reinforced walls reached from ceiling to floor and went back another twenty feet. The sides were lined with small steel-gray doors. It looked exactly like the safety deposit room of a large bank. Except these doors had no locks.

Musa reached out tentatively and with his fingertips touched a door at eye level. It was warm but not hot. He turned the handle and opened the door. Inside was another handle. The handle of a strongbox. It slid out easily, but it was long and heavy, and when it came free he had to hang on to it with both hands. Gingerly, he carried it outside and into the light, where he could see it properly. Then he opened the lid and looked inside. The others all closed around him.

Inside was a maroon velvet box the size of a small shoebox. Embossed on the padded lid was the lion and the unicorn. He opened the lid and stared. Nestled on a thick cushion of maroon-colored satin was a slender crescent of metal. The metal seemed to glow with a radiance of its own. Platinum, Musa realized. Platinum and diamonds. It was a tiara made entirely of platinum and diamonds. His quickest calculation told him there were at least fifty, perhaps sixty stones. Most of them small though flawless and perfectly cut. And in the midst of the centerpiece was a lone diamond. A diamond the size of a swallow's egg.

Musa lifted the tiara out and turned it carefully in his hands. The diamonds snatched at the weak electric light, split it into atoms, multiplied it, magnified it, and fired it back like rainbow-colored lasers.

"Allahu Aqbar," Musa breathed. "I could get ten million American dollars for the stones on their own."

He turned and looked at Doyle, his hands trembling with excitement.

"There are more than millions in here," he whispered reverentially in the presence of such wealth. "There are hundreds of millions."

Musa spent the next hour looting every drawer in the strong room. He found three more tiaras, necklaces, and pendants from the queen's collection. He found maroon velvet bags filled with loose stones. He found the gifts she had received during the voyage; a brooch made of white gold with sapphires and emeralds, a solid gold statue of a hawk with rubies for its eyes . . . and he found the golden camel that had been a gift from the King of Arabia.

It was so heavy it took two men to move it.

They also found two strongboxes containing cash. One box held four million pounds sterling. The other, four million dollars U.S., all in large bills. Money to service the *Britannia*'s hard currency needs while abroad. After the gold and diamonds the cash came almost as an anticlimax.

It took Javad and Youssef more than an hour to move it all upstairs to join their growing hoard in the queen's drawing room. When they were finished, the five of them stood for a moment in the drawing room and surveyed the pile of treasure, all but Doyle awestruck by the size of the fortune they had stolen. There were more than a hundred strongboxes arranged in a pyramid as high as a man's chest, every one of them containing cash or treasure. Some of the bigger items, gifts of gold statuettes, diamond-encrusted novelties and toys, and the *Britannia*'s solid gold cutlery, were packed crudely in suitcases. There was no need to be gentle, Musa had said. All of it would be broken down or melted for resale on the Arab world's many clandestine bullion markets.

"How much?" Doyle asked Musa quietly.

Musa shrugged.

"It will take years to break it all down and get rid of it," the Palestinian hedged. "Even so . . ."

Doyle gave him a hostile look.

"Two hundred, perhaps two hundred and fifty million American dollars," Musa said. "That is after it has been melted down. The way it is at the moment it is worth more . . . and it is worth nothing. It cannot be sold like this."

"A queen's ransom," Michael Kenney breathed without a hint of irony.

"Yes," Doyle agreed softly. "And we've still got the queen."

He turned to Musa.

"Wait till after dark," he said. "Then put it on the big launch. You might have to get ashore in a hurry."

Musa nodded.

"There's more than enough here to keep our comrades in Yemen happy," he said. "Enough to buy us a safe haven for the rest of our lives."

Doyle snorted and looked as though he was about to say something, but he was stopped by a burst of static from his radio. He plucked it from his belt and put it to his face.

"Yes?"

"The *Hotspur* wants to talk," Patsy Ryan said urgently.

"I'm on my way," Doyle answered.

A minute later he strode onto the bridge and picked up the ship-to-ship transmitter.

"Commander of the *Britannia* here," he said. "We want proof of concession."

There was a short pause, and then a cultured English voice responded in the studied tone of a man who wished only to be reasonable. The immediate effect it had on Doyle was to antagonize him. Eddie Doyle's accent might have been British. He might have had the manners and the looks of an Englishman. To all intents and purposes he might have been one of them. But he wasn't. They had seen to that. Edward Doyle was as Irish as his name. Catholic Irish. Born and raised in Belfast until his family had moved to Liverpool when he was eleven years old. And the voice that came over the ship's radio inspired only hatred in Eddie Doyle. Not reason.

"This is Walter Pryne on board the *Hotspur,*" the voice from the British warship added. "I've been asked to negotiate the arrangements with you if that's all right—but you've got to give me something to work with. Can you give me a name? A code name? Anything? I have to call you something."

Doyle bowed his head and chuckled softly to himself.

"Sorry, old chap," Doyle answered, his voice leaden with sarcasm. "Afraid I can't do that . . . but I'd be most awfully grateful if you could get to the point."

There was a pause while they considered his response. Doyle chuckled softly to himself as he thought of the confusion his voice and accent must be causing at the other end.

"I've been given the authority to make a deal," the voice floated back. "I'm sure we can work something out between us, you and I."

"Oh . . ." Doyle took a malicious pleasure in drawing out his response. "I don't think so, old chap. You see, I don't think you're in any position to ask for concessions. But I will tell you this. We're watching all the news here on the telly. And when we see British troops pulling out of Northern Ireland and when we get confirmation from our people that it is a genuine withdrawal, then we'll talk about what happens next, all right?"

"Yes, of course," Pryne persisted soothingly. "But we have to work out some kind of a time frame. Seven days isn't long enough to do what you want. You've got to try and give me something to work—"

"You're really not getting this, are you?" Doyle interrupted, injecting his voice with all the condescension he could muster. "It's really very simple, even for an Englishman. Either you do as we tell you to do, by noon on the twenty-third, or this ship goes to the bottom of the sea and the queen and the Duke of Edinburgh go with it. No deals, no compromises. Oh, and one last thing. If you or any other smug, patronizing bastard from the psychology division try to talk to us again—we'll give you another hostage to pick up. Do you understand?"

There was a baffled silence at the other end. Doyle switched off the mike and put it back in its cradle.

"They never learn, do they?" he muttered vaguely as the others on the bridge stood silently by. "They think they're so damn clever. They think they're so much better than everybody else. This time they'll learn. This time . . ."

WASHINGTON. 14.22 HOURS

"Good afternoon, Sir Malcolm. I've been expecting your call. I understand you have a shopping list I might be able to help you with?"

General Coburg was alone in his office at the Department of Defense. The call he had been expecting had just come through. He pushed the button on his speaker decoder then punched out a command into his computer keyboard and called up a file picture of Sir Malcolm Porter onto the screen so he could see the face of the man with whom he was speaking.

"It's good of you to help us, General," the polished British accent of the man in the picture chimed clearly into the room. "Though I think I'd better warn you—it's a pretty hefty shopping list."

Coburg allowed himself a small chuckle. He had been reassured when he had first seen the picture of Porter. The man who looked back at him had a strong, lean-featured face and a commanding expression in his eyes. It was not the face of some florid-faced, overweight armchair quarterback. It was the face of a soldier. His record reassured the general even more. It was pure bias, Coburg knew. But it made him feel better.

"The President has ordered me to assist you in every way possible, short of putting American personnel into the firing line," Coburg answered.

"We can take care of that end of things," Porter answered.

"Though there are one or two highly specialized items that would come in handy, considering the delicate nature of the operation we have in mind."

Coburg nodded. It was a promising sign. Whatever political posturing might be taking place in public, the Brits were serious about taking back the *Britannia.* If they were successful, the situation would be resolved quickly and British troops would remain in Northern Ireland. That pleased the general. He had no desire to see American soldiers dragged into another quagmire.

"Tell me what you need, Sir Malcolm," he said.

"A squadron of Blackhawks to begin with," Porter answered amiably.

Coburg pursed his lips. The guy wasn't kidding when he used the word *hefty.*

"We can't allow them to be used in a direct combat role," he cautioned.

"They'll operate in a purely supportive capacity," Porter answered. "We need them as invisible air platforms for our special forces. I promise you, they won't approach within two miles of the *Britannia* and the only shots will be fired by our people."

Coburg hesitated. He could see what Porter was driving at. But the Blackhawk pilots would still be American. If one of them were hit by enemy fire it could prove embarrassing when questions were asked in Congress about the part played by American forces in the operation. Coburg knew that the President was walking a thin line, and while he wanted to help the British, he didn't want to inflame the situation at home by antagonizing the Irish-Catholic constituency.

"To the best of my knowledge, we have two squadrons already in Saudi Arabia," Coburg decided. "I can have one of them on the *Carl Vinson* within, oh . . . three hours suit you?"

"That'll do us very nicely indeed, General."

At his Ministry of Defence office in London, Sir Malcolm swiveled his chair so he could put his feet up on the windowsill and enjoy a view of the budding plane trees as they marched down Horseguards Parade to the Thames. For the first time in three days he indulged himself in a smile. Both the view and the conversation had lifted his spirits.

"We've ruled out a direct air assault," he went on. "Even a stealth machine like the Blackhawk can be seen and heard when it gets close enough, and it still takes many precious seconds to get men from the chopper to the deck of the *Britannia.* We can't afford to take the risk. That is why the main assault will be launched from the water. And that requires an underwater approach. I've been looking at scooters and minisubs, but I've run into a problem because we don't have anything that can't be picked up by the *Britannia*'s sonar. Unfortunately that is where our ten-mile exclusion zone works to the advantage of the hijackers. If any aircraft or vessel ventures inside that circle, in the water or under it, the hijackers get trigger-happy. We've already seen how unpleasant they can be when that happens."

"Yes," Coburg acknowledged soberly. "I heard about Admiral Marchant. It's a goddamn outrage. I can't tell you how sorry I am, how sorry we all are . . ."

"Thank you, General," Porter answered. "That's reassuring to hear. We're all so scared we haven't had time to feel sorry. That's a luxury that will have to come later."

"What minisubs have you looked at?" Coburg went on, eager to help.

"We've got a couple of SDV-Mark 8s we bought from your people in Naval Special Warfare last year," Porter answered. "The big drawback with them is that their top speed is only eight knots. The hijackers zigzag and change speed all the time. They had her up to twenty knots at one point. They never drop below eight. Slow enough to conserve their fuel but fast enough to frustrate an underwater approach. Certainly too fast for a swimmer to hang on. We need something that will get our chaps alongside the *Britannia* without being seen or heard and that can remain there, as a stable platform, for several minutes while we get our men on board. That's where I was hoping you might help us. I know your people have been working on something."

"You probably know more than I do," Coburg conceded. "I'm army and my interest in new technology leans in that direction. I'll have to make inquiries with my colleagues at the Navy Department —see what they've got."

"Actually, General, I think I know what you've got," Porter continued without missing a beat. "I believe your chaps with the Defense and Advance Research Planning Agency have exactly what we need."

Coburg sniffed.

"Tell me what it is and I'll see what I can do," he said.

"It's the SDV-Mark 12," Porter added. "I believe there are only two of them in existence, the prototype and a spare. Your special weapons test unit at Norfolk has already put them through their paces—we had a chap from SBS there as an observer last year—but I believe both subs have been dry-docked these past few months. If either of them is operational, we'd like one in theater within forty-eight hours."

"You want me to get a minisub from Norfolk to the Middle East within forty-eight hours—assuming it's in operational working order?"

"Exactly." The single clipped word echoed around Coburg's office.

The general took a breath.

"It's designed to fit into the hold of a Starlifter," Porter said helpfully.

"The hell you say," Coburg muttered. So far Porter's shopping list ran to only two items—but its cost was well into the billions.

"We'll also require a SEALs team to operate the sub while we put our men on board the *Britannia,*" Porter added. "According to my information, the commander of the unit that tested the prototype is already here in the United Kingdom on private business. With your permission, we'll draft him into the operation at this end. He can hook up with the rest of his people in theater."

"Tell him his orders come direct from the commander in chief via me," Coburg responded. "If he needs confirmation, I'll be happy to speak to him personally. Meantime, I'll communicate with the admiral of Battle Group Charlie. I assume you'll be using the *Carl Vinson* as your operations platform?"

"Indeed we will, General," Porter confirmed. "It was first on my shopping list."

"Pardon me for saying so," Coburg responded, "but it would probably be cheaper if you were our fifty-first state."

"Does this mean all is forgiven and you're inviting the monarchy back into the colonies?" Porter rejoined. "Her Majesty will be pleased."

Coburg's leathery face creased into a broad smile.

"I think I better get off this line while I can still count all my fingers," he said. "I'll get back to you about the sub just as soon as I have something to tell you, Sir Malcolm."

"Pleasure doing business with you, General," Porter answered. "I'll be waiting for your call."

The line went dead. Coburg leaned forward and flicked off the phone switch.

"Jesus H. Christ," he muttered as he thought about all that had been asked of him, all that could go wrong and how it all had to be done within the passage of a mere forty-eight hours. He punched a button on his intercom.

"Janet," he spoke urgently to his secretary. "Get me the secretary of the navy, would you? And I don't care if he's on the goddamn moon. I want him now."

BALLACHULISH, SCOTLAND. 16.58 HOURS

Colin Lynch and Tom Bonner leaned against the dry stone wall outside the cottage and savored the warmth of the late spring sunshine on their faces. Lynch's kit bag was propped against the wall. Bonner's few spare clothes were in a blue canvas overnight bag at his feet. The rest of his things were at the hotel in London. He'd have to pick them up later.

"So," Bonner mused out loud. "Thought any more about my offer?"

Lynch chuckled softly and squinted into the sun as it dropped toward the purple-slashed hilltops on the other side of Loch Linnhe.

"Red," he murmured, "You don't know when to quit, do you?"

Bonner shrugged.

"I'd sure hate you to think I was being mercenary—this being the queen an' all," he drawled his reply. "But even a fool could see that if we work this one right, why, God almighty, we'd be able to write our own goddamn ticket. There wouldn't be a shipping line in the world would say no to the guys that got the Queen of England off of her own yacht."

"It hasn't been done yet," Lynch said soberly.

"It will be," Bonner replied.

Lynch turned to look at his friend.

"By appointment to Her Majesty . . . is that it?"

"They put it on their jelly jars here, don't they?"

Lynch smiled thinly and looked away. He had tried his damnedest to explain how he felt to Bonner, but still he hadn't gotten it across. He doubted he ever would. He wasn't entirely surprised. Queen and country was a quaint notion these days, even to him.

"You lay your life on the line for the President, don't you?" he tried one last time.

"What, are you kidding me?" Bonner sniffed. "You wouldn't catch me putting my ass in the line of fire for any goddamn politician."

Lynch stared at him, openly skeptical.

"I do it for me," Bonner explained. "I've always done it for me. Number one. You ask most guys why they sign up and, if they're honest, they'll tell you—it's the money. They do it to make things better for themselves. Sure, you get some assholes say they're doing it for the flag, God, mom, and apple pie. But most guys do it for themselves. See, that's what makes the American military different from the British. The American military is an army of cantankerous individuals. Always has been. It's our greatest strength and our greatest weakness. Somebody tells us to fight, first we figure out if it's worth fighting for. You can go right back to the American Revolution if you want. What did you have? A whole goddamn army made up of rebels. They were fighting because they figured they'd be a whole lot better off if they could get the British off their backs. Look at the Civil War. Guys on both sides fought mighty hard 'cause they had a difference of opinion on the right way to run the country. Second World War, no problem. Guys knew damn well that if they didn't fight, the Germans and the Japs were going to come on over and cut their nuts off. And that, my friend, is how we lost the war in Vietnam. We lost it not because we couldn't win it. We lost it because we decided it wasn't worth winning. And when we decided that, the President couldn't do shit. That's the difference between the Americans and the British, pal. We won't stand up and fight just because some President or queen says that's what we're supposed to do. We like to figure it out for ourselves first. And if we decide a thing is worth fighting for, well, you better get the hell out of the way . . . and I think the whole world knows that."

Lynch hesitated before answering.

"I don't think we're so different," he said finally.

Bonner looked at him.

"I know what I'm fighting for," Lynch added. "And when the day comes that I have to take the uniform off—I don't think I can put a price on it and sell it to some guy in a suit sitting behind a desk."

Bonner slowly shook his head.

"Then you're a fool, my friend," he said. "Because in this world that is the only way you get to enjoy the things you've been fighting for."

An awkward silence settled between the two men, and they stood side by side for a long time without saying anything more. Lynch was concerned. He felt a barrier coming between them, and it saddened him. But he didn't know what more he could say. He couldn't change the way he was. In some ways he wished he could. His legs still ached from the marathon run to Ben Nevis and back. And his rump was still tender from the minor roasting Bonner had given it. Mortality seemed to be staring at him from every which way. He shifted and leaned away from the wall to stretch his legs.

"Goddamn . . ." Bonner began suddenly as though he had thought of something else to say, but Lynch held his hand up to silence him. The big man hesitated, puzzled. Then he realized what Lynch was doing. He turned his ear to the wind and listened. Then he heard it too. A distant drone that deepened rapidly into a heavy, rhythmic thud and rushed down the wind-rippled hillside toward them.

"Over there," Lynch said, nodding to the northeast.

The helicopter appeared suddenly over the crest of the mountain and boomed down the hillside toward them. It was a big chopper, a Sea King from the base at Holy Loch. The two of them squinted into the rotor wash as the chopper slowed, banked around, and hovered a mere fifty yards away before settling. A side hatch slid open and four Marine commandos jumped and fanned out protectively across the hillside. They were followed a moment later by an officer.

"Commander Lynch, Lieutenant Commander Bonner?" he yelled above the roar of the chopper as he approached.

Both men nodded their response.

"Sir Malcolm Porter sends his regards and requests that you both join him at once in London."

"We've been expecting you." Lynch shouted his response. Then the two of them bent down, picked up their bags, and followed the officer back to the chopper and their appointment with Her Majesty.

HMY *Britannia.* 01.05 hours

Gault padded along the royal corridor to the head of the elevator shaft, where Judy Stone was waiting.

"Soon as I exit the bottom of the shaft, you switch the circuit breaker back, okay?" he whispered. "Give me four hours, then flip it back for fifteen minutes. After that, you alternate it at fifteen-minute intervals for the next hour, like I said. If I'm not back in that time, lock it up for good. I'm not coming back . . . for whatever reason."

She nodded but said nothing. She seemed unexpectedly tense and there was a look in her eyes he hadn't seen before. If he didn't know her better, he would have thought it was worry. Professional concern only, he was certain.

He unsheathed his combat knife, prised it under the armored screen, and lifted. With the power shut off, it was held down only by its own weight and Gault moved it easily. He was surprised at how light it was and how thin. A highly compressed sandwich of titanium and Kevlar only three millimeters thick. But strong enough to absorb and deflect the most high-powered bullets, resilient enough to deflect the most powerful explosions.

Judy held up the screen while he sheathed his knife and opened the door to the elevator manually. The elevator car was dark and empty and had two emergency escape hatches, one in the roof, another in the floor. He stepped inside and knelt down to open the hatch in the floor.

"Gault," Judy whispered urgently. He looked up and saw that she was beckoning him to come back. Puzzled, he took a breath, then stepped back out into the corridor. And then he saw why. The Duke of Edinburgh was there, wearing a blue dressing gown over pajamas. His thin, bony face looked sallow, and there were circles under his eyes.

"Couldn't let you go without wishing you luck," the Duke said self-consciously, and extended his hand. Gault felt awkward though he knew he shouldn't. He was dressed for work; black combat suit, face smeared with camouflage grease, knife sheathed at the hip, pistol in his ankle holster. The duke had seen him like this before during the hostage rescue exercises in the killing house at Hereford. Except this time it wasn't a rehearsal. There wouldn't be whiskey and soda and laughs all round in the officer's mess afterward. He shook the duke's hand. It felt cold and dry. Like a dead man's hand.

"Thank you, sir," Gault said. "With luck, I'll be back well before morning with some useful information for my trouble."

The duke hesitated, as though there were something more he wanted to say, but then he stopped himself, gave Gault a reassuring pat on the shoulder, and turned back along the corridor toward his stateroom. There was simply nothing more he could say to a man who might be dead before morning, and both of them knew it. Gault watched him go, knowing that the duke was someone else who wouldn't be getting much sleep this night.

"Just come back in one piece, okay?" Judy whispered suddenly to Gault. He looked at her, surprised by the note in her voice. He assumed he was mistaken. It was only professional concern. Then she surprised him. She stood up on her toes and kissed him on the lips. It was just a touch, barely enough to smudge the camouflage grease. But it was a kiss nonetheless.

"You certainly know how to pick your moments, Lieutenant."

"So do you, Captain." She smiled. "So do you. And perhaps next time you think you might want to lie on top of me, you could try asking first."

Gault looked into her eyes for what seemed like an age, trying to see whether she was playing with him. Instead, he saw all his questions answered at once.

"I'll be damned," he breathed. Then he turned and ducked back down into the elevator car.

Like everything else on board the *Britannia,* the floor hatch was impeccably maintained and opened the first time, smoothly and without making a sound. A ray of light spilled down into the shaft like the beam of a flashlight, illuminating the smooth, dark walls. Gault studied the layout inside the shaft, noting the placement of the steel supporting struts, the doors to the decks below, and the oily hydraulic jacks and cables that operated the elevator car. He gave Judy one last parting look, then swung down through the hatch and was gone. Judy waited a moment, then leaned in and closed the trapdoor noiselessly after him. She backed out of the elevator car and pushed the doors shut. Then she looked at her watch and walked back down the royal corridor. He had five minutes before she would reset the circuits that would lock all the armored screens in the elevator shaft. After that Gault was on his own.

Inside the shaft, Gault worked his way down to the bottom deck in total darkness, relying only on touch and memory for footholds and handholds. In less than a minute he was standing in the shaft well, fingertips pressed to the doors that opened out onto the household staff cabins. He put an ear to the door and listened carefully. There was nothing unusual. Only the distant hum of the engines. He unsheathed his knife, slid the tip of the blade under the armored screen, and lifted it up until he could crouch underneath and prise open the outside door that opened directly onto the corridor. This was the dangerous part. If the hijackers had been careful, they would have rigged booby traps or alarms to every elevator door on every deck. He inserted the blade of the knife and prised the door open a fraction, looking for the threadlike glimmer of wires. The door slipped from his grasp and began to slide open on its own momentum. And that was when he saw the wire, growing tighter as the door slid back.

There was no time for anything but reflex. If it was plastique, the force of the blast directed into the confined space of the elevator shaft would kill him. He slipped his head and one arm through the widening gap and scanned both sides of the doorway. He saw it immediately. It was the most basic kind of booby trap. A grenade inside a Coke can with the pin removed so the sides of the can held the detonator lever down. The can was taped at an angle to the bulkhead. The wire stretched from the grenade to the door handle. When the door started to open the wire tightened, pulled the grenade out of the can, and freed the lever.

Gault rolled through the opening door, reached up, and caught the grenade in his outstretched hand just as it popped out of the can and the lever started to spring. His fingers closed tightly around it and pressed the lever back down. He lay still for a moment and looked around. There was no one in sight. Then he examined the grenade in case there was something more. The silver line of the joint between the fuse cap and the casing was clearly visible through the grime. The cap had been unscrewed recently, he realized. The fuse must have been reset. Shortened, no doubt. From the usual five seconds to one. It had been that close.

He got to his feet and looked around. The security screen had slammed shut behind him. In a few moments Judy would activate its lock. He eased the grenade back into the Coke can with the wire still attached so that it looked as though it had not been disturbed. Then, very carefully he slid the outside elevator door shut again. He wouldn't forget it on the way back.

Standing in the brightly lit corridor, Gault felt naked and exposed. He started along the corridor, past the staff mess, moving forward toward the engine room. If the *Britannia* was wired to explode, the engine room was the place to plant charges to make sure the blast broke the ship's backbone. It was also a likely strong point and would be guarded by one or more of the hijackers. Gault knew that taking control of any ship was relatively simple once the hijackers had gotten on board. All they had to do was hold the bridge and the engine room. Her Majesty's loyal forces might take the rest of the yacht with ease, but it wouldn't change a damn thing as long as the hijackers still controlled those two critical areas.

The door to the engine room was open. The only way Gault could approach was along a short corridor with no doors, no hatches, no means of escape. If someone should see him, he would make an easy target. He slipped his pistol from its holster, readied himself, and started forward. The moment he moved, he heard a voice from inside the engine room, a man's voice.

". . . going to take a look around . . ." it said. "Back in a few minutes."

Gault knew the accent. It was the accent of the Belfast street. He'd heard it often enough over the years. He backtracked hurriedly, ducked into the staff pantry, and waited behind the door. A moment later he saw a man walk past. Tall, thin, dressed in black and carrying an Armalite. He walked confidently, carelessly. An easy mark. A radio spurted static from the man's belt. Gault waited. There was no way of knowing if the man was actively communicating with someone on the radio or in the engine room. He would let him go. For now.

The SAS man stepped out into the corridor and started toward the engine room again. It was empty. He scanned it quickly but saw nothing to indicate where charges might be hidden. The fact that the engine room had been left unattended told him something else. The charges weren't there.

But the door to the boiler room was closed.

Gault opened it a millimeter at a time. Immediately he found two wires. One at the bottom, one at the top. Two more grenades. He allowed himself a small smile. This was more like it. The charges had to be in there. Slowly, delicately, he unhooked the wires from the door and stepped inside. The moment he looked around his face fell.

He was right. The charges were in that room. But the man responsible for them had come up with an ingenious method of hiding them. He had hidden them out in the open, where they could be seen easily—but were still invisible. The pipe carrying the yacht's central communications cable had been sliced open and the wires pulled out in a tangled rainbow-colored nest. A score of wires had been knitted into the nest and braided into a loose rope that led across the gangway and down to the deck below, where they snaked back and forth in a bewildering mosaic. Obviously some of the wires led to explosive charges. But some of them didn't. There was simply no need for that many charges. Some of the wires would be live. Others wouldn't. Some might be rigged to set off an alarm when cut. Others might be booby-trapped to trigger the charges. And there was no way he could determine which were which. He couldn't touch any of them without risking discovery or disaster.

"Bastards," Gault muttered to himself.

He was right on top of the hijacker's main cache of explosives and there wasn't a thing he could do to defuse it.

At that moment, a hundred feet away and one deck up, the man who should have been guarding the engine room had something more satisfying in mind. Jimmy Mulcahey yanked the fire ax away from the staff cabin door and stepped inside. The young woman who huddled beneath the bedclothes looked up miserably.

He had been to see her twice since he had bundled her in there more than twenty-four hours earlier. He had brought her food and drink and talked to her soothingly each time. And he had told her what she must do if she wanted to survive.

"Hello, darlin'," Mulcahey grinned at her. "I'm home."

He set his rifle down in a corner and pulled a paper bag from his tunic. Inside were a few pieces of bread and cheese from the galley. It was the only food she'd seen since morning. There was a tiny cubicle in the corner of the cabin with a shower, a toilet, and a hand basin, where she got her only drinking water.

Mulcahey had been careful. He had given her just enough food to keep her from starving but not so much that she could avoid the pain and the desperation of hunger. At first she had been sullen and defiant and refused to speak to him. She had expected him to force himself on her earlier and had steeled herself for the ordeal. But Jimmy Mulcahey was no rapist. He did not want to take her by force. What he wanted was a willing partner. More than a partner.

He wanted complete subjugation to his will. A slave who would do everything he demanded and beg him for the privilege of pleasing him. Especially an upper-class bitch like this. Now he knew the time was right. He could see it in her eyes. Defeat had replaced defiance. She was almost there.

He put the bag down on the dresser while he pulled off his balaclava and rubbed his fingers through his greasy yellow hair. Then he looked down at her.

"You goin' to tell me your name yet, darlin'?" he asked softly.

She looked no more than twenty. She still had not brushed her thick red hair and her eyes had cried themselves dry. Still she wouldn't answer.

"You want the food?" he asked.

She looked down at the bed covers for a moment. Then she nodded her head without looking back at him.

"Sorry, darlin'," Mulcahey added. "I didn't hear ye. Do you think you could speak up a bit?"

There was a long pause, and then she said something. It was so faint he hardly heard it.

"You'll have to do better than that if you want to eat tonight, girl," he said. He picked the bag up from the dresser and turned to go.

"Please . . ." she said suddenly, her voice a plaintive whisper.

Mulcahey stopped and looked back at her.

"What?" he asked.

"Please," she repeated, her voice slightly firmer. "I'll do . . . anything. Please give me the food."

"Anything?" Mulcahey taunted her. He walked over to the bed, sat down, and set the bag near the foot of the bed, beyond her reach.

"Yes," she answered after a while. "Anything."

"You can start by showing me your lovely face again," he coaxed. "And you can tell me your name."

She raised her face and looked at him. There was something there, he thought. Resignation maybe. The realization that it would all be so much easier if she cooperated. Gave him what he wanted, put an end to the torture, got it over with. But it wouldn't be that easy, Mulcahey knew. It wouldn't be over that quickly. It had been a long time since he'd had a woman. And never in his life had he made love to a woman this young. This beautiful. He wanted to make the most of it, draw it out, enjoy every delicious moment. He waited, as though he had all the time in the world.

"It's Susan," she said. The tremor had left her voice. Replaced by something else. Something flat and lifeless.

"You got a second name?" Mulcahey asked as though teasing a girl he had just met at a party.

"Latimer," she said. "My name is Susan Latimer."

"Ahh," Mulcahey sighed. "A pretty name that. A very . . . English kind of name, isn't it? I wonder what your daddy does for a livin', eh, Susan? What does your daddy do? Does he work? Does he have a job? Or does he just live off the land, mebbe?"

"He owns property," she answered, a spark of anger flaring briefly.

"Ah-ha," Mulcahey murmured. "A man of property is he? Probably been in the family a long time, eh? And your daddy knows the Queen of England too, does he, Susan? Well enough to get you a soft little job like this. A bit of fun. See the world, then settle down with some chinless wonder called Reginald or Percy somethin'. Was that the plan, Susan?"

She lowered her head so her hair fell forward and covered her face.

"Well," Mulcahey added, "there's been a slight change of plan for you, Susan."

He reached out, took hold of the bed covers, and pulled them sharply away from her. She flinched but did not cringe back from him the way she had done earlier. Instead, she sat still, her legs drawn protectively up to her chest, arms folded over her knees. The long rip in the side of her nightdress was still there. He could see the side of one breast and as far down as the curve of her hip.

"Put your legs down, Susan," he said, his voice growing hoarse.

She hesitated, then slowly straightened her legs. Her arms stayed folded across her chest.

"And the arms." Mulcahey smiled.

Slowly, she unfolded her arms and let them fall slackly by her sides. The nightdress had a high neckline, though there was another small rip at the front. Just enough to reveal the deep cleft at the top of her breasts.

"Take your nightdress off, Susan," Mulcahey ordered.

She hesitated, but only for a moment. Then she hitched herself up and pulled the nightdress over her head, letting it fall into her lap in a tiny shriveled heap. Mulcahey reached forward, prised her fingers from the nightdress, and threw it into a corner. She kept her head bowed while he looked at her, his eyes wandering over every exposed inch of her flesh. He had never seen skin so white. Her breasts were large and firm, the way only a young woman's breasts could be, and her nipples a pale, innocent pink. Her belly was a creamy curve that led down to a reddish nest of curls between her thighs. Mulcahey felt himself growing hard.

He stood up and quickly pulled off his clothes. When he was naked he knelt back down on the bed, closer this time, his erect penis hovering only inches from her face. Still she would not look at him.

"Now, Susan," he said, his voice thick with anticipation. "You're going to be a good girl, aren't ye? And you're going to tell me how much you want this."

She looked away but he reached out, grabbed her by the hair, and forced her to turn her face to him. She shuddered and gave a small sob. Mulcahey smiled and wrenched her hair harder to make her look. She gasped and grabbed at his wrist with both hands to stop him twisting her hair. Mulcahey held his penis in his other hand and guided it closer to her face, brushing it against her cheek, aiming it toward her mouth. She tried to jerk her face away from him, but he twisted his hand viciously in her hair and she screamed. A shrill, piercing scream that cut the air like a knife and echoed hauntingly along the deserted corridor outside.

Mulcahey's temper flared. She wasn't supposed to scream. That wasn't part of it. He slapped her. Hard. She screamed again. Instinctively his hand balled into a fist and he drew his arm back to hit her properly. Instead, his arm kept going backward, gripped suddenly by some terrible force. Mulcahey gasped with pain as he felt himself hoisted off the bed and lifted into the air. The cabin spun past his face in a blur and he saw a wall rush toward him. The thing that was holding him let go, and Mulcahey hit the wall with his head and shoulder. There was a jarring spasm of pain and then a crack like the sound of a branch breaking as he felt his neck snap. Then he was on the floor and he could feel nothing. He could not tell whether he was lying facedown or faceup. All he could see was darkness. And he couldn't breathe. The darkness rushed into his eyes, nose, and throat like something warm, liquid, and comforting. Then the last flicker of consciousness slipped away, his heart fluttered and stopped beating.

"Bugger," Gault swore. He hadn't wanted the hijacker dead. He wanted to ask him a few questions. Now the man lay on the carpet like a broken doll, his head skewed at a bizarre angle, his mouth open and eyes staring blindly at the ceiling.

Gault turned and looked at the girl. She had pulled the bed covers back around her as if they alone could protect her. Her face was a mixture of terror and incomprehension. Gault had seen that look before, on the faces of other hostages. It was the look of people who hovered on the edge of insanity.

"It's all right." Gault tried to sound comforting, knowing how threatening he must look with the same black uniform as the hijackers and his face streaked with paint. "I'm security and I'm going to get you out of here. Put something on . . . fast."

There must have been something in his voice that reassured her. She pulled the sheet tightly around her and struggled from the bed.

"There's nothing," she said numbly. "He took everything away."

Gault stepped back to the door, glanced down the corridor, then disappeared. He returned a moment later with a pair of khaki trousers and a dark green sweater from the cabin next door.

"Don't worry if they don't fit," he said. "They're just to cover you while I get you somewhere safe."

He turned his back while she dressed. It gave him just enough time to decide what to do with the body of the hijacker.

"Are you part of a rescue party or something?" Susan Latimer asked hopefully, behind him.

"Wish I were," Gault answered. "I'm on-board security. I'm taking you up to the royal deck, where it's safe. They can't get at you up there."

When she was ready, he took her hand and led her quickly down the corridor toward the staff mess. He opened the door and ushered her inside. She looked fearfully back at him.

"It's all right," he promised. "Stay here till I get back. Keep the lights off. I won't be long. Just try to be brave."

"How long—" she began.

"Just wait," he interrupted her. Then he closed the door and was gone.

It took Gault almost an hour to get Jimmy Mulcahey's body up to the main deck without being seen. Once, he heard voices on the deck above and had to freeze halfway up the stairs until they had passed. When he finally made it to the upper deck, he heaved the body across his shoulders and lugged it to the lifeboat station near the stern, where he would find one vital piece of equipment. Something to make sure the body would float. He put the body back down on the deck while he pulled a bright orange life jacket from a metal chest. It took him only a few minutes to strap the life jacket onto the body. Then he dragged it to the ship's rail and lifted it over the side. He didn't wait for the splash. Instead, he ducked back inside the gangway that led down to the staff mess on the lower deck, moving as quickly and as quietly as he could.

But when he opened the door to the staff mess and looked inside, Susan Latimer had gone.

7 Reptiles Rising

HMY *Britannia,* May 19. 04.05 hours

"There's some guy trying to get through on the UHF," Dominic Behan said, leaning through the doorway from the radio shack to the bridge. "Says he's a TV reporter from New York. Name of Dunbarry. Says he wants to talk to the top man."

"Does he indeed." Doyle sighed. "Tell him—" Then he stopped himself. "No," he decided, "I'll talk to him."

Doyle told Ryan and Deveny to wait, then followed Behan into the radio room and leaned down to speak into the transmitter.

"What do you want?" he asked curtly.

"It's not what I want." Dunbarry's brash barroom voice flooded into the room as though he were speaking from next door. "It's what I can do for you, my friend. You want to make a point to the world —I'm going to help you do it."

"How did you find this frequency?" Doyle asked, irritated.

"Contacts, my friend," Dunbarry explained. "I assume we're being listened to, so I won't say too much."

He was hunched over a telephone in the conference room at the

Flash office in Manhattan. It was a little after six at night in New York. Dunbarry had received the number half an hour earlier from London, courtesy of a lover of one of the royal yacht's former radio operators. The door to the conference room was locked and Sheila Scutter was outside by the switchboard, standing over the operator to make sure she didn't lose the line. On the table in front of Dunbarry, next to the phone, were an open pack of Marlboros, a full ashtray, a gold-plated Zippo, and a tape machine. The machine was plugged into the phone and the spools turned steadily, picking up every word that was said.

On the other side of the world Doyle smiled coolly.

"Perhaps there is something you can say on my behalf," he said.

"Anything you want, my friend," Dunbarry answered quickly. "Anything you say is news."

Adrenaline surged through his veins and, despite the air-conditioning, sweat beaded on his forehead. He couldn't go wrong now, he knew. He had it made. The story of the century.

"The British government hasn't told the full story," Doyle said. "They've been holding back."

"Wouldn't surprise me at all, my friend," Dunbarry said, sucking hard at a cigarette. "You tell it like it is, and we'll run it like it is."

"Three days ago," Doyle went on, "we gave the British government an ultimatum. That ultimatum has not been made public and the British have done nothing to meet our demands. We are not terrorists. We are freedom fighters. We have legitimate political demands that must be recognized by the British and by the United Nations."

"I'm listening," Dunbarry panted. "I'm with you, my friend. All the way."

"We gave the British government seven days to declare an end to their illegal occupation of the northern provinces and to begin an orderly withdrawal of their forces," Doyle said. "That deadline was effective from noon, Greenwich Mean Time, Tuesday, May sixteenth, and will expire at noon, Greenwich Mean Time, Tuesday, May twenty-third. If the British have not begun their withdrawal to our satisfaction by that deadline, we will blow up the *Britannia* and all on board."

"You must know that would be suicide, my friend," Dunbarry answered, struggling to keep his voice calm.

"We are committed to the legitimate political goal of a united Ireland," Doyle added. "This process cannot begin until all foreign troops have been removed from Irish soil. We are all patriots here. We are prepared to die for our beliefs."

"Obviously, my friend, you're a very committed man," Dunbarry said. "A very brave man. And I can tell that you're an educated man, if I might say so. Tell us something about yourself. Who are you? What has brought you to this moment in history? How about the queen and the Duke of Edinburgh? Are they safe? Have you spoken to them . . . ?"

Doyle reached forward and switched off the radio.

It didn't matter. Dunbarry had what he wanted. He leapt to his feet, pounded the table with his fist, and gave a whoop that echoed the length of the floor. He threw open the conference room door and strode out into the newsroom, mashing the air with his fist. Reporters, production assistants, researchers, and secretaries got to their feet and applauded on cue. Sheila Scutter walked out of the switchboard room, a reluctant smile of admiration on her face.

"Goddamn!" Dunbarry grabbed her by the arms. "The old guy's done it again, eh? What did I tell you, Sheila? The story of the bloody century, and we've got it. An exclusive interview with the leader of the hijackers on board the *Britannia*—and he blows the whistle on the Brits with a bloody ultimatum."

He paused and stepped back.

"You know what he said? If they don't get their arses out of Northern Ireland in four days—boom! The boat goes up and Liz and Phil go with it. What a fucking story."

Dunbarry was so excited his whiskey-reddened face had grown even redder and there were flecks of spittle at the corners of his mouth.

"Dave," he yelled to one of his reporters, "get on to the British embassy in Washington now. I want to do a live cross to the ambassador at the bottom of the show. Sheila, let's get a response from the palace in London. Let's see if we can get a comment from Downing

Street too . . . and the White House. Christ, wait till this hits the airwaves. The whole bloody world will shit itself."

Something caught his eye, and he stopped to look at a battery of TV monitors mounted along the back wall of the newsroom. It was six-thirty in the evening in New York, and all the network news shows were going to air. Two TVs were tuned to CNN, their usual twenty-four-hour news service and their headline news. Dunbarry strode across to the monitors, turned, loosened his belt buckle then dropped his pants, and bared his bony buttocks to the battery of screens.

"Kiss that, you bastards," he yelled over his shoulder. "You're going to be seeing a lot of that after seven o'clock tonight."

Fifteen thousand miles away, on the perimeter of the exclusion zone in the middle of the Red Sea, a junior intelligence officer in the communications room on board HMS *Hotspur* finished his notes and took off his earphones.

"Bloody hell," he muttered, looking at his colleagues in disbelief. "Better get the boss out of bed. Some American TV reporter just got through to the hijackers."

Five nautical miles away, Doyle stepped back onto the bridge to finish what he had been doing when Dunbarry's call had interrupted him.

"What did you say your name was?" he said, looking back at the terrified girl in the ill-fitting khaki pants and dark green sweater.

LONDON. 00.35 HOURS

John Traynor hesitated before knocking on the door to the Prime Minister's bedroom. The PM had retired only minutes earlier in the hope of getting his first uninterrupted night's sleep since the crisis had begun. Traynor knew his master better than anyone outside the PM's immediate family. He knew only too well what effect the crisis was having on the mental and physical health of the Prime Minister. It made his heart ache to see it. The Prime Minister was a good man. An honorable and unpretentious man whose simple decency impressed everyone who knew him. And the crisis on board the *Britannia* was destroying him. Traynor took a deep breath and knocked on the door.

There was a moment's delay, then a weary "yes?" from inside the room.

Traynor opened the door and stepped inside. The Prime Minister was seated on the edge of the bed. The covers were down, he had removed his slippers, and the sash of his dressing gown hung loosely in his hands.

"I am truly sorry to disturb you, sir," Traynor said softly. "I'm afraid I've got Admiral Bryden on the line from Northwood. He says there have been some rather ominous developments on board the *Britannia.*"

The Prime Minister bowed his head for a moment. He felt like weeping. Instead, he sighed, refastened his dressing gown, and slid his slippers back on.

"Switch it through here, will you please, John?" he said dully. Traynor nodded and closed the bedroom door. The Prime Minister sat on the side of the bed and waited for the call to be switched through to his bedside phone. He usually shared the bed with his wife, but she had left Downing Street two days earlier to stay with their eldest daughter at Chequers until the crisis had passed. More and more since the hijacking had taken place, Number Ten had come to resemble a besieged military bunker. Senior military people came and went at all hours. The Prime Minister worked around the clock, snatching a couple of hours sleep here and there, whenever he could. This would have been his first opportunity to get anything resembling a full night's sleep. Now it looked as though he would be deprived of that too. The bedside phone chimed softly.

"This is the Prime Minister."

"Admiral Bryden, sir. More bad news, I'm afraid."

The Prime Minister waited.

"According to intelligence, the explosion we heard from the *Britannia* yesterday indicates the hijackers have broken into the yacht's strong room."

"What good will that do them?"

"Our best guess is that they're going to try to move some of the contents ashore, possibly to the People's Republic of Yemen."

"And what would be the value of those contents, Admiral?"

"According to the palace, the queen took a substantial amount of personal jewelry with her. She also received several official gifts during the voyage. The Saudis in particular tend to be rather ostenatious about royal gifts. The palace can't give us an accurate figure yet, but the best estimate comes in at around half a billion pounds."

"Good God," the Prime Minister gasped. "Does the *Britannia* usually have that sort of wealth on board?"

"Apparently the paintings alone are worth around fifty million pounds, sir," Bryden answered. "Some items are considered irreplaceable . . . priceless."

"So," the Prime Minister murmured, "our hijackers are not acting from purely political motives—they're pirates too."

"Rather looks that way, sir," Bryden replied. "They may be looting the *Britannia* as a form of insurance. They're going to need safe haven somewhere. Their political connections and the treasure from the *Britannia* might make them welcome guests in Yemen. The government there has been hostile toward us ever since independence. We have no extradition treaty with them. If the Yemenis do accept the terrorists and their plunder, it could take the threat of military intervention on a large scale to make them change their minds."

"So we're looking at the possibility of a military operation against Yemen now?"

"It's a political matter before it becomes a military matter, sir."

"Yes, Admiral. What else?"

Bryden hesitated, knowing that the news he was about to impart would shatter whatever was left of the Prime Minister's hope for a few hours' rest.

"An American TV reporter spoke to the terrorists on board the *Britannia* about forty-five minutes ago."

"What?" The shock jolted the Prime Minister to his feet.

"The man who appears to be the hijack leader told him of their demand that we pull all our troops out of Northern Ireland by noon on the twenty-third. We're getting more intelligence on the reporter as quickly as we can. All we know so far is that his name is

Dunbarry, first name Pete or Peter, and he is the anchorman of a nightly half-hour current-affairs program that is syndicated throughout the United States. It is a widely watched program with a heavy emphasis on the sensational."

"Dear God in heaven," the Prime Minister groaned. He knew it would be futile to call the President of the United States to see if anything could be done to stop Dunbarry putting the information to air. The US did not have anything like the Official Secrets Act, which could be used so effectively to muzzle the British media. And even if there was something the President could do, the Prime Minister would not ask. What Bryden said next confirmed all his worst fears.

"Dunbarry's program goes on the air in a few minutes, New York time, sir," the Admiral added. "There seems little we can do to prevent him making the ultimatum and the deadline public knowledge."

"No," the Prime Minister agreed. "Anything else, Admiral?"

"That's all for the moment, sir."

The Prime Minister hung up the phone and sat quietly back down on the bed while he absorbed the shock of this latest string of disasters. In a few minutes news of the hijackers' murderous ultimatum would be flashed all around the world. The situation in Northern Ireland had only just settled into a sullen standoff between troops and rioters, with both sides temporarily exhausted. This development would inflame the violence anew. Only this time an explosive new element would be added to the equation. The Protestant militias of Ulster would become dramatically aware of the true scale of the threat against them.

The Prime Minister got up and walked to the door. John Traynor was talking quietly with a secretary in the hallway. He looked up when the PM appeared.

"I want you to get me General Richards in Belfast on the line now, please, John," the Prime Minister said. "Then I want you to contact Malcolm Porter and see if you can get him over here now. And then I want you to change tomorrow morning's meeting of the War Cabinet to a meeting of the full Cabinet. You can tell the media to expect an announcement tomorrow at noon."

"Yes, sir," Traynor answered. He dismissed the secretary and walked slowly up to the Prime Minister, his own blood-rimmed eyes fixed on the Prime Minister's lined and shrunken face.

"Are we going to send in more troops, sir?" he asked.

"No," the Prime Minister declared flatly. "We're going to start pulling them out."

BELFAST. 05.35 HOURS

"Come on, lads." Lieutenant Hodges roused his men from their beds in the red brick junior school the army had commandeered on the Crumlin Road. "Looks like we've got another spot of bother to attend to."

The soldiers responded, as all exhausted soldiers do, with much muttering and curses and then by doing as they had been ordered. It was only a few hours since they had turned in, after making their last patrol of the burned and abandoned barricades of Andersontown. They had heard the news about the hijackers' demands a little after midnight and had been ordered onto the streets to quell the anticipated riots of renewed support. There had been none. The Catholics had stayed indoors, perhaps afraid of the backlash everyone knew was coming from the brooding Protestant ghettos of West Belfast. Instead of filling with rioters, the streets of Andersontown had been filled with an uneasy silence. Like the lull before a bigger, more ferocious storm.

It took the troops only a minute to get ready. They had slept in their uniforms on thin rubber mats laid on the floor, rifles loaded and ready by their sides. As tired as they were, they were luckier than the two men on sentry duty outside who now had to go back on duty with no sleep at all.

"Back to Andersontown, sir?" one of the men asked.

"Not this time," Hodges responded, buckling on his Plexiglas-visored helmet. "Shankhill Road. It seems the UDA has called a march to show support for the queen and our continued presence in Northern Ireland."

The Ulster Defence Association was one of the biggest and most radical of the Protestant militias.

"Nice to know somebody wants us," one soldier said.

"Yeah," another commented. "They have a funny bleedin' way of showing their gratitude though."

"You don't think there's any chance the government will order a pullout, do you, sir?" the first soldier asked as he passed Hodges on the way outside to the waiting armored cars.

Hodges gave a short, caustic laugh. "Dream on, private," he said. "We're going to be here for a while yet."

"Ah, well," the soldier grumbled as he kept on walking. "Can't blame a bloke for wishing."

Half an hour later the three Winged Pigs pulled into the bottom end of Shankhill Road and stopped, as ordered, beside a British Army roadblock. It was a few minutes past six and the sun was just coming up, but Shankhill Road was already filled with marchers. They seemed to be well organized with men in white armbands acting as marshals, gathering the marchers into groups under separate banners. As well as the gaudy banners of the loyalist lodges, there were other placards which proclaimed OUR QUEEN, OUR COUNTRY and NO SELLOUT TO THE IRA.

Hodges climbed out of the Pig and reported to Colonel Blythe, who seemed to be the officer in charge.

"How many do you think there are, sir?" he asked as they both surveyed the massing ranks of marchers.

"Too many," Blythe answered bluntly.

"Do we let them pass?"

"No," Blythe answered. "Our orders are to keep them here. It's an illegal march and it will not be allowed to proceed."

Hodges looked at him.

"There must be four . . . five thousand of them, sir."

"Probably."

Hodges looked around, his face apprehensive. There were six armored cars drawn across the road, leaving a gap in the middle big enough to allow the passage of a single car. Hodges estimated there were two hundred troops in full riot gear from his regiment and three hundred RUC men. Most of the RUC men also wore riot gear and had been deployed in front and behind the barricade. The gap in the middle was plugged by a solid phalanx of about fifty soldiers protected by high Perspex shields. The others waited in the rear with gas grenade launchers and the fat-barreled riot guns used to fire rubber bullets, which threatened severe pain at long range but which could be lethal at short range. Down a nearby side street Hodges could see perhaps another hundred soldiers and another two hundred RUC men held in reserve beside a line of police trucks and Army Land Rovers. Like Hodges's men, these soldiers were armed with assault rifles. There were also a large number of RUC men patrolling both sides of Shankhill Road in a vain attempt to defuse the mood of the crowd. Many of them had friends and neighbors among the marchers and they traded jibes with one another with a kind of forced jocularity that betrayed the underlying tension. There was something different about this day, Hodges sensed. Something in the air. A sense of menace. A sense of history. Everyone could feel it, and it charged the cool morning air like static electricity.

"Where do you want me, sir?" Hodges asked.

"Put your Pigs behind the roadblock," Blythe added. "Deploy the wings to give the men a bit of cover in case things start to get a little boisterous. How many men did you bring?"

"A full squad, sir."

"Armament?"

"Gas, rubber bullets, and rifles, sir."

"Good." Blythe nodded. "Let's hope the gas is all we need, eh?"

An hour passed, the sun climbed into a clear sky and brought a beautiful spring day. The crowd swelled to seven, perhaps eight thousand marchers and still they poured in from the side streets along Shankhill Road. It was a little after eight when two solemn-faced middle-aged men in dark blue suits detached themselves from the crowd, fifty yards away, and approached the roadblock. Hodges recognized one of them as Gerry Laughlin, president of the UDA and one of the province's leading firebrands. Colonel Blythe stepped forward to meet them as they drew closer. Hodges was just close enough to hear a few snatches of the exchange. What he heard gave him a queasy feeling in his gut.

"So . . ." Laughlin began in his usual bombastic manner. "Is the government planning to sell us out, Colonel?"

"Politics are not my concern," Blythe answered sharply. "But the public order is. This march is illegal, Mr. Laughlin. My orders are to see that it does not proceed. In the interest of public safety, you would be well advised to call off your protest and disperse this gathering."

Laughlin grinned, muttered something to his colleague, then looked back at Blythe.

". . . a day of shame for the British Army," Hodges heard him say. "But we don't need you to look out for our interests, Colonel. This is our home. We fought for it once and we'll fight for it again if we must."

Colonel Blythe answered him, but the first few words of his sentence were drowned out by the noise in the street. The only words Hodges picked up this time were ". . . in the name of common sense . . ."

Laughlin's reaction was to throw back his head and laugh in Blythe's face.

"In the name of common sense, you say? Tell that to the Catholics, Colonel. That's where your duty lies today. Tell them they've tried our patience long enough. That traitor government of yours and the papists in Dublin have taken our restraint for weakness. Well, I tell you on this day that we will stand for it no longer. We will claim what is ours. We will march where we want to march, and if the taigs know what's good for them, they'll get out now. Because when you and your men have all gone, they'll find out that God is on our side and his wrath is our wrath."

He finished with a defiant toss of his head and turned to rejoin the waiting marchers, his lackey hurrying to keep up with him.

"Stupid bugger," Blythe muttered as he walked slowly back behind the barricade. "He won't be satisfied till he's seen blood flow, and I don't think he cares too much whose blood it is."

"Yes, sir," Hodges said. "Trouble is there are plenty like him on both sides. All they want is a chance to go for each other's throats."

"Looks like they're going to get it, lad," Blythe answered soberly. "It looks like they're going to get it."

Hodges swallowed and looked down the road at the swelling, threatening crowd. His stomach growled again. Whether it was from hunger or fear, he couldn't be sure. He pulled a chocolate protein bar from his shirt pocket and took a bite. It wasn't the ideal breakfast for a man about to face an assault by several thousand loyalist fanatics, but it would have to do.

The next hour passed slowly, and Hodges estimated that the crowd along Shankhill Road had grown to almost ten thousand. The noise they made was like the grumble of an angry sea that echoed back and forth between the red brick houses on both sides of the street. As the final few minutes before nine o'clock ticked by, the tension grew until it infected the air like a bad odor. Hodges reached beneath his bulletproof vest and tugged his shirt away from his back. It was soaking wet.

At nine o'clock a drum roll sounded from somewhere in the midst of the marchers. Others joined in. A rapid syncopated countdown into the Protestant anthem "The Sash My Father Wore." The drums were joined by the shrill clamor of pipes, a great roar welled up from the crowd, and the first rank of marchers started forward, their banners raised high and defiant.

The RUC men and the soldiers in front of the barricade pulled on their gas masks and braced themselves. Blythe had done all he could. A solid roadblock, tear gas, and rubber bullets would be enough to discourage any ordinary march. But this time, Hodges knew, it was different. This time the loyalists were marching for the right to survive. And if they got anywhere near the Catholic ghettos of Belfast on this beautiful spring day, their fury would be terrible.

The gap between marchers and soldiers closed quickly. Hodges watched, mesmerized. Laughlin and his cronies were right up front, and they were marching briskly toward the barricade as though they expected to walk right through it, like ghosts through a brick wall. Perhaps they would, Hodges thought. His fingers wandered over the butt of his pistol one more time.

"Give 'em the drill, lads," Blythe called out, walking back and forth behind the front squad of soldiers. "Just give 'em the drill."

The last few yards melted away, and the marchers broke upon the thin blue line of the police and the Perspex shields of the soldiers like an ugly black tide. Laughlin faded to the side and was replaced by a wedge of bigger men who brought the massed weight of the crowd to bear on those fragile transparent shields. It had all been planned, Hodges realized. The biggest men in the crowd bore down on the soldiers like a Greek phalanx. The policemen on either side of the road were engulfed, disarmed, and shoved to the rear of the crowd. The soldiers at the barricade pushed back. The line swayed. The shields began to flex and wobble. The first punches were thrown by the marchers. The soldiers struck back with riot sticks. Suddenly, the air between the two opposing forces filled with a spray of thrashing arms and sticks carried on waves of shouting white faces.

The first line of soldiers buckled beneath the onslaught and started to give ground. Blythe gave the order to fire, and a score of gas launchers coughed in unison. The canisters painted woolly white vapor trails in the clear blue sky as they arced sharply upward, then dropped into the crowd, fifty to sixty yards away. Moments later, thick white clouds of gas rolled down Shankhill Road as Blythe tried desperately to rob the marchers of their momentum.

Something small and shiny appeared in the air above the crowd and curved over the barricade to land amid the soldiers at the rear. It erupted in a vivid blossom of flame, scattering those soldiers waiting to reinforce the men at front. Another firebomb exploded and then another. The third exploded near Hodges, spattering him with burning droplets of gasoline. He spun away, beating at the pinpricks of heat on his arms and legs. Two of his men rushed forward to help him put out the flames. His battle dress was riddled with tiny charred holes.

"Jesus . . ." he muttered inside his gas mask. Things had escalated from fearful anticipation to full-scale madness in a matter of minutes. The smoke from the firebombs merged with gas to create a blinding, toxic fog. Hodges returned to the barricade in time to see a man in a dark suit and a marshal's armband clambering over one of the armored cars that made up the roadblock. The man was wearing a gas mask and waving to others to follow.

They had come ready. With a plan. With gas masks. With weapons and with an unstoppable resolve. The loyalists had been smoldering for days, weeks, years. They wanted to vent all their rage and frustrations on the Republicans now, and the British Army wasn't going to stop them. Hodges saw the man in the dark suit leap onto a policeman from the roof of the armored car. He was quickly wrestled away by two RUC men. Then there were half a dozen more loyalists climbing over the armored cars. The marchers had turned into a mob. Hodges caught a glimpse of Blythe shouting orders but couldn't hear his words above the roar of the crowd. One of the armored cars began to rock. The massed blue ranks of the RUC men rushed forward to reinforce the barricade. Hodges ordered his own men to assist. He saw more gas grenades leap into the air. Then he saw a sight that would remain with him for the rest of his life.

The smoke and gas cleared for a moment and Hodges saw a dozen loyalist men swarming over one of the Pigs. One man stopped, a hand cupped to his roaring mouth, the other waving his comrades on. He was a young man with long brown hair and a thin face lit by the fire of battle. For a moment Hodges was reminded of a painting he had seen of the storming of the Bastille. Then half the man's head disappeared in a gout of blood as a rubber bullet fired from point-blank range tore his skull to pieces. The man's body froze where it was for a moment, his arms still raised in a grotesque parody of life, then he collapsed like a broken toy and disappeared back into the crowd. The marchers hesitated, but only for a moment, then they surged forward with a roar of renewed fury that sent a ripple of dread through the thinly massed ranks of soldiers. A moment later one of the armored cars teetered slowly over, then rolled on its side with a crash that made the pavement shudder.

Hodges drew his pistol and ran forward to meet the onrushing mob. It was already too late. Two hundred and fifty British soldiers and three hundred RUC men were not enough to stop the furious loyalist tide that morning. All around him Hodges saw soldiers and policemen thrown aside or pushed to the ground by the onrushing mass. He pointed his pistol into the air and fired two shots in quick succession. He barely heard them above the tumult. Something hit the side of his helmet hard and he staggered. He fought back but there were too many. A hundred fists seemed to pummel him all at once. He felt his helmet go. Someone punched him in the face. Desperate hands clawed at his fist. He felt a savage pain as his finger broke, and then his pistol was gone.

A few moments later the worst of it was over. The front of the crowd had passed. A stampeding mob of triumphant, cheering faces that would not be stopped. Hodges staggered to his feet, blood streaming from a gashed cheek, his broken hand clutched to his body. The crowd ignored him now, swept him aside as though he no longer mattered. He saw others, soldiers and RUC men, equally battered and dazed, stripped of their weapons, pushed to the side of the street as the mob surged past in a tidal wave of blood lust.

Hodges pushed his way to the other side of the road, looking for Blythe. He saw the colonel a moment later, helmet gone, bleeding from a cut over his left eye, trying to regroup his men down a side street. Hodges ran over to him, fighting to ignore the pain that lanced up his arm with each jarring step.

"They've got some of our weapons," he panted.

"I know," Blythe answered. "But we never came under direct fire. I couldn't order our men to shoot into a crowd like that . . . I couldn't."

"If they get to Andersontown in that mood, there'll be slaughter," Hodges said.

"I've informed HQ of the situation here," Blythe answered. "The bulk of our forces have been concentrated around the Catholic ghettos to try and keep the silly buggers from murdering each other. Our job was to stop the march if possible . . . or at least take some of the steam out of them."

"Take some of the steam out of them?" Hodges echoed. "We've just warmed them up."

"Come here." Blythe said abruptly, taking Hodges by the shoulder and steering him out of earshot of the troops.

"There isn't much more we can do with the men we've got, and we're not getting any reinforcements. In fact, the word is . . . we may be pulling back altogether."

"Pulling back?" Hodges stared at him in horror. "What do you mean, pulling back?"

"The situation throughout Northern Ireland is rapidly becoming unmanageable," Blythe added. "We've only got eighteen thousand men in Belfast and we need twice that many if we're to have a hope in hell of keeping a lid on it. In the meantime, we may have to withdraw, at least for a few days, while this thing burns itself out."

"Burns itself out?" Hodges shook his head, unable to believe he had heard correctly. "If we step back and let them get on with it, there could be hundreds dead by morning."

"Well, what the hell would you do, Lieutenant?" Blythe snapped at him, suddenly losing his temper. "How many British soldiers are you willing to sacrifice? God knows what our casualties will be from this little episode, and I have no idea what is happening in other parts of the province or in Londonderry, where they're even more seriously undermanned. We can only thank God if we haven't had any fatalities yet."

"Sir, I—"

"I know, Lieutenant," Blythe interrupted, struggling to regain his composure. "At this stage we are just trying to keep a lid on the situation. But my orders are that if things deteriorate to the point where my men are in danger of being overwhelmed, then we withdraw and leave the bastards to it. And you've already seen how quickly that can happen. We can only hope that sometime in the next twelve hours both sides will come to their senses. Otherwise they'll have the bloodbath they've been threatening for years."

Hodges turned away, stunned.

Twelve hours. That was all that stood between them and anarchy in Northern Ireland.

LONDON. 10.10 HOURS

"Gentlemen."

The Prime Minister began his announcement the moment he had seated himself in the Cabinet Room.

"Events have reached a stage where I must commit this government to a course of action. I have decided, therefore, to issue the order at three o'clock this afternoon that will commence the withdrawal of British troops from Northern Ireland."

There was a collective gasp from around the table.

Charles Ingham, secretary of state for Northern Ireland, was first to respond.

"Prime Minister," he asked, "will you be making this announcement to the House personally?"

"No, Charles," the Prime Minister answered. "You will."

Ingham looked stunned. Then he slowly shook his head.

"The secretary of state for Northern Ireland will make the announcement to the House on behalf of the government, immediately prior to question time," the Prime Minister went on. "The same announcement will be released by my office at three o'clock in the form of a written press statement. I have already apprised General Richards in Belfast of my decision. I have further advised him that commencement of the withdrawal should not begin until midnight tonight, when it will take the form of a general return to barracks. That will give the RUC time to adjust to the demands of the new situation. General Richards has informed me that the first troops should be airlifted out of Northern Ireland within twenty-four hours. By that time I hope we will have reopened negotiations with the hijackers to establish an appropriate timetable for an orderly withdrawal and the subsequent release of hostages. The next seventy-two hours will be critical, and I do not expect to be able to leave Downing Street. Therefore, the deputy prime minister will lead question time for the government in the House this afternoon"—he paused and looked directly at Ingham—"and I expect you to be there, Charles, to help him deal with the Opposition."

"I shall be there, Prime Minister," Ingham responded coolly. "But not in my capacity as secretary of state for Northern Ireland."

The Prime Minister waited, his gray face unreadable.

"I cannot make this announcement on behalf of the government," Ingham added. "Because I do not believe in it. I have slept very little in the past few days, like everyone else at this table, I imagine. And I have used the time to examine my conscience fully. My heart goes out to every member of the royal family, as it would to any family in a similar situation, but I cannot support any policy of appeasement toward terrorists that involves the sacrifice of Northern Ireland. It is my understanding, Prime Minister, that you have spoken with the queen directly and that Her Majesty has already conveyed to you the view that she does not wish this government to enter into a dishonorable negotiation with the hijackers on her behalf. It is also my understanding that this same view has been expressed to you by Prince Philip and Prince Charles."

The Prime Minister stared at Ingham but said nothing to refute his words. A number of ministers stirred around the table.

"As terrible as the implications may be," Ingham went on, "I believe this stand by the royal family to be both courageous and well-considered, and most certainly should be allowed to enter into the decision-making process. I for one could not think of a more dishonorable act than for this government to come to an arrangement with terrorists and murderers that would condemn Northern Ireland to anarchy and bloodshed. The IRA has long been excluded from the peacemaking process, and this is a dastardly attempt by them to sabotage that process. It should, under no circumstances, be allowed to succeed. If British troops are pulled out, it will create a security vacuum that can only be filled by blood. This is a decision that you and you alone have made, Prime Minister. It is not the decision of this Cabinet and therefore it cannot be said to be the decision of this government. I certainly cannot defend it in Parliament. Therefore" —he paused just a moment to give his words added emphasis—"I have no alternative but to resign. I shall see that my resignation is on your desk, in writing, before three o'clock this afternoon."

Ingham gathered his papers and got up to leave. The room was so still, so silent, even the rustle of paper sounded unnaturally loud.

"Would you like to hear the latest casualty reports on our troops in Northern Ireland, Charles?" the Prime Minister asked blandly. He pulled a slip of paper from the file in front of him.

"As of eight o'clock this morning, two soldiers confirmed killed in Belfast, twenty-three wounded, eleven of those seriously. In Londonderry, one soldier killed and seventeen wounded, nine seriously. In Armagh, one soldier killed, three wounded, all seriously. If we leave them there, more will die. So will the queen, Prince Philip, and every other hostage on the *Britannia.* I am faced with a choice of evils, Charles. I have chosen what I consider to be the lesser evil. If you would care to reconsider your position, at least until this meeting is over, I would be glad—"

"With respect, Prime Minister," Ingham interrupted. "You do not need me. You did not extend to me the courtesy of forewarning me that you would be speaking to General Richards. You have already made up your mind. The only purpose you have for me now is to do your dirty work in the Commons, and I'm not prepared to do that."

He paused and looked around the room while his insult hung in the air like something tangible.

"I wish you . . . I wish you all the greatest good luck, gentlemen," he added. "Because you will be fortunate indeed to emerge from this shameful capitulation with your good names."

Ingham left the room and closed the door quietly behind him. The Prime Minister sighed, leaned back in his chair, and turned to Alexander Rose, the deputy prime minister, who sat next to him.

"Alexander," he said, "you will take over Charles's portfolio until further notice."

An aging Tory elder serving out his last term of office, Rose looked mortified by the realization that he would go down in history as the secretary of state for Northern Ireland who presided over its bloody demise.

"Don't look so worried, old chap." The Prime Minister gave him a weary smile. "I don't think you'll be burdened with it for too long. I think we can all prepare for a general election once this is over."

"He'll be on the phone to the leader of the Opposition in five minutes, you know," the Home Secretary, Nigel Shepherd, remarked suddenly, nodding to the door where Ingham had just made his exit. "The moment Alex makes the announcement in the House, the Opposition will start a motion of no confidence against you."

"I know," the Prime Minister answered. "I'll be talking to the chief whip after this meeting. From what I understand, it's going to be a pretty full session this afternoon anyway. Even if we allow for half a dozen absentees and the same number of defections, we've still got a twenty-seat majority."

"Perhaps," Shepherd mused. "Perhaps not."

"You think more than a few of our people will cross the floor?" the Prime Minister asked.

"Yes," Shepherd answered. "I do."

"How many?"

"I don't know for sure. All I know is what I hear. This crisis has created the most unexpected divisions . . . across all party lines. We're looking at Tory realpolitik, Prime Minister. There are people on our side who don't want to see Northern Ireland go at any cost, probably because it's not their necks that are on the block. I was talking to one of our backbenchers in the bar last night, and once he'd gotten a few whiskeys into him, he said the old girl has had a good innings and it wouldn't make any real difference to anybody if Prince Charles got the job sooner rather than later."

The Prime Minister's face seemed to blanch even more.

"Heard the same talk myself," Teddy Lawson added. "There's a surprising lack of sentiment out there, when you get right down to it. There are a few chaps I know who are saying privately that we can afford to lose the queen more than we can afford to lose Northern Ireland."

"Good God," the Prime Minister mumbled.

"To balance that," Shepherd went on, "there are a few Labour people I know who don't like the idea of using this crisis to force an election. They might win—but look at the blood they'd have on their hands. A murdered monarch or anarchy in Northern Ireland. They're quite happy to let us bugger this one up on our own, then tell us what we did wrong later. They're convinced they'll win the next election, whatever happens. All they have to do is be patient and let us take all the blame for this mess."

"So you think we could get a few Labour defectors crossing to our side of the floor?" the PM asked.

"Prime Minister," Shepherd added, "the only certainty about this crisis is that no one has any idea what is going to happen. It is a no-win situation for anyone. Everyone loses. What I can tell you is that there is not a man in Parliament or in the entire bloody country, for that matter, who wants to be sitting in your chair at the moment."

"Or sitting too closely to me?" The Prime Minister smiled faintly.

"That too," Shepherd conceded.

"If I may say so, Prime Minister . . ." Francis Grey, the foreign secretary, spoke for the first time. "Charles Ingham may have hit on one vital issue that it may well be in your best interests, and the best interests of this government, for you to address."

"Yes, Francis?" The Prime Minister waited.

"No one outside Cabinet, or your immediate circle of advisers, has heard from you since this crisis began. You haven't spoken to the House on the matter. You haven't given a press conference. You haven't addressed the nation. There is a perception outside the walls of this office, Prime Minister, that you are vacillating, and in this vacillation you are being pushed by the momentum of the situation into an unwise decision."

"What would you have me do, Francis?" the PM inquired softly.

"We can all appreciate that you don't want to get distracted by grubby House politics at this time, Prime Minister," Grey added. "And those of us who consider ourselves loyal servants of the Crown are willing to do our bit to keep the hounds at bay while you manage this crisis. However, some newspapers and television commentators are starting to criticize your apparent nonhandling of the situation. They are calling you the invisible man. We have to put an end to that sort of thing. I am of the opinion that it would be a good idea if you were to make a televised address to the nation sometime very soon. Tonight . . . tomorrow night at the latest. Either live or with a prerecorded statement. Whichever you feel up to. But I do think the country needs some form of reassurance from this office that you are still very much in charge and you are doing what you believe to be best for the queen and for the nation. They might not like it, they may not understand it, and a great many of them probably won't agree with it. But this is a historic crisis, Prime Minister. The country is in shock. The people need to hear from you."

"In short, Francis," the PM responded, "you believe I owe the country an explanation?"

"That would be putting it bluntly, yes, sir."

"And how does everyone else feel on that score?" The PM glanced around the table.

"I think it's absolutely essential," Teddy Lawson said.

"I'm inclined to agree," Nigel Shepherd added.

"Prime Minister, we all feel it would be a good idea," Alexander Rose said. "The crisis is taking its toll on the nation. There is a degree of despair in the national temper that has not been apparent before. A feeling of hopelessness that we must dispel. An appearance by you now with a few Churchillian phrases about difficult times and the courage to make the hard decisions, that sort of thing . . . it could make a world of difference to the mood of the people."

"And it might buy us a little time," Nigel Shepherd added. "If the government falls before noon on the twenty-third, what hope would there be for Her Majesty then?"

The Prime Minister raised both hands to indicate that he'd heard enough. The room fell silent.

"Gentlemen," he said. "Nothing pains me more than the knowledge of what this crisis is doing to our country. The outrage, the despair, the mood of helplessness, I can assure you, I feel it all and I feel it as deeply as anyone. However, I must ask you all to have faith in me and to bear with me just a little longer. Regrettably, I do not believe the interests of the nation would be best served at the moment by my taking the time to make a television appearance to mouth a few well-chosen platitudes. I have already made it clear that I will take whatever steps I believe are necessary to safeguard the life of the sovereign, even if that should mean the end of my own political life. The things you are telling me now have all been taken into consideration. It is my decision to proceed with the course of action I have described. British troops will be withdrawn from Northern Ireland, starting from midnight tonight. That information will be conveyed to the hijackers forthwith and it is my hope that negotiations will begin then for an orderly timetable of withdrawal, followed by the release of hostages. Then, and only then, will we worry about the future disposition of power in Northern Ireland."

The Cabinet meeting broke up a few moments later in a mood of sullen despair. The foreign secretary hung back a moment and gently drew Shepherd and Lawson aside while the others filed from the room.

"What do you think?"

"I think we're in more trouble than we realized," Shepherd answered dully.

"He's lost something," Lawson added. "His edge, his political savvy . . . something."

"It's hardly surprising," Shepherd shrugged. "From what I've heard, he's had about twelve hours' sleep in the past four days. Nobody thinks clearly under that kind of strain."

"No," Grey agreed. "All the same, it worries me that he won't go to the House or the nation on this, even for the sake of damage control. He's running scared and it shows. I think we may have to face up to a few things."

"Such as?" Shepherd raised an eyebrow.

"Do you think it has to be handled like this?" Grey asked. "Do you think we have to pull the troops out? Surely, there's something else, something . . ."

"My biggest fear is that the Opposition will get a no-confidence motion up before midnight," Lawson mused.

"That's what I mean," Grey said. "We can't allow that to happen."

"We can always try to stall, I suppose," Shepherd added. "We're down to four days as it is. If we can stall the vote for seventy-two hours—"

"I don't think that's a viable strategy," Grey cut him off.

"Well, what do you have in mind?" Shepherd looked at him.

"Leadership challenge."

"What?" Shepherd's voice went up a level.

Grey glanced furtively around. The three of them were alone in the Cabinet Room, though the doors were open and they could hear the murmur of others waiting outside. Only John Traynor looked in briefly, then disappeared again.

"It's a hell of a lot better than going to an election," Grey argued. "And maybe we can come up with something better than the PM can. I'm not convinced that caving in completely is the only way to go, are you?"

"No," Shepherd murmured. He hesitated for a moment, then made up his mind.

"Whom do you have in mind?" he asked.

"Rose would be the logical choice."

"Won't go along with it," Shepherd said. "He's the PM's man. He hates it as much as we do and he's the messenger who's going to get his head cut off in the House this afternoon but he won't be part of any plot to oust the Prime Minister."

"Charles Ingham, then?"

Shepherd paused.

"That's who I was thinking of," he said finally.

"He's the logical choice, given the circumstances," Grey added. "I suspect he's just waiting for somebody to make the suggestion."

"Think we can get the numbers?"

"I think we have to find out," Grey said. "Between the three of us, we ought to be able to get some idea before three o'clock this afternoon."

Shepherd nodded, then finished packing his briefcase and followed Grey and Lawson quietly from the room. Most of the others had already left and the door to the Prime Minister's office was closed when they passed. All three Cabinet ministers assumed the Prime Minister was talking to the chief whip, the party executive responsible for the turnout of members in the House and strict adherance to the PM's line.

All three were wrong.

The PM kept the whip waiting in another room a few minutes longer while he took an important call. A call from Byron Blair, director of MI5.

"Yes, Byron," the Prime Minister said, alone in his office. "What can I do for you?"

"I think I may have some rather interesting news for you, Prime Minister," Blair said.

"Go on."

"One of our more reliable assets in Belfast has been in touch."

The PM smiled despite his exhaustion. He knew damn well that Blair had not deactivated all his agents in the province. He waited, expectantly.

"This whole thing has been very well handled by the IRA, I must admit," Blair continued. "It would appear that two new cells, perhaps more, were organized at least a year ago to orchestrate the hijacking, and they've been in quarantine ever since. Nobody in the Provo rank and file knew this thing was coming. That's why nobody got a whisper. These cells have operated independently of each other and it's only now that the hijacking is under way and the support cell has gone into action that its involvement has become apparent."

"Do we know who they are?" the Prime Minister asked urgently. "Do we know where they are?"

"We know who they are," Blair answered. "I'm afraid we don't know yet where they are. Our asset has been working deep cover for three years, but it's not a situation that allows for hour-by-hour contact."

"But at some point," the PM responded, "the hijackers will have to make contact with their support cell to confirm that their demands on the ground have been met?"

"That is what we expect, sir," Blair replied.

"Excellent." The Prime Minister nodded his approval. "Until that contact has been made, you don't make a move, Blair. Understood?"

"We have to shut down that cell at some point," Blair protested. "At least when the rescue operation gets under way—"

"There may not be a rescue operation," the Prime Minister interrupted. "Just because I have ordered a contingency plan into place doesn't mean it will be enacted. I'll tell you what I've told everybody else, Blair. If I have to make a deal to save the life of the monarch, I'll do it. Even if it means pulling our troops out of Northern Ireland."

"I stand to lose a fine agent if we keep buggerizing around like this," Blair protested.

"The moment you know the location of that cell, you let me know, Blair. And you don't make a move until I say so. Understood?"

"But, Prime Minister—" Blair started to argue.

"Understood?" the PM angrily cut him off.

There was a long pause.

"Understood," Blair acknowledged, his voice flat, resigned.

The Prime Minister hung up the phone and Byron Blair slumped back in his seat.

"Jesus," he muttered to himself. What the hell did the Prime Minister think he was playing at? Perhaps the rumors he'd heard from the War Cabinet were right after all, he thought. Perhaps the PM did deserve to be dumped . . . and soon.

LARNE, NORTHERN IRELAND. 15.33 HOURS

In the darkened sitting room of a rented summer cottage, a couple of streets back from the dingy sea front at Larne, three people huddled over a transistor radio, faces tense as they absorbed every incredible word of a BBC news flash. When it was over, Matty Byrne switched the radio off and looked first at McDermott, then at Jilly.

"Sweet Mary, mother of Christ," he breathed. "They're pullin' out. After all these years—they're finally pullin' out."

He got up slowly from the table, pushing the chair back with his legs, the beginnings of a grin spreading slowly across his fleshy red face. He reached out with both arms and McDermott got up and joined his longtime comrade in arms in an emotional embrace.

"God almighty," Byrne mumbled, slapping McDermott repeatedly on the back. "We've done it, Sean. We've bloody well done it."

The two men held on to each other for a long time, snuffling tearfully into each other's shoulders and swaying like drunks, as though they might topple over at any moment. Then McDermott reached down and pulled Jilly up to join them, and the three of them held one another tight, caught in the euphoria of a historic moment none of them dreamed they would see in their lifetimes.

"Jesus Christ," McDermott mumbled, and pulled himself away, dabbing self-consciously at both eyes with the heel of his hand. "You're sure it's real? You don't think it's another stunt by the Brits?"

"You heard the man," Byrne said, nodding at the radio. "The Prime Minister gave the order today. They start pullin' out at midnight tonight. Unconditional surrender, Sean. That's what it means. Unconditional bloody surrender."

"God." McDermott peeled himself away from the others and walked around the room, shaking his head, dazed. "I can't . . . I still can't believe it."

Jilly stared at them both, then shook her dirty blond hair, sat down, and lit a cigarette.

"You two . . . you're part of it, aren't you?" she said slowly, as though it were all just becoming clear.

McDermott and Byrne grinned and looked at each other.

"I knew it," she said, smiling slyly at the two of them. "You're in on it, aren't you? You knew this was coming?"

"Now, now, Jilly sweetheart," Byrne said. "Don't you go worryin' about how much we know and how much we don't know."

"I told you before, Jilly," McDermott said warningly. "What you don't know . . ."

"Can't hurt me, I know," she finished the sentence for him. "But I'm not completely stupid, you know. You two have been like a couple of school kids with a big secret ever since we got here. I knew somethin' was up. I knew you didn't just bring me up here to get away from all the shit in Belfast."

Jilly was straying onto dangerous ground, but she was too stupid to realize it. McDermott tilted his head to one side and looked at her.

"What do you know, Jilly?" he asked softly.

She looked back at him through eyes that were thick with mascara and insolence. Then she got up and walked slowly across the room toward him on her bare feet, putting just enough emphasis into the sway of her hips to send a familiar, provocative message. McDermott watched her, his face expressionless except for the tightly knit brows and the hint of a sneer. Jilly was wearing a loose top that stopped a few inches short of the waistband of her skirt, showing a slender white waist. Byrne could see that she wasn't wearing a bra under the top. And, instead of her usual skin-hugging jeans, she wore a denim miniskirt that accentuated her bottom and showed off her long, bare legs. When she reached McDermott, she molded her body gently to his, pressing her crotch against him, brushing his chest with her nipples. She stared directly into his eyes, then slowly, lewdly, she ran the tip of her tongue over his lips.

"I know that I don't want you gettin' yourself hurt," she murmured. "I know that it's best when there's just you an' me."

She lowered her voice to the tiniest whisper so that Byrne could not hear.

"And I know I don't want him hangin' around watchin' us all the time," she said. She slid her hand between their bodies so that Byrne could not see and lightly traced the outline of McDermott's hardening cock beneath his jeans.

McDermott laughed despite himself. He wrapped his arm around her waist, pulled her hard against him, and kissed her sloppily on the mouth.

"You're a bad, dangerous girl, Jilly Cahill," he told her. "You just mind your curiosity and do what you're told."

"I always do what you tell me to do," she said, still playing with him.

"Look, Sean," Byrne interrupted from the other side of the room, sounding uncomfortable. "I'd be happy to leave you two to get on with it, but we've got business to attend to."

Jilly leaned back from McDermott, leaving her crotch pressed against him, a pleading look in her dark eyes.

"You got some money, Matty?" McDermott asked.

"Yes," Byrne answered.

"Give Jilly a few quid, then, would you? She can nip down the pub and pick up something to drink. We should be havin' a party tonight."

Byrne turned and reached into the inside pocket of his jacket on the back of a kitchen chair. He pulled out his wallet, took out three twenty-pound notes, and handed them to Jilly.

"Pick us up some grub while you're out," he said. "And get a couple of dozen cans of lager, a bottle of Bushmills. There should be a bit left over to get yourself some vodka."

He picked up his car keys and threw them to her.

"Mind and drive careful now . . . and don't go makin' any new friends."

"I'm choosy about my friends, Matty," she answered. Then she slipped on her shoes, opened the back door, and stepped out into the warm spring sunlight. The two men sat back down at the table as the sound of her footsteps clicked past the kitchen window.

"You sure she's all right?" Byrne asked.

“I told you”—McDermott shrugged, trying to ignore the heat that ebbed reluctantly from his crotch—“she’s a fuckin’ bimbo. All she cares about is havin’ a good time.”

Byrne still looked unsure.

“She doesn’t like you much though,” McDermott added, getting to what he believed was really niggling Byrne. “She thinks you listen to us fuckin’, outside the bedroom door.”

A guilty shadow crossed Byrne’s eyes and McDermott grinned as he realized he’d scored a bull’s-eye.

“She thought she was comin’ up here for a few days’ holiday with me, for Christ’s sake,” he added. “Look, she knows I’m a Provo man. She knows that you and me have been pals since we did time in the Kesh. She knows I’ve done a few jobs for the Provos.”

“Shit,” Byrne swore. “She knows you’ve topped a few fellers?”

“She knows I’m no fuckin’ choirboy,” McDermott answered dismissively. “There’s at least a hundred other people in Northern Ireland who know that and ninety-nine of them are your fuckin’ relatives. But she doesn’t know about you bein’ quartermaster. And she doesn’t know shit about Doyle and what’s happenin’ now. She thinks we’re happy because we’re good IRA men and the Brits are gettin’ out of Northern Ireland and that’s all.”

“I hope you’re right,” Byrne responded grudgingly. “Because if I thought the bitch—”

“You know what I think?” McDermott interrupted harshly. “You can’t stand the sight of your missus, and you wish it was you that was fuckin’ Jilly and not me, now, isn’t that the truth, Matty? Isn’t it?”

McDermott folded his arms, scraped back his chair, and waited for an answer. A long, sullen silence descended between the two men. It was Byrne who gave in first.

“Ah, sweet Jesus,” he muttered. “I’m not going to waste another minute on the stupid woman.”

Instead, he reached behind him and pulled a thin strip of waxed paper from a slit in his jacket lapel. He opened it carefully, pressed it flat on the table, and read it in the light that filtered through the curtained windows. There were two short paragraphs. He read them quickly, then pushed the paper across the table. McDermott looked at it blankly for a moment. Then he pushed it back to Byrne.

"What does it say?" he asked.

Byrne stared at him.

"Jesus Christ," he said, "you still can't bloody read, can ye?"

"Not real writin'." McDermott shrugged.

"That's printed."

"Just fuckin' read it, Matty, okay?"

Byrne sniffed and picked the piece of paper up again.

"It says, 'This is a statement on behalf of the liberated people of Northern Ireland. We hereby appeal to the United Nations to send a peacekeeping force to Northern Ireland immediately to safeguard the transfer of power in the six counties to the legitimate government of the Republic of Ireland.' And that's all of it. That's what Doyle wants us to release to the TV and the papers."

McDermott nodded but said nothing.

"You have to do it," Byrne added. "Not me. And we can't make the calls from around here. They have to be made from different call boxes around Belfast . . . and they have to be done now. Today. So everything looks right."

McDermott nodded.

"I can memorize it," he said. "That's what I always do. Go over it with me a few times and I'll remember it."

"Jesus," Byrne hesitated. "You're sure?"

"Of course I'm bloody sure," McDermott snapped back at him. "Get on with it, for Christ's sake, or I'll never get out of here."

Half an hour later Jilly returned with two bags packed full of groceries, beer, and liquor. McDermott had just finished putting on his motorcycle leathers.

"Where are you goin'?" she asked, setting the bags heavily on the table.

"None of your business," McDermott grumbled.

"Can I come?" she asked, a plaintive note creeping into her voice.

"No, you fuckin' can't," McDermott snapped. He picked up his helmet and brushed angrily past her toward the door.

"When will you be back—"

"When you see me, Jilly, that's when." McDermott cut her off and opened the door.

"Jesus, Sean," she called after him. "What did I do?"

McDermott spun around and grabbed her T-shirt so hard that it ripped in his hand.

"Sometimes you just fuckin' breathe wrong, Jilly," he growled. She blinked as flecks of spittle sprayed in her face. Then he pushed her away so that she bumped into the table and the two grocery bags fell over, spilling their contents across the table. Byrne jumped up and helped her catch the rolling cans and bottles before they fell to the floor. McDermott slammed the door so loudly behind him it seemed for a moment that it might have splintered.

"What happened, Matty?" she asked, looking angrily at Byrne.

"You know Sean." Byrne shrugged, a glint of malign pleasure in his eyes. "He's a man of many moods."

8 The Moving Finger

BOSTON, MAY 20. 12.05 HOURS

The crowd on Boston Common was smaller than Noraid's organizers had hoped. Only about three thousand people so far. Most of them familiar faces from the waterfront unions and the city's Irish-American clubs, their numbers augmented by a sprinkling of professional protestors from a ragtag coalition of left-wing organizations and the usual rabble of street toughs drawn by the promise of trouble. A couple of dozen uniformed police officers and a half dozen mounted policemen patrolled the edges of the crowd, making their presence known but trying hard not to be too obtrusive. Another fifty or so waited along nearby Park and Tremont streets, and there were two hundred more in reserve, hidden in buses in the back streets, including two tactical response groups in case things got ugly. Agents of the FBI and the Secret Service circulated anonymously through the crowd, taking photographs whenever they could.

Noraid's organizers had assured the city they planned a peaceful rally followed by a march to the British consular offices at Federal Reserve Plaza on Atlantic Avenue, where they would deliver a petition calling for the withdrawal of British troops from Northern Ireland. But, because it was a Sunday, the building was closed and the organizers had been advised they would have to content themselves with turning over the petition to the police captain in charge of security at the plaza for delivery to the consul the next day. Orders to the police were clear. They had come down to the chief of police via the mayor and the governor from the President of the United States. Protest was fine. Violence was not. Attacks on British property or personnel would not be tolerated. The President had added that he expected the highest degree of professionalism from the Boston police department despite the large number of Irish-Americans on the force and the sympathy they might have for the cause of Irish unity. The governor, the mayor, and the chief of police understood perfectly. Their asses were all on the line.

A short, balding, pug-faced man in his early fifties by the name of Roy Maguire had assured the city that once the petition had been turned in, the marchers would disperse. Maguire was chairman of Noraid's Boston chapter. It was Maguire who sat closest now to Senator Pat Callaghan on a makeshift stage, where the two of them could look out over the bobbing heads of the crowd. It was Maguire who had helped Callaghan make his run for the Senate in the late 1970s. It was Maguire who had taken Callaghan's place as president of the longshoremen's union. It was Maguire who had seen to it that Callaghan's voting base among all the waterfront unions remained intact.

The two of them sat on a couple of folding chairs at one side of the stage, smiling, talking, and chatting to friends and supporters. Hundreds of banners and placards waved and danced among the crowd, some showing the Union Jack streaming blood, others calling for the immediate withdrawal of British troops from Northern Ireland. To the right of the stage a table had been set up where volunteers collected signatures for their petition. Bag ladies, punks, drunks, kite fliers, skateboarders, and children were all encouraged to lend their names to the Cause. The center of the stage was occupied by a five-piece band from the Shamrock Social Club. Their repertoire was an emotive blend of boisterous rebel songs, maudlin ballads, and passionately delivered poems about British soldiers who bayonetted babies in their cribs, raped fair Irish maidens, desecrated churches, and whose scarlet tunics were dyed red from centuries of Irish blood.

Maguire stopped tapping his foot for a moment and looked at his watch. It was time to begin the speeches, he decided. He had hoped for a bigger crowd, but it wasn't bad considering he'd had only a few days to organize. He could always bump the estimates up to ten thousand later. No one could prove otherwise, and three thousand noisy demonstrators could look like an awful lot of people to a TV camera. Maguire noted with satisfaction that there were at least five news crews covering the event and there were more people drifting onto the Common all the time, most of them spectators and curiosity-seekers, but they helped pad out the numbers.

He signaled to a union aide that he wanted the band to finish after the next song. The aide walked around to the front of the stage and whispered to a bearded man with a fiddle who was the bandleader. The bearded man nodded. A moment later the song ended and he announced that the next song would be the last. There was a smattering of boos from the crowd, but they quickly dissolved into cheers as the band segued into the opening bars of "The Wearing of the Green," the anthem of Irish expatriates all over the world. It was a stirring piece of music, and on this day it was delivered with such raw power and emotion that it was impossible for anyone who was there not to feel moved. When it was over, Maguire was inspired to dab a tear from the corner of his eye. Callaghan regretted that he hadn't thought of that first. He contented himself by giving Maguire a sympathetic pat on the shoulder to show that he shared the same depth of feeling.

The bandleader introduced Maguire as a legend in the union movement, a great American, and a champion of the oppressed classes on both sides of the Atlantic. Callaghan applauded and nodded his approval. In the past ten years, he knew, Maguire had sent two million dollars worth of arms and ammunition to the Emerald Isle.

Maguire spoke for half an hour. In that time he canvassed every British crime and atrocity, real or invented, that had ever been perpetrated on Irish soil from the time of Cromwell onward. For good measure he threw in the idea that the great potato famine was due to a blight imported from Britain and was therefore the earliest example of germ warfare used against a civilian population. When he mentioned the IRA he spoke of the moral justice of its cause and omitted any mention of its excesses, especially its bombing of department stores at Christmastime. Nor did he mention the hijacking of the *Britannia.* It had been agreed earlier that he would leave that to Callaghan. Sensing the crowd was growing restless, Maguire concluded his speech with the solemn declaration that there could be no peace on earth until Ireland was whole again. Then he turned to his long-time union pal, Pat Callaghan.

"And now, my friends," he announced through the booming speakers. "It is my privilege to introduce to you the only man who ever went to Washington to do an honest job of work. A man of principle. A man of courage. A man of hope. A man who was never afraid to stand up for what is right, even when he had to stand alone . . ."

Callaghan was the only national figure on the platform, and the crowd began to buzz in anticipation.

"Friends . . ." Maguire's voice rose to a crescendo. "I give you the lone voice of reason in the United States Senate, the honorable senator for Massachusetts, Mr. Patrick Callaghan."

Callaghan stood up to an orchestrated roar of approval from the crowd nearest the platform. A lumpy man with a lumpy face, he walked purposefully to the microphone, his canopy of long white hair lifting photogenically in the spring breeze. He had no notes, no papers, no cue cards. He knew exactly what he wanted to say. He thrust one hand into a jacket pocket and leaned forward into the microphone in a characteristic pose of jut-jawed aggression. With the other hand he waved the crowd into silence, as though he were too serious a man to waste time with frivolous displays of adulation.

"Good people of Boston," he began, his voice somber and portentous. "It gives me no pride to stand here before you today . . ."

The crowd became still and quiet. They had been prepared for Callaghan's usual eloquent blandishments. He was known as a provocative speaker. He had a reputation as a loose cannon on the ship of state. At the very least he could be expected to deliver good entertainment value. This time he had taken them by surprise. There was something different in his voice. Something that reached into them and infected them with a sense of occasion. This was not just another demonstration. This was momentous. They had come to a turning point in history.

"Instead," he added, "I am filled with shame. I am filled with shame and despair for what has happened on the high seas."

Roy Maguire shifted uncomfortably on his seat. Callaghan hadn't told him exactly what he intended to say, and the union boss wasn't certain that the senator was headed in the right direction.

"The British are about to pay a high price for their four hundred years of wickedness," Callaghan continued.

"They are about to discover that the sins of the fathers are indeed visited upon the sons. They are about to discover the terrible consequences of what can happen when good men are driven insane by four centuries of oppression and injustice."

Maguire nodded, relieved. He was listening to a master at work.

"And that is why I can take no pride in the events that are unfolding before us today," Callaghan went on. "That is why I can feel only shame and despair that the stubbornness and the stupidity of my fellow man has brought us to this terrible moment in history. For four centuries the British have refused to heed the voice of reason. For four centuries they have been deaf to the cries of our people. For four centuries they have scorned our pleas for justice. And today they understand the price they must pay for their arrogance. Today is their day of reckoning. Today they must come to terms with the full and dreadful knowledge of what they have brought down upon themselves. And, in all conscience, my friends, I have to tell you that it gives me no satisfaction to stand here and say to the British: 'I told you so.' Nor can I stand here and say to them: 'You were not warned.' They were warned—and it was they who chose to ignore those warnings."

Scattered yells of agreement rang out among the crowd.

"And that is why I am here today," Callaghan continued. "I am here to make one last plea for reason. I am here to sound the final warning before it is too late. I am here to say to the British that the time has come for them to end their illegal occupation of Northern Ireland . . ."

His voice was drowned out by a chorus of cheers.

"The troops must go!" he bellowed into the microphone, his pointed finger stabbing the air, punctuating his words as they boomed out over the speakers. "Too much blood has been spilled already. The green fields of Ireland are stained red with the blood of the innocent. Not another drop should be shed. The British have it in their power to end the bloodshed now if they would only do what is right and take their soldiers home. And, instead of sitting in the White House and wringing his hands, the President of these United States should add his own voice to the voices of reason. He should tell the British it is in their own best interest—it is in the interests of peace and justice—for them to end their long and damnable occupation of the six counties."

The crowd erupted again, and this time Callaghan was happy to let the cheers and the applause drag on for almost a minute. It was only when he sensed they were beginning to wane that he raised his hand to demand silence once more.

"Good people of Boston," he added. "Two hundred years ago our forefathers threw chests of tea into Boston Harbor to protest the tyranny of the British. It was the beginning of a struggle that climaxed in the birth of the greatest nation the world has ever seen. Today it is time for the people of Boston to send another message to the British. The time for tyrants is over. The time has come for the birth of a new nation. British soldiers must leave the six counties as once they left the thirteen colonies. They must put an end to this disgraceful chapter in history and they must do it now. The time has come for the people of Ireland to fulfill their own dream of manifest destiny. The time has come for Ireland to be whole again. The time has come for Ireland to take its proper place in the world. United, independent, and free . . . one nation under God."

Roy Maguire was first to his feet, leading the cheers and the applause that crashed around them like breaking waves. He strode to the front of the stage and pumped the senator's hand. Then he hoisted Callaghan's arm in the air, and the two of them posed together, like candidates for presidential election, basking in the adoration of the crowd. The band wasted no time and kicked into a spirited reprise of "The Wearing of the Green."

"And now, friends . . ." Maguire leaned into the microphone and yelled above the roar of the crowd. "It's time to send the British a message they can't ignore. It's time for another tea party!"

The band marked time while Maguire and Callaghan climbed down from the platform. Then, with the two of them striding confidently in the lead, the march got under way. With pipes wailing and placards waving the marchers poured off the Common, across Tremont Street and headed south along Summer Street toward Atlantic Avenue. The police struggled vainly to marshal the rowdy mass into a single lane, but it was hopeless. The crowd spilled across all the traffic lanes, tying up traffic on both sides of the street.

Down at Federal Reserve Plaza, Captain Fuller heard the first warnings on his radio. The protestors were on their way and the march was barely under control. Fuller snapped his radio off and listened. He could already hear them, half a dozen blocks away. He glanced around at the forty men he had with him and doubted they would be enough. He decided to order up his reserves. In the street behind the plaza, eighty officers in full riot gear filed out of their buses and quickly took up positions around the Federal Reserve Building.

It took less than a quarter of an hour for the first marchers to reach the plaza. For a few minutes Maguire, Callaghan, and the march organizers did nothing. They simply staked out their territory at the forefront of the plaza, faced off with the police, and waited for the main body of protestors to catch up with them. The streets around the plaza quickly became choked with people. They surged around the giant pillar of the Federal Reserve Building in waves, filling the concrete canyons with an angry, threatening rumble. The riot police on the perimeter of the plaza nervously fingered their billy clubs. A few mounted officers tried to barge their way through the crowd, provoking angry confrontations with the protestors.

At last Maguire and Callaghan decided it was time to present their petition. They walked up the few steps from the sidewalk to the plaza and approached Captain Fuller. TV crews swarmed in around them, eager to record every detail.

"'Afternoon, Captain," Maguire greeted Fuller.

"Mr. Maguire," the policeman answered coolly. "Senator Callaghan."

"We have a petition here from the people of Boston calling for the withdrawal of the British army of occupation from Northern Ireland," Maguire added officiously. He flourished the sheaf of papers in his hand as though they were a warrant. "We wish to present it to the British consul."

The consular offices were on the twenty-fifth floor. It was clear what would happen if the crowd got inside. They would ransack the entire floor. Or they would try. The FBI had two dozen armed agents up there in case the protestors got that far. Assuming they had any energy left after climbing twenty-five flights of stairs because the elevators were locked. But that was a contingency plan. A last line of defense. And there were other federal offices in the building that might be invaded. Fuller knew his career was on the line. He could not allow a single protestor to set foot inside the building.

"I'll be happy to take it off your hands, gentlemen," the police captain answered politely. "I'll see that it reaches the proper authorities."

"I'm sorry, Captain," Maguire responded. "But we intend to see that our petition is delivered to the consul and no one else."

Fuller took a long, deep breath. This wasn't supposed to happen. This wasn't how it had been explained to him. He had been told that the march organizers had agreed to leave their petition at the door.

"If you want to see the consul, you picked the wrong goddamn day, and you know it," he said, a note of exasperation creeping into his voice. "The consul ain't here and the offices are closed. I have been ordered to take receipt of your petition here. So, if you don't mind, gentlemen . . ."

He held out his hand to receive the petition.

Maguire hesitated.

"Come, come," Callaghan interjected. "One small deputation can't do any harm, Captain. What do you think we're going to do, take over the building?"

A few of the marchers laughed and hooted derisively at the police. The TV cameras whirred. Flashbulbs strobed.

"You're on federal property, gentlemen," Fuller insisted. "My orders are that no one enters the building."

"We leave our petition at the door to the consul," Maguire insisted, his voice rising. "Not the door to the goddamn building."

Fuller hesitated, wondering if a mistake had been made, if a few wires had been crossed somewhere. It didn't matter. His orders were clear. Whatever promises the march organizers claimed had been made, they weren't to be admitted to the building. He turned his attention to Callaghan, leaned in closer to him and lowered his voice, hoping the news crews wouldn't pick it up.

"Senator," he said. "I can't let you do this. I can't let you in here. Talk to them, will you, for Christ's sake? Make them see reason before people get hurt."

Callaghan's eyebrows shot up as though shocked that anyone would suggest such a thing. He turned to Maguire.

"I'm sorry, Roy," he said with an exaggerated shrug of resignation. "But it looks like the police have their orders."

A few people in the crowd saw the senator's gesture. A rumble of indignation spread through the crowd.

"They won't take the petition," somebody yelled. A roar of anger welled up around them.

"Let us through or it's on your head," Maguire shouted at Fuller.

Fuller saw what was happening. He had been in this situation before. He could smell the violence in the air. Taste it in the back of his throat. It always happened like this. It always came apart faster than anyone expected.

"Gentlemen . . ." he tried again, standing his ground.

"Fuck you . . ." somebody yelled.

"Fucking Fascist . . ." another voice added.

The chorus of abuse grew stronger. Then there was a sudden movement in the crowd. Maguire, Callaghan, and Fuller turned to see what it was. Somebody had produced a Union Jack. Somebody else held it up by one corner and lit it with a lighter. The filmy material flared up suddenly. A mounted police officer was nearby, and his horse reared up at the sudden blaze of fire, its hooves flailing at the air. A woman was struck a glancing blow and she fell, blood streaming down her face. People screamed. It was just the spark the crowd needed to ignite its passions. They surged toward the police lines with a roar of uncontrolled fury. Captain Fuller retreated hastily, bellowing into his radio for reinforcements. Police billy clubs rose and fell in a futile attempt to beat back the onrushing mob. Maguire and Callaghan were bustled away by a protective huddle of aides. Their work was done for the day.

JIDDA, SAUDI ARABIA. 06.35 HOURS

The Royal Navy Nimrod banked eastward over the Red Sea and began its descent toward King Abdul Aziz International Airport 28,000 feet below. A brilliant blaze of light rippled like flashbulbs through the portholes along the left side of the plane as it tilted into the rising sun. Lynch turned away from the glare, wishing he could sleep like Bonner, behind him. The big man had been snoring peacefully since they lifted off the ground at Portsmouth, six hours earlier.

The door to the cockpit opened, and Sir Malcolm Porter appeared looking rather dapper in his olive-green flight suit. He walked down the side aisle past tightly packed banks of surveillance electronics and the attentive crewmen who watched over them and took the seat next to Lynch.

"I've just been speaking to the PM," he said, raising his voice just loud enough to be heard over the roar of the engines. "And I think there's something you ought to know. He's having a little bit of bother with Cabinet."

Lynch waited, concerned. He had known Porter professionally for ten years and before that he had known the former chief of the SAS by his reputation for imperturbability. What he might describe as "a bit of bother" others might describe as imminent disaster. Until now Lynch had not had an inkling that there was anything less than perfect unanimity in the government.

"A no-confidence vote has been set for tonight's session of Parliament," Porter added. "The PM isn't sure the government will survive, so he's going to try to get the party hacks to extend the debate as long as they can. If they can drag it out for another forty-eight hours, we can launch the operation. Otherwise, everything goes on hold."

"Until what . . . ?" Lynch asked, his voice filled with disbelief. "Until the deadline expires?"

"Probably."

"If they do that," Lynch added slowly, "it will be the first time the Parliament has caused the death of a British monarch since Charles the First."

"Yes," Porter reacted coldly. "And God forgive them if they do . . . because I won't."

There was a sudden loud rumble, and the floor vibrated beneath their feet as the landing gear slid out of the plane's underbelly and locked in place.

"I'm afraid there's worse," Porter added.

Lynch wondered how much worse it could get.

"The PM thinks he might be able to hold off the vote in the House, but that still leaves him with another, more immediate threat."

Lynch waited, apprehensive.

"He's expecting a leadership challenge in Cabinet," Porter added evenly. "It seems not everyone in the government appreciates the way he's handling the situation either."

"Good God," Lynch muttered. "What the hell do they think they're playing at? The government should be united on this one. The life of the monarch is at stake . . . you do whatever it takes."

"I'm afraid it's no longer that simple," Porter sighed. "It's a choice between the life of the queen and the future of Ulster. The government is split. Seems some people are willing to sacrifice Her Majesty rather than pull out of Northern Ireland. They don't seem to care that if they don't make up their minds in the next forty-eight hours, the decision will be made for them."

"So, meanwhile, they're playing politics?"

"If the leadership challenge is successful," Porter added, "we could have a new Prime Minister by nightfall. All it takes is a vote in

Cabinet, an ambush, if you like—and he's been holding Cabinet meetings daily, since the crisis began. If he tries postponing the next Cabinet meeting for a day or two, it could be just what his enemies need to move against him anyway."

"So, what has he decided?"

"He's going to face the bastards down in Cabinet today. Challenge them to see if they've got the numbers."

"You think he's got the numbers?"

Porter slowly shook his head.

"I don't know, Colin," he sighed. "I really don't know anymore. The world is mad beyond my understanding, and this is just another symptom of its madness. I don't think anybody can say with any certainty what will happen anymore. All I can tell you is that we should know by the end of the day whether we have a new Prime Minister or not. Maybe a new leader will allow the rescue operation to proceed. Maybe he won't."

"Who's the most likely candidate for the job?"

"Charles Ingham," Porter answered. "Secretary of state for Northern Ireland. Pragmatist. Not a devout monarchist. Wants to hang on to Northern Ireland at all costs."

"So." Lynch paused. "He'd squash any deal the Prime Minister has made that puts Ulster at risk?"

"That's right." Porter nodded.

"You think he'd approve a rescue attempt?"

"Oh, I'm sure he'd be willing to let us try," Porter said. "Assuming there would be anything left for us to rescue once he'd announced that the deal was off and more troops were on their way to Northern Ireland. I am quite certain that Ingham wishes Her Majesty no harm and would prefer to see her come out of this in one piece. But if she didn't, it wouldn't change the outcome one whit as far as he is concerned. There'd be a rather grand state funeral, a lot of noble rhetoric about not capitulating to terrorism whatever the cost, and the status quo would prevail in Ulster."

The nose of the plane dropped sharply and Lynch's eye was drawn back to the porthole and the spectacle of a milky blue sea yielding to the rose pink shoreline of the Arabian peninsula a few hundred feet below.

A moment later the plane touched the runway with a shriek of rubber. Tom Bonner jolted awake in the seat behind. He rubbed his face roughly with both hands and looked out of his porthole at the desert sand and the glittering Jidda skyline in the distance.

"Looks just like Vegas," he mumbled dismissively, and leaned back in his seat.

The plane coasted to the end of the runway, turned, and taxied to a restricted area, out of sight of the main terminal. On the tarmac Lynch saw armed Saudi soldiers, armored cars, and what looked like a small official welcoming party. The plane rolled to a halt, bobbed a couple of times, then settled. The pilot cut the engines and the Nimrod's crew busied themselves covering their sensitive computer equipment with protective plastic covers. There were few elements in the world as dangerous to computers as dust, and Saudi Arabia was nothing but dust. After a few minutes they were finished. A Navy lieutenant cranked open the cabin door and a gust of warm air wafted through the cabin. There was a loud metallic clang as a gangway bumped against the side of the plane.

Porter was first to step outside followed by a ministerial aide with a briefcase. Lynch and Bonner grabbed hold of their bags and followed a moment later. Three Saudi humvees full of soldiers had pulled up nearby, and Porter stood in the midst of them, talking to three senior officers. Two of the men were Saudis, a major general and a colonel. The third man wore Royal Marine battle dress with insignia that identified him as a general. Lynch and Bonner waited at the bottom of the gangway until someone noticed them. A moment later the Saudis exchanged salutes with the Royal Marine general, walked back to their humvee, got in, and drove away, leaving their guests in the care of a captain and half a dozen soldiers.

"Guess I didn't need my passport after all," Bonner muttered.

"Gentlemen." Porter signaled them to join him and the general. The two of them straightened up and walked quickly over to the second humvee, where Porter and the general waited.

"General," he began the introductions, "I'd like to present Commander Lynch, commanding officer Two Section, SBS, Poole, and Lieutenant Commander Bonner, United States Navy, commanding officer SEALs special weapons program, Norfolk, Virginia."

Both officers saluted smartly. Their salute was returned by General Aubrey Sharpe, Commandant General, Royal Marines.

"General Sharpe already has a unit from Comacchio on board *Hotspur.*" Porter explained. "As you chaps are aware Comacchio will provide backup for you on this operation. The general very kindly came out to meet us in his own helicopter. He is going to give us an aerial tour of the situation at sea on the way back."

Lynch was impressed. In seventeen years with the Royal Marines and the SBS, this was the first time the Commandant General had thought to greet him personally. But then, it was a rather unusual occasion. It was Her Majesty, the queen, the corps' royal patron, who was at risk.

"With respect, sir," Bonner interjected. "I ought to report in to the United States regional commander before I go too much farther. I've still had no official confirmation from Washington that I'm even supposed to be here."

"Of course, Commander Bonner," Porter acknowledged. "We'll be going on to the USS *Carl Vinson* from HMS *Hotspur.* I believe you'll have all the confirmation you need when we get there. But if you have any doubts in the meantime, General Coburg did advise me that you can speak to him personally. I'm sure we can patch you through to Washington from the chopper. . . ."

"Absolutely," Sharpe agreed. "General Coburg and I know each other quite well, actually. I'd be delighted to get him on the line for you, Commander?"

Bonner smiled. Another thirty days and he would be a civilian who would need all the goodwill in Washington he could muster. This was not the time to be awkward.

"Thank you, General," he added. "I'm happy to do all I can to help you guys out here."

Lynch smiled but said nothing. He wasn't sure what worried Bonner most. The fear that he might have to take part in such a dangerous operation only weeks before he was due to retire, or the fear that he might blow it and with it his lucrative future in the maritime security business.

"All right, gentlemen," Porter decided briskly. "Let's get going, shall we?"

They climbed into the waiting humvees, and a moment later their little convoy was speeding across the tarmac toward a far corner of the airport, where a Royal Navy EH-101 waited. Ten minutes later they were airborne again, this time heading out over the Red Sea. According to Sharpe, the *Britannia* was 180 nautical miles southwest of Jidda and, within the last half hour, had turned south again. The seven British warships in the accompanying fleet had performed their own about-face, and now the whole armada was heading back toward the Gulf of Aden at a steady eight knots.

Lynch followed the radio chatter on his headphones as the helicopter pilot talked to the *Hotspur* and informed the British flagship that they would be making a circuit of the exclusion zone before landing. Then the pilot took the chopper down from three thousand feet to one thousand. A moment later General Sharpe motioned to his passengers to move forward, where they could look through the cockpit windows at the spectacle that had begun to unfold beneath them.

They could not have asked for a more perfect day. The sky was cloudless and visibility limited only to the haze on the horizon. From their vantage point they could see how narrow the Red Sea really was. Both its shores were clearly visible, the pale pink ribbon that was Saudi Arabia in the east and the murky brown that was Ethiopia in the west. Below and in front of them, on the glittering metallic surface of the water, seven warships of Her Majesty's Royal Navy described an elegant ellipse around the solitary needle of blue and white that was the *Britannia.*

Lynch was struck first by how innocent and picturesque it all looked. A grand vista of ships on a shining sea. As graceful as a royal regatta on the Solent. But, as the chopper circled slowly around the perimeter of the ten-mile cordon, the picture assumed another, more sinister dimension. This was not a pageant or a celebration. The *Britannia* was not making a royal progress with an escort of lesser ships dancing attendance like so many loyal courtiers. She was alone out there. Small, fragile, and vulnerable. Like a child's toy stranded in a pond. And all around her, thousands of soldiers, seamen, and airmen waited and watched helplessly, bound by the knowledge that one wrong move would spell her immediate destruction.

Lynch spotted another EH-101 a few miles off to their port side, patrolling the perimeter of the exclusion zone. He scanned the horizon, and far to the west he thought he saw a flash of reflected sunlight from another aircraft, then another.

"What's all the air activity on the western side?" he asked the pilot through his helmet mike.

"News media," came the answer. "Every coastal city on the Red Sea, from Cairo to Port Sudan, Jidda, and Djibouti is swarming with them. They've chartered every light plane and helicopter they can get their hands on. We've identified one hundred twenty-seven so far. Usually they keep their distance, skim around the edges for a couple of hours, trying to see something, using their super lenses to get shots of us and the *Britannia.* If they come in too close, we warn them off and they usually respond. Very few of them seem willing to die for a good picture. The Japanese have been the biggest pests so far. Day before yesterday they tried to swamp us with six helicopters they'd air-freighted in from Tokyo. We had to put a few bursts of fire across their noses to show them we were serious."

He took one hand off the yoke and jabbed a thumb down at the sea.

"There are at least a couple of hundred small craft down there too," he added. "The Saudis have been helping us keep them at bay. Got to expect it, I suppose. Story of the century and all that. Bastards make it harder than it needs to be though."

The pilot banked to port as the helicopter completed its circuit of the TEZ and began its descent to the deck of HMS *Hotspur.* Lynch and Bonner watched in silence as seamen scurried below to clear the helipad on the afterdeck. A moment later they touched down with a bump and a half dozen sailors scurried forward through the rotor wash to tie the chopper down. General Sharpe exited first, followed by Porter, then Lynch and Bonner. The sailors eyed the two last men out of the chopper curiously. They knew special forces types when they saw them. Obviously, the sailors realized, things were warming up.

The *Hotspur*'s intelligence officer, Lieutenant Gage, was waiting to greet the new arrivals. There was a brief flurry of introductions before he asked them to follow him below to the operations room where, he explained, Captain Purcell was waiting.

"You'll see in a moment why we're delighted you're here, sir," Gage said to Porter as he led the way through the warship's narrow gangways. "We've had rather a busy night."

Bonner sniffed. He knew the British penchant for understatement. "Rather a busy night" could mean anything from mutiny to mass murder.

Captain Purcell got up from the small conference table to meet his guests as they entered the operations room and apologized for not being on deck to meet them. There were three other men with the skipper of the *Hotspur;* Walter Pryne, the Cambridge psychologist and negotiator attached to Naval Intelligence for the duration of the crisis; Lieutenant Drewe, the ship's communications officer; and Colonel Quillan, commanding officer of the SAS. Once the introductions were over, Purcell invited Sir Malcolm to take the head of the table, in recognition of his authority as chief of operational planning.

Lynch and Bonner parked themselves at the opposite end of the table and gazed around at their new surroundings. The room was small and crowded with a conference table, a dozen metal chairs, and a battery of telephones adjacent to a computer console. On the wall behind Purcell was a large TV screen linked to the ship's computer. The screen could display intelligence information, maps, graphics, satellite images, or live television relays. For the moment it showed a slowly evolving television picture of the *Britannia* relayed from a camera aboard one of the choppers that patrolled the security cordon continuously. If anything happened aboard the *Britannia,* they would be among the first to see it, in living color.

"Perhaps," Sir Malcolm said, snatching everyone's attention back from the screen, "it might be a good idea if I kicked things off with a little good news."

Lynch was surprised. His impression from Porter on the plane had been that there was no good news.

"I spoke to the Prime Minister about an hour ago," Porter added. "He told me that late last evening he received a call from the Prime

Minister of Ireland, Mr. Caughey. Mr. Caughey advised the Prime Minister of two facts. The first was that he was putting the Irish Army on alert at midnight to correspond with the return to barracks of British troops in Northern Ireland and that this was a purely cautionary measure. The second was that his government would not recognize any attempt to integrate the six counties of Ulster with the Irish Republic through this or any other act of terrorism."

Quillan and Sharpe exchanged skeptical glances. Pryne, the negotiator, leaned forward in his chair, an anxious expression on his thin, bespectacled face.

"I hope they don't intend to announce that publicly yet," he said.

Porter acknowledged Pryne's concern with a nod of his head.

"The Prime Minister expressed his great gratitude to Mr. Caughey and asked if he would mind holding off any public announcement of that fact until the crisis had passed."

"Thank God for that," Pryne breathed. "If the hijackers hear there's no chance of getting what they want, even with us out of Northern Ireland, they'll blow up the yacht in an instant."

"What about the request for United Nations troops?" Colonel Quillan asked.

"The Security Council stands by its original resolution condemning the hijack and calling upon the hijackers to end the crisis peacefully," Porter answered. "As you know, the UN has also called on the IRA to renounce terrorism as a means of achieving its political goals. They won't respond to the hijackers' request to send in troops because it has no legitimacy."

"They could change their minds if the situation over there gets much worse," Quillan remarked.

They had all seen the latest news footage of the violence that had swept Northern Ireland in the past three days. Protestant mobs battling Catholic mobs in the streets of Belfast and Londonderry. Houses burning, people dying, the Royal Ulster Constabulary overwhelmed and not a British soldier to be seen anywhere. And it wasn't only Northern Ireland that was in turmoil. There had been massive demonstrations and violent clashes in London, Birmingham, Liverpool, and Manchester as supporters of a united Ireland clashed with outraged monarchists. In the US too there had been violent pro-unity demonstrations at British consular offices in Boston, New York, Chicago, and San Francisco and outside the British embassy in Washington.

"Yes," Porter responded soberly. "But I may have some promising news on that front too."

Lynch shook his head in wonderment. If it had been some anonymous little old lady who had been taken hostage by terrorists, the world would have been united in its condemnation. But because this little old lady sometimes wore a crown, the world had gone mad and strangers fought each other in the streets over whether she should be saved or whether she should be left to die.

"It is true that the situation in Northern Ireland has been rather dire for the past forty-eight hours," Porter continued. "In point of fact, I can give you the latest figures myself."

He leaned over to his aide, who sat quietly nearby, guarding Porter's briefcase.

"These are current as of seven hours ago," he added, producing a single sheet of fax paper bearing the insignia of the British Army GHQ, Belfast. "So far we can confirm there have been seventy-two civilian deaths and more than six hundred injured, many of them seriously. We can't give a breakdown on Catholic and Protestant casualties. Those are the figures for both sides. In addition, five RUC constables have been killed and fifty-eight injured."

He paused.

"British casualties so far stand at seventeen soldiers killed and forty-one wounded. Troop casualties are firm as of midnight last night, GMT, when all British troops in Northern Ireland returned to barracks. There may be more British casualties to come, of course, but all indications are that the IRA has its hands rather full at the moment. Certainly too full to worry about attacking British Army installations. Yesterday was the worst day of the crisis by far. Ulster loyalists staged an illegal protest march through West Belfast. Their strength was put at around ten thousand, which made it the biggest demonstration seen in the city in years. The marchers breached security force lines and marched on the Bone, which, some of you may know, is an isolated Catholic ghetto in Protestant West Belfast. They spent most of the afternoon driving Catholic families out of their homes and then set fire to their houses. The count so far says something in excess of three hundred homes were destroyed. While that was going on, the IRA mobilized its forces and counterattacked. At one point a large number of shots were fired into the Protestant crowd, causing many casualties. By early evening the loyalists had regrouped and they continued on to Andersontown, where there were several violent exchanges and a great many shots exchanged between both sides, despite the presence of a large number of British troops and RUC officers. That is when the bulk of the casualties were inflicted on all sides.

"And then"—he paused—"it seems something rather extraordinary happened. As the hour of the troop withdrawal approached, we were able to impose a little sanity on the situation. Thanks to some very timely intelligence from MI5, General Richards, the British troop commander in Northern Ireland, was able to talk a little sense into the Protestant leadership. He was able to convince them that their assault on the IRA was a little premature.

"You see, gentlemen"—Porter glanced around the table—"according to MI5, the hijackers don't have the full blessing of the IRA army council for this little operation of theirs."

Tension in the room moved up a degree.

"Our mistake," Porter added, "was to take the hijackers at their word from the beginning. When they said they were IRA, we were inclined to believe them. And why shouldn't we? Everything seemed to fit. The Belfast accent, the standard IRA demands for troop withdrawals and unification with the south, the follow-up calls to the BBC in Belfast demanding United Nations intervention. It all suggested the whole thing was a thoroughly well-coordinated plot by the IRA. Now, it seems . . . it wasn't. Our intelligence sources tell us that the hijacking of the *Britannia* has split the Provos right down the middle."

"Well, that explains it," Lieutenant Gage interrupted animatedly.

Everyone at the table turned to look at him.

"So far we've heard from two hijackers," he added quickly. "One with a Belfast accent, the other with an English accent."

"English?" Porter queried. "You're sure about that?"

“Oh,” Pryne intervened in support of Gage. “Middle class English or educated Irish. No doubt about it.”

“Well,” Porter went on, “that would seem to confirm the other information we’ve received so far. What we’re dealing with here is an extremist faction inside the Provisional IRA. A faction with links to other terrorist organizations here in the Middle East that helped them engineer the hijack of the *Britannia.* It also explains why we were able to arrange a truce between Protestants and Catholics in Northern Ireland. Not a perfect truce, mind you, and we don’t know how long it will hold, but certainly a better situation than the mayhem that prevailed until eleven o’clock last night.”

“You mean they’ve stopped killing each other?” Sharpe asked.

“For the time being,” Porter confirmed. “Though you must remember, it is only around three o’clock in the morning there. The truce is still in its infancy. What General Richards was able to do was persuade the loyalists to pull back inside their own areas for seventy-two hours on the understanding that the Catholics would remain in theirs. Richards was able to extract a promise from the IRA that, in return, they would keep a lid on their areas. You might also be interested to know that Joe Keegan, commander of the Belfast Provo brigades, sent word to the loyalists via Richardson that he was as unhappy as they were with the hijacking and its implications for the Catholic population.”

There was a sharp intake of breath around the table.

“And you think you can believe anything Keegan says?”

It was Colonel Quillan, and he spoke for all of them.

Porter shrugged.

“It seems Red Joe got a bit of a fright last night when the loyalists finally went for this throat,” he said.

“The loyalists wouldn’t take his word on it, would they?” Quillan queried.

“No,” Porter conceded. “But they believed General Richards. And I think there was something else that played a part in their decision too.”

Everyone in the room waited.

“I think they may have frightened themselves,” Porter added. “There was a terrible amount of bloodshed yesterday, even for

Northern Ireland. I think what happened is that they went to the brink of the abyss and they looked inside and saw what waited for them there . . . and they pulled back."

"Either that or they just wore themselves out with their first real frenzy of hate and they've gone back to regroup," Quillan observed dryly.

"Undoubtedly there's a bit of that too." Porter nodded. "But the fact remains that British troops returned to their bases throughout Northern Ireland peacefully at midnight last night. Since then the security of the province has been entirely in the hands of the RUC, and apart from a few minor, isolated incidents there have been no major confrontations—and not a single fatality."

"It won't last," Sharpe said. "It can't last. The suspicion and the hatred goes too deep. We've just seen round one. Both sides will be using the time to gather their resources for the big one."

"Unfortunately," Porter said, "I have to agree with you on that. But Richards has done bloody well to get them off each other's throats even for a little while. The truce has to hold for only seventy-two hours. If we haven't resolved the situation successfully in that time, then the sovereign will be dead, the government of Great Britain will have fallen, Northern Ireland will be in flames, and we shall all be back at this table, wondering which of us should be the first to commit hara-kiri."

A somber silence settled anew around the table.

"Now"—Porter turned to Captain Purcell—"I'm curious to know what you've heard from the *Britannia* in the past few hours. Have they made contact with anyone on shore yet?"

"No," Purcell answered. "Radio traffic between the hijackers and the outside world has been minimal. They seem to prefer it that way. They talk to us only when they want to and they seem content to monitor the rest of the situation on their own. Obviously they have full access to international radio and television broadcasts, so they can see what effect the hijacking is having on Northern Ireland, the UK, and the rest of the world. When we tried to open negotiations through Professor Pryne here, they broke the contact off with the threat to execute more hostages. They've taken one call from that lunatic American reporter Dunbarry, because it suited their purposes, but that's all."

Purcell paused, but Porter only nodded and waited for him to go on.

"I'm interested to know what our position will be if we do discover complicity between the hijackers and the Yemenis," Purcell added. "Especially if the hijackers try to take hostages or the *Britannia*'s treasure ashore and we have to make a decision in a hurry."

"Yes," Porter acknowledged. "I spoke to the Prime Minister about this yesterday. "He had the foreign minister summon the Yemeni ambassador and warn him that any evidence of complicity between his government and the hijackers would be treated as a hostile act against the government of Great Britain."

"And how did the ambassador respond?" Purcell asked.

"Well," Porter sighed. "I hate to say this, but—you know what they're like. The ambassador denied all knowledge of the hijacking, said his government didn't know anything about it, had no idea what we were talking about. According to him, they didn't know there was a royal yacht, didn't know where it was, and didn't know what it was doing."

"We've picked up a few of their patrol boats on ELINT," Lieutenant Gage added again. "The closest they've come to the cordon so far has been fifty miles, but they've been showing plenty of interest. They know what's going on all right."

"If they come too close or if they are stupid enough to try to assist the hijackers in any way, you are authorized to use force to stop them." Porter directed his gaze at Captain Purcell. "You do know that, don't you?"

"And if the hijackers try to take hostages or treasure onto Yemeni territory?" Purcell asked.

"You stop them," Porter said simply. "By any means possible—fair or foul."

"Suppose the hijackers do manage to get ashore and the Yemenis do give them safe haven," Quillan asked. "What then?"

"Unconscionable," Porter answered. "Can't be allowed to happen."

"Hypothetically?" Quillan persisted.

"Then we'll have to insist that the Yemenis give them up, won't we?"

"And if they don't?"

Porter smiled faintly.

"They'd have to be pretty bloody stupid not to have learned the lessons of the Gulf War by now."

An uneasy silence descended. So far no one had raised the possibility that the hijacking of the *Britannia* might somehow lead to a wider conflict in the Middle East.

Porter leaned quickly into the silence and steered the conversation in a new direction.

"I believe you've had rather a busy night of it yourselves," he said.

Captain Purcell nodded.

"I think Lieutenant Gage might be able to give us a little more on that," he said.

Gage leaned forward and opened the intelligence folder on the table in front of him.

"Our colleagues on the *Carl Vinson* have been rather busy on our behalf," he began. "In the past forty-eight hours they've obtained satellite shots and thermal image profiles of seven of the *Britannia*'s hijackers. This is what they came up with after they'd put them through digital enhancement."

He fanned out a series of black and white laser-printed photographs of seven male profiles taken from a number of angles. Three of the photographs showed men with clearly defined Arab features. Two of them had mustaches. The third was a thin-faced man with long hair and a blurred goatee.

"That's Abu Musa," Porter said the instant he saw the picture. "He's one of the most senior men in the PFLP General Command."

Gage nodded.

"The Americans put a tentative ID on him before they sent these over. Our own people confirm it. Presumably, sir, you know him?"

"Oh, yes," Porter answered quietly. "We've been after him for a long time, along with half a dozen other western intelligence services, including the Americans. He's the organizing force behind some of the worst terrorist acts ever committed in the West. He never ventures out of the Middle East though. Too dangerous for him. He has bases in Lebanon, Tunisia, and Iran. Put a lot of money through BCCI before the balloon went up. If I'm not mistaken, he's spent most of the past two years in Mashhad in northern Iran. It's a training base for terrorists; the PLO, Hezbollah, and the PFLP-GC, obviously. They've got a very sophisticated infrastructure up there, including a real airliner to help them rehearse hijack operations. The IRA have put quite a few of their people through Mashhad in the past twenty years too."

"Could they have a mockup of the *Britannia* there?" Quillan asked.

Porter looked up at him.

"They could," he acknowledged. "Assuming they had accurate plans. It would be relatively easy to lay out taped deck plans of the *Britannia* providing you had enough floor space, an airplane hangar or something like that."

"That would explain the involvement of the IRA and the PFLP-GC, then, wouldn't it?" Quillan added. "It's a joint operation between two of the world's nastiest terror groups."

"Good God," Porter breathed, and leaned back in his chair. "They've done each other favors for years. They train together. They swap intelligence. They trade arms and explosives. They smuggle weapons and people back and forth across Europe all the time. But who would have dreamed they were capable of something of this magnitude?"

"All it takes is one man," Lynch added quietly. "One man who thinks big enough."

"Who are the other two?" Porter asked, gesturing to the photographs of the remaining two Arabs.

"So far we've got them pegged as a couple of Jordanian migrant workers," Gage added. "Saudi intelligence tell us, according to their immigration files, their names are Javad Malik and Youssef Shaheen. They've both lived in Jidda for about five years and their records are spotless. Model citizens until now."

"I think you'll find they're false IDs," Porter added. "If they're tied up with Musa, they're almost certainly Palestinian."

"Sleepers?" Quillan remarked.

"Got to be," Porter said. "Easy enough to do, especially in the Middle East."

He switched his gaze back to Gage.

"What about the other four?"

"We're pretty sure about three of them," Gage answered. "The other one is a complete mystery man, I'm afraid."

Porter pulled the prints of the other four hijackers toward him. Three were clearly Caucasian, though one of them could have been an Arab with his mass of black hair and dark, grainy features.

"That's Dominic Joseph Behan," Gage said. "We've matched him with shots from MI5 and Special Branch and there's no mistake. He's IRA all right. Born in Belfast, 1957. Catholic. Was a builder's laborer for a while. Interred in Long Kesh on suspicion of terrorist activities from 1976 to 1978. No employment record after that. Been with the Provos most of his adult life."

"I know that bastard," Quillan said. "We've got a shoot-on-sight order on him in the province. Complete fanatic. Kills without conscience. He's responsible for the death of at least four British soldiers that we know of."

Porter quickly scanned the rest of the intelligence report.

"It says here he was on the Provo army council. Obviously he wasn't only a thug. He had political aspirations too?"

"He may have had political ambitions at one point," Gage concurred. "Seems he's changed his approach somewhat since then."

"The political route was probably a bit too slow for him," Porter mused. "Obviously he prefers something a bit more direct."

He paused for a moment, then added: "It does fit the general intelligence picture from Northern Ireland though, doesn't it, gentlemen? Our Mr. Behan here may have hungered after the leadership of the army council for some time but became frustrated with the slow pace of Provo politics. They're always squabbling among themselves about what gets the best results, political pressure or wholesale slaughter. So, being the man of action that he is, our Mr. Behan took it on himself to circumvent the army council and to embark on a more dramatic approach with the assistance of his colleagues in the PFLP-GC."

"Talk about a marriage made in hell," Quillan murmured.

"Quite," Porter agreed. "But that explains why the Provo leadership in Belfast has been so quick to agree to a truce. They don't want to distance themselves entirely from Behan until they see how the whole thing turns out. If he's successful and forces a troop withdrawal, the army council has to be able to say they supported him all the way. Its always been Provo policy to get the British out no matter what the short-term cost. In the meantime, they have to find a way to weather the first round of Protestant attacks. Because, assuming Behan is unsuccessful and the troops stay, somebody has to be there to pick up the pieces and carry on."

"So," Quillan added, "he's boxed his own people into a corner too. They have no choice but to support him while this thing is under way. And if he's successful . . ."

"He goes back to Ireland a conquering hero," Porter finished for him. "And the leadership of the army council is his for the asking."

"You've got to hand it to him," Gage added grudgingly. "He's got an eye for the big picture—and he's got the balls to go for it."

"For a little while longer," Quillan observed quietly.

A smile passed fleetingly around the table. It was the first time anyone had smiled since they sat down.

"And the others?" Porter continued.

"We've got positive IDs on two of them," Gage answered. "Both longtime Provo gunmen. One is a Mr. James Mulcahey, the other is William Deveny. Both of them are longtime associates of Dominic Behan. There's nothing especially impressive about either of them. Deveny operated with Behan on the continent for a while, blowing up cars and buses carrying the wives and children of British servicemen in Germany. Mr. Mulcahey, in particular, was a low-level thug. This would have been the most ambitious operation he's been involved in by far."

"It's the biggest operation any of us are likely to be involved in," General Sharpe observed.

"Was?" Porter chimed in, looking at Gage. "You referred to Mr. Mulcahey in the past tense. Is he no longer with us?"

"In a manner of speaking," Gage answered mysteriously. "I'll come back to Mr. Mulcahey later. In the meantime, we're building profiles on Behan, Deveny, and the Arabs in case we get a chance to turn the screws."

"That's another thing that worries me about those bloody Arabs," Porter mused aloud. "We've got so little time and there are still so many damn pieces of the puzzle missing."

A bleak silence descended around the table as Porter's gloomy thoughts were reflected in the shadows on his face.

"Abu Musa never takes an active role in these operations," he went on. "The fact that he's put his own life at risk by boarding the *Britannia* indicates a major change in his thinking . . . a major change."

"Perhaps he has a major incentive," Bonner remarked quietly.

Everyone in the room turned to look at the American, who had so far remained silent.

"You've already talked about the kind of money that's on that boat," Bonner shrugged. "A few hundred million dollars still goes a long way in the world."

Lynch smiled. He wasn't surprised that Bonner had homed in on the mercenary possibilities of the hijacking before anyone else in the room.

"Exactly," Porter agreed, and he rapped the table softly with his knuckles. "It's a hell of a sum of money if they can get themselves into a position where they can use it."

"Such as an outlaw state like the Republic of Yemen," Purcell added.

"A couple of hundred million into the Yemeni treasury could buy them a bit of time," Porter agreed. "And that would be only the beginning. They could move on from there very quickly. If they make it back to Iran, we've lost them. And they'd still have a fortune left for whatever other purposes they have in mind."

"You think Musa is only in it for the money?" Gage asked.

"No," Porter answered. "Not for its own sake. And neither is Behan. But let's just pause for a moment and look at the personalities of the two major players here. We've got Behan—former slum kid, IRA fanatic, totally dedicated to the cause of Irish unity, apparently fearless and quite willing to get his hands bloody. Then we've got Abu Musa—ruthless, cunning, completely amoral but prefers to do his killing by remote control. A longtime survivor in a terrorist organization not noted for the longevity of its leaders and a man with connections in half a dozen Arab states. What does this operation mean to both of them?"

"Well," Gage volunteered, "if they both get what they want, Behan gets the British out of Northern Ireland, he becomes a hero to the Cause—and he gets his hands on an awful lot of money to buy arms for the subsequent confrontation with the Protestant militias. And Musa gets virtually the same thing in this part of the world. If he pulls it off, presumably he'd be in a very strong position to assume the leadership of the PFLP-GC. That would make him one of the most feared and influential power brokers in the Middle East."

"Exactly," Porter added. "It's power, gentlemen. The power to move nations. The power to shape history. That is the prime motivator behind this unholy alliance."

"Perhaps," Lynch sounded a cautionary note. "But what about the mystery man? The man with the English accent? What's his part in all of this?"

Porter singled out the one remaining photograph and pulled it closer to him. If anything, it had a higher quality of resolution than the others. It showed a lean-faced man with light-colored hair and regular caucasian features who could have been aged anywhere between twenty-five and thirty-five.

"You say we've been unable to turn up anything on this character at all?" Porter looked at Gage.

"Nothing," Gage answered. "He doesn't exist on any photo file that we've tapped into so far. Initially we assumed he was an IRA man with a clean sheet. We changed that assessment though . . . after Admiral Marchant."

Porter seemed to hold his breath.

"Is this the bastard who shot Marchant?" he asked quietly.

"Yes," Gage answered. "Shortly after he went on board. It seems that Behan and Musa are both willing to defer to him. Despite what you have told us, Sir Malcolm, it would appear that this is the man who is really running the hijack of the *Britannia.* And Behan and Musa are only his accomplices."

"The one man who thinks big enough to put something like this together," Porter said, looking at Lynch. Then he looked around the table.

"Who the hell is he?"

"That," Purcell interjected icily, "is what we would all like to know."

"Musa would make an alliance with Satan himself if it would get him what he wanted," Porter muttered vaguely, his face a mask of bewilderment. "And so, I dare say, would Dominic Behan."

"Perhaps they have," Lynch added quietly. "In a manner of speaking."

Lynch's words seemed to smolder in the air. Porter shook his head to clear it of the encroaching madness and looked at Pryne, the negotiator, searching, probing for some kind of opening.

"You say this man has no accent, no trace of an accent at all?"

"I didn't say that," the professor answered quickly, eager to qualify his earlier information. "I've listened to the tape of our conversation quite a few times since then. He's very cool, very authoritative. He speaks clearly and precisely, as though he is used to giving orders. But there's a slight inflection on a few of his *R* words. That's why I mentioned educated Irish as a possibility."

"Pretty unlikely," Porter added.

There was a murmur of agreement around the table from those who knew the social milieu from which the IRA drew its support.

"It's very subtle," Pryne added. "If I had to take a stab at it, I'd say it's a northern English inflection."

"That pins it down," Gage muttered.

Pryne shot him a wounded look, then added: "Not the northeast. It's not Yorkshire or the northeast. I'd know them. They're almost impossible to disguise. At a rough guess I'd say Cheshire, Lancashire, or Liverpool . . . but I wouldn't expect you to hold me to it."

Porter smiled faintly and looked at Gage.

"You're still looking?"

"Of course," Gage answered. "We're cross-referencing all intelligence photo files we can get our hands on. Our friends aboard the *Carl Vinson* are doing the same. If this character has had a driver's license or a passport in any western country in the past twenty years, we should be able to turn it up. It's only a matter of time."

"We don't have a lot of time," Porter added.

"The computers are fast," Gage answered. "But not that fast. It still takes time to do photo fits."

"Have you tried one of the mainframes at Northwood?"

"Would the Admiralty give us sole use of a mainframe?" Gage asked.

"They will now," Porter said. "It would help us a great deal if we could get a profile on this beggar sometime in the next twenty-four hours. Then we'd have a better idea of what kind of psychological approach to take."

"I'm sorry," Pryne said, "but I'm not very optimistic on that score."

Porter looked questioningly at him.

"Every time something happens that they don't like, a hostage dies. Whether it's our fault or not. The way our mysterious friend here left it last time, we only have to try talking to them again and a hostage will be killed."

"Yes," Porter acknowledged Pryne's concern. "I realize that. But we've got to be ready—even if we get a chance to sow a few seeds of confusion only at the last minute. We have to get some idea of the dynamics involved here, how the hijackers are likely to interact with each other when things start to get hairy. If there's even a chance that we could introduce some sort of division . . ."

Pryne nodded and leaned back in his chair, but the expression on his face said he was unconvinced.

"Have you tried service files?" Lynch asked abruptly.

"What . . . ?" Gage looked at him. "You mean armed forces . . . our armed forces?"

"The devil comes in many different guises," Lynch said. "This chap seems awfully comfortable in this environment. He could be ex-military turned mercenary. Mercenaries aren't always particular where their paycheck comes from, you know. And somebody had to be working for the IRA in England. Somebody got hold of the *Britannia*'s deck plans. Somebody got their hands on large quantities of GBX gas and Demex. Those aren't things the IRA has traditionally been able to get its hands on in the past."

"You're right," Porter agreed. "He could be an ex-serviceman.

We've seen a couple of them turn traitor over the years. We can't afford to ignore any possibility at this juncture."

Bonner smiled to himself at the use of a word like *traitor.* To him it sounded quaint, medieval almost. But no one else in the room was smiling.

"I'll get on it as soon as this meeting is over," Gage added. "In the meantime, there is one more positive terrorist ID I can give you. At least it confirms our satellites are working to order."

He slid one last photograph into the middle of the table. It was the infamous picture of the hooded hijacker on the bridge of the royal yacht. The picture that had flashed around the world to become the instant symbol of the hijack of the *Britannia.*

"As most of us know, we've been in regular contact with Captain Gault on the *Britannia* since the first hours of the hijacking."

Lynch leaned forward at the mention of Gault's name. He knew John Gault well. They had trained together many times on joint SBS-SAS air-sea exercises. It was Gault who would have to lead him to the location of the explosives on board the *Britannia.* Lynch had a vested interest in his welfare.

"Captain Gault and Lieutenant Stone were assigned bodyguard duty for the royal tour and they remain with the queen and Prince Philip in the secure section of the yacht," Gage explained for the benefit of the three newcomers. "A little over twenty-four hours ago Captain Gault went on a little reconnaissance mission on our behalf and he sent us back a little present . . . the body of one of the hijackers."

Porter, Lynch, and Bonner waited, their faces mirrors of the tension that permeated the room.

"Captain Gault was quite apologetic when he radioed in to tell us the body was on its way," Gage continued. "He had hoped to question the hijacker but, apparently, the situation called for the use of some force and Captain Gault accidentally broke the man's neck. We picked the body up sixteen hours ago. It was in excellent condition apart from the broken neck, so we got good prints and a photograph. A positive ID came through from London a couple of hours ago. The body is that of James Mulcahey. Age thirty-three. Catholic. Born in Strabane, Ulster. Active in the Provisionals since 1981, first in Londonderry then Belfast. Did two years in Long Kesh, disappeared around the middle of 1991. Believed involved in several killings and bombings. MI5 speculated that he had been murdered during factional fighting in the Provos from 1990 to 1992. In view of what has been said here today, it would seem that is mistaken and he switched loyalties to Dominic Behan's side and ultimately became part of the hijack operation."

"One down, eight to go," Quillan remarked, beating Lynch by a microsecond.

"There is one more piece of news, sir," Gage added, looking at Porter. "But it's not good."

Porter waited.

"About three hours ago we picked up another body," Gage continued. "Another hostage. We assume it was revenge for the killing of Mulcahey, though the hijackers haven't said so."

"Who was he?" Porter asked quietly.

"Actually, sir, it wasn't a he," Gage answered. "It was a she. A young woman. Shot through the back of the head at close range in full view of everyone . . . just like Admiral Marchant."

He paused while he distributed a series of photographs that showed the face of a girl on the stern of the *Britannia* with a hooded figure behind her, holding a pistol to her head.

"Jesus Christ . . ." Porter whispered.

There was a sharp intake of breath around the table. Every man who looked at the photograph knew it was an image that would stay with him for the rest of his life. It was a photograph of a human being who had been driven into madness in the dreadful moment before her death.

"Her name was Susan Latimer," Gage went on quietly. "She was attached to the wardrobe department of the household staff. Captain Gault found her and tried to take her back to the royal apartments. Unfortunately, he had to leave her on her own for a while and it seems the hijackers found her."

"Do we know the identity of the man who shot her?" Lynch asked.

"Not exactly," Gage answered obliquely. He gestured to the photograph of the unidentified hijacker.

"It's him . . . the same bastard who murdered Admiral Marchant."

For a moment there was only silence in the small, crowded room. Lynch was the first to venture into the void.

"Perhaps," he said, "it is a picture of the devil after all."

NORFOLK, VIRGINIA. 14.20 HOURS

Otis Birnbaum watched the US Navy Sea Stallion descend from a clear blue sky like a chariot from the gods. It hovered briefly over the grassy apron that fronted the research center, then touched down with a light bounce. The engines shut off, the rotors whined to a standstill, and a side hatch slid open. A Marine guard appeared in the door and lowered the folding steps down to the grass. Then he disappeared. A moment later three of the gods of war stepped out.

First to appear was General Kurt Coburg, chairman of the joint chiefs. The second was the secretary of defense, Ron Grierson. The third was Admiral Thorson Davies, commander in chief, Central Command, or CINCENT. Birnbaum knew them by sight though he had never seen them all together before, and it made for an unnerving spectacle.

Birnbaum exchanged an uneasy glance with Admiral Freeman, who stood alongside, waiting to meet their VIP guests. The commanding officer of the Norfolk naval base, had been advised by the chairman of the joint chiefs' office only a half hour earlier that the VIP chopper would be coming in direct from the Pentagon, 160 miles away. Admiral Freeman had been told that its passengers were operating under presidential edict and wanted to conduct an urgent examination of the program currently under way at the Navy's defense research and test facility hidden away in the secure heart of the Norfolk base, home of the US Second Fleet and the biggest naval base in the world. As the director of the facility, Birnbaum had been summoned to show his guests around and give them anything they wanted. It was that last phrase that worried Birnbaum. Giving them anything they wanted could mean only one thing.

The three VIPs advanced out of the dying rotor wash in a phalanx of raw power. Birnbaum swallowed. He was a small, mousy man in glasses and a white coat, and to him these men were like titans. Admiral Freeman stepped forward and saluted. General Coburg and Admiral Davies returned the salutes. Freeman was about to conduct the introductions, but Coburg preempted him by stepping forward and fixing Birnbaum with a stern gaze.

"Professor Birnbaum?"

It was a statement, not a question. The scientist nodded.

"General . . . sir—" he began.

"I believe you have something I need, Professor," Coburg interrupted. "And it's not like we have a helluva lot of time to stand around here, talking about it."

Birnbaum's heart sank. It was exactly as he had feared. There had been only one major test program under way at the facility for the past year. Until now he had been getting ready to shut it down in accordance with the Pentagon's orders. Suddenly it seemed they had changed their minds. Again. Suddenly they wanted to know all about the revolutionary new minisub he had designed—the Swimmer Delivery Vehicle, Mark 12.

"It hasn't been tested to full operational capability yet," he protested lamely. He looked around at the four men who towered around him. He felt like a kid who had strayed into a grown-up game of football by mistake. And he had the ball.

"According to my information, it has performed pretty damn well," Coburg declared. Again it was in a tone of voice that dared Birnbaum to tell the General he was wrong.

Suddenly the penny dropped inside Birnbaum's brain with a resounding clang.

"My God," he blurted out. "You're going to use it to put men on the *Britannia!*"

Coburg smiled an odd, mirthless smile.

"You have a quick mind, Professor," he said quietly. "Now show me how quick you really are."

For a second Birnbaum's mind reeled. His pulse fluttered and the palms of his hands felt clammy. Then he caught himself. He wiped his hands on his trousers and looked back up at General Coburg, forcing himself to keep a smile off his own face. It was exactly the kind of operation the SDV-Mark 12 had been designed for. And, God forgive him, a big part of him was thrilled just at the prospect.

"Gentlemen," he said shakily. "It will be an honor."

The director turned and led his visitors up a short flight of steps to the reception area. The VIPs were passed quickly and efficiently by Marine guards eager to show how well they did their job regardless of the visitor's rank. Then the group marched noisily down a series of long, shiny corridors until they came to a pair of red metal doors marked HIGH SECURITY AREA—NO VISITORS PAST THIS POINT.

Birnbaum slipped his plastic pass card into the computer lock, punched in a code, and pushed the door when it buzzed. They stepped onto a steel gantry that girdled a large, brilliantly lit bowl-shaped chamber. The whole room was air conditioned to a temperature at least ten degrees cooler than the temperature in the rest of the building. Below, on the flat bottom of the bowl, half a dozen men in white coveralls tinkered over two sleek gray vessels that looked like scaled-down versions of conventional submarines. Each sub was thirty-two feet long, eight feet across, had a stubby conning tower, a rudder, and a prop. Both of them were enmeshed in a web of electrical coils connected to batteries of computers set against the walls. On the opposite side of the room was a slipway and a pair of large steel doors. On the other side of those doors was a test chamber sixty feet long, forty feet wide and thirty feet deep, filled with water pumped in from the open sea.

"You see them like this and they look so goddamn puny," muttered the secretary of defense.

"Don't be deceived, Mr. Secretary," Birnbaum assured him. "They're built to take a pounding, believe me."

The scientist invited his guests to follow him down a flight of metal stairs to the floor of the lab. Birnbaum felt a little more comfortable now. He was in his domain. These men might have the power. He had the knowledge. He gestured to his colleagues to continue their work, then turned back to his visitors, letting his eyes rest on Coburg.

"I don't know how familiar you are with the SDV series, General . . ." he began.

"My knowledge is confined to the information I received from Admiral Davies on the way here," Coburg admitted.

"Oh." Birnbaum sighed, unable to conceal his dismay.

"Keep it short and keep it simple, Professor," Coburg added. "And I'll probably be able to keep up with you."

"Of course, sir." Birnbaum nodded, used to the brevity of the military mind. "I don't know how much Admiral Davies told you about our earlier generations of SDVs, but, basically, their shortcomings were that they suffered from low speed, low underwater endurance, and minimal payload capacity. The best SDV we built before this, the Mark 8, managed a maximum speed of only eight knots, a maximum range of eighty miles while submerged, and carried a maximum of four swimmers. It could get swimmers in and out of hostile territory well enough, but it was no good for interceptions at sea. It could not pursue or intercept even the slowest of surface craft and it could be hunted easily because it could not dive deep or take swift evasive action. It also suffered from the same problem as conventional submarines—it could be picked up by advanced sonar."

He paused and looked at Coburg.

"I presume the *Britannia* has advanced sonar?"

"We shall presume so," Coburg answered blandly.

"Well," Birnbaum continued briskly, "we have learned the lessons of the past and we have applied all that we have learned to the Mark 12."

The visitors followed Birnbaum in a slow circumnavigation of the sleek and sinister craft.

"The Mark 12 is a wet-dry minisub with a hull of aluminum-titanium-Kevlar construction," Birnbaum explained. "Its engines are based on hydride fuel cell technology which give it three times the speed and three times the range of the Mark 8. The Mark 12 has a cruising speed of ten knots and a sprint speed of sixteen knots. It has a range of two hundred miles and it can carry six swimmers. It has an ablative coating that absorbs and deflects sonar so that it remains invisible in the water. It won't show up on enemy sonar screens at all. The only way it can be detected is when its engines are running and the enemy sonar operator is actively listening for it. To counteract that we've been developing a system whereby we bracket the target vessel with sonobuoys to tell us when the enemy is conducting sonar sweeps for engine noise. The moment he starts sweeping, the sonobuoys pick up his pinging pattern. That information is transmitted to an AWAC circling overhead and relayed instantly to the Mark 12. What the sub does then is shut down its engines and lie dormant in the water. The moment the sonar operator stops sweeping, the pinging stops and we alert the minisub. It switches its engines back on and commences a fresh approach. In this way the sub can sneak up on the target vessel in a series of short sprints—absolutely undetectable."

"What if the target vessel were to sweep constantly for underwater engine noise?" Coburg asked.

"If it did," Birnbaum replied, "it wouldn't be able to use its conventional three-hundred-sixty-degree sonar with any reliability—and that is what gives early warning of approaching objects. Basically, it's a matter of range. Wide-scan sonar gives you early warning of hostile objects in the water. Directional sonar gives you a much clearer fix on the object you've detected. If it's a sub, you can listen to it and identify it by the noise its screws make in the water—its signature. If the sub is big enough and it comes close enough, you can hear it without instruments. However, if the sub is small and invisible to wide-scan sonar and makes almost no noise at all, it is impossible to know when it is sneaking up on you. If you don't know it is there, how do you know when and where to look for it? Besides, the hijackers on the *Britannia* don't know about the SDV-12. They don't know that there's any such thing as an invisible minisub with the range and power to catch a fast surface ship. Nobody does. If they're smart, they'll run occasional sweeps in case the British try to sneak up on them in something big. The rest of the time they keep their eyes on the wide-scan sonar. Under normal circumstances that would be all they'd need to tell them the British were trying something."

"How have the SEALs tests worked out so far?" Coburg asked.

"The hard part is the design," Birnbaum said. "Once they're built, they're actually very straightforward machines to operate. All tasks in our open water trials scored a ninety-nine percent completion rate."

"Only ninety-nine percent?" Coburg said, raising an eyebrow.

"We don't accept perfect scores here," Birnbaum said.

"How long before you can get both these beasts operational?" the general asked.

Birnbaum took a breath.

"Well," he began. "As you know, the project was put on hold—"

"Please, Professor Birnbaum," the general interrupted. "Don't quote budget policy to me right at this moment."

"They're actually in the best shape they could possibly be in right now," Birnbaum added hastily. "We were getting ready to put them away, but we wanted them in mint condition first. All we have to do now is reinstall the batteries."

"How long will that take?"

"Two, maybe three hours."

"Good." Coburg nodded. "Because I want both these machines, and the SEALs teams that trained on them, in Saudi Arabia in twenty-four hours."

A look of panic crossed Birnbaum's face. His voice assumed a plaintive note.

"These are the only two in existence, General. They're first and second prototypes. If you lose or damage both of them—"

"Wrap 'em up, Professor." Coburg cut him short. "They're coming with me."

Birnbaum opened his mouth to protest again but thought better of it. He nodded and stayed silent. Then he remembered something.

"Oh," he said apologetically. "There is something else about the Mark 12 that I've forgotten to mention."

Coburg waited.

"It is the world's first air-deployable submarine," Birnbaum added. "You don't have to launch it from a ship or a dock. You can launch it out the back of a plane at 40,000 feet. Because the hull is ablative coated, it can't be picked up by radar or sonar. It is invisible in the air, on the water, and under the water. You could drop it right next to the *Britannia* and as long as the hijackers didn't see the splash, they wouldn't know it was there. That might be important, General—if you're pressed for time."

Coburg looked at him.

"Have you tried that yet?"

"No," Birnbaum answered. "It was next on the program."

Coburg looked first at Admiral Davies, then back to Birnbaum.

"I'll let you know what happens, Professor," he said.

HMY *Britannia.* 13.06 hours

"Looks like serious movement to me, Eddie."

"Maybe," Doyle murmured. "Maybe not. I thought you'd have learned by now, Nick. You can't believe everything you see on television."

Dominic Behan sat at the sonar console in the radio room of the *Britannia* with Eddie Doyle leaning in the doorway behind him. Both men had their eyes on a TV monitor mounted on the bulkhead. Doyle had tuned in to the latest CNN broadcast from Atlanta to see pictures of British soldiers preparing to pull out of Northern Ireland. The report had opened with shots of RAF Hercules transports arriving at Aldergrove Airport in Belfast to pick up the first of the departing troops. That had been followed by aerial shots of the roads surrounding the airport, showing them jammed with military traffic. TV crews on the ground showed pictures of armored cars, APCs, and trucks filled with soldiers. Some of the soldiers flashed peace signs at the camera and seemed to be happy to be leaving.

"Get them away from their officers for a few minutes, and they'd be thanking me for getting them out," Doyle murmured.

There was a time when Behan might have doubted that. But that was before he had met Doyle. Eddie Doyle had changed his mind about a lot of things. Behan opened his mouth to respond, then caught himself as the broadcast switched live to the streets of Belfast. Both men tensed, and their eyes followed the camera closely, hungry for confirmation. It was late afternoon on what looked like a warm, overcast day, and the CNN crew had set themselves up in front of a massive barricade that blocked one of the main thoroughfares into Andersontown. The barricade was a mass of burned-out cars and trucks that reached almost as high as the rooftops of the houses on both sides of the street. Clearly visible on top of the barricade were half a dozen hooded men with automatic rifles. Behind the TV reporter the occasional RUC man wandered into view, seemingly oblivious to the armed men on the barricade.

"Barricades such as this have sprung up all through Belfast," the reporter was saying. "Symbols of anarchy in a city divided by hate. Armed militiamen from both sides now carry their weapons openly in an obvious display of contempt for the thinly stretched forces of the Royal Ulster Constabulary, the only authority left in Northern Ireland now that the unthinkable has happened and the British have begun their withdrawal."

The camera panned around to show a street littered with rubble, the blackened hulks of burned-out trucks and cars, and dozens of gutted houses. Furniture from many of the houses had been thrown into the street and smashed or burned. A group of kids had set up a couch, a chair, a dead TV, and a bedroom dresser with the mirror miraculously intact in the middle of the road, like a mock living room. A hundred yards away a couple of blue RUC Land Rovers were visible and half a dozen RUC men wearing bulletproof vests and carrying rifles. The defeated expressions on their faces showed the hopelessness of their situation.

"Behind this barricade," the reporter went on, "the tricolor of the Irish Republic can be seen hanging from windows and flying from flagpoles and lampposts. Behind this barricade the IRA is the only law. Behind this barricade the Catholics call their territory Free Belfast. And the situation is the same in every other Catholic ghetto throughout Northern Ireland tonight. The situation across town in the Protestant ghettos is the same. The only differences are the symbols and the names. Instead of the IRA it is the UDA and the UDF. Instead of the tricolor it is the Union Jack and portraits of the queen. Instead of Free Belfast it is called Loyal Belfast. Everywhere the mood is the same. The tension so thick it fills the air like a fog. A fog of sectarian hatred that hangs over the entire province as the countdown continues to what now looks like certain civil war in Northern Ireland."

Behan turned his attention back to the solemn-faced Doyle.

"Give yourself a bit of credit, man," he said. "This is history we're watchin' here. The Brits are pullin' out. Joe Keegan has no choice but to go along with us or get left behind. Another few weeks and things will be so bad the UN will have to go in. And everybody knows it's the Yanks who tell the UN what to do—and they're on our side. So it's only a matter of time before the country is whole again and those black Proddie bastards can go back across the Irish Sea to where they came from."

Doyle looked doubtful.

"If there's one thing I learned about the Brits," he said, "it's that you can't believe a filthy word they say. They're the smoothest of the smooth, Nick. They smile in your face, they pile on the charm, and the moment your back's turned they stick in the knife. They're famous for it. They've double-crossed their way through history. I wouldn't trust the bastards if they told me the world was round. Let's just wait till we've spoken to the boys on the ground in Belfast, shall we? Then maybe we can believe it's real."

Behan shook his head. There had been a time when he believed that nobody could hate the British as much as he did. Then he had met Doyle. Doyle's hatred was pathological and all-consuming and left little room for anything else. Not friendship, not women, not even politics. Behan had long ago formed the opinion that the emancipation of Northern Ireland was only a sideshow as far as Doyle was concerned. The real show was on board the *Britannia,* where Doyle could hold the Crown to ransom and inflict on the British the greatest humiliation in their history.

"They had their doubts about you, you know," Behan remarked abruptly. "Right until we left for Mashhad. I don't think they ever expected to hear from us again."

Doyle looked at him.

"Who?"

"The boys," Behan added. "They went along with it only because I said so. A few of them still thought you were a plant. That's why I had to keep your name out of it until the last minute. Jimmy and

Billy and Michael and Patsy nearly shit themselves when you came on board."

Doyle's lips tightened in what might have been a smile.

"You think they believe in me now?" he asked, his voice cold and passionless, as if he didn't care whether they believed in him or not. Those who remained now that Mulcahey was gone, lured to his death by his own primitive lusts.

"I think the whole bloody world knows you're serious after that bit of business with Marchant and the girl," Behan added quietly.

He switched his attention back to the TV screen and the images of yet another European country tearing itself apart at the seams. Except this time it was his country. His nation. His Ireland redefining itself through a baptism of blood and fire. And all of it made possible by the strange, foreboding figure who stood silently behind him. On the rubble-strewn streets of Belfast, Behan knew, it was he who would be celebrated as a hero. As the man who provided the spark, the catalyst for unification. But the real architect of the moment was Doyle. None of it could have happened without Doyle. It was his plan. His idea. His vision. All of it. As devoted to the Cause as Behan was, he had been forced to concede many times over that he could never have attempted anything quite so audacious as the hijacking of the royal yacht without Doyle to show him how. Without Doyle to propel him every step of the way. Sometimes he found himself wondering. Wondering if at last he had fallen in league with the devil as so many of his cronies in the Provisionals—allies and enemies alike—had predicted he would. Because, until Doyle had come along, Behan had been ready to quit. Close to exhaustion, sick and tired of the endless petty feuds within the IRA, ready to give up the struggle after a decade of fighting and running and hiding and getting nowhere. So weary of it all that in the dark of night he had found himself again and again silently offering his soul up to the devil if he could only find a way to break the deadlock of history. To stand the world on its head. To find the mechanism that would hurl the British out of Ireland forever. And then the night had come when he had awakened to find a still, dark figure standing at the foot of his bed, watching him. As his eyes had adjusted to the darkness, he realized that the figure was real. A real man with a real nine-millimeter pistol aimed at Behan's head.

Behan was staying at a girlfriend's flat at the time. It was on the tenth floor of a high-rise building in the heart of Turf Lodge, a Republican stronghold in the middle of Belfast. An area the British never entered unless they were at platoon strength or more and protected by a couple of armored cars. Behan could hardly have felt more secure. He had a dozen places in Belfast where he could lay his head, and this was one of the safest. There were a couple of teenage boys who lived in the building and worshipped him as a hero. They were happy to stay up all night to act as lookouts for him.

Until that night Behan had complete confidence in his survival instincts. Doyle shattered that confidence. Forever. The most wanted man in the IRA awakened to find his girlfriend unconscious on the floor beside the bed and Doyle watching him in the darkness. His first reaction was that his time had come. He knew he had been targeted for an SAS hit and now they had found him. There was no time for fear. He could only watch the shape at the foot of the bed and wait for the impact of the bullets. Instead, Doyle had spoken to him, spoken to him in a voice so calm and reasoned they might have been strangers exchanging greetings in a park on a sunny afternoon.

"If I wanted you dead," Doyle told him in that soft English accent, "you'd be dead now."

At first Behan didn't believe him. The bastard was toying with him, that was all. He'd seen it himself in situations where he and a few of the boys had to take care of a tout. Pure contempt. Then again, he had thought, maybe it wasn't a hit. Maybe they wanted to take him back in one piece. Beat some information out of him. Put him on trial. Score a big propaganda victory. His next thought was for his pistol beneath the pillow. He moved his hand slowly behind him, hoping it wouldn't be noticed in the darkness.

"Don't be stupid," Doyle said. Behan lay still. Okay, he told himself, all he had to do now was keep his mouth shut and stay alive. No matter what they did to him. As long as he was alive, anything was possible. Then Doyle stepped over to the light switch and turned on the light. It took a moment or two for Behan's eyes to adjust to the glare. Then he looked over the side of the bed at his girlfriend,

Doreen, on the floor. She was on her side, naked, a breast folded against one arm. She didn't seem to be breathing. Behan felt an unaccustomed stab of fear. He had slept soundly through it all. Hadn't known a thing until then. Whoever this bastard was, he was right. He could have done anything he'd wanted while they were both asleep.

"She's okay," Doyle reassured him. "I just stopped her pulse for a minute while she was asleep. Shut off the oxygen to her brain. She'll come round in an hour or so. There shouldn't be any lasting damage."

Behan looked closer. The guy was telling the truth. She was breathing after all, though barely. He looked back at his visitor. He was dressed entirely in black, his hair covered by a black woolen cap, his face streaked with grease. He had to be SAS.

"How did you get in here?" Behan asked. He thought of the door. Two bolts and a deadlock. He had heard nothing.

Doyle smiled and nodded in the direction of the bathroom window.

"Up the side of the building," he said.

Behan caught his breath. The side of the building was nothing but rough brick studded by narrow bathroom windows. Only special forces training could equip a man for a climb like that.

"Okay," the IRA man asked. "What happens now?"

Doyle smiled and moved around to the side of the bed. In one hand he held an automatic. In the other he held Behan's short barreled stainless-steel Ruger. He flicked out the chamber and shook all six nine-millimeter cartridges onto the covers. Then he let the pistol fall to the bed beside them.

"Nothing," he said finally. "Nothing happens now. I wanted to give you a message, that's all."

"You've done that," Behan muttered.

Again Doyle made that odd, thin-lipped grimace that seemed to be his idea of a smile.

"My name's Eddie Doyle," he added abruptly. "I'm not SAS. I'm better than that. Royal Marines actually. Arctic and Mountain Warfare Cadre."

Then Behan had understood. The Royal Marines had been in

Northern Ireland for six months on one of their periodic tours of duty in the province. After the Paras they always spelled bad news. Especially in Armagh, where they liked to beat the IRA at their own ambush game. But there had been one time when Behan had turned the tables on the marines and laid an ambush that had killed four. Kids, all of them. Not one of them older than twenty. Not like this bastard. Not a hardened professional. That could mean only one thing. It wasn't a sanctioned hit after all. It was private. The settling of an old score. And all the time these thoughts raced through Behan's mind, Doyle only seemed to enjoy his pain.

"Fuck you, then," Behan spat back at him. "Fuck you and get it over with."

"I don't want you dead, Nick," Doyle answered quietly. "But I do want you to understand something."

He paused for a moment to give added weight to his words.

"I want to come over."

Behan stared back at him in silent disbelief.

"You see," Doyle explained. "This isn't far from where I started. I was born at St. Mary's. Spent the first eleven years of my life right here in the Lodge. Of course, these blocks weren't here then. Just streets. Row houses. Mile after mile of them. I'm Catholic, just like you, Nick. Not that I give a shit. For the church or the Pope. My family moved to England in '71. Liverpool. They thought it would be better than here. It wasn't. Still no work, you see. Not for the likes of us. I joined up in '79. My parents thought I did pretty well to get into Royal. They told me to lie about my religion. About what I was. I did. It didn't do me any good though. All these years and still only a lieutenant. Talk about disappointment, eh? Talk about frustration? Now my time is just about up. And I've come to a decision, Nick. I've decided I'm coming over . . . to your side."

"Bullshit . . ." Behan had sputtered back, his voice a derisive half laugh. "You're out of your fucking mind. You think we're stupid or something?"

"I tried to fit in, you know," Doyle continued, as though Behan hadn't even spoken. "Did pretty well for a time too. Learned the talk. The manners. The style. Went to officer training school. Almost became one of them. An officer and a gentleman. But not quite. You see, the truth is . . . they didn't want me. I was good enough to fight for them. Good enough to go to the South Atlantic and fight the Argies. Good enough to help turn the Argies' flank at Mount Harriet. Good enough to kill three and take a dozen prisoner. But not good enough to get a medal. Not even a mention in dispatches. My platoon leader did that for me. Took the credit and everything that went with it. I tried to put it right, and all that happened was that I got put on a charge. Took seven years after that before I got my commission. And even then it was clear I wasn't going any further. Just not good enough to become one of them, you see, Nick. Wrong side of the water. Bad Irish stock."

"Sure," Behan had muttered. "Whatever you say, pal."

There had been a long pause before Doyle had spoken again.

"I didn't expect you to believe me," he said. "Not tonight. But you're going to be thinking about it in the next few months, aren't you, Nick? Won't be able to help yourself. I could have killed you tonight. But I didn't. And I'll remind you of that in the next few weeks. I'll always know where to find you, Nick. And I can take you out anytime I want. But I won't. And from time to time I'll send you a message. Let you know I'm thinking about you. And then we'll talk again."

And with that he switched off the light and disappeared from the room. Behan stayed perfectly still for a while. Then he fumbled for his Ruger and the shells, loaded it quickly, and crept quietly out of bed and through the darkened apartment. And all he found was the door to the flat wide open . . . and no sign of his visitor. He pulled on a pair of pants and a shirt and went outside in search of his lookouts. One of them was at the top of the stairs from where he could watch the elevators and the stairwell. The other was downstairs in the lobby. Neither of them had seen anyone.

Behan hadn't told anyone what had happened. He didn't want them to know. He knew what they would think. Then, two weeks after his first visit from Doyle, Behan had left a pal's house in Ballymurphy one morning and got into his car. He was halfway to Strabane before he noticed a note attached to the sun visor.

Look under the hood, it said.

That scared him. It couldn't be a bomb because he had been driving for a couple hours. He cursed himself for his carelessness and then he got out of the car and, slowly, carefully, he opened the hood. There were a couple of highway flares attached to the car battery. And another note.

If this was a bomb, it said, *you'd be dead.*

There was no signature. It was a message that didn't need one.

That had shaken Behan. This time he had to do something. He told the rest of the guys on the army council. It was a few days before word came back. There was a Lieutenant Doyle serving with the Royal Marines in Belfast at the time. Behan could scarcely believe it. The bastard was using his real name. The guys on the army council suspected he was running a con. They made Doyle a target for assassination. But he proved too smart for them. He avoided all the usual traps. He never went to the pubs where the Catholic girls could seduce him and lure him to a place where the boys could kill him. He seemed to have no off-duty life at all. But he had been right about one thing. All the time Behan was thinking about him.

Then Doyle had sent the army council a message. It happened at a checkpoint in south Armagh. Doyle was in charge of a patrol stopping cars and checking for smuggled arms from the south. One of the cars was driven by Sean McDermott and he was bringing in a dozen M-16s for Matty Byrne, all of them dismantled and hidden in the car. Doyle had prised open an inside door panel and found an M-16 stock. McDermott knew he was gone. Instead, Doyle had looked him in the eye and said: "Tell the boys. Tell Nick Behan . . . this one is a present from Eddie Doyle."

There were other things too. Times and places when Doyle went easier than anybody else in situations where a bit of force might have been expected. The word was getting out among his troops too. Doyle was soft on Catholics.

And then, near the end of his tour of duty, Doyle had turned up again. This time he had walked into a pub in the Short Strand where Behan was having a drink. He was wearing civilian clothes, he appeared to be unarmed, and he had walked right up to Behan, who was sitting at a table with Patsy Ryan and Michael Kenney. And he looked at Behan and told him straight out: "I'm leaving for England in four days. I'll be out of the service in six weeks. Then I'm on my own. The next time we talk will be in Dublin."

He had been as good as his word. A letter arrived at Behan's girlfriend's flat, telling him where and when they should meet. The army council had warned Behan against it. They said they wanted no part of Doyle, and they would not tolerate him being brought into the organization. Behan had gone anyway. He couldn't help himself. He had thought about little else but Doyle for months and had come to the conclusion that he might just be on the level about crossing over. He had already shown how useful he could be. Behan wanted to hear him out.

They had met at Dunphy's bar on a sunny Saturday morning in June. And it was there that Doyle had quietly revealed his plan. His plan to hijack the *Britannia.* Behan remembered how disappointed he was. His earlier assessment was right. Doyle was a rogue bull, a lunatic. Then Doyle had opened his jacket and pulled a long white envelope from his inside pocket. Inside the envelope was a piece of paper. When he spread it on the table it was about the size of a broadsheet newspaper page. Behan saw that it was some kind of blueprint, but he couldn't tell exactly what it was supposed to be.

"So," he had asked. "What is it?"

"It's a copy of something that might interest you," Doyle answered. "It's a deck plan of Her Majesty's royal yacht, the *Britannia.*"

Now, two years later, Behan still found it incredible. Even as he sat in the sonar operator's chair on board the *Britannia* waiting for the counterattack that could come at any moment. He knew now that Doyle was not mad. Not in the way that Behan understood it. Though he hadn't entirely ruled out the possibility that Doyle was an agent of the devil.

"I'm going to catch up on some sleep," Doyle said suddenly. "Anything happens, you tell me."

"No problem." Behan nodded. He turned back to the sonar scanner, put on the headset, and sent out another sweep. The probe pinged off into the depths, faded, and vanished. The green circular screen in front of him stayed blank.

Doyle stepped out onto the bridge. It was deserted. Patsy Ryan was asleep on a cot in the chart room. The ship was on autopilot, steering Ryan's preprogrammed course southward at a steady eight knots. Billy Deveny was with Michael Kenney in the engine room. Musa, Javad, and Youssef were asleep in the cabins next to the admiral's day cabin, where the officers remained imprisoned. Brady and O'Brien were patrolling the lower decks to deter any more incursions from the royal apartments. He paused to check the galvanometer taped to the shelf beneath the bridge console. Two wires from the galvanometer led up through a hole in the console and were spliced into the ship's primary communications cable. The handle of the galvanometer was taped down. A single turn of that handle was enough to send an electric pulse humming down to the boiler room—and all five charges would explode at once.

Doyle ran the tip of his forefinger lightly over the handle, almost as if he were caressing it. He didn't care what deals the British made or how many of his demands they accepted. The *Britannia* was going down. And the bloody Queen of England was going down with it.

9 Operation Scepter

HMY *Britannia,* May 21. 01.05 hours

Doyle felt a hand on his shoulder and was instantly awake.

"That Yank TV reporter is on the line from New York again," Behan whispered. "Says he has to speak to you."

"Damn," Doyle swore. "Who the hell does he think he's playing with?"

"He says he's got a deal."

"What kind of deal?"

"He won't say. Says he has to talk to you. Says you and him have an understanding. Says he trusts you . . . you know the kind of shit reporters say."

Doyle got up reluctantly from the chart room cot, padded back out to the bridge in his stocking feet, and snatched up the radio handset.

"Make it fast," he snapped.

"Good evening, my friend." Dunbarry's voice slid onto the line. "Or is it morning already where you are?"

"You've got one minute," Doyle answered. "Make it count."

"That's more than enough for what I have to say," Dunbarry answered with just enough firmness to show that he too could play with the hard men.

"I'm coming out there to see you, my friend," Dunbarry announced. "I want to do an interview with you, live, from the decks of the *Britannia.*"

"Jesus," Behan muttered. "The guy's got his balls where his brain should be."

Doyle leaned back down to the transmitter, that grimace forming on his lips again.

"And exactly how do you propose to do that?" he asked softly.

"I'll fly out to the yacht by helicopter," Dunbarry answered. "There will be three people on board. Myself, the pilot, and one man to do pictures and sound. We'll use the helipad on the afterdeck of the royal yacht. Just myself and the cameraman will get out of the chopper. We'll do a live-to-air interview with you. The whole world will hear what you have to say. Unedited. Uncensored. No tricks. I give you my word of honor."

Doyle hesitated. It wasn't long, but it was long enough for Dunbarry to sense that he had his opening. A new note of urgency crept into his voice as he realized that the gamble of his life was about to pay off. An exclusive interview with the hijack leader in the final hours of the countdown. It would be his greatest scoop. It was like getting Hitler in the bunker just before the fall of Berlin. And only he had the wit to think of it . . . and the nerve to carry it off.

"You get to tell your story to the world, my friend," Dunbarry went on. "No bullshit. What you say will go straight out over the airwaves. You can say anything you want to say and nobody will touch it. A lot of people might not like what I'm doing, but that's a chance I'm willing to take. I'm talking to you man to man, my friend. You know that I don't know who you are or where you come from. But you've got a cause that you are willing to die for, and in my books that makes you an important man. A courageous man. A man of conviction. You've got something to say and I am going to give you the opportunity to say it to a billion people around the world. Just think about that for a moment, my friend. You can't walk away from that. . . ."

"You know what it's like out here?" Doyle asked.

"I know," Dunbarry answered. "But I'm willing to take that risk the moment you give me the word. You are our guarantee of safe passage, my friend. Nobody will touch us if you say so. Right now you've got the power. You're holding all the aces and you might as well play them for all they're worth."

"All right," Doyle decided abruptly. "Do it. You want a story . . . I'll give you a story."

"I'm on my way, my friend," Dunbarry said. "See you in a few hours."

But Doyle had already gone.

Five miles away, on board the *Hotspur,* the duty intelligence officer signaled his colleague to take over surveillance. Then he put down his headset and called through to Lieutenant Gage.

HMS *Hotspur.* 10.59 hours

"Gentlemen . . ." Sir Malcolm Porter began the meeting the moment he sat down in the operations room. "I think we may have put a name to our devil."

He paused to survey the expectant faces gathered around the table: Captain Purcell, General Sharpe, Colonel Quillan, Professor Pryne, Lieutenant Gage, Commander Lynch and Lieutenant Commander Bonner. All of them summoned to a meeting that was scheduled to have begun three hours earlier.

"First, I want to apologize for messing all of you around this morning," Porter added in a conciliatory manner. "However, Lieutenant Gage and I have been rather busy these past few hours and I think you'll appreciate that the wait has been worthwhile. Some rather interesting material came in from Northwood around five o'clock this morning."

His aide handed him a plain buff file and a sheaf of photographs.

"As soon as we had a positive ID, we pulled in every file on this chap that we could get our hands on. I gave copies to Professor Pryne a couple of hours ago and he will give us the benefit of his own insights a little later on. I also took the time to make a few copies of this photograph."

He fanned the copies out across the table and paused for a moment to let each of them study in detail the face of the man who looked back at them. It was a flattering photograph even though it was a service record shot. A picture of a man in his late twenties with lightly tanned skin, even features, a strong jaw, good nose, and sandy-blond hair cropped to military length. The only discordant features were his eyes. They were sharp, clear, and intelligent. But there was something else in them that demanded closer inspection. Something odd and unsettling. A pinpoint glimmer of light in the pupils that seemed to have burned right through the camera's lens and into the print itself so that whichever way the photograph was turned he was looking directly at you, mocking you.

"Good God al-bloody-mighty."

They all lifted their eyes from the photograph and turned to General Sharpe. Even the mask of his well-weathered features wasn't enough to disguise the shock on his face. Lynch knew what was wrong. He had seen it too, the second he had looked at the picture. It wasn't much. The collar and epaulettes of an ordinary khaki shirt, the kind that any British soldier might wear. Except for the shiny metal nubs at the edge of one epaulette. A crown and a letter *R*. The second letter wasn't visible. It wasn't needed. Both Sharpe and Lynch knew what it meant.

"I can't believe it," Sharpe breathed. "This man is a Royal Marine."

"Was a Royal Marine," Porter added hastily, seeking to ease the general's sense of betrayal. "It seems Commander Lynch's hunch was right. The hijackers are being led by a mercenary. A mercenary who has a great deal of specialized knowledge about the royal yacht, about the way we think, and about the way we operate."

Sharpe slumped back in his chair as though wounded. Lynch, too, felt betrayed. He had been a Royal Marine before he had moved up to the SBS. To a large extent, part of him still was a Royal Marine and always would be. And try as he might, he could not remember a single instance of any other Royal Marine who had ever turned against the Crown.

"His name"—Porter's carefully measured words seemed to echo between the gray metal walls—"is Edward Joseph Doyle. Until two years ago he was a lieutenant with the Royal Marines."

"Are we absolutely certain about this?" Colonel Quillan interrupted, struggling to find some scrap of consolation for the devastated General Sharpe.

"I'm afraid so," Porter confirmed briskly. "There's no doubt about his identity . . . and there's worse to come."

The mood in the small room became funereal. Porter looked down at the top sheet of papers he held in his hand.

"Our Mr. Doyle is thirty-three years old and was born in Belfast. He had one younger brother. His father was an electrician. The family migrated to England in 1971, when he was eleven years old, and settled in Liverpool. He left school at fifteen, worked as an apprentice electrician for a year, decided it wasn't the career for him, and went to night school to finish his high school education. After getting his CSE it seems he applied himself to the task of getting into the armed forces. He made two attempts to join the Royal Marines and was successful on his second attempt. He got through Lympstone without too much difficulty and his service record remains clear until the second year, when his commanding officers noticed certain characteristics that made them doubt his suitability for advancement in the corps. It appears that he had a propensity for getting into fistfights with his comrades, often over insults that were more imagined than real. He was counseled exhaustively during this period and, apparently, responded quite well because his sheet is clean for the next two years. However, his career almost came to an abrupt halt during the Falklands campaign in 1982, when his platoon commander suspected him of shooting POWs. Apparently he performed very well throughout the campaign and acquitted himself courageously on several occasions. If it weren't for the suspicions involving his treatment of the POWs, he would have been recommended for decoration and promotion. He kicked up a stink at the time until the CO told him that if he didn't shut up, he'd be booted out of the corps. After that he kept his mouth shut and knuckled down to straightforward soldiering again, though it would appear he harbored some considerable resentment over his treatment by the corps. He was recommended for a commission in 1987 but rejected on the grounds of psychological unsuitability. Though he was a good marine, his leadership abilities were considered poor. He was recommended again and rejected again in 1988, which probably served only to fuel his resentment. He was recommended again in 1989 and accepted. He got through the officer training program well enough at Dartmouth, though there was some recurrence of the type of behavior that marred his second year in the corps. Disputes that often ended in violence. It seems he came close to getting bounced back down to the ranks. Nevertheless, he completed officer training and graduated about midway in his class. After he received his commission, he went straight to the Arctic and Mountain Warfare Cadre and again acquitted himself quite well. Still, it seems Mr. Doyle read the signs quite accurately and decided he would go no further in terms of promotion. After he left Dartmouth he spent spent less than eighteen months in the corps before resigning his commission. What is particularly interesting to us is that he spent his last year on a tour of duty in Northern Ireland."

Porter paused for a moment and looked up. Everyone in the room was still and silent though their eyes were fixed on him with an intensity he could feel.

"What is so interesting about our Mr. Doyle's tour of duty in Northern Ireland is that it is remarkable for its lack of incident," Porter went on. "And, as most of us are aware, it is most unusual for any unit of the Royal Marines to spend an entire year in Northern Ireland without becoming involved in at least one major incident. If anything, Doyle was criticized for excessive caution—which had hardly been a prominent characteristic of his in the past. His men said he was soft on Catholics because he himself was a Catholic although he lied on his first application to the corps and put himself down as Protestant. It may have been a problem with him, but there is no evidence of any religious behavior in his record at all."

"Strengths?" Lynch asked.

Porter nodded and quickly scanned Doyle's service charts. He understood what Lynch wanted. After all, it was Lynch who might have to go toe to toe with Doyle.

"Good marksman," he announced after a moment. "Good swimmer. Excellent climber."

Lynch sniffed. They were all the preferred activities of the individualist. Activities that precluded teamwork and allowed a man to excel on his own and on his own terms.

"What happened after Northern Ireland?" Colonel Quillan asked.

"Resigned from the corps," Porter answered simply. "Six weeks after his return to England."

"There's nothing on suspicious contacts with IRA people during his tour of duty?" Quillan asked, incredulous.

"Nothing more than I've told you already," Porter replied. "Although we've got a record from immigration showing that he flew from Birmingham to Dublin in June of 'ninety-two."

"Do we know what he did while he was there?" Sharpe asked.

"No," Porter answered flatly. "At the time there were no grounds for suspicion. There was nothing to alert anyone to the possibility that Doyle could be a rogue element."

"Nothing but his penchant for shooting POWs," Purcell remarked acidly.

"I know how you must feel, Captain Purcell," Porter responded evenly. "But if you'll allow me to play the devil's advocate for a moment, it has to be pointed out that there was a considerable body of opinion in the military at the time that held that the occasional shooting of POWs was not wholly unforgivable in a war where the enemy used phosphorous grenades against our men. The suspicions about Doyle were handled according to the standards that prevailed at the time. It must also be said that when the media came sniffing around afterward, trying to dig up dirt about British war crimes, there was a resultant closing of the ranks that obviously worked to Doyle's benefit by shielding him from further investigation."

"Obviously," Purcell remarked dryly.

"We keep tabs on some of our special forces people when they leave the service," Porter added defensively. "But it could hardly be called close surveillance. It's neither possible nor practical to keep an eye on everybody. Nor is it desirable. We are a democracy, after all."

"So," Quillan interjected, "we don't know whom he met while he was in Dublin, where he went . . . ?"

"According to our sources, he was there for four days," Porter answered.

"Then what?" Sharpe asked.

"The best we can say is that he appears to have returned to Birmingham where he lived for about ten months and then . . . he vanished."

"What . . . ?" Sharpe looked accusingly at Porter. "You mean there's no record of where he went?"

"No employment record, no unemployment checks, no hospital records, no further use of his passport—nothing."

"It's easy enough to get a new passport," Lynch added. "A thousand pounds will get you any passport you like made to order in Brussels. The genuine article costs a little bit more."

"And . . ." Porter went on, "the moment he had a new passport he could have gone anywhere he wanted . . . no one would have known."

"What was the bugger doing for money all this time?" Purcell asked. "He scarcely qualifies as independently wealthy."

Porter smiled faintly. For a Royal Navy skipper, there were times when Purcell could sound extraordinarily naive.

"He took his Navy pension in a lump sum," Porter answered. "It came to about twenty-eight thousand pounds. Quite enough for one man to live on for a year as long as he didn't engage in any conspicuous consumption. And he may have had other savings we don't know about. Then, of course, there's every policeman's nightmare . . ."

"Policeman's nightmare . . . ?" Purcell echoed.

"Special forces operate the most advanced schools for criminals in the entire world," Porter explained. "When a man is accepted for special forces training, he learns how to use explosives, how to break into buildings, how to steal cars and boats and airplanes, how to kill people. They make the best cat burglars, the best thieves, the best hold-up men, the best . . ."

"Hijackers . . . ?" Purcell finished for him.

"We do our best to weed out the psychotics," Porter went on. "Character is a fundamental part of the selection process. The reviews are constant and rigorous. Both Colonel Quillan and General Sharpe can attest to that. Not everybody gets the benefit of special forces training and not everybody gets through it either. In the past we've been pretty successful in screening out the bad apples. Every now and again, even in the best of systems, one of them slips through. It's unavoidable. What is especially terrifying to me is knowing how clever this bastard must be to have done it—because it isn't easy."

Professor Pryne saw his cue and gave a small cough to signal Porter that he had his own insights to offer into the kind of psychology they were dealing with.

"Of course," Porter responded. "Professor Pryne has had a couple of hours now to study Mr. Doyle's records. I think we might all benefit a little from his wisdom."

"I'll try to keep it simple," Pryne began with the kind of easy arrogance that always irritated men like Lynch. The SBS commander exchanged glances with Bonner and saw that he was not alone.

"Of course it's easy to recognize a pattern now," Pryne continued in his supercilious way. "The long periods of calm between storms. The years when Mr. Doyle was a loyal and obedient servant of the Crown whose service was marred only occasionally by displays of inappropriate behavior."

Lynch smiled to himself. He wondered if "inappropriate behavior" was politically correct jargon for the shooting of POWs.

"This pattern, however, has taken fourteen years to emerge," Pryne went on. "So we can hardly fault the marine corps for missing its underlying significance. Examining this man's behavior today, with the benefit of hindsight, we can see that most, if not all, of his outbursts occurred at times when he was under intense and prolonged stress. His first years in the corps, when he would have been trying to prove that he belonged, the alleged shooting of POWs during the Falklands War, the incidents at Dartmouth when he was trying to get through officer training. The impression I get is of a rather poorly formed, immature personality with pronounced feelings of insecurity and personal inadequacy."

Lynch gave an imperceptible nod. He might not like Pryne, but he knew the type the professor was talking about. He had encountered a few of them in his early years in the corps. Men who had all the confidence in the world on the surface but who were hollow on the inside. Men who desperately wanted to belong to the Royal Marines in order to prop up their own shaky self-image. Porter's earlier comments had been right. Types like that rarely lasted.

"Doyle belongs to a personality type that is often drawn to the military way of life," the professor went on. "Not only by the structure and discipline that is offered but by the implicit promise that once he has been accepted, he will one day have the power to tell others what to do. We call it a passive-aggressive type of personality. It may sound like a contradiction, but it isn't. It is essentially an insecure personality that craves discipline and order. It has to attach itself to a powerful, clearly defined image because it draws its own self-worth from that image. Let me explain it another way. A man like Doyle doesn't want to go to the trouble of establishing his own persona because it is simply too difficult. Too many moral dilemmas for the immature psyche. It is much easier for him to acquire a successful, potent, ready-made personality. In this case the persona of the man-at-arms. And, if you're going to go shopping for that kind of persona, it follows that you will want the best that money can buy. In this case the Royal Marines with their attendant opportunities for advancement to special forces and all the glamour and mystique that seems to bestow."

"Very flattering," Lynch murmured.

Pryne heard him and gave him his most baleful look.

"I think we all know of at least one individual who has devoted his entire life to the service of a large and powerful organization and who identifies with it to such an extent that once he retires, he goes into a very rapid decline because he has ceased to exist in any viable sense."

Lynch shifted awkwardly in his chair and caught Bonner grinning at him.

"Still," Porter interjected, "it doesn't explain this little display of initiative, does it?"

Pryne nodded and switched his attention back to Sir Malcolm.

"Doyle was uprooted from everything with which he was familiar when he was eleven years old," the professor continued. "That's a highly impressionable age. The trauma would have been considerable and its effects almost certainly repressed, given what we know of the family circumstances. In Liverpool he was part of a migrant community that was kept at the bottom of the social ladder and was widely looked down upon. The only way for him to acquire any self-esteem was to borrow it from a highly respected organization like the Royal Marines. When he was in the marines he probably tried very hard to belong. The fact that he lied about his religion and, no doubt, other aspects of his background, is an indication of how hard. In a perverse way the execution of POWs—the total annihilation of the enemy—was his idea of winning the approval of his comrades in arms. I also noticed in his file that his mother died in 1986, yet he did not seek compassionate leave to attend the funeral. There appears to have been no subsequent contact with his father or brother. This confirms the scenario of the embittered loner. The personality that wants very much to belong to something or somebody but is continually thwarted. Undoubtedly he saw his only family as the marine corps and yet the corps repeatedly spurned him—to his way of thinking. Even when he was accepted for officer training it was only after repeated rejections which, to him, would have been incomprehensible. At Dartmouth he would have been one of the oldest officer candidates and, given his modest origins, he probably stood out from the other candidates in other ways, bearing in mind that the majority of them would have come from well-educated, middle class backgrounds. Undoubtedly it only made him feel more of a misfit. Ultimately his feelings of rejection were compounded. He came to believe that the institution he depended upon for self-affirmation had continually let him down. He'd given his best and the corps had scorned him. Betrayed him, if you like. Given these feelings of betrayal, it is a very short leap to a personality that has become hell-bent on revenge."

"So he goes from betrayed to betrayer?" Porter queried.

"He wouldn't see it that way, of course," Pryne answered. "As far as he is concerned, he is the victim of a terrible injustice. Consequently, he has set out to procure justice for himself. Naturally, he wants to avenge himself against the corps . . . but that is not all."

"He wants to take it out on the queen . . . the throne of England?" Sharpe added.

"That is exactly what he has done," Pryne answered flatly. "The queen is the titular head of the corps, the symbol of all that is British . . . everything he has come to despise. I doubt if he gives a damn what happens in Northern Ireland. The people involved in this disaster are pawns in his game. As are the IRA. As are the Arabs."

Pryne paused for a moment to give his words final emphasis: "I stated at the beginning that I believe him to be a passive-aggressive type of personality. Slave-dictator is another way of putting it. He is quite content to do what he is told when he belongs to a strong, rigidly controlled structure. However, when he feels he does not belong, when things do not perform according to his expectations, he has to exercise control in some other way. By dominating it, if necessary. By becoming the dictator of events rather than the follower."

"Let me get this straight," Quillan mused out loud. "As long as this chap had somebody kicking him up the arse, he was happy. But as soon as that stopped, he had to make a bloody nuisance of himself and try to run everything, is that it?"

"In a manner of speaking," Pryne sighed.

"Sounds more German than Celt," Sharpe reflected quietly.

"What our Mr. Doyle has orchestrated here," Pryne continued, "is a situation he can control. He has gone from being a loyal servant of the Crown to a situation where he is its master. But only for a limited period of time. He is master only of the moment."

"Assuming he isn't completely mad—" Porter began.

"He isn't," Pryne interrupted. "Not in any clinical sense. Rage would be a more accurate way of describing it . . . pathological rage."

"He's mad enough for me," Purcell commented to a mutter of agreement around the table.

"Well . . ." Porter resumed. "Assuming he isn't completely mad, he must know that the moment can't go on indefinitely. He's the one who imposed the deadline. He's the one who's sticking to it."

"Absolutely," Pryne agreed. "And all the deadline does is confirm his mastery of the moment. When the moment ends, his dominance ends. His world ends . . . and so, I suspect, does ours."

"What do you mean by that?" Sharpe asked testily.

"He'll revert to type," Pryne responded. "The immature psyche will take over. He'll throw a tantrum, lash out at everything and everyone who has ever harmed him . . . try to destroy them all."

"You mean he'll blow up the royal yacht no matter what?" Porter asked.

"Yes," Pryne answered quietly. "In his sub-conscious it has already been decided for him."

BELFAST, MAY 21. 11.25 HOURS

Sean McDermott threaded his motorbike carefully through the traffic jam in front of the main passenger terminal at Aldergrove Airport. Attached to the back of his bike was a black box that bore the logo of the United Parcel Service. Inside was a package wrapped in UPS paper and tape containing a dozen rolls of exposed film showing scenic shots of Northern Ireland. It was addressed to a company in London that published calendars. For good measure McDermott had added a couple of UPS stickers to the sides of his helmet so that anyone who saw him would assume he was just another of Belfast's many motorcycle couriers.

The airport was a mess. All the major airlines had added extra flights to cope with the tide of people rushing to escape Northern Ireland. The line of cars, taxis, and buses stretched from the departures terminal as far back as the main road, two miles away. Most of the approaches were restricted to two lanes because military traffic jammed the third. The footpath in front of the terminal was clogged with people squabbling over luggage carts, trying to move children, elderly relatives, and mountains of baggage. Occasionally, the odd, beleaguered RUC man could be seen, trying to impose some order on the chaos, though there was no mistaking the undercurrent of panic that simmered beneath it all. The scene was reportedly the same at every major ferry terminal on the coast. The looming threat of civil war had prompted a rush of refugees to the British mainland. Forty thousand had fled in the past two days and that number was expected to double before the deadline expired. By noon on the twenty-third, it was estimated, at least one hundred thousand refugees would have fled Northern Ireland. Most of them Protestant families, exhausted by decades of sectarian warfare and fearful of what was to come once the British had completed their withdrawal. Thousands of Catholic families had fled south by road into the Irish Republic and new rumors had surfaced that the Irish Army would close the border soon, until the crisis had passed.

McDermott grinned behind the protective mask of his motorcycle helmet, thrilled by the anarchy he had helped create. He maneuvered his bike around an awkwardly parked TV news van with a camera crew on the roof, and slowly wormed his way out of the logjam. When he was clear of the main terminal, he turned onto a service road that led to the air express depot, next door to the section of the airport that was reserved for military transport. The traffic was lighter there and he picked up speed as he followed the pavement beside a high chain-mesh security fence that guarded the runways. A line of hangars and service buildings blocked his view for most of the way, but as he came closer to the depot, he found a wide gap between buildings and glimpsed the gray-green tails of three Hercules military transport planes.

Then, in front of him, he saw the first British soldiers he had seen for three days. They had set up a roadblock with a couple of armored cars near the air express depot. McDermott assumed it was a preliminary checkpoint because he could see a number of TV vans and press cars nearby and there were news crews and photographers taking pictures of the transports through the fence. He slowed down and coasted to a halt as a soldier motioned to him with a rifle.

"Business?" the soldier demanded.

McDermott pulled off his helmet, pushed back his hair, and smiled his friendliest smile.

"Parcel for UPS," he said, and nodded to the building a few yards away. It was a long, single-story brick building that housed a dozen air freight companies and the UPS office sign was clearly visible among them.

"Let's see some ID," the soldier said.

McDermott unzipped his jacket, fished around for a moment, and pulled a driver's license out of his inside pocket. The license was valid but the name said Thomas O'Neil and the address was in Protestant West Belfast. The soldier looked at it, then handed it back.

"Open it up," he ordered, gesturing with his rifle at the parcel box.

"It's open," McDermott said.

"You open it," the soldier said.

McDermott sighed, got off his bike, put down the stand, and flipped open the compartment.

"Open it," the soldier ordered when he saw the parcel.

"Ah, Jesus . . ." McDermott grumbled. It was never wise to give in too easily.

"Open it," the soldier grumbled back.

McDermott took out the parcel, tore open the neat wrapping, and peeled back the paper to reveal a plastic Kodak box inside filled with neatly stacked rolls of exposed film. The soldier poked a finger inside, picked up a couple of rolls at random, sniffed them, then handed them back.

"Make it snappy," he said, and nodded at McDermott to pass through.

"Got to wrap it up again now," McDermott complained as he climbed back astride his motorbike.

The soldier shrugged and turned away. McDermott pulled on his helmet, kicked his bike back into life, and cruised the last fifty yards to the UPS office. He parked the bike and took the parcel inside. There was only one person behind the counter, a girl no more than twenty with long brown hair and bad skin. McDermott waited while she rewrapped the parcel and did the paperwork. It didn't matter that the company for which it was destined would have no idea what it was for or where it had come from. It had gotten McDermott where he needed to be.

"So," he said, making conversation. "It's right enough. The British are pulling out."

"Aye," she answered, giving him an anxious look. "It's hard to believe, isn't it? The planes were here when I started and they've been loading them all morning. There's hundreds and hundreds of soldiers out there, you know. It's a bit scary, do you not think? What's going to happen?"

McDermott wanted to tell her the truth, but he had to assume she was a Protestant.

"I know what's going to happen," he said mischievously. He leaned over the counter, flexed his eyebrows, and gave her his best James Dean look.

"Oh, you do, do you?" she said, smiling.

"We're all going to have to find somewhere nice and safe to hide," he said. "And somebody nice to hide with."

"Aye." She nodded. "I've told the boss I'm taking my holidays on Saturday and I'm going to stay with my sister in Newport till I see what happens."

McDermott stood back from the counter.

"Well"—he shrugged—"if you get lonely and you think you might need a strong shoulder . . ."

"I don't think my boyfriend would like it," she answered. Her tone was flat, but there was a flirtatious look in her eyes.

"Tell him to find his own strong shoulder." McDermott grinned.

The girl giggled but said nothing more, fearing she was straying into dangerous territory. McDermott was smart enough not to push it. He had what he wanted. He'd made contact. She seemed to trust him.

"Think they'd mind if I take a look see at what's happening there?" he asked idly, nodding in the direction of the military planes.

"I don't see why," she answered. "Everybody and his dog has been out there taking pictures . . ."

"Is there a back door?" he added.

"Sure," she answered innocently, and waved him around the counter to the parcel dispatch room at the rear. McDermott passed through a small, cluttered room where two middle-aged men sorted parcels for the next flight. He gave them both a nod and slipped out the back door. He found himself on a narrow strip of asphalt between the back of the air freight building and the security fence. There were gates in the fence every few yards where the trucks came to pick up their express cargo. All the gates were closed and padlocked. Inside there were sentries and MPs with dogs.

McDermott strolled along the fence for a few yards, trying to look like another nosy spectator, his eyes fixed on the security area a couple of hundred yards away behind another, higher fence. On the inside of that fence he could see more armed sentries, and beyond them the three Hercules transports. What excited McDermott most was the number of British troops, hundreds, it seemed, lined up at the rear doors of each aircraft, ready to embark. He continued his stroll until he had passed the end of the air freight building and crossed onto a narrow grassy strip where a crowd of reporters had gathered to record the first mass departure of British troops from Northern Ireland. Half a dozen TV crews had set up on the roofs of their vehicles and were trying to shoot over the fence. Others wandered back and forth, killing time, looking for better positions from which to take their pictures. McDermott sauntered into their midst, his motorcycle helmet dangling from one hand. He picked a small, balding man fiddling with his camera on the hood of a car.

"Hard to believe they're really leavin', isn't it?" McDermott remarked lightly.

The bald man glanced up at him and shrugged.

"Hard to believe a lot of things these days," he said. "But they have a habit of coming true."

"How many do you reckon are goin' out today?" McDermott asked, trying to sound casual.

"Nine hundred, I heard," the photographer answered. "Maybe twelve. Hard to say really. There's a lot of them out there though. I've been here since eight last night and the trucks were bringing them in for about three hours in the middle of the night."

There was a sudden commotion and everyone swarmed up onto the roofs of their vehicles or rushed for the stepladders they had set up along the fence.

"They're moving," somebody called out.

The bald man forgot about McDermott and scrambled onto the roof of the car and aimed his camera. McDermott looked around and walked back to the fence to blend in with the others. About 200 yards away he saw them. The first column of troops to be pulling out of Northern Ireland—forever. Without any kind of ceremony and with only a few faintly heard commands, they marched across the tarmac, up the ramp, and into the belly of the first Hercules. McDermott tried to count them, but it was too far and they were moving too fast. He guessed there were close to two hundred. A few minutes later he saw another column moving out to the second Hercules and then the third. A sharp thrill of excitement coursed through his body. History was taking place in front of him.

A few minutes later the rear doors on the first Hercules closed, the engines started up, and the big plane began to taxi toward the runway. McDermott watched, enthralled, as cameras whirred and clicked all around him. From the breathless, disbelieving comments, he knew there were others who were equally affected by the spectacle, though for different reasons. For them it was the end of an era of British power and the beginning of a new era of uncertainty and almost certain bloodshed. For him it was the vanquishing of an army of occupation. It was freedom, unification . . . and immortality.

The Hercules disappeared from view for several minutes, and when it reappeared it was almost a mile distant. Slowly, it lumbered down the main runway, then gathered up speed and hoisted itself ponderously into the air, as though reluctant to leave. McDermott held his breath as he watched it climb, turn slowly eastward toward England, then disappear into the cloud, never to return.

It was all the IRA man needed to see. He turned and walked back to his motorbike, struggling to keep the spring out of his step and the smirk of triumph from his face. Calmly, beneath the watchful gaze of British soldiers, he put on his helmet, climbed onto his bike, and rode slowly back toward the main highway. Back to Larne to await the call that would come any time now.

USS *Carl Vinson.* 17.40 hours

The trio of Royal Navy EH-101s thudded southward, out of the Red Sea, through the straits of Bab al Mandab, and into the Gulf of Aden, where the biggest warship in the world waited to receive its guests. A few minutes after they had passed the dusty headland known as Ras al Arah on the southernmost tip of the People's Republic of Yemen, the pilot in the lead helicopter pointed through the cockpit window and Lynch, Porter, and Bonner leaned forward in unison to see the *Carl Vinson.*

The giant aircraft carrier loomed out of the ocean like an island of steel, a great blue-gray fortress whose ramparts were lined with war planes that reminded Lynch of crossbows. Crossbows armed with lightning bolts. Guarding the fortress like an encircling reef of metal were the carrier's eleven escort ships, a nuclear missile cruiser, three guided-missile destroyers, frigates, and support ships. Lynch smiled to himself. This single battle group was a bigger armada than the entire Royal Navy had mustered to save the Queen of England.

Unlike some of his colleagues in the British armed forces, Lynch felt no pang of envy at the sight of such colossal wealth and power. No ache of nostalgia for the glory that once had been Britain's. He had worked with the U.S. Navy so often over the years he felt only the familiar reassurance of a man who knew he was back among friends. Powerful friends.

The helicopter pilot radioed down to the *Carl Vinson* and was cleared to land. A few moments later they bounced lightly down onto a flight deck the length of two football fields. Porter slid open the side hatch and climbed out first. He was met by a welcoming committee that included Admiral Howe, the commander of Battle Group Charlie, and Captain Boyd, skipper of the *Carl Vinson.* A moment later the other two helicopters landed and the group was joined by Captain Purcell and Lieutenant Gage from the *Hotspur,* General Sharpe, Colonel Quillan, and the captains of the remaining British warships.

It took only a moment to get the formalities out of the way. Everyone understood the urgency of the situation and no one wanted to be accused of holding things up. The *Carl Vinson*'s executive officer steered everyone into the command tower, and a moment later they were all riding the elevators below decks. The moment he stepped out of the elevator Lynch's nostrils were assailed by a sweet, buttery aroma that cut through the smell of men, metal, and engine oil. He smiled. It had been a while since he had been at sea on a US warship this size. He had forgotten that there was one ritual that never changed. It was suppertime aboard the *Carl Vinson,* and, in addition to the thousands of meals that were being served, popcorn dispensers were filling up all over the warship. The U.S. Navy was the only navy in the world whose ships filled with the sweet aroma of buttered popcorn, free for the asking, when the sun went down.

He followed the group along a corridor that looked as if it stretched ahead of them for a mile. Just before they were about to leave the blue zone, that section of the ship whose walls and deck were painted sea blue instead of battleship gray to distinguish the command center from the rest of the ship, they turned a sharp left. A moment later they found themselves in the admiral's quarters, a big, roomy cabin furnished as a combined lounge and dining room where the admiral of Battle Group Charlie could entertain his officers and other VIP guests at the end of the day. On a table in the lounge was a coffee urn and a tray filled with doughnuts. In the dining room a large U-shaped table had been set with starched white linen, silverware, and place settings for twenty-four guests. A melange of cooking smells drifted from the galley. The Americans were generous hosts and planned dinner for their British guests when their war council was over. Both Lynch and Bonner paused to grab coffee and doughnut each, then followed the others next door, through the admiral's private cabin and into the war room. It was there that the operation to free the *Britannia* would be finalized.

Admiral Howell, a handsome, pink-cheeked man with a small white mustache, sat at a blue-topped conference table in a matching blue leather chair emblazoned with a white star. To his left sat Captain Boyd and the *Carl Vinson*'s chief intelligence officer, Lieutenant Harper. To his right were Sir Malcolm Porter and Captain Purcell. Also arrayed around the table were General Sharpe, Colonel Quillan, and Lieutenant Gage. The table was too small to accommodate everyone, and a second row of chairs had been arranged for the remaining American officers and their British counterparts. Lynch and Bonner chose the outermost chairs in the second row.

Under other circumstances the room would have been filled with the easy banter of friends and allies, the senior officers of two navies who took pleasure in each other's company. But this was not another exercise. The fate of the British monarch depended on the decisions that would be taken by the men gathered together in this small room, and their mood was somber. And, though none of them would have admitted it, there was another guest at the table. A guest called fear. Not fear of the harm that could come their way. This was the deeper, gnawing fear of how history would judge them if they failed.

"I'm sure I speak for all of us in Battle Group Charlie when I say that I wish we were meeting our British colleagues under happier circumstances," Admiral Howell began in a voice that reflected the gravity of the moment.

"But we all know why we're here. We know that time is against us and we want to do all we can to help bring about a swift and successful resolution to this crisis."

He added: "I have been directed by the commander in chief to commit the full resources of this strike force in support of an operation to secure the safety of all those persons held hostage on board the *Britannia.* I have also been advised that, as far as is practicable, we should limit the potential for US service personnel to become involved in direct combat."

The admiral paused and addressed himself directly to his British guests.

"Gentlemen," he said. "I'm sure I don't have to spell out the reasons for the President's concern."

Lynch and Porter exchanged knowing glances. They knew all too well what the President was up against. It was one thing to commit material and resources to help the British deal with the hijackers of the royal yacht. It was something else entirely to have to explain American casualties in support of British political aims.

"Accordingly," Howell continued, "I invited the officers and men of Battle Group Charlie to express their own views of the situation. I put it to them yesterday that if there was any member of this strike force who felt he could not give himself wholeheartedly to the task of rescuing those people on board the *Britannia,* to advise his senior officers and he would be relieved of any responsibility in the operation. There are approximately fifty-three hundred men in Battle

Group Charlie. As of this moment, gentlemen, we have approximately fifty-three hundred volunteers for active duty."

A certain tension had crept into the room when Howell had opened with his cautionary remarks about the President's political concerns. That tension evaporated in a silent ripple of smiles as the British registered their appreciation of Admiral Howell's remarks. A slight smile tugged at Howell's neat white mustache before he turned toward Porter.

"Now," he said, "I believe Sir Malcolm has a few words to say about the exact nature of this operation."

Porter thanked Howell, an undertone of relief apparent in his voice. Then he leaned forward with his hands clasped loosely on the tabletop in front of him.

"The code name for the operation," he began, "is Operation Scepter. It will take the form of a joint air and sea assault on the royal yacht launched simultaneously by helicopter-borne units of 22 SAS and waterborne units of the Special Boat Squadron and O Group Comacchio, Royal Marines. The objective is to overwhelm all opposition on board the royal yacht so quickly and so completely that the hijackers will not have time to detonate the explosives they have planted. At the very least, if we hit them hard enough and fast enough, their reaction time ought to be impaired enough to delay or stop them from detonating all the charges.

"To help accomplish this objective, SBS will make up the advance force and Comacchio will make up the main assault force. The SBS team will be led by Commander Lynch. Commander Lynch's task is to board the *Britannia* and rendezvous with Captain Gault of the SAS, who is already on board and will assist Commander Lynch and his team in the identification and neutralization of all the explosive charges. While this is taking place, Comacchio's main assault force will board the *Britannia* and liberate the hostages in the forward section of the vessel. We shall also be ready with a second assault wave in helicopters and fast boats to saturate the area, provide combat reinforcement where necessary, and pick up hostages in the water.

"Our greatest enemy in this operation is not the hijackers," he added. "It is time. We have to prevent or delay the detonation of the explosive charges on board the *Britannia* long enough to insure the rescue of the sovereign. Captain Gault has already identified six sets of charges. There may be more. There are certainly a large number of booby traps scattered around to discourage the rapid advancement of our forces. The main charges are located amidships in the boiler room, where they will do the most damage. They appear to be connected by electrical wiring to some kind of trigger on the bridge. It was hoped that Captain Gault would have disabled some of these charges on his own, but that has not been possible. The main charges appear to have been booby-trapped and Captain Gault is not a bomb expert.

"Therefore," Porter went on, "we must prepare for the contingency that Commander Lynch and his team will not be able to prevent the detonation of some—or perhaps all—of the charges on board. In which case we would expect the *Britannia* to sink and to sink very quickly. According to our calculations, a vessel the size and tonnage of the royal yacht, which has had its back broken by a large and powerful explosion, can be expected to go down in two minutes . . . perhaps less."

He paused, deliberately, to give his next words added emphasis.

"We can put a helicopter over the yacht, drop an SAS team on deck, and get both royal hostages off the *Britannia* within three to four minutes . . . as long as the hostages are ready."

There was a distinct intake of breath around the table. Porter ignored it and calmly went on.

"The plan we have put in place will insure that the moment the assault begins, all communication between the hijackers on the bridge and the hijackers in the boiler room is terminated. Also, all electrical circuits that connect the bridge with the rest of the yacht will be terminated. Therefore, in the unlikely event that any of the hijackers were to survive the assault on the bridge, they would not be able to send a signal to detonate the charges below. Assuming, however, that there are individuals below decks who are capable of acting independently and who are prepared to give up their own lives to achieve the destruction of the royal yacht, it is possible they would reset or detonate the charges themselves . . . once they were aware that an assault was under way. We can assume that the hijackers below decks will be confused by the shock of the assault and the subsequent loss of communication with the bridge. Under the circumstances we must give them the benefit of the doubt and expect them to react with extreme swiftness. Our experts tell us it would take several minutes to reset enough of the charges to create an explosion with sufficient force to break the back of the ship. If the hijackers elect to blow the charges manually, then, obviously, it will take much less."

"How much less?" Admiral Howell queried.

"A minute," Porter added. "Two at most."

Howell turned his attention to Lynch, and everyone else in the room followed his gaze.

"So," the American admiral added quietly, "Commander Lynch and his team have four minutes to get onto the yacht and down to the boiler room to stop the remaining hijackers blowing it up while your SAS team goes in to lift off the queen and Prince Philip?"

"Correct," Porter answered flatly.

Howell nodded but said nothing more. He didn't have to. The look on his face said everything for him.

Lynch remained motionless in his chair. He knew what they were all thinking. If anything went wrong. Just one little thing . . .

Porter glanced around the conference table. He could see the flaws in his plan too. If something did go wrong, as it very well could, the queen and Prince Philip stood only an even chance of rescue. The remaining hostages stood no chance. Two hundred and seventy two innocent people would go down with the *Britannia*—and many of their would-be rescuers with them.

"I know it means we will be operating within a rather slender margin of error," he added calmly. "But we're used to that . . . it's what we do best."

Lynch allowed himself a small smile. It was the closest he had ever heard the old man come to a boast.

"Naturally," Porter went on in his brisk, businesslike manner, "the success of the operation will depend on the level of surprise we can achieve and the speed with which we can coordinate and execute the assault once it begins. To assist us in that regard, we have been provided with some rather sophisticated hardware by our American colleagues. At this moment we have a C-141 standing by in Saudi Arabia with two SDV-12 minisubs on board. Our assault teams will rendezvous with the C-141 onshore this evening. Once the operation commences, we're going to need some pretty smart coordination between units. Perhaps Commander Bonner could advise us precisely what form that coordination will take."

Bonner seemed surprised that he had been chosen to outline the American component of the operation. He had already spoken by radiophone with Howell and mapped out his requirements. He coughed and sat up so that those who did not know him might see where he was.

"We'll need sonobuoys on both sides of the Red Sea to pick up the *Britannia*'s sonar sweep," he said. "Then, of course, we'll need our own AWACS in the air to monitor the sonobuoys and tell us when the hijackers are looking for us."

"I understand all that," Admiral Howell confirmed. "Just tell us when, Commander."

"Wouldn't hurt to put 'em in the water now," Bonner replied. "That way, if there's any glitches and we have to make another run, we've got the time."

Admiral Howell nodded to his XO, and the officer got up and left the room."

"It's under way," Howell said.

"We should also have a couple of Tomcats in the air to safeguard the 141's approach when it comes in to drop the Mark 12," Bonner added. "Just in case somebody in one of those funny countries out there does something stupid."

Howell looked at Captain Boyd.

"We can coordinate that with our friends in the Royal Navy," Boyd confirmed.

Bonner allowed himself one small smile. There was no doubt about it. It was thrilling to have an admiral, an aircraft carrier, ninety war planes, and a strike force of fifty-three hundred men at his beck and call. He wouldn't tell Lynch, not just yet anyway, but he was going to miss all this when he retired.

"Good," Porter added, and resumed control of the meeting. "All that remains is to set the jump-off time for the operation."

“It’s your party, Sir Malcolm,” Howell responded agreeably. “You tell us where you want us and what time, and we’ll try to oblige.”

Porter smiled. He hadn’t dared put a figure to the amount of money the Americans had spent already in support of the British effort. But it wasn’t cheap. And all they’d get at the end of it was a vote of thanks from the British government and possibly a knighthood for the admiral. Porter intended to make the recommendation personally. If he wasn’t too busy making arrangements for a state funeral.

“Let me be frank,” Porter said in the voice of a man with his back against the wall. “Unfortunately, we have political considerations to bear in mind too.”

The war room became so quiet that the only sound was the dull background drone of the ship.

“I don’t think it is a secret that our government is in some difficulty over its handling of this crisis,” Porter went on. “Only yesterday the Prime Minister survived a leadership challenge in Cabinet by a very narrow margin. Even so, a debate is under way in the House of Commons at this very moment that could result in a no-confidence vote against the government. At this point we can count on the Prime Minister’s support. However, he may not be in a position to give us that support for much longer—and we have only thirty-six hours before the hijackers’ deadline expires. If the government of Great Britain falls in the next few hours, the political situation could change so quickly and so drastically that this operation might be robbed of all chance of success. It may even be cancelled altogether.”

Porter noticed as the Americans exchanged awkward glances with one another. He knew what they were thinking. They were scarcely able to believe that any government would allow politics to interfere with an operation to save the head of state.

“My view is that we can’t afford to waste any time at all,” Porter added finally. “As soon as we’re ready, I say we go. My preference would be for the assault to commence before dawn tomorrow.”

There was an audible intake of breath around the table. Howell looked grim and was about to say something, but Bonner got to his feet and spoke first.

"Sir, permission to speak, sir?" he said in a voice that was cordial but strained.

"Go ahead, Commander," the admiral responded, suspecting that Bonner might be about to save him the embarrassment of saying what was on his own mind.

"Sir." Bonner directed his attention at Sir Malcolm. "With respect, sir, I don't think it's a good idea to schedule the assault for tomorrow."

Porter took a deep breath and slowly shook his head.

"I share your concerns, Commander, but—" he began.

"I—I think we all understand the political pressures involved here, sir," Bonner cut Porter off. "And we could get into a position to jump off in twelve hours."

Even as he said it, everyone knew it was a horrifically short time in which to mobilize all the men and machinery that were needed for such a massive and complex operation.

"But we're going to get only one shot at this . . . right?"

A yawning silence answered his question for him.

"I think we need twenty-four hours to get everything in place for this," he added. "I've looked at every little detail of this operation, and it's a good plan. But its success depends on split-second timing and a lot of slick coordination between a lot of people. There's no time for any rehearsals here, no dummy run. We get only one chance to do it right. And if just one component is missing the mark when this operation goes down, we could blow the whole thing. Now, I know the SDV-12 better than anybody except the guy who built it. It's a great minisub, but it's not a miracle machine. If we rush into this now, there's a chance we might not be in position to launch the assault from the water at exactly the moment you want."

Bonner stopped for a moment to let Porter digest the enormity of what he was saying.

"Sir," he added, "I understand that the pressures to move quickly now must be enormous. But whatever you have to do to keep London off your back for the next twenty-four hours—and I mean anything—I suggest you do it. Because this operation will work. But if we do it now, we're going to need an awful lot of luck. And if it was me who was running this thing, I'd have to tell you—I wouldn't want luck playing any goddamn part in it."

Bonner sat down again, his face flushed by the passion that underscored his words.

Lynch nudged him gently.

"I thought you were a cool, dispassionate professional," he whispered. "That sounded awfully close to sincerity to me."

Bonner shifted in his seat.

"The people on that yacht are real," he whispered back. "We can get them out of there, I know it. But I don't want any goddamn politicians from our side or yours telling us how to do it."

Lynch nodded and leaned back in his chair.

"Face it, Tom," he murmured. "You're a closet idealist."

"It's cutting things awfully fine . . ." Porter was saying.

"Sir Malcolm," Admiral Howell added, "I have to agree with Commander Bonner. I think that extra twelve hours is vital to the success of the operation."

Porter fell silent, his face clouded with worry.

"Do it," Bonner said under his breath. "Just lie to those fuckers in London. Lie to 'em . . ."

"All right, gentlemen . . ." Porter sighed, the Prime Minister's final cautionary words echoing ominously inside his head. "I recognize your concerns and I shall defer to your judgment. Operation Scepter will commence at 0400 hours on the twenty-third."

HMY *Britannia,* May 21. 19.20 hours

John Gault sat in the corridor outside the Duke of Edinburgh's sitting room, put his head back against the wall, and closed his eyes for a moment. He hadn't slept or eaten much in the twenty-four hours since Lieutenant Gage had told him of the death of Susan Latimer. He had tried not to dwell on it—she had ignored his orders to stay hidden—but had panicked and paid a terrible price. He could still see her face when he had left her. The way she had looked at him. Like a beaten and frightened child who wanted to cling to him for safety. He should have known she was too scared to stay there, on her own, in the dark. He should have taken her up to the armor-plated sanctuary of the royal apartments, then gone back to dump the hijacker overboard.

"Try some of this."

He opened his eyes and looked up to see Judy Stone holding a cup out to him.

"Scotch broth," she explained. "Fortnum and Mason. Very nice."

"Sorry," Gault apologized, getting to his feet, "I'm not hungry."

"What has that got to do with it?" she said sharply. "Make the effort. Then try to get some sleep. We're into the last two days of this thing. It's going to get very busy around here—and I don't want you conking out on me again."

Gault sighed but accepted the cup and took a sip. She was right. It was good. He took another deeper swallow and felt its warmth seep soothingly, restoratively, down into his empty stomach.

"You angry about what happened?" he asked, looking up at her.

"No," she answered lightly, her face giving away nothing.

"You haven't said a word about it since I got back."

"I don't have to," she said.

He studied her, trying to see what was going on her mind. He had expected some reaction from her about the girl. Something. Anything but indifference. But there was nothing. Nothing in her voice or manner to give him a clue. Not even the disparaging humor he had come to expect. Instead, there was something else. Something gentle, conciliatory.

"I should have brought her back here," he said. "She was scared and in shock. I shouldn't have left her on her own."

Judy kneeled down beside him and put a finger gently to his lips. He looked at her, startled by the sudden intimacy of the gesture.

"You know what happened?" she said.

He waited.

"You got unlucky," she said quietly. "It's what I was afraid would happen. It was what you said wouldn't happen. But it happened and there's nothing you can do to change it. So now you have to live with it. That's the price for being unlucky . . . and I feel for you."

"Is this your idea of sympathy?" he asked.

She smiled and settled down beside him with her back to the wall.

"What we do is . . . pretty perverse," she said. "What we are actually trained to do is to preserve life. But a lot of people don't see it that way because, sometimes, to save a life we have to take a life. Politically, it's very incorrect. We decide that the life of a good person is worth more than the life of a bad person and it's up to us to decide who is good and who is bad—and we dispense summary justice to back up our judgment. But I can live with it. The difference between you and me is that I could not make a decision that could lead to the death of an innocent person. But you did. And you know what?"

He waited, watching her stark white face, looking into the eyes that took their color from her name.

"I don't believe you really thought about how it would affect you if it went wrong."

He turned his face away from her.

"You were so confident you could go out there and handle everything that came your way," she went on. "And you were right. They don't come much better than you, Gault. But you forgot one thing. You forgot about the things you can't control. Like the way a young girl might panic and run. Like . . . bad luck."

She put her hand gently on his forearm to make him look back at her.

"I've watched you these past twenty-four hours," she said. "And my heart has gone out to you. Really . . . it has. Not just because you have to live with what happened to that girl. But for what it's going to do to you a few years from now. I've seen what happens to men who stay too long in this business. The kind of men who get to the top because they've learned how to harden their hearts to others. The kind of men who talk about collateral damage when what they really mean is dead babies. And I'd hate to see that happen to you. Because you're not here for the fun of it. You're not here for the glory or the pay. You're here because you're a good guy. And because you're strong. I just hope you're strong enough to deal with this without turning into something hard and ugly."

Gault handed back the half-empty cup.

"And I thought the psychology screenings at Hereford were tough," he muttered.

"Don't be glib," she said, fixing him with a matronly look. "It doesn't suit you."

"I didn't realize you'd been paying such close attention," he added quietly.

"I notice a lot more than I would ever admit." She smiled. "Usually."

"One thing?" he said. "And whatever your answer, I promise I won't raise it again until we're off this bloody boat."

She waited.

"Dinner at Le Gavroche when we get back?"

"I've got a better idea," she answered. "How about dinner at my place . . . I have a psychiatrist's couch big enough for two."

Gault hesitated a moment. Then he cupped his hand behind her head, gently drew her close, and kissed her. This time she gave him no trouble at all.

At that moment, 150 feet away in the *Britannia*'s radio room, Dominic Behan leaned away from the sonar screen and tiredly rubbed his face. He hadn't shaved in a week and his skin felt rough and raspy to the touch. His eyes ached for want of sleep and his mouth tasted foul. He got up with a grunt and stepped out onto the bridge to stretch his legs. As usual, Patsy Ryan was at the wheel. He, too, had hardly slept. The two of them took it in turns, grabbing a couple of hours whenever they could. Doyle was asleep on the cot in the chart room. He had been there for hours. Behan wondered how he could sleep so well through it all. Then he pushed his doubts to the back of his mind and checked his watch. He had an important call to make soon. A very important call.

"How's she look, Patsy?" he asked.

Ryan glanced at the radar scanner.

"Same as usual." He shrugged. "Watchin' us every step of the way."

Behan opened his mouth to respond, but a sudden burst of sound from the radio speaker stopped him.

"This is the *Hotspur,*" it said. It was the negotiator's voice. Ryan looked to Behan for instructions and Behan shook his head.

"If Edward Doyle won't talk to us, we want to talk to Dominic Behan," the voice added.

"Jesus," Ryan muttered. "How do they know your name?"

"We know you're there, Behan," the voice persisted. "All we want to do is set up a point of negotiation. We have to talk to somebody."

Behan stayed where he was. Doyle had warned him about this. The British would use all manner of tricks to step up the psychological pressure, to divide and weaken the hijackers, to undermine their resolve. The only protection was to resist all contact. They had issued their ultimatum. There was no need for further contact. Once they started to deal, they gave the British a way in.

"I understand if you're afraid of Doyle," the negotiator added. "You have every reason to be."

"Fucking bastards," Behan sniffed.

"You must know that Doyle will double-cross you," the voice continued. "He's double-crossed everybody he's ever worked with. If you have any hope of making this deal work, Behan, you have to talk to us. Doyle doesn't have to know. Just make contact with us. Anywhere, anytime, any way."

Then the radio went dead.

Ryan looked at Behan.

"Tricks." Behan shrugged. "They're getting desperate, that's all."

Behan's face was a mask of impassivity. His eyes, as usual, were unreadable. Still, Ryan couldn't help but notice. There was one small tic at the bottom of Behan's jaw that hadn't been there before.

LARNE, NORTHERN IRELAND, MAY 21. 23.20 HOURS

"Gin!" Eddie Byrne gave a triumphant grunt and slapped down a card to take the last suit of the game. McDermott shot him a disinterested look, pushed his own cards away, and emptied his beer can of the last mouthful. He had never much cared for card games, and he was bored. There was no TV set in the cottage. His only amusements were drinking, listening to the radio, or humping Jilly, and he was tired of all three.

“Fetch us another Harp, would ye, Jilly darlin’?” he growled.

Jilly lay on the couch, a few feet away, asleep.

“Hey,” McDermott yelled suddenly at her. “I said get me another fuckin’ beer.”

Jilly jumped and looked around, startled, her dirty-blond hair tangled on the side where she had been sleeping. She rubbed her face, got unsteadily to her feet, and slouched into the kitchen to get McDermott’s beer.

“You’re a bit rough with the girl, y’know,” Byrne said reprovingly. McDermott looked at him. It was hard to know whether Byrne was being serious or not.

“She’s a lazy slag,” McDermott grumbled. He had finished close to a dozen cans of beer and he was sliding into a black mood. He hated being cooped up in the dingy seaside cottage, waiting for a single phone call from Behan before they could get back to where the action was. Northern Ireland had rarely been safer for people like him. There were no British soldiers to be seen anywhere, the RUC was grossly undermanned, and the Protestant militias were keeping to their own territory while the cease-fire lasted.

“She does nothin’ to earn her keep,” he rambled on. “All she does is lie on her back and twitch her fanny a bit, and she doesn’t do a very good job o’ that.”

Byrne poured himself another nip of whiskey and took a swallow. He wanted it over with too. They were all starting to get on each other’s nerves. But Behan’s orders were clear. This was the safe house they had agreed upon. This was the only number he would call. Byrne picked up the phone and listened. The tone whirred maddeningly in his ear. A general state of panic and disorder might be creeping across the province, but at least the telephone lines were still up. He put the phone down with a grunt of annoyance, gathered up the cards, and began shuffling the deck again. Jilly returned with McDermott’s lager. He snatched it from her without a word and took a long pull. Jilly turned and went back to the couch.

“Another hand of gin rummy?” Byrne asked.

McDermott gave him a poisonous look but said nothing. Byrne shrugged, put down the deck, and got up to stretch his legs. He walked over to the back door and opened it wide to let in some fresh salt air. The night was cool and cloudless and a bright three-quarter moon lit up the mean little houses that crowded in all around them. Byrne stepped outside, cleared his lungs, and listened for a moment. All he could hear was the muted crash of waves from the sea front, two streets away.

Then the phone rang.

McDermott snatched it up and put it to his ear.

"Yeah?"

Byrne stepped back inside, closed the door quietly, and looked expectantly at McDermott. McDermott looked back at him, his scowl gone, face animated. He nodded.

"Aye, Nick," McDermott said, struggling to keep the slur out of his voice. "Everythin's all right. It looks like the genuine article. I was at Aldergrove yesterday and they were pullin' out, just like the TV and the papers said. Hundreds of the bastards. I saw three planeloads take off myself, and there were pictures in the paper this mornin' of them getting off the plane in England. It's the real thing, Nick. They're gettin' out all right. You should see the state of the place. You should feel the mood over here. You could cut it with a fuckin' knife."

He paused for a moment while Behan said something back, then he handed the phone to Byrne.

"We've got a lovely Windsor Knot here, Nick," Byrne said. It was the code name they had agreed upon before Behan had left. If anything had gone wrong or if they were speaking under duress, Byrne was supposed to say the word *palace.* At this stage they knew it wouldn't matter that they used Behan's real name. All that mattered was that he make this one call to Larne for confirmation. The fact that the British might be listening in was irrelevant. Byrne and McDermott would be on their way within minutes, well before the RUC had time to react to a request from the British—assuming there was anyone left in the British garrison to make a request.

"God bless ye, Nick," Byrne added quickly. "This is a proud moment for all of us. . . ."

He stopped in mid-sentence, looked awkwardly at both of them, then put the phone down. Behan had gone.

"Come on," McDermott said. "That's it. Let's get the fuck out of here."

He hurried into the bedroom and began stuffing his clothes into the tote bag he had left open on the bed. Jilly followed him, an expression of concern on her face.

"Are we leaving now?" she asked.

He looked at her with open contempt.

"If you're comin' with me, you've got five minutes to collect your things," he sneered.

Jilly looked back at him, shrugged, and turned away. She walked out of the bedroom, across the living room, and into the bathroom. On the way she saw Byrne through the doorway of the second bedroom, greasy hair hanging over his red face, hurriedly packing his suitcase for the drive down to the Irish Republic, where he planned to hide while Northern Ireland tore itself apart. A moment later McDermott strode back into the living room, threw his bag and his motorcycle helmet together on the table, and plucked his motorcycle jacket from the back of his chair. He zipped it shut, picked up the remaining can of lager, and poured it down his throat. From the corner of his eye he saw Byrne emerge from his bedroom with his suitcase in his hand. They both glanced around the room. The cottage was a mess but they would leave it as it was. Full of fingerprints on beer cans and strands of hair on the sheets. None of it mattered anymore. Law and order was coming to an end in Northern Ireland. Soon there would not be a power in the six counties that could touch them. McDermott glanced toward the bathroom and saw that the door was closed.

"Come on, Jilly," he called impatiently.

There was no answer.

Stupid bitch, McDermott thought. It would be just like her to stop and put on makeup.

"Jilly?" he shouted, angrier this time. If she wasn't out in ten seconds, he decided, she could go to hell. He would leave without her. He took a few steps toward the bathroom door and listened. There was nothing. No radio. No sound of running water. There was a window in the bathroom, and it must have been open, because he heard the sound of a car passing outside. He looked at Byrne and

Byrne looked back at him. Something registered in both their eyes at the same moment. Byrne's face started to contort from confusion to realization to fear. McDermott roared with rage and threw himself back across the room toward the bag on the table, where he carried his pistol, loaded and ready.

Every door and window in the tiny cottage exploded inward at the same moment, showering the room with splinters of glass and wood. The cottage was drenched in a blinding white light, and McDermott felt his eardrums buckle under the impact of a shattering explosion. Fragments of glass and wood ripped and tore at his motorbike leathers. He hit the edge of the table hard and fell blindly to the floor, fingers scrabbling for his gun. A man dressed in black appeared through the window and brought the butt of his submachine gun down hard on McDermott's fingers. The IRA man screamed, fell back to the floor, and lay still, blinded and bloody.

Matty Byrne was hunched over and running, trying to ignore the burning pinpricks that stabbed at his back and shoulders, aiming for the refuge of his bedroom. Then a creature from his darkest nightmares materialized in front of him. A man in black carrying a submachine gun with a scope on top that swept the room with a needle of red light. Byrne saw the pinpoint of red dance across his chest, then up to his head, and he knew what it meant. He dropped to his knees, hands behind his head, and opened his mouth to plead for his life. But fear had tightened his throat and the only sounds that came out were pitiful croaking sobs. Then he felt something warm and wet streaming down his thighs, soaking through his trousers and onto the floor.

It was seven long minutes before McDermott had recovered sufficiently from the shock of the stun grenade to stand on his own feet. His vision was still hazy and there was a tinny ringing sound in his ears when they brought him out into the street. His bike leathers had been turned into blood-smeared rags. His hands were cuffed behind him, the fingers of his right hand were smashed and bloody, and there was an ugly wound on the right side of his head, where he had hit the table and from which blood still trickled. He blinked his eyes to try to clear the blur. They cleared fractionally as his captors led him down the footpath to an RUC paddy wagon in the middle of the street. Farther out he could see police cars blocking both ends of the street and dozens of RUC men holding back crowds of curious onlookers. But the men who held him, the men in black, with balaclavas, armored vests, and submachine guns—they weren't RUC, he knew. They were Special Branch, CTC, or maybe even SAS.

Then he saw Jilly.

She was wearing a borrowed black raincoat and was standing a few yards away beside an unmarked car with a middle-aged man in a light blue raincoat. But there was something different about her. Something about the way she held herself and stared confidently back at him. Something he had never seen in her before. Instead of dumb submission, there was only confidence and triumph. Even her face, the light in her eyes, looked different. She wasn't the same woman he had known these past ten months at all.

"You fuckin' tout," he spat at her as he was dragged into the nearest van. "You'll die for this, you fuckin' bitch."

Jilly glanced at the man in plain clothes, then took a few steps toward McDermott.

"You know what was the worst part about the past year, Sean," she said casually. "The worst part was that you weren't even a decent screw."

Then she turned and walked back to the car and got in beside her boss, Byron Blair, director of MI5.

10 A Bloodied Crown

HMY *Britannia,* May 22. 09.33 hours

Five miles was not a great distance at sea. A speedboat could cover it in ten minutes. An attack helicopter could leap that far in a minute. A missile traveling at Mach 2 would cover the same distance in twenty seconds. Doyle played with the numbers in his mind as he stood on the compass platform on the starboard side of the bridge and watched the warships circling in the distance, like great white sharks looking for a meal. He had expected them to come last night and had kept everyone in a high state of alert. Behan searching on the sonar, Ryan watching the radar, both of them safe behind the reinforced bulkheads of the bridge, out of sight of long-range snipers. Deveny, Brady, and O'Brien were outside, hidden about the upper deck in case of a parachute drop. Michael Kenney was in the engine room, guarding his one-minute fuses in case somebody cut the wires. Musa, Javad, and Youssef were in the chart room, finalizing details for their departure. It had been a long, tense night for all of them. Something in Doyle had been disappointed that the attack hadn't come. But it would come tonight, he knew. It had to. It was their last chance before the deadline expired. He turned and stepped back onto the bridge.

"How far are we from Turba Mayun?" he asked Patsy Ryan at the wheel.

Turba Mayun was the first landfall in the People's Republic of Yemen.

"One ninety," Ryan answered.

"How long to get there at this speed?"

They were still doing eight knots to conserve fuel.

"About forty-eight hours."

"How are we on diesel?"

"Tanks are still half full."

"All right," Doyle said. "Let's take her up to ten knots, shall we? That should get us there at just about the right time."

He heard a noise and turned to see Musa with Javad and Youssef emerging from the chart room.

"You've got the crown jewels ready to go?" he asked.

"Everything is on the launch," Musa answered unsmilingly. The strain was beginning to tell on the Palestinian terror boss. His long hair was greasy and lifeless, his clothes rumpled and stained with sweat, and there were dark, puffy pouches beneath both eyes. Doyle's mouth tightened. He had enjoyed watching the Arab sweat. Men like Musa should know how it felt to go through something like this, instead of orchestrating the violence from the sanctuary of his villa in Mashhad.

"If we get through the next few hours okay, you should be ready to go an hour before midnight," Doyle added.

"You think they will come tonight?" Musa asked.

"They don't have much time left before the deadline," Doyle answered coolly, enjoying Musa's suffering. "They have to come soon."

"Sometimes," Musa said, "you sound as though you want them to come."

Doyle shrugged.

"I know how they think," he said. "I know they'll come. They have to."

"Why, Eddie? Why do they have to come?"

Doyle turned to see Behan standing in the doorway to the radio shack. He had been watching, listening. Until now Behan had gone along with everything Doyle had wanted. He had put together the team, brought Doyle into the terrorist underworld, taken him to Mashhad and introduced him to Musa. For his part, Doyle had delivered everything he had promised. He had turned over the plans he had copied during a nighttime visit to the archives of John Brown's shipyards in Glasgow. He had delivered the GBX gas and the Demex. He had shown them how to take the yacht, told them what they could expect in the way of resistance. He had trained them, turned them into a team, modeled them along special forces lines. He had gotten them fit, taught them how to climb and how to scale ships at the old coast farm in Clare. Later, at Mashhad, he had taped out scale maps of the *Britannia*'s deck plans on the floor of a munitions warehouse and shown them how to move around the yacht quickly in the midst of a blinding fog. Until now Behan had no reason to doubt Doyle's dedication to the mission. Because he had been right about everything. He had been right about the hijack. He had been right about the reaction of the British. And he had been right about all the events that had subsequently unfolded in Northern Ireland. But now, like Musa, Behan found himself wondering about Doyle. Wondering whether he shared the same ultimate objective as the rest of them. Or whether he had improvised a new agenda now that it was all coming to an end.

"You heard Byrne and McDermott," Behan added quietly. "They said the pullout was genuine. They've watched it happen right in front of their eyes. We've seen it here on all the TV channels. Surely they couldn't fake somethin' that big?"

Doyle shook his head, irritated by Behan's sudden and unexpected questioning of his authority.

"Don't you try and tell me about the British," he growled. "I lived with the bastards, remember? They'll try something. They have to. They can't let the deadline expire. They know what will happen if they do."

Behan nodded but only because he wanted to keep Doyle mollified for the moment.

"Maybe we should talk to them," he added. "Tell them we're keeping the deal. When the withdrawal's done we get safe passage to Yemen and they get the yacht and the queen back, unharmed. That was the deal, Eddie, remember? That was always the deal. But if they pull out and we still blow the ship, there won't be anyplace we can hide on the planet."

"No." Doyle almost shouted. "No talk. No negotiation. We give them nothing."

Behan paused. His eyes shifted warily to Musa, to Ryan, then back to Doyle. Javad and Youssef watched from a safe distance. They had seen this kind of thing happen before. Their leaders squabbling as the pressure mounted. It nearly always ended in bloodshed.

Behan stepped out onto the bridge and approached Doyle slowly and deliberately. Doyle watched him come, his face expressionless. But nobody was fooled. They all noticed as his body became tense, poised for sudden violent action. Behan was surprised by how calm he felt. He had never been afraid of any man, but common sense had told him to be afraid of Doyle. Now, strangely, he felt no fear at all. He stopped when he was barely two feet away from Doyle and looked directly into his eyes. The mood on the bridge had become electric. Javad and Youssef stood perfectly still. Patsy Ryan had become robotized at the wheel. Only Musa made any kind of a move. He began to edge his right hand inside his jacket toward the little nine-millimeter Beretta he always carried. If something started, he knew what he would do. He had never liked Doyle.

"Are you sure we're all still on the same side here, Eddie?" Behan asked quietly.

Doyle could barely keep the contempt out of his voice when he answered.

"What are you worried about, Nick?" he said. "Worried that the Queen of England never took swimming lessons?"

"The Brits won't keep their end of the deal if we blow the boat," Behan responded evenly. "They've no reason to . . . and all this will have been for nothin'."

"The Brits won't keep their end of the deal . . ." Doyle growled. "Whatever happens."

"You're planning to blow the boat anyway, aren't you?" Behan said.

Musa's fingers closed around the pistol butt. Ryan chanced a quick sideways glance. Like Behan, he had reason to be wary of Doyle. But if something started, he had no doubt where his loyalties lay. Doyle was on his own. And no matter how capable Doyle might be, he couldn't fight five men.

"They'll have time enough to save their boat and their queen," Doyle said softly. "Once we're all safely away."

"How much time?" Behan pressed. Like the others, he had heard an unfamiliar note of conciliation in Doyle's voice. Though it wasn't enough to reassure him completely.

"Just enough to keep them occupied while we get away," Doyle answered. "Assuming that's all right with you, Nick?"

Doyle's face was so devoid of expression it was almost immobile. Inside, he was boiling with repressed fury. He wanted to kill Behan. Wanted to rip him apart with his bare hands. And he would. But not now. For a moment Behan looked as though he were about to press Doyle further. But he didn't. He knew instinctively he had gone as far as he dared. And he, too, knew what he must do to neutralize Doyle. Behan nodded and took a step back. The electricity started to leech slowly out of the air.

There was a sudden burst of static from the bridge radio, then the sound of a man's voice trying to punch through the interference. They all switched their attention to the radio.

"This is Pete Dunbarry calling the *Britannia,*" the voice said, clearer now. "Can you hear me? I'm about half an hour out from you guys. Am I clear to land, *Britannia?* Come in, *Britannia.* Can you hear me?"

"Jesus Christ . . ." Behan swore softly.

Doyle smiled, then stepped forward and picked up the mike.

"This is the *Britannia,*" he said calmly. "You can come in, Dunbarry."

"Glad to hear you're still in one piece, my friend," the TV newsman said. "We're coming in just like we said. No tricks. Just the three of us. I'm putting a lot of faith in you, my friend."

"I've got him," Ryan interjected. He nodded down at the radar screen. There had been two helicopters in the air, circling the *Britannia,* just outside the security zone. Now there were three. The third helicopter a small luminescent dot approaching from the direction of the Egyptian coast, far to the northwest. Doyle slapped the mike back into its cradle and walked back out onto the compass deck.

Five miles away on the *Hotspur,* Lieutenant Drewe hurried anxiously out onto the bridge to see Captain Purcell.

"Sir, we've just picked up an exchange between the hijackers and an approaching helicopter," he said. "It's that newsman, Dunbarry. It looks like he's going to try to crash the exclusion zone. The hijackers have told him to come in."

Purcell looked at Drewe, then crossed quickly into the operations room, his face grim.

"The *Nimrod* picked him up an hour and ten minutes ago when he took off from Khalij," Drewe added. "They tracked him down the coast for a while. There's been a helluva lot of media air traffic the past week, sir, as you know. Some of them test us a bit, but they usually respond when we warn them off. This one presented himself as a bit more of a problem when he started making a beeline for us. Then we picked up the exchange between them and the *Britannia.*"

"How long before they get here?" Purcell asked.

Drewe looked to the radar operator.

"At their current speed, about eleven minutes, sir."

"See if you can raise them, Lieutenant," Purcell ordered.

Drewe hesitated.

"Do you want us to order a helicopter intercept, sir?"

"No," Purcell answered. "That won't stop them. We know what they're up to. Get them on the air. Now."

Drewe signaled to the radio operator and bent down to the microphone while the operator switched to all-frequency transmission.

"This is Her Majesty's Ship *Hotspur* to Dunbarry aircraft," Drewe said, snapping his words off clearly and precisely so there could be no mistake. "You are approaching a military exclusion area. You must turn back immediately. Confirm."

They waited but there was no answer. Drewe tried again. Purcell glanced at the radar screen. The glowing green dot was drawing closer.

Fifteen miles away and two thousand feet over the Red Sea, the

South African pilot of the chartered helicopter turned to Dunbarry and spoke through his helmet mike.

"The Royal Navy just told us to turn back," he said.

Dunbarry nodded.

"Now we come to the interesting part," he said. "Just ignore them. We knew this would happen. It'll be just like I told you. If they think we can't hear them, they won't do anything. They'll be really pissed off at us, but they won't do anything. They know who we are."

"Shit," the cameraman swore behind Dunbarry. "You better be right, Pete. This is the hairiest goddamn stunt I've ever pulled to get a story."

"Hey." Dunbarry waved at him to be quiet. "You leave your balls at home or something? If it was easy, anybody could do it."

The pilot turned again to Dunbarry. This time there was a nervous catch to his voice.

"I've got the navy again," he said. "They're warning us that if we don't turn back, they'll shoot us down."

"They're bluffing," Dunbarry said evenly. "They have to say that. They won't shoot down a civilian aircraft. Don't answer. Fuck 'em."

"I'm not so sure about—"

"You're getting twenty grand to do this, friend," Dunbarry cut him off. "That's more money than I make for a day's work, I can tell you. Now, you goddamn well earn it."

The pilot took a deep breath and turned back to the stick, a light sheen of sweat forming across his forehead.

"They're not responding, sir," Drewe said on board the *Hotspur.*

"Can they hear us?"

Drewe looked to the radio operator. The man nodded.

"If they've got their radio switched on," he said, "they can hear us."

Purcell looked back at the radar screen.

"How long now?" he asked.

"Two minutes, sir," the radar operator answered.

"Activate missile systems," Purcell said. "Lock on and prepare to launch."

Drewe stared at him for a moment.

"Sir . . . ?" He let the question hang in the air.

"I know they think we're bluffing, Lieutenant," Purcell said, his voice cool and firm. "But those bastards on the *Britannia* aren't bluffing . . . and I won't give them an excuse to kill another hostage."

Instantly, Drewe saw the ghostly image of Admiral Marchant on the afterdeck of the *Britannia* and the violent spurt of blood as he was shot in the back of the head. Then he saw the bodies being hauled from the water, the dead marines in Jidda harbor, the innocent girl from the queen's household staff.

"Yes, sir," Drewe acknowledged. He turned and repeated the captain's orders to the missile systems officer.

"One minute," the radar operator called out.

"Systems activated," the weapons officer said. "Locked on and ready to launch at your command, sir."

Purcell took a breath.

"Give them one more warning, Lieutenant," he said.

Drewe leaned down to the microphone and tried to put a new note of urgency into his voice.

"This is HMS *Hotspur* to Dunbarry aircraft," he said. "You are about to enter the total exclusion zone. This is your final, repeat final, warning. If you do not turn back now, you will be shot down. Do you understand?"

The operations room fell eerily silent as everyone watched the small green dot on the screen cross the invisible line into the exclusion zone.

"Launch," Captain Purcell ordered.

"Launch missile," Drewe repeated.

The weapons officer thumbed the firing button on the panel in front of him.

"Missile away, sir."

There was a sinister rumble from the forward section of the ship, then silence. Purcell walked back out onto the bridge and lifted his binoculars to his face. The missile was clearly visible as it stitched a woolly white thread across a clear blue sky. Drewe held his breath. All sound and movement stopped on the bridge as everyone watched the Sea Wolf surface-to-air missile streak toward its distant target.

"Jesus Christ," the helicopter pilot screamed as he saw the spurt of flame from the *Hotspur* and then the vapor trail of the missile as it leapt toward them. He pushed the joystick forward and hard to starboard. The chopper wheeled and went into a steep dive as the pilot tried to shake the missile off. If he could get the helicopter down to wave height, he knew, they might have a chance. The missile's radar might get confused and carry it into the sea. Then he could skim the waves into shore before they fired another—and to hell with this lunatic Dunbarry and his twenty thousand bucks.

But there wasn't enough time, and he knew it.

He turned and spat at Dunbarry, his face contorted into a mask of fear and hatred. In the seat behind them they heard a long, anguished howl as the cameraman slumped forward and buried his face in his hands.

Dunbarry stared through the cockpit as the missile zigzagged toward them, still unable to comprehend the reality of what had happened. His infallible judgment had finally failed him—and he was about to pay with his life.

"Oh, shit," he mumbled. His last thoughts were of his epitaph on the evening news, the prurient glee his death would cause throughout the industry. The drinks that would be raised mockingly to his memory in the bars of Manhattan.

The missile tore through the chopper like a burning spear through a paper kite. The warhead detonated and the sky blossomed with a brilliant crimson fireball. And then there was nothing but a brief fiery rain.

A few seconds later the thunderclap of the explosion echoed across the water to Doyle on the compass deck of the *Britannia.* He watched impassively while the last burning fragments of the destroyed chopper fell into the water. Then he turned and looked at the others, the glow of the fireball reflected in his eyes.

"I think he should have stuck with the press pool." He smiled.

USS *Carl Vinson.* 12.01 hours

Colin Lynch leaned against a companionway rail on the portside of the *Carl Vinson* and watched the milky blue water swirl past, ten stories beneath his feet. The wind scoured his hair and tugged at the navy flight suit he wore for the short air hop he and Bonner would be making soon to the Saudi air-navy base at Jaizan, where Lynch's SBS squad and Bonner's SEALs waited with their special cargo aboard a C-141 transporter. Above and behind him there was a deafening roar and a screech of rubber as an EA-6B Prowler smacked down onto the flight deck, having completed its turn in the round-the-clock air patrols the carrier had mounted ever since it had arrived in the Gulf of Aden. A few seconds later there was another roar as the catapult on the launch deck hurled another war plane into the sky, this time a Hawkeye. In the near distance Lynch could see a Sea King hovering over the waves, ready to pick up any pilot unfortunate enough to ditch in the sea. It had been like that all morning. Noise, bustle, exquisitely synchronized tumult as planes landed and took off every few seconds. The whole ship humming with a sense of expectancy as the countdown continued. Nine Blackhawks had arrived during the night and were lined up near the command tower, watched by Marine guards. Lynch had seen Colonel Quillan and a dozen SAS troopers in and around the helicopters engaged in intense discussions with their crews.

The previous night's war council had continued until three o'clock in the morning with only one break for a late supper at 2200 hours. Porter had since returned to the *Hotspur* with the rest of the skippers from the Royal Navy task force. Lynch and Bonner had spent the night in guest cabins aboard the carrier. Lynch had slept well enough, though it hadn't been as long as he would have liked and so he had stolen off for a few minutes now to clear his head and to focus himself on the task that lay ahead.

He sensed rather than heard someone approaching and turned to see Bonner climbing the steps to join him in his little eyrie on the side of the giant warship.

"We ready?" Lynch asked.

"Few more minutes," Bonner replied. He took a position at the rail and followed Lynch's gaze out over the water. It was a beautiful day. Warm and clear with a cooling wind and a brilliant sun polishing the sea to a sapphire sheen. It was the kind of day when they should have been at the beach, Lynch thought, not riding this massive war machine, getting ready to inflict sudden death on men on the other side of the horizon.

"Thought you might have been planning to desert," Bonner added amiably.

Lynch chuckled.

"Give me enough time to think about it, and I probably will," he said.

"How do you feel?" Bonner asked.

"Fine," Lynch answered. "You?"

"Another day, another dollar." Bonner shrugged.

"That isn't how it sounded last night," Lynch added.

"Just doing my job, boss," Bonner answered in a hayseed's mocking drawl.

Lynch smiled.

"It isn't just the money against the odds, is it?" he said, turning to look at the big Texan. "It's easier for you to pretend that it is. But it isn't . . . is it?"

"It isn't?" Bonner feigned surprise.

"You want to help the people out there on that yacht as much as I do," Lynch said finally.

"I do?" Bonner echoed.

Lynch smiled again and turned away. He knew what he had seen in Bonner the previous night.

"Funny thing," he added. "But it's hard not to admire a man like that. I guess I might even want to work for a man like that someday."

Bonner turned and looked at him.

"You limey sonovabitch," he said.

Lynch chuckled but said nothing more.

"Okay, smartass," Bonner added. "You tell me something. You've been feeding me that stuff about honor and Queen and country for a long time now, and I haven't had a helluva lot of choice except to believe that it's true. That maybe you stuffed-shirt limeys do have some kind of national code of honor, some noblesse oblige that just might be missing in us crass, vulgar Americans."

Lynch grinned at Bonner's use of the expression *noblesse oblige.* Nobody could murder a French accent better than Red Bonner.

"So," Bonner was saying, "I can believe it coming from you. Leastways I can believe that you believe it's true. But what about this guy Doyle? What about him? Did he just kind of slip through the system unnoticed, or did the system let him down? You tell me. Did all your fancy ideas about honor and duty just go over his head because he's a bad apple—or is it the system that's rotten? Because I've seen the way you guys operate, and I have to hand it to you, most of the time it works pretty good. But I also know that guys who talk nice and come from the right family and who go to all the right schools have a habit of going a helluva lot further than guys who talk bad and come from the wrong side of the tracks. So you just tell me now, what do you think the story is with this guy Doyle? Was he always nuts or was it that fancy system of yours that made him nuts?"

Lynch was silent for a long time. He hated to admit it, but there was a lot of truth in what Bonner said. He had spent a lot of time thinking about it ever since he had seen Doyle's file and read his psychological profile. He turned and looked back at Bonner.

"The truth is, I don't know," he admitted. "I don't know if anybody will ever know for sure. But you're right. Either scenario could be true. I've met psychopaths in the military . . . and I've seen the military destroy men. I've seen it drive good men mad. The way I deal with it is by reminding myself of one thing. Every man's soul is his own and it's up to him what he does with it. I really believe that. No matter what happens to you, no matter what the bastards do to you, they cannot take your soul. Not unless you choose to give it to them. You don't have to sell your soul to the devil . . . you don't have to."

Bonner nodded and fell silent for a moment.

"I'll tell you one thing," he said finally. "If this guy did sell his soul to the devil, he got a helluva price."

LONDON. 22.35 HOURS

"Thank you for coming in to see me at this late hour, Charles," the Prime Minister greeted Ingham amiably in his office at 10 Downing Street.

"I'll let you know in a moment whether it's a pleasure," Ingham answered coolly, and sat down.

"Would you like a drink?" the Prime Minister inquired pleasantly as John Traynor hovered discreetly in the background.

"Actually," Ingham answered, "a small whiskey would be an excellent idea."

"Good." The Prime Minister smiled. "I might even join you."

Ingham studied the Prime Minister carefully while Traynor brought two small whiskies. He still looked tired, but there was something different about him. He looked like a man who had reached a difficult and momentous decision that had nevertheless resulted in a great weight having been lifted from his shoulders.

"You haven't decided to throw it in after all, have you?" Ingham ventured, taking the glass from Traynor.

He thought he saw a glimmer of a smile in Traynor's eyes before the Prime Minister's aide turned away, slipped quietly from the room, and closed the door behind him.

"Oh"—the Prime Minister smiled—"I think Sunday's vote in Cabinet was decisive enough, don't you?"

The Prime Minister had survived Ingham's leadership challenge, orchestrated by Shepherd, Grey, and Lawson, fifteen votes to eleven. One more crisis within a crisis for the front pages of the nation's newspapers.

"Ah," Ingham nodded. "For a moment there, I thought you'd called me in to offer me your job."

"I don't think so, Charles," the Prime Minister said, enjoying his little duel with the man who had attempted to stab him in the chest and the back, both at the same time.

"How goes the debate in the House?" he asked mildly.

"I think there'll be a vote before morning," Ingham answered. "It's been thirty-seven hours and everybody's pretty buggered. Even the diehards are starting to wilt."

"That's what the chief whip tells me," the Prime Minister murmured. "How do you think it's going to go?"

Ingham sighed and took another sip of whiskey.

"I haven't got a clue," he answered.

The Prime Minister smiled. It was his first real smile in days. He loved it when politicians were so desperate they had to resort to telling each other the truth.

"If I had to summarize the tactical consequences," Ingham volunteered, "I'd say it's backfired badly on the Opposition and it's caused a great deal of unnecessary anxiety throughout the nation. But, having gone this far they all know they're up to their necks in blood and ill will, so I think they'll see it through and not only will you be out of a job tomorrow morning, but England will be looking for a new government. I told you, you should have stepped aside. I could save the party. There's still time."

The Prime Minister shook his head.

"I have something else in mind," he said.

Ingham waited.

"I would like you to go back to the House and table a special statement on behalf of the government," the Prime Minister said.

Ingham shuffled uneasily in his chair, wondering what exactly the Prime Minister was up to.

"I'd like you to inform the House that at midnight tonight the withdrawal of British troops from Northern Ireland will cease. Those units that have already withdrawn will return to their duties in the province. Those units still in barracks will recommence normal operations from six o'clock tomorrow morning. And our current strength will be increased immediately by ten thousand more troops. Those units are already on their way."

Ingham was so shocked his drink almost slipped from his fingers. He caught himself and put the glass down on the Prime Minister's desk. Outwardly the Prime Minister remained expressionless. Inwardly he was delighted by the look of sheer stupefaction on Ingham's face.

"Having a little difficulty working this one out, Charles?" The Prime Minister allowed himself one small indulgence. "A clever chap like you?"

"What's happened?" Ingham said quickly. "What have you heard from the *Britannia?* Has she gone up?"

"Actually, no," the Prime Minister answered. "The truth of the matter is that I don't know what is happening with the *Britannia* at the moment and it will be several hours before I do know. All I can tell you is that an operation is currently under way to rescue Their Majesties and all the other hostages from the royal yacht. And now that there is no further need for secrecy, there is no further need to maintain the pretense that we have complied with the hijackers' demands . . . and we can restore some real law and order to Northern Ireland."

Ingham sat stunned.

"So we still don't know whether the queen is alive or dead?"

"I'm afraid not," the Prime Minister answered quietly. "And I would appreciate it if you did not address that issue in the House. What I want you to do is to resume your portfolio as secretary of state for Northern Ireland and make the announcement that the troop withdrawal has been reversed. And I don't want you to make that announcement until after midnight. By which time I will know the outcome of the rescue operation."

"My God," Ingham breathed suddenly. "You had no intention of making a deal with the hijackers at all, did you? The whole thing was a ploy to keep them foxed until we could get a rescue operation up. You'd already decided that we would hang on to Northern Ireland whatever happened."

"That's the wonderful thing about the military," the PM said innocently. "It's very portable, you know. Entire planeloads of soldiers can go almost anywhere. They can take off from Belfast, for instance, fly to Manchester, have their pictures taken on the tarmac by the world's press, then go for a cup of tea and fly back when no one is looking. It only takes a few hours."

Ingham picked up his glass and threw the rest of the whiskey down his throat.

"Mind if I have another?" he asked.

"Help yourself."

Ingham got up, poured himself a fresh drink from the cocktail cabinet, and gestured with the bottle to the Prime Minister. The PM shook his head.

"When did you change your mind?" Ingham asked, a fragile note of composure creeping back into his voice.

"Immediately after they executed Admiral Marchant," the Prime Minister said soberly.

"My God," Ingham whispered. "That's been a well-kept secret."

"There's been worse, Charles. There is much about this hijacking that has been kept secret and must forever remain so. But I can tell you this. From the conduct of the hijackers so far, and from the intelligence profiles that I have seen on them, there was never much hope of making a deal that would stick. They're the dregs of the terrorist world. Outlaws among their own kind. The ringleader is a man called Doyle. Edward Doyle. He's from Belfast originally. Served fourteen years with the Royal Marines. But he went bad somewhere along the line, slipped into the terrorist underground via the IRA and joined forces with Abu Musa. We believe Doyle will blow up the *Britannia* whatever happens. According to our intelligence, this isn't about Northern Ireland. This isn't about politics at all. It's about revenge. Doyle is unbalanced. He despises Britain and everything Britain stands for, and he found the ideal way of getting back at us."

Ingham sat quietly for a long time, absorbing all that the Prime Minister had told him. Then he looked at his watch. It was just after eleven.

"Well," he decided, "I don't believe you've left me a great deal of choice in the matter."

"No," the PM concurred. "I don't believe I have."

"All right," Ingham added. "If I'm going to get back to the House in time to make an announcement as secretary of State for Northern Ireland, I suppose I'd better get a move on. This is going to cause an absolute bloody uproar when it breaks, you know. You'll turn everything upside down. And we still won't know for a few hours whether the queen is safe or not."

"I expect to know something before morning our time," the Prime Minister answered. "If I hear anything sooner, I'll see that you're informed before you get up to speak. Though you will save that announcement for me, whatever the news. Good or bad."

"Gladly," Ingham said. He hesitated a moment, still absorbing the impact of all he had been told. When he spoke again, it was with new respect for the man he had so grossly underestimated.

"God, but you played a cool hand this time," he said. "And to think, we thought you were cracking under the strain."

"Perhaps I was," the PM answered.

"You lied to us all, you know," Ingham continued. "And you wanted me to go into the House at the beginning of this thing and tell them we were pulling our troops out even though you knew it was all a subterfuge. The whole thing was a lie and it could have cost me my career for misleading Parliament."

"I thought it would sound better coming from you," the PM answered blandly. "Besides, I doubt they'd hold it against you in the midst of all the confusion."

Ingham chuckled quietly and got up to go. His hand was on the handle when the last penny dropped, and he froze.

"You crafty bugger," he said, turning to look back at the PM. "That's why you wouldn't go to the House. That's why you wouldn't go on television to address the nation."

"Charles," the Prime Minister murmured reassuringly, "I could lie to you, I could lie to Cabinet, I could even lie to the House. But I could hardly lie to the nation, now . . . could I?"

HMY *Britannia,* May 23. 00.01 hours

It was the call Gault had been waiting for. The call that told him their seven-day ordeal was coming to an end. He hadn't spoken to Colin Lynch in more than a year, but he recognized his voice with its faint Scots burr immediately.

"0400 hours," Lynch told him. "We'll come in over the fantail. Some cover would be nice, if you can manage it. Once on board, you have to get us down to the boiler room bloody smart to knock out those charges. Lieutenant Stone must have HRH One and Two ready for SAS airlift from the helipad. Whatever you do, stay the hell away from the bridge."

"Confirm," Gault responded. "One more thing. The bad guys are wearing black. They look like SAS. Make sure you wear ID. Shoulder flashes . . . anything. And make sure you wear full gas cover. They used GBX to take the ship, and they have plenty left."

"Roger that," Lynch responded. "See you for an early breakfast, John."

"Looking forward to it," Gault answered. The radio fell silent. He turned to Judy Stone. Tony Stevens and Lady Sarah were waiting with her.

"You heard," he said. "Time to break the news to their royal highnesses."

Lady Sarah and Tony Stevens hurried back along the corridor. Gault and Judy followed a moment later, each of them carrying a bulletproof vest. Prince Philip and the queen were waiting in the queen's sitting room. They sat together on the same small sofa and were dressed as though they were ready to take a quiet turn around the deck.

"Your highnesses," Gault said, trying hard not to sound like the Lord High Chamberlain making a proclamation. "We will be taking you off the royal yacht at approximately 0400 hours. You will be leaving by helicopter and you must be ready to move very quickly. Lieutenant Stone will advise you when it's time to go. You should wear warm but light clothing and you should not take anything with you."

He paused and laid the two bulletproof vests on a nearby chair.

"They're rather heavy and uncomfortable, I'm afraid," he said. "But you must put them on, at least half an hour before 0400."

There was an awkward silence as everyone was reminded of the threat that could still exist when the royal couple made the short open dash from the shelter of the royal apartments to a waiting helicopter. All it would take was one unlucky bullet, one unlucky grenade. Gault pushed the image from his mind and looked at the queen. She was wearing a pair of loose beige slacks and a matching sweater.

"I think it would be a good idea if you kept the slacks on for your departure, ma'am," he said.

"Thank you, Captain," the queen responded with a faint smile. "I was thinking of doing that."

"I'm sorry, ma'am." Gault realized he'd just made another blunder. "I meant . . ."

"I know what you mean, Captain Gault," the queen reassured him. "Now, what about the crew?"

"We'll be trying to take them off at the same time, from the front section of the ship," he answered. "We're preparing for a rapid mass evacuation. I can't pretend there aren't any dangers. But we have a plan that we believe has a very high chance of success."

"So," the duke said, "they're still in charge up there."

"I'm afraid so, sir," Gault answered. "But not for much longer. They are about to discover just how unpleasant the consequences can be for an act of this nature."

"I hope so," the duke added, no longer trying to conceal his anger. "I bloody well hope so."

The queen glanced reproachfully at her husband, then turned back to Gault.

"We have every confidence in our armed forces, Captain Gault," she said.

Gault wondered briefly if she was speaking for both of them or whether she had lapsed into the royal *we.*

"You said Lieutenant Stone will escort us from the ship," Prince Philip added. "Where will you be?"

"I shall be leaving in a moment to help pave the way for our guests, sir," Gault answered. "I'm going to try to advise the other hostages too, so they'll be ready to go at 0400."

The duke nodded, then got up, walked over to Gault, and offered his hand.

"I hope we don't have to make a habit of this, Captain," he said dryly. "Good luck to you."

"Thank you, sir."

Then her royal highness got up from the couch and followed her husband. She stood in front of Gault and looked at him with those gray brown eyes that seemed both penetrating and wise. She was wearing flat shoes, and everyone in the room was reminded how physically small she was. But even though he towered over her, Gault felt diminished in her presence. He realized that he was not only standing in the presence of history. He had become part of history. The queen reached out and lightly shook his hand.

"Good luck, Captain Gault," she said. "No Queen of England ever had a more courageous officer."

Gault held her hand momentarily, lost for words. At the same time, a shiver ran through his whole body and the hair on the back of his neck prickled up. Then he recovered himself, saluted, and left the royal presence for what could well be the last time.

At that same moment, far above their heads, in the yawning silence of the stratosphere, far above the sweep of the *Britannia*'s radar, a giant USAF C-141 Starlifter banked into a steady circling pattern while the men in the back prepared to jump. The hold of the Starlifter was flooded by a sickly green light that illuminated a dozen grotesque creatures who looked like invaders from a hostile planet. All wore bulky space helmets and glossy black bodysuits that could double as wetsuits, and full-length combat suits. A spinoff from the space program, the suits were only a quarter-inch thick and made from a flexible thermal active blend of Gore-Tex and acrylonitrile compounds designed to resist the impact of grit-size meteorites during space walks. It was a feature that had the added advantage of making them resistant to all but the most powerful bullets. Each man's helmet was fully enclosed and equipped with a full night-vision visor with a holographic heads-up display linked to a computer inside the helmet that provided the wearer with a constant stream of data on altitude, speed, direction, and relationship to local geographic features, and gave them a constant fix on the minisub. Each man also carried a rebreather on his chest, a parachute on his back, and a pair of swim fins attached to his belt. They stood in two lines of six alongside a pair of black bomblike cylinders mounted on skids and waited patiently for the signal to jump. The only sounds inside each man's helmet were the drone of aircraft engines and the answering hiss of air from his rebreather.

Lynch was third man from the front. Bonner and a SEALs lieutenant were ahead of him. Behind him were three SBS men. They would go out after the first minisub. On the other side of the hold was the team that would man the second minisub; two SEALs officers and a four-man Comacchio squad. Lynch thumbed the display button on the side of his helmet. A scrollwork of glowing red figures leapt into view at the bottom of his visor. He checked his rebreather gauge and noted that he still had fifty-four minutes left. More than enough time. His eyes flicked to the altitude gauge. They were at thirty-eight thousand feet. The highest HALO jump he'd made before this had been twenty-eight thousand. He swallowed. His throat felt dry. It was probably the canned air.

The green light blinked to red. There was a high-pitched hydraulic whine, and the rear doors of the massive cargo plane swung slowly outward to reveal a starry spectacle that could have been a window into deep space. The minutes passed slowly as the pilot throttled down to 160 knots and circled once more over the drop zone. The red light started to pulse. Lynch watched as two crewmen with oxygen masks and survival lines worked their way down to the skids where the minisubs sat. A moment later there was a rapid series of loud bangs as they freed the skid locks, followed by a squeal of metal as the first minisub rolled toward the open hatch. A moment later the skids hit the floor chocks and tilted. The first SDV-12 slid forward, over the lip of the exit ramp and, like a mammoth bomb, it plummeted into the darkness. The line started moving as they shuffled out after it. Bonner stepped out first and disappeared. Then the SEALs lieutenant. Then it was Lynch's turn. He came to the edge of the ramp, leaned forward into the void, and let himself go. A moment later he fanned his arms and legs out for stability and dived through space at 140 miles per hour. The figures on his visor seemed to go haywire. Lynch ignored them and counted down the seconds in his head.

One thousand . . . two thousand . . . three thousand . . .

At twenty thousand he opened his 'chute and felt himself snatched back up into the sky by the hand of God. The numbers on the altitude gauge slowed to a saner count as he began a gentle, controlled descent through the night sky. Through his night-vision visor the sky looked just as it would through the naked eye. Blackness punctuated by brilliant pinpoints of light. He switched his focus to the sea below and briefly glimpsed the passing figure of another sky diver. There was no sign of the minisub yet, only the waiting black maw of the sea.

Far below him the first SDV-12 hit the water with a smack that sounded like a small explosion and promptly headed for the bottom of the sea. The huge parachutes that had carried it safely down to the surface filled with water and quickly turned into anchors. The velocity and impact of the landing carried the minisub down a hundred feet before the seawater flooded the bolts that held the parachutes in place. Each bolt was set with an explosive charge primed to detonate on contact with saltwater. The bolts fired in unison, the giant twin parachutes sprang free and continued their descent through the ocean depths. The Mark 12 found its natural buoyancy and headed obediently upward. When it broke surface, it leapt like a playful porpoise, then bobbed back down into the water and settled, its homing beacon pulsing steadily out to the following sky divers. A moment later its ghostly green chem-lights switched on, bow and stern, invisible to the naked eye but easily picked up on night-vision masks.

Tom Bonner hit the water two hundred yards away. He dumped his parachute, rolled onto his back, detached the swim fins from his belt, and pulled them onto his feet. Then he turned slowly in the water, looking for the others. Somebody splashed down a few yards away, then another and another. Bonner counted them as they landed, all of them within a hundred-yard circle. So far so good, Bonner thought. Then he turned and started finning through the water toward the SDV-12.

HMY *Britannia.* 00.20 hours

"How far to friendly territory, Patsy?"

Ryan looked down at the radar scanner.

"We're about twenty miles from land," he told Doyle. Then he gestured to a small island that lay off the coast of Yemen. "We're getting pretty close to Perim. That's friendly country, too, right?"

Doyle looked at the screen but said nothing. The *Britannia* was closer to shore than at any time since they had left Jidda. The circle of British warships that had followed them so closely for the past seven days had rearranged itself into a crescent. A blockade that stretched twenty miles from north to south and locked the royal yacht between it and the coastline of Yemen.

"There's a few new boats on the shore side," Ryan added. "Looks like the Yemenis have a few patrol boats out watching us. There's nothin' else near 'em."

"All right," Doyle decided. "We're close enough. Let's do it now."

Ryan reached for the ship's telegraph and signaled Kenney to cut the engines. A moment later the drone that had been with them night and day for a week fell to a whisper and the *Britannia* began its glide to a dead halt in the water.

"Anybody see or hear anything?" Doyle asked.

Ryan looked at the radar screen again.

"She's clean," he said. "Nothin' for miles."

Doyle turned his attention to the radio room.

"Nothing here," Behan answered from his seat at the sonar scanner.

"They're out there," Doyle growled to himself. "I can feel the bastards getting closer."

He turned his attention to Billy Deveny, who stood nearby.

"Everything ready?"

"Musa and his two pals are down at the launch," he answered. "They've got everything but the furniture and fittings."

"The hostages?"

"We had to give 'em another whiff of gas to make sure they didn't rush us," Deveny answered. "We got twelve of them out okay. None of 'em are moving too quickly."

"As long as those bastards out there can see them," Doyle muttered, indicating the surrounding forces who watched every move from afar.

He picked up his rifle and strode from the bridge with Deveny following quickly behind. It was only one deck down to the admiral's day cabin, where twenty men had been held captive for a week; Colonel Grant of the Royal Marines and nineteen of the *Britannia*'s senior officers. Brady and O'Brien waited on a narrow shelf of deck space in front of the cabin with twelve men at riflepoint. Their arms were bound tightly behind them and they lay on the deck in varying stages of distress. Some had fouled themselves or emptied their stomachs. None of them were in any condition to put up a fight. Traces of the gas still clung to them and stung Doyle's eyes and nose.

"All right," he ordered. "Let's get 'em down to the launch."

A chorus of groans erupted as the four hijackers began dragging and kicking the hostages down to the main deck. As sick and as helpless as they were, all were conscious and every one of them feared the worst. They believed their time had come. They were about to follow Admiral Marchant.

They were wrong. Doyle and Abu Musa had other plans.

It took ten long and brutal minutes to manhandle all the hostages down to the main deck, where Musa waited anxiously with Javad and Youssef. It pleased Doyle to see how wretched Musa looked. His eyes were bloodshot, his face sallow. His nerve seemed all but gone even though the riskiest part had yet to come. By comparison, Javad and Youssef looked quite calm. They were veterans now. They had proven themselves under fire. The launch was filled with treasure and the lights of Yemen were visible from the island of Perim. To them it seemed the worst was over. They were almost home. And now they had hostages to guarantee their safety over the last few miles of open water.

One by one the hostages were lifted into the launch. One by one they were bound to the rail so that they formed a living shield around the outside of the boat. The three Palestinians would ride in the middle. If anything went wrong, the launch, the twelve hostages, and a half billion dollars in royal treasure would go to the bottom of the sea. Doyle had assured Musa many times over. Human life was more important to the British than the treasure. For that reason alone they would not attack.

At last the launch was ready. The *Britannia* was almost at a dead stop.

"You've got one minute to get it in the water," Doyle snapped.

Javad hurried to the winch control. Gradually the royal yacht came to a standstill, and then there was only the sound of a light slop against the battle-scarred hull. Javad hit the winch button. The electric motor started to hum. There was a loud creaking sound as the mechanical joints of the derrick lifted the launch out over the side of the yacht. Then the winches kicked in. Thick cables of knitted steel played out from each end of the derrick and the launch descended smoothly toward the water.

Doyle glanced around, listening, watching. It was a warm and cloudless night. The sea was calm, the sky serene and empty. Doyle wasn't deceived for a moment. He knew they were out there. Invisible. Threatening. Moving closer and closer with every minute that passed. It wouldn't be long now, he told himself. Not long at all.

One deck down, beneath Doyle's feet, John Gault made his way silently toward the front of the ship and the petty officer's mess where the 253 hostages from the yacht's crew and the queen's household staff were held prisoner. Gault heard the winches turning as he slipped past. Something inside him urged him to investigate, but he kept going, his MKP5 clenched in his right fist, the P7K3 in his ankle holster.

He moved quickly but carefully along the deserted, brightly lit corridors and gangways, eyes and ears alert for booby traps or hostile footfalls. It was the cannister taped to the door to the first mess that told him he had found the hostages. The door was locked and held fast with an iron bar. The cannister was tucked behind the bar with a length of wire leading from the trigger to the bulkhead. The moment somebody moved the door or jolted the bar from the inside, the wire would jerk the trigger and the cannister would go off. Gault recognized the cannister, and it made his skin crawl. More GBX. If the hostages inside had tried to break out, they would have triggered the cannister and the corridor would have filled with gas and they would have subjected themselves to more pain and paralysis.

Delicately, Gault disconnected the wire from the pin and put the cannister on his belt, to be replaced when he left. When he was finished, he pressed an ear to the bulkhead and listened. There was nothing. They might all have been asleep. But he doubted it. Somebody would be awake in there, aching for an opportunity to escape—or to exact a lethal revenge against their captors.

He tapped gently on the door. Still there was no response. He had an idea. He tapped again, a sharp, rhythmic tapping this time. Clear and precise. Over and over he tapped out the letters SAS in Morse code. All the time he kept glancing anxiously over his shoulder. The hijackers were out there, he knew. Somewhere. More minutes passed and he began to grow frustrated. Then he heard it. An answering tap. Unmistakable. OK, they signaled. He tapped out one last message. SAS-OK. Then, slowly, he removed the iron bar, turned the door handle, and slipped inside.

It was pitch black. For a moment he was blinded.

"It's John Gault," he said clearly. "Captain Gault, SAS. Prince Philip's bodyguard. Some of you people know me."

Suddenly, the lights went on. Gault blinked and looked around. He was alone on the wrong side of a barricade built from metal chairs and tables. On the other side of the barricade he saw a man with something that looked like an elephant gun.

"It's okay," the man said loudly. "I know him. It's Gault."

There was an audible release of tension in the room as the man stepped out to shake Gault's hand.

"Bloody hell," he swore. "Am I glad to see you."

Gault recognized one of the remaining Royal Marines from the yacht's complement. A big, burly man called Hackham with a bristly blond crew cut. Gault shook his hand, then looked down at the bizarre device that dangled from Hackham's left hand. It was a metal tube with a trigger and a couple of hoses running up to a gas canister that had been attached to a crude frame on Hackham's back.

"What the hell is that?" Gault asked.

Hackham hefted the gun proudly and grinned.

"Flame thrower," he said. "They took all our guns. We had to make something. I was wondering whether it would work."

Gault shook his head.

"Glad I wasn't the first to find out," he said. He looked around as the room filled up with people.

"What's happening?" one man asked.

"Is it over?" asked another.

It was the signal for a flurry of anxious questions. Gault put up a hand for quiet.

"No," he told them, "it isn't over yet."

The room was filled once more with a tense, expectant silence.

"Who is the senior officer?" Gault asked.

"We're all sort of Communists now." Hackham grinned. "They put the officers somewhere else. We're more or less all lumped in together. We've been deciding things through a committee."

"Good." Gault nodded. "I hereby appoint you committee chairman. Can we get everyone together for a meeting somewhere, quickly and quietly?"

"Shouldn't be any trouble doing that," Hackham answered. "Come through to the rec room. That's where everybody is."

Gault followed Hackham through the petty officer's mess, past the sergeant of marines mess and the marine barracks into the long, open recreation room. It was packed with people whose disappointed expressions showed they had been hoping for the best but already knew the worst. It wasn't over yet. Among the sea of unshaven male faces he saw a few female faces. Women from the household staff. They all looked tired and drawn and the room had a stale, sour smell.

"How is her royal highness?" one of the women asked suddenly. The disappointed murmuring that had filled the room stopped suddenly.

"She's fine," Gault said. "They're both fine."

He lifted his hand to stop the hubbub that followed.

"For God's sake, don't start cheering or anything. The hijackers are still on board and the yacht has been wired to explode. Both the queen and Prince Philip are still hostages like you. I'm here to tell you that rescue is coming soon and you have to be ready."

"How soon?" someone asked.

"Please, everybody," Gault said, trying to inject some calm back into the atmosphere. "We've all come through this pretty well so far. Let's not blow it in the last few hours. All I can tell you is this—be ready to leave the yacht at 0400 hours. Do not leave this area until you are told to leave by me or somebody like me. It is very likely that there will be shooting in many parts of the yacht, and we don't want to lose any more people than we have already."

He paused as his words sank in and a more subdued mood settled over the crowd.

"All the doors and hatches to this area have been barred and booby-trapped," he went on. "And I can't remove them in case it tips off the hijackers that something is up."

"What if they blow the yacht?" a seaman asked. A murmur of renewed anxiety followed his question.

"We're doing everything we can to stop them doing that," Gault added, trying to sound like a man who traded in understatement. "But I won't lie to you. If any charges do go off, then the yacht could go down very quickly indeed. That's why you all have to be ready at 0400 hours. I promise you, I will not leave this yacht without you—even if I have to blow the bloody deck off to get you out."

"Don't think that'll be necessary, squire," Hackham remarked behind him.

Gault turned. Hackham beckoned him closer.

"We had to do something to pass the time," the marine whispered. "When they locked us in here, they locked us in with the shipwright's cabin. There's all kinds of tools in there. That's how we made my little zippo. We made something else too."

Gault waited.

"An escape hatch," Hackham added.

Gault stared at him, uncertain whether he should be impressed or alarmed. Hackham saw the look in his eyes and hurried to reassure him.

"We cut an eight-foot section out of the hull," he added. "It's still in place, but all we have to do is give it a good shove and bingo! We've got a six-by-eight escape hatch. I reckon we could get two hundred people through it in a hurry—if we have to."

Gault's face creased into a smile of approval.

"Make it a twenty-foot escape hatch," he said. "The moment the rescue operation starts, this yacht will be rushed by helicopters and rescue craft. Just tell everybody to jump and swim like hell. They won't be in the water long."

He turned to go, then stopped and pulled the P7K3 from his ankle holster.

"Here," he said. "Just in case. It's got thirteen rounds in it. Might be more reliable than your flame thrower."

Hackham grinned.

"Always a pleasure to work with the SAS," he said.

SDV-12. 00.35 HOURS

"They've come to a dead stop," SEALs Lieutenant Mike Nichols said. He sat crouched over the radar screen in the aft section of the minisub, eyes fixed on the little red blip that was the *Britannia,* 3700 yards away. He adjusted his headphones and called up the AWACS, circling 31,000 feet overhead, from the *Carl Vinson.*

"Yeah, copy that, *Triton One,"* the communications officer aboard the AWACS answered. "Looks like they stopped to put a small craft in the water. Stand by."

"Rats deserting the ship, maybe," Nichols murmured, and glanced over his shoulder at the men who crouched nearby. Bonner was at the helm. Lynch sat next to him, then the three SBS men. No one spoke. Somewhere nearby in the water, they knew, the second team in *Triton Two* was following instructions from the same AWACS.

A moment later the AWACS issued a fresh order.

"Go, *Triton One."*

"Go," Nichols echoed. Bonner started the engine and pushed the throttle up to sixteen knots. Everybody hung on as the minisub powered smoothly through the water at a depth of thirty-three feet with only a faint whine from its engines.

"Thirty-six." Nichols counted the distance down in hundreds for the benefit of the others. "Thirty-five. Thirty-four."

They were at 2200 yards when the AWACS came through on Nichols's headphones again.

"Cut, *Triton One,"* the operator ordered. "Stand by."

"Damn," Nichols grumbled.

The others looked at him.

"Britannia's moving again."

They waited, wondering how much distance the royal yacht would put between them before the sonar operator had finished his new sweep. Lynch looked at his watch. Two-thirty. Another ten minutes ticked past. The longest sweep yet. The AWACS officer watched the *Britannia* increase speed to twelve knots. Nichols saw it on the radar screen too.

"Goddamn," he swore.

Another ten minutes passed before the pinging on the sonobuoys stopped.

"Go, Triton One," the AWACS officer said. "Make this one count."

Nichols nodded to Bonner again, and the Mark 12 pulsed forward, its ablative coating soaking up and diffusing the sweep of the wide-scan sonar, rendering the minisub invisible in the vastness of the ocean.

"Thirty-three . . ." Nichols began. They had lost almost all the ground they had gained. If the *Britannia* kept that speed and the sonar operator kept up such long directional sweeps, Lynch knew they would never catch the royal yacht.

"Nineteen," Nichols called.

It was the first time they had gone under two thousand.

"Eighteen. Seventeen. Sixteen."

This time they made it to 1470 yards before the *Britannia* switched back to listening. They were within a mile of the royal yacht. The minisub sat silently in the water, the only noise the sound of men breathing. This time the sweep seemed endless. The minutes added up relentlessly. Half an hour passed.

"He knows," Lynch muttered. "The bastard knows."

He looked at his watch. It was after one o'clock. Less than three hours to get alongside the royal yacht.

Somewhere over their heads, above the surface of the sea, in the crystalline darkness of night, other secret forces were moving silently into place. On every ship in the fleet, men tensed and waited. Fountain boats, capable of reaching eighty knots, hugged the moving warships, blending their radar signature in with the bigger craft, so the hijackers on the *Britannia* would not detect the slightest changes in the configuration of the fleet. Each boat was filled with armed marines from Comacchio, all of them eager to avenge their dead comrades dumped in Jidda harbor. Helicopters were poised on the deck of every warship filled with silent, waiting men, faces blackened, eyes aglow with a hunger that could be satisfied only by decisive action. On board the *Hotspur* a troop of six SAS men waited in their chopper. They would be first in to pick up the queen and Prince Philip when the assault began at 0400.

The minutes ticked past. Slowly, painfully, they turned into an hour. Then another.

At 0300 hours, 120 miles to the south of the British fleet, the first Blackhawk lifted off the deck of the *Carl Vinson* and took up a hovering position half a mile out at one thousand feet. One by one the others followed. At last all nine were airborne. They maneuvered themselves into attack formation and waited. A few minutes later Sir Malcolm Porter, on board the high, circling AWACS, signaled the *Carl Vinson.* Captain Boyd relayed the go signal from the command tower and the Blackhawks started northward, hissing through the night toward the straits of Bab al Mandab and their rendezvous with the *Britannia.* On board each helicopter were three men: the pilot, a gunner, and an SAS trooper.

Minutes later the AWACS operator called down to the SDV-12.

"Go, *Triton One.*"

"Go," Nichols repeated.

Bonner gunned the engine and the minisub leapt forward one more time.

Lynch looked at his watch. The minute hand ticked past 0300. Less than an hour to go and they were still well short.

"Twenty-five." Nichols started counting again. "Twenty-four. Twenty-three."

"Blackhawks will be in position in thirty minutes," the AWACS operator called down.

"Copy," Nichols said.

Lynch looked at Bonner.

"Are we going to make it?" he asked.

"I don't know," Bonner answered. "You're right about this guy. There's never been this much sonar activity before. It's like he knows we're here."

"Damn," Lynch swore.

"Twenty. Nineteen fifty. Nineteen." Nichols's voice counted down the distance in a dead monotone.

The yards seemed to click past as slowly as the second hand on Lynch's watch.

"Eighteen fifty. Eighteen. Seventeen fifty. Seventeen. Sixteen fifty."

All over the fleet, on the water, under the water, and in the air, thousands of synchronized watches marched past 0330 hours.

The Blackhawks skimmed up to the security cordon at wave height and broke formation without exchanging a word, each to a preassigned position on the fringes of the exclusion zone. The pilot in the lead Blackhawk throttled back as the *Britannia* shimmered clear and bright in the distance. He pushed back his night-vision goggles. He didn't need them. The *Britannia* was lit up like a Christmas tree.

"Eye on," he said, alerting the gunner and the SAS trooper behind him.

The Hughes Agile Eye mounted on the Blackhawk's rotor prop blinked on. The Eye was a 360-degree night sight and thermal imager fully integrated with the Blackhawk's on-board computer designed to feed a steady stream of crystal-clear images to the pilot. Except this time it wasn't the pilot who needed it.

The SAS trooper in the back climbed into an oddly shaped seat that looked like the product of an unholy alliance between a barber seat and an electric chair. Gymbal mounted, it bounced lightly as it took its weight, then settled. The trooper strapped himself in. To all intents and purposes he was now suspended weightless inside the chopper. No matter what happened to the Blackhawk, whether it was buffeted by a sudden gust of wind or it shifted up or down a degree, he would remain stationary. He turned to the gunner and nodded.

The gunner acknowledged with a nod of his own, then leaned down and opened a long, rectangular metal case on the floor. He reached inside and took out a fifty-caliber customized Macmillan-Barrett sniper rifle with scope. Then he took out a cartridge a little bigger than a twelve-gauge shotgun shell, except this cartridge was shaped like a high-powered rifle bullet and appeared to be constructed of high-tensile steel. It was known as a Bolfus round. An armor-piercing, pyroforic, high-cyclonic cartridge packed with spent uranium. The round weighed almost a quarter of a pound, and it took the gunner a moment to load it into the breech. Then he helped the SAS man attach the rifle to the arm-mounted tripod on the shooter's chair. When they were ready, the SAS man uncoiled a line from the sniper scope and plugged it into the Blackhawk's computer via an outlet on the arm of the chair. Immediately the SAS man was interfaced with the Blackhawk's computer and the 360-degree prop-mounted image intensifier and thermal scanner up top. Then the gunner slid open the chopper's side hatch.

The trooper swiveled the rifle around and adjusted the tripod arms so that the scope fitted neatly to his right eye. The *Britannia* was ten miles away. It leapt into view as clearly as if he were holding a photograph at arm's length. He found his quadrant and locked in. Shooters on six other choppers did the same with quadrants of their own. The shooters on the three remaining Blackhawks waited in reserve. Then the trooper signaled the gunner. The gunner signaled the pilot. The pilot radioed their readiness to the circling AWACS. A moment later the order came down from Porter on board the AWACS. All nine Blackhawks eased forward into the exclusion zone at the same moment, silent and menacing, their ablative coats diffusing the radar emissions of every ship in the area.

Lieutenant Drewe had been watching the Blackhawk nearest the *Hotspur*. He looked on from the flying bridge as it thrummed quietly past, then stepped inside to check the radar screen.

"Jesus," he whispered.

According to the warship's radar, there was nothing out there.

The Blackhawks closed in on the *Britannia* like robotic birds of prey forming an ever-tightening arc. The distance between them and the royal yacht shrank from ten miles to five. Then four. Then three. They stopped at two. There was still no sign of alarm from the *Britannia.*

The pilot of the first Blackhawk checked the time.

"Eight minutes," he said.

The SAS trooper used the scope to roam over the *Britannia*'s superstructure, letting the computer and the Agile Eye do all the work for him. There was also a laser-sighting range finder in the Eye that compensated for the differences in angle and elevation between the Eye's position on the rotor and the shooter's position in the cabin, and computed the information directly into the shooter's sights. The Eye's thermal imager and intensifier probed through the cold metal of the *Britannia*'s superstructure, seeking out warm bodies hiding behind thick bulkheads believing they were safe. The shooter found the huddled mass of captives in the admiral's day cabin easily. He hesitated a moment, then moved back up to the bridge. He already had his target. There was a man standing at the wheel. From the configuration provided by the intensifier, it was the same man who had steered the *Britannia* most of the time since the yacht had been hijacked. Intelligence had put a tentative ID on him. Patsy Ryan, a longtime IRA footsoldier. The intensifier presented Ryan so clearly the trooper could calculate his height, weight, and build. The sniper made one final pass across the bridge. He didn't think Ryan was alone in there. A moment later he confirmed his suspicions. There were two more outlines. Blurred and faint perhaps, but identifiable as live targets. He surmised that they weren't on the bridge at all but behind two bulkheads in the radio room, which was the reason for the weaker trace. Not that it mattered much. Not with the ammunition he was using. They only had to be in the vicinity when the Bolfus round went through the bridge. The sharpshooters in the other Blackhawks had slightly different ordnance. Their rifles were loaded with mercury-filled rounds tipped with titanium that could punch holes in steel plate and obliterate whoever was on the other side.

"Four minutes," the pilot called.

"Goddamn," the American gunner muttered. "Why does everybody else get to have all the fun?"

The SAS man pushed a small button on the side of the scope. A set of double cross hairs flicked on. One red, one black. He steadied himself and took careful aim. He decided to be charitable. The cross hairs merged over Patsy Ryan's heart.

Little more than two miles away, on the stern side of the royal yacht, Lieutenant Nichols counted down the remaining yards. They still weren't close enough.

"Five hundred," he chanted in a steely monotone. "Four fifty. Four hundred."

"Cut, *Triton One,"* the AWACS operator said.

Nichols looked at the time. The seconds were ticking down to 0400. The long-range snipers on the Blackhawks would open fire at any moment.

"Jesus," he swore, and looked at Bonner.

"We're four hundred short," he said. "They're listening now. Air Control says stop."

He switched his attention to Lynch.

"Your call," he said.

Bonner eased down the throttle and turned away so that Lynch couldn't look in his eyes. He didn't want anything in there to influence Lynch one way or the other.

"Keep going," Lynch said.

"Hot damn," Bonner growled, and turned the throttle back up to full.

Lynch and his men bent down to pick up their helmets and MP5 submachine guns.

"I said cut it," the AWACS operator bellowed into Nichols's headset. "They're tracking. They'll hear your engines. You're right underneath them."

"We're too close," Nichols snapped back. "We're going in."

"Ah man . . ." the AWACS operator's voice went up a notch. "Stand by, I'm advising the Blackhawk to hold . . ."

"Don't you fucking . . ." Nichols started to yell back at the AWACS officer.

At that moment the SAS trooper in the lead Blackhawk fired. In the confined space of the helicopter the noise sounded like a cannon going off. Even though he was ready for it, the recoil from the fifty-caliber rifle drove the SAS man back into the thickly padded sniper seat with a kick like a sledgehammer. He gave an involuntary grunt, then realigned the rifle and peered through the scope as the Bolfus round howled over the waves toward the *Britannia.*

Dominic Behan leapt to his feet in the radio room and tore the headset loose.

"There's something coming up on us," he yelled. "It sounds like a fuckin' torpedo."

Doyle grabbed the headset, pressed it hard against his ear, and listened. It was loud and steady. The whining, rhythmic churn of approaching props.

"They're coming in from behind," he said. "Get up top with O'Brien and stop them."

Behan grabbed his M-16 and followed Doyle out onto the bridge.

"Take her up to full speed," Doyle snapped at Ryan. "Then put her on autopilot . . . and get ready to jump."

"Holy shit," Ryan muttered. His fingers closed over the handle of the ship's telegraph. Doyle reached for the galvanometer. Behan stopped just as he was about to step off the bridge.

"Don't . . ." he yelled at Doyle.

Doyle looked back at him.

"I'll give you time to save your skin," he said, no longer bothering to hide his contempt. He took hold of the galvanometer and snatched it from its taped mounting under the console. Then he stared at it in mute incomprehension. The wires leading from the galvanometer had been cut.

"I couldn't let you do it, Eddie," the IRA man said quickly. "All I ever wanted was a deal. I don't kill for the sake of killing."

Doyle stared at Behan, his eyes filled with murder.

"You . . . stupid . . . Irish . . . ape . . ."

His voice was a low growl, and every word he spoke was dipped in hatred. He hurled the useless galvanometer at Behan. It hit a steel stanchion, bounced to the floor, and skidded across the deck with a high metallic squeal.

"They haven't kept the deal . . ." Doyle screamed at Behan. "Don't you understand . . . they haven't kept the deal . . ."

Then he leapt at Behan. The IRA man lifted his rifle, but it was too late. Doyle hit him full force. The impact carried both of them off the bridge and down the gangway steps to the deck below.

At that moment the Bolfus round sliced through the bridge, hit Patsy Ryan on the left side of the chest, and detonated with a searing blast of light that vaporized everything for a radius of twenty feet. One moment there was a man at the wheel of the *Britannia.* The next there was nothing. Only a blinding inferno that consumed flesh, metal, and plastic as if they were tinder. The bulkheads groaned. The ragged edges of a tear in the roof began to melt and drip into the fire. A vivid plume of smoke and flame poured from the shattered husk of the bridge and stained the night sky.

Declan Brady was amidships on the top deck, hidden safely between two steel deck lockers when the bridge vanished in a blast of heat. He saw nothing of it. Nor did he hear the bullet that killed him. It cut through the steel walls of the locker beside him and exploded with a force that pulped every organ in his body. O'Brien was less fortunate. He lived a moment longer. He had secreted himself behind the dome of the elevator shaft atop the royal apartments, from where he could cover the afterdeck. The first bullet hit his right arm and blew it and his M-16 into a thousand spinning fragments. His scream of shock was brief. The second bullet hit him in the lower torso and cleaved him in two.

Three men were dead in less than a second. Not one of them had seen or heard a whisper of the silent forces that had killed them.

Eight miles away in the heavily laden launch, with its cargo of hostages and treasure, Abu Musa, Javad, and Youssef heard the crackle of gunfire followed by the sound of a loud explosion aboard the royal yacht. They turned to see a violent fire on the bridge and a lurid column of smoke boiling into the sky. Some of the hostages had recovered sufficiently from the gas to turn their heads and look. There was a collective moan of despair.

"The madman has got what he wanted," Musa muttered in Arabic to his two companions. "He has destroyed the English queen."

The three of them were huddled in the well of the launch. Youssef was at the wheel. Javad had his rifle trained on the hostages who surrounded them, still bound tightly to the launch rail. Then they heard something else. New sounds. The unmistakable thump of helicopter rotors on the night air. The sound of more gunfire. There was a new mood among the hostages, a ripple of elation.

"She's not sinking," somebody shouted in English. "They're taking her back."

Everyone struggled to see. It was true. It wasn't the explosion they had feared. The *Britannia* hadn't been destroyed. Only the bridge was aflame. The rest of the royal yacht appeared unscathed as she sailed defiantly across the near horizon, her dressing lights still stubbornly aglow. Somebody gave a weak cheer. Others joined in with what little strength they could muster.

"Shut up," Musa screamed in English. He took out his pistol and brandished it in their faces. "You have nothing to celebrate . . . ."

Javad leaned forward and slammed his rifle butt into the two hostages nearest him, cowing them into silence. Anxiously, Musa turned his gaze back to the lights of Perim Island, now less than a mile away. Doyle and Behan and those other madmen could die on board the *Britannia* if that was what they wanted. He never had any intention of joining them in their martyrdom. There was no cause on earth that could command his life. Another half hour and he would be on dry land, safe in the protection of his Yemeni allies. There he would turn over the hostages and one third of the *Britannia*'s treasure. In due course the Yemenis would return the hostages to the British while denying all knowledge of the treasure. Musa would be back in Iran with the rest of the treasure within the week. That was the deal he had made. And his friends in the Yemeni government had never let him down.

The launch moved sluggishly through the water. Musa willed it to go faster. Youssef said they were overladen and he was afraid they would burn out the motor or capsize. Musa kept his eyes on the lights ahead and, for the hundredth time since they had left the royal yacht, he pledged his soul to Allah.

"A boat is coming," Javad grunted abruptly.

Musa strained to see through the darkness. They were so close to Yemeni territory they could expect to run into Yemeni patrol boats at any time. But the British were out there too, he knew. Even this close to land. Perhaps, he thought, his allies were playing it safe, unwilling to risk a military confrontation with the British. Perhaps this was a British vessel.

Gradually it materialized, the dark outline of a patrol boat a hundred yards to starboard. Unlike the *Britannia,* it carried only steering lights and it was impossible to see whether it was British or Saudi or Yemeni. Whatever its nationality, it was steering toward them on an intercept course.

"Stand up," Musa ordered the hostages in English. "Stand up where they can see you."

No one obeyed. Either from weakness or a resolve to make some show of resistance. Javad grabbed the man nearest, hauled him to his feet, and propped him against the rail. The man screamed with pain as the ropes twisted into his skin and tore his flesh. Javad seized another man by the shoulder and dragged him to his feet, then another. Musa crouched down to the deck, where he could not be seen from the approaching vessel, and pressed the barrel of his pistol to the chest of a hostage.

The patrol boat closed in until it seemed that it would cut across their bow. Then it cut its speed and turned around to keep pace with the royal launch. A distance of only fifty feet separated the two craft. Someone on the patrol boat switched on a searchlight. Its beam swept the royal launch, lighting up the haggard faces of the hostages. Then Javad saw what he wanted to see. A flag at the stern with a red star and red, white, and black stripes. Also visible on the stern were the Arabic words for "Star of Aden," the name of the patrol boat. At that moment a man carrying a loud hailer and wearing the white uniform of a Yemeni naval officer appeared on the foredeck of the patrol boat.

"You have entered the territorial waters of the People's Republic of Yemen illegally," he called out in the guttural Arabic of south Yemen. "You must stop and identify yourselves immediately or we will open fire."

As he spoke, a dozen sailors fanned out along the bulwarks of the patrol boat, carrying rifles. A sailor at the bow trained a pair of deck-mounted machine guns on the royal launch.

"Allahu Aqbar," Musa murmured to himself. He was safe.

"Stop the engines," he ordered Youssef. The Palestinian obediently pulled back on the throttle and the launch slowed dramatically. Musa cupped a hand to his mouth.

"I am Abu Musa," he shouted back. "I am a friend of the People's Republic and I have been guaranteed safe passage by your government."

There was a pause while the officer conferred with someone on the bridge. A moment later he reappeared.

"Stand to," he ordered. "We are coming aboard."

The patrol boat's engine rumbled. It spurted through the water and pulled up smoothly alongside the launch. The gap between them narrowed to ten feet, though the patrol boat sat a good six feet higher in the water. A dark-skinned Yemeni sailor stood ready near the patrol boat's stern with a line. As the gap narrowed, he leapt nimbly down to the royal launch and secured the line to the bow of the royal launch.

"Salaam," the officer called down. "Your name is known to us, Abu Musa."

"Salaam, brother," Musa answered with a relieved smile and a wave. His eyes roamed along the friendly Arab faces that lined the patrol boat's deck. They had put away their guns. A few of them smiled and waved back. The fear and tension evaporated from Musa's body and were replaced by delicious sensations of triumph and relief. He turned and squeezed Javad's arm. They had done it. They were home.

The officer jumped down onto the bow of the royal launch and was followed by two sailors. One of them went to give Javad a friendly slap on the back. But instead of stopping, his hand kept going, driving Javad's face into the brass cockpit rail. There was a heavy thud and, as Javad lost consciousness and slumped to the deck, the sailor snatched away his rifle. Musa whirled around in time to see the second sailor pulling Youssef out of the cockpit by the head and shoulders as though he weighed nothing. The sailor threw him onto the bow, bounced his head once off the solid timbers, then put a foot in the back of his neck.

Musa's fingers closed around his pistol. He was too late. The officer took him by the throat with one hand, slammed him against the bow rail so hard that every scrap of breath was jolted from his body, and wrenched the pistol from his grasp.

"Frightfully sorry, old chap," the Yemeni officer said in perfect English. "But I don't think you'll be needing that anymore."

Musa's eyes widened in horror as the rest of the sailors from the patrol boat swarmed the royal launch. They spoke English too. Another cheer went up from the hostages, ragged and feeble perhaps, but lustier than before. The patrol boat gunned its engines once more, the bow line tightened as they described a wide arc and began heading back out to sea.

"Do you want to know something interesting," SAS Captain Jeremy Bright added, pausing only to wipe away some of the skin stainer that irritated his eyes. "Her Majesty's government retains the death penalty for only two crimes. Treason . . . and piracy on the high seas."

At the precise moment that Abu Musa, Javad Malik, and Youssef Shaheen learned that their fate was to die on a British gallows, the minisubmarine *Triton One* broke surface twenty yards from the *Britannia*'s stern. Lynch twirled the release handle of the exit hatch and climbed out of the conning tower, followed by his men, their MP5s trained on the deck rail. There was no one waiting for them. Lynch saw a thick plume of white smoke billowing from the direction of the bridge. They had only minutes to get to the boiler room before the charges could be reset.

He steadied himself on the rolling deck of the sub, switched on his helmet light, and aimed the beam up at the stern. The gold figurines of the lion and the unicorn on the royal coat of arms shone back at him. Then Lynch noticed something else. There were splotches of dark red on the crown. They weren't rust, he realized. They were blood. This was the spot where Admiral Marchant and the girl had been executed.

He turned and took a canister the size of an aerosol can from one of his men. The gap between the minisub and the yacht narrowed as Lieutenant Nichols kept the Mark 12 snug in the *Britannia*'s wake and a steady one knot faster than the royal yacht. Lynch waited and calculated, knees flexing, hips swaying to compensate for the pitching and yawing of the narrow deck. It was only a matter of seconds now. Still, it was a dangerously long time to be so exposed. All it would take was one man left on deck to get off a single burst and they would be finished.

The gap narrowed to a few feet and the deck rose. Lynch knew it was his best chance. He braced the canister against his hip and thumbed the button. There was a loud hydraulic hiss and the canister jumped back as it pumped a twenty-foot telescopic tube up to the deck rail. The claw at the end of the tube hooked onto the deck rail and closed like a mechanical fist. At the same moment, a series of metal rods sprang out from the sides of thc tube to make a ladder.

Lynch jumped onto the first rung and held fast. He swung hard into the stern of the *Britannia* and bounced. But he was ready and the ladder held. Quickly, he climbed the steps until his head was almost level with the deck. Then he braced himself to snatch a look. If any of the hijackers on the upper deck had survived the murderous assault of the SAS sharpshooters, this was the moment when Lynch could expect to get his head blown off.

His caution was entirely justified. Two men remained on the top deck. One of them was Dominic Behan. But he was on the forward deck and in no condition to fight. He lay sprawled at the bottom of the gangway steps where Doyle had left him, his eyes glazed with shock, his back broken. The other man was better situated to put up a fight. Edward Doyle had been lucky. Behan had been between him and the worst of the blast. He had made his way back to the roof of the deck and taken up a position atop the veranda from where he could control all movement on the afterdeck. There would be no more sniper fire, he knew. Not now that the assault had begun. He could hear the roar of the oncoming helicopters. Any moment now they would come, streaming out of the sky on drop lines, swarming over the deck rails from fast assault craft. Doyle knew that for him it was almost over. But first he would make them pay.

A helmet appeared over the stern rail. Doyle fired a burst from his M-16. A section of rail vanished in a blizzard of wooden shrapnel over Lynch's head.

"Shit," he swore.

As planned, the destruction of the bridge had severed all communication between the bridge and the boiler room. But there were still booby-trapped charges to be negotiated below decks. Every second the charges were live and the queen and Prince Philip were trapped inside the royal apartments, they were at risk. Lynch knew he had no time. He looked back down at the men waiting behind him and signaled that he was going to go. He readied himself with one hand and poised himself to swing up onto the deck. With the other hand he lifted his submachine gun over the lip of the deck and blindly fired a long, wild burst.

Doyle watched as the bullets thudded harmlessly into the armored apartments of the royal deck. A moment later Lynch swung up onto the fantail. Doyle leveled his rifle and squeezed the trigger. A fusilade of bullets smashed into the deck where Doyle lay, stitching a long, deadly path beside his body. Instantly he forgot about Lynch, threw himself sideways, dropped down to the next deck, and dived into the queen's drawing room.

The instant Lynch was on deck he scrambled to his feet, sprinted for the protection of the royal veranda, and crouched behind an elegant gold and white binnacle that had once graced the deck of another monarch's yacht, *The Royal George.* Quickly he scanned the area and gave his men cover as they followed him on board.

"Welcome aboard, Commander," a friendly voice called down from above.

Lynch snapped up his rifle.

"Password?"

"Miter," the voice answered prompt and clear.

Lynch had heard Gault on ship-to-ship communications several times in the past twenty-four hours, and he recognized the voice.

"Show yourself," he ordered.

Obligingly, John Gault swung down onto the veranda deck and

landed lightly on both feet. Lynch got up and nodded to his SAS counterpart.

"Thanks for getting me on board in one piece," he said.

"Glad to have you here," Gault said. "Didn't get the bugger though. Just scared him off."

"We'll get him," Lynch added. "First, let's take care of those charges, shall we?"

Without another word Gault turned and quickly led Lynch and his men down to the queen's drawing room.

Moments later the men from Comacchio climbed on board from the second minisub and fanned out quickly along the upper decks. Then the first two Sea Kings thundered overhead. They wheeled tightly around the royal yacht and hovered over the newly secured afterdeck. Lines spilled from their open hatches, and SAS troopers fast-roped down to the deck of the royal yacht.

Dominic Behan watched them come in from his position below the charred and blackened bridge. He heard them before he saw them. The roar of their heavy rotors battered through the cold mist of darkness that crept over him in ever-increasing waves. He blinked the haze from his eyes and looked up as the first chopper passed overhead. It was so close he could see the faces of the men inside, dark and threatening and full of malice. To him they looked like angels of death. He willed his right arm to move and fumbled weakly at his belt. Then his fingers found what he was looking for. He took one last breath, then pulled the pin from the grenade.

"Rule Britannia," he croaked, his lips angling into a smile of deadly irony.

The sound of the explosion echoed through the night, sending the *Britannia*'s rescuers scurrying for cover. It echoed down through two decks to the recreation space in the bow, where marine private Hackham and eleven of the burliest crew members on the royal yacht braced themselves against a twenty-foot section of the hull.

"Now," Hackham shouted.

The blast sounded terribly close. It could be the one that would send them all to the bottom. They lunged at the crudely cut steel plate at once. For a moment nothing happened, and Hackham feared that they hadn't cut it enough. Then he felt it begin to give.

"Again," he urged.

Once more they threw themselves against the hull, this time with all the strength they could muster. There was a dull metallic groan that escalated sharply to a shrill, rending screech and the three-quarter-inch-thick section of plate started to topple outward. It fell slowly at first, clinging stubbornly to the remaining few threads of steel at the bottom. Then there were two loud bangs, as sharp and as startling as pistol shots as the remaining metal fibers gave way and the whole section of plate fell out from the *Britannia*'s hull and splashed heavily into the water.

"Okay," Hackham urged. "Everybody out."

All the women and some of the men wore life jackets. The only life jackets they had been able to round up, and they had gone to the non-swimmers. There were twenty-eight of them, and they stood nearby, preparing themselves for the leap into the dark.

"Remember," Hackham yelled. "Jump as far as you can and keep clear of the sides. You'll all be picked up in a few minutes."

The first few hostages hurried forward, braced themselves, then jumped through the gaping hole and into the rushing water below. Some hesitated and were pushed from behind.

"Don't panic now, for Christ's sake," Hackham shouted. "Just jump and swim like hell. . . ."

"Dave!"

Hackham spun around when he heard his name called. It was another marine.

"One of the bastards is trying to get in through the door!" he yelled.

"Jesus," Hackham muttered. He pushed his way back through the crowd and hurried after his buddy. As soon as he left the recreation area he heard the shots coming from the direction of the petty officer's mess.

"They blew the door a minute ago and started shooting," the second marine told him. "We kept 'em back with the pistol but we're running out of ammo."

Hackham took it all in as they hurried along the passageway, through the marine barracks toward the makeshift barricade they had set up in the petty officer's mess.

"Did you use the zippo?" Hackham asked.

"Are you kidding?" the marine said. "Nobody but you wants to touch that bloody thing."

"Okay," Hackham decided. "Now's the time we find out."

He ducked into the mess as another fusillade of bullets hammered into the bulkhead over their heads. Outside in the corridor, Billy Deveny screamed as he fired, his voice approaching the pitch of madness.

"Get out here, you bastards," he screamed over and over. "Get out here . . ."

"He must think we're stupid," Hackham chuckled.

Another marine was hunched down behind the barricade with Gault's pistol, the makeshift flamethrower by his side. He looked up as Hackham appeared.

"I've got five left," he said, gesturing with the pistol.

"All right," Hackham grunted, squatting down beside him. "When I give the signal, let him have the lot, nice and steady, keep his head down for just a minute."

Hackham picked up the frame with the gas canister cradled in it upside down. He put his arms through the straps and hefted it onto his back. Then he reached behind his back and opened the valve on the gas canister a fraction. Next he took a plastic lighter out of his pocket and held it to the open nozzle of the makeshift gun. Nothing happened for a moment, but then the gas caught and blossomed into a loose, sloppy flame. He nodded to his two mates, then held the gun in front of him and nodded to the marine with the gun.

"Now," he said.

The marine started shooting. Not too fast, not too slow. The shots whined through the open door and hammered around the walls of the corridor outside, forcing Deveny back for a minute. Hackham steadied himself and turned the valve on the gas canister all the way. Then he pulled slowly back on the trigger, releasing a jet of compressed air from the canister attached to the barrel. There was a sudden, terrifying whoosh of flame and a vivid scarlet claw reached out across the room.

"Whooeee . . ." Hackham bellowed.

He stepped around the barricade, walked ponderously to the open door, and pulled the trigger back as far as it would go. A jet of fire rushed out of the barrel, through the open door, and gathered into a gigantic ball of flame that swept the length of the corridor with the roar of an enraged animal. The scream that came back was a combination of terror and excruciating agony. Suddenly the flame died as quickly as it had begun, all the gas in the canister exhausted in a few short seconds.

But it was more than enough.

The marines stood transfixed as the figure of a man stumbled back down the corridor wreathed in ribbons of fire. His screams drowned out all other sounds as he bounced from wall to wall, flailing blindly at the flames that enveloped him. He stumbled and fell to the floor. The flames flared even brighter, burning through his clothes, setting fire to his hair, and melting his flesh. He got to his hands and knees and tried to crawl, but even the strength of terror had deserted him and he sank slowly back to the floor.

At last he lay still while the flames licked at his body like the tongues of ravenous beasts. Hackham slid the flame thrower from his back and set it down on the floor. Then he turned to the marine with the gun and held out his hand. There was one bullet left in the magazine. Hackham took the pistol, stepped out into the blackened corridor, and approached the still-smoldering body on the floor. The smell of burned meat rushed into his nostrils. He aimed the gun and fired a single shot into the back of Deveny's head. Then he walked back to his two mates.

"It's more than they did for us," he said.

At that moment Lynch, Gault, and the three SBS men were working their way amidships along the corridor that connected the household staff cabins. They moved swiftly and silently, watching for booby traps, leapfrogging one man forward at a time while the others gave cover. Occasionally they heard gunfire from different parts of the yacht punctuated by the odd explosion. It told them the hijackers weren't giving up quietly. Lynch could understand why. If Comacchio or the SAS took any prisoners, it would only be by accident.

Most of the corridor was behind them. Ahead, through an open door, lay another empty stretch of corridor that led to the engine room. Lynch crouched in a cabin doorway while Gault waited in the doorway opposite, ready to follow the next man forward. From where he stood he could see the door to the staff mess swinging loosely on its hinges in the next corridor, reminding him of the doomed girl he had left in there. The lead man scurried forward into the next section of corridor and dropped to one knee, submachine gun ready. There was no one waiting. He signaled the next man to follow. Gault leaned forward.

There were three deafening bangs, and the lead man flew backward as though hurled by a giant fist. He slammed against a bulkhead, tumbled to the floor, and lay still. Lynch glimpsed three massive hollows in the man's chest as he fell. The combat suits were strong, but they couldn't save a man who had been shot at point-blank range with an assault rifle. Beneath the material his chest was shattered and shards of broken bone had carved his heart into pieces. Gault hit the floor and returned fire. The others opened up in unison. A stream of bullets poured through the mess room door, where the shots had originated. There was no answering fire. Lynch signaled everyone to stop. An eerie silence settled. Gunsmoke drifted sinuously along the corridor like lazy airborne serpents. Lynch broke cover and moved forward at a fast crouch, past Gault, past the body of the lead man on the deck. In a situation like this the rules were simple. An ambush favored the ambusher. The only way out was to fight a way out. He charged the mess room door, snapping off shots as he ran.

An arm appeared and hooked a grenade at him. Lynch threw himself through the nearest cabin door. The grenade detonated before he made it. He was lucky. It wasn't high explosive. It was GBX. The gas filled the corridor with a thick swirling fog. Lynch thumbed his helmet switch and his visor switched onto night sight. He glimpsed a blur of heat through the fog in the shape of a running man at the end of the corridor and squeezed off a burst. Too late. Their attacker had vanished.

Behind him John Gault hastily pulled a mask over his face. A moment later the first oily tendrils of gas coiled around his body. Behind the protection of the mask he thought he could taste its bitterness. His stomach recoiled at the memory and he almost retched. He reminded himself that he was covered from head to toe. The gas shouldn't be able to reach his skin. He suppressed a shudder and crawled forward along the cold deck, looking for Lynch.

Armed with his night-sight visor, Lynch moved quickly down the last stretch of corridor. There was a junction with another corridor that ran past the engine room door. Another good spot for an ambush. Lynch stole a quick look around the corner. Both corridors were empty. Their assailant had gone. All he had wanted was to stall them. To buy time. And Lynch knew why. The charges must have been reset with timers by now. They had only a few minutes left to find and disarm them. Maybe not that long.

He turned and looked back along the corridor for John Gault. The gas had already begun to clear. He saw the others coming toward him through the haze. The two SBS men, then Gault . . . then somebody else. There was no mistake. There should have been only three shapes. Lynch saw four. Their attacker had doubled around behind them. Lynch dropped to one knee and tried to aim past the first three men.

"Get out of the way," he yelled, his voice strident and metallic through the helmet speaker.

The first three men dropped to the deck, leaving the last man open and exposed. Lynch's finger tightened on the trigger.

"No, no, no . . ." another robotic voice rang out along the corridor. "It's me—Tom Bonner. Don't shoot me, for Christ's sake."

Lynch's finger froze on the trigger.

"Jesus . . ."

Another fraction of an inch and he would have cut Bonner in two. Lynch lowered his gun and got back to his feet. The others followed suit as Bonner hurried past them.

"I could have killed you," Lynch added, his voice a brittle mixture of anger and accusation. "I came that close . . . that goddamn close . . ."

For a second, but only a second, Tom Bonner looked abashed. Then he shrugged it off.

"I thought I might be able to help," he said in his best aw-shucks manner. Lynch recognized the tone. It was the closest Bonner ever came to an apology.

“Your orders are pretty bloody clear,” Lynch added sharply. “No combat role for Americans. Don’t you even listen to your President?”

“I ain’t planning on shooting anybody,” Bonner grunted. “But maybe, just maybe, I can help you with those charges.”

Lynch hesitated. There wasn’t time to argue. Besides, he had to concede, Bonner was the best explosives man he had ever known. Instead of arguing, he should be counting himself lucky.

“Anyways,” Bonner added slyly, “I have an investment to protect here.”

“Jesus . . .” Lynch shook his head. He turned away and contemplated the locked door to the engine room for a moment.

“All right,” he decided. “We have no idea what the hell is waiting on the other side of this door . . . so how about you help us find out?”

Bonner obligingly leaned forward and studied the door.

“Is this the only way in and out of here?” he asked.

“As far as I know,” Gault said, his voice muffled inside his mask.

“It doesn’t look like it’s wired,” Bonner pronounced. “Unless it’s been done from the other side. In which case, whoever did it is still in there.”

“And willing to go down with the ship?” Lynch said.

“Either that, or he didn’t have time to do the job and get out before you guys got here,” Bonner said.

He leaned away from the door.

“Give yourselves some credit,” he added. “You got down here pretty fast. If you trapped somebody inside, this door isn’t wired and he wants to get out a lot worse than you want to get in.”

Lynch thought about the ambush. Maybe their assailant hadn’t bought enough time after all. He gestured to the others to take up positions on either side of the door. Then, gingerly, he tried the handle. It moved easily. There was an audible click as the lock turned. He eased the door open a fraction. The bass thump of the engines flooded into the corridor. Lynch looked carefully. There were no wires or tapes. No sign of booby traps. He took his hand away, readied himself, and nodded to the others. Then, in a single fluid motion he kicked the door open and dived inside.

He landed on a steel gantry, rolled quickly, and flattened himself against the engine casing against the opposite bulkhead. Nothing happened. There was no explosion. No answering fusillade of shots. He looked around both decks of the pounding, cavernous engine room but saw no one. He signaled the others to follow. They came in quickly and spread out across the top deck while Lynch scanned the room for any sign of threat. Still there was nothing.

Wordlessly, Lynch signaled his men to secure the bottom deck. It took them only a moment. They found no one. The only obvious hiding place left was a washroom on the second level. Lynch stood on one side of the door, Gault on the other. Carefully, Lynch tried the door and opened it a sliver. The washroom was empty. He checked for booby traps but found none. The engine room was clean and secure. Satisfied, he strode quickly down the gangway to the engine room floor and crossed to the emergency cutoff switch on the main control board. He punched the button hard. Instantly the thudding monotone of the engines altered, descended to a moan, and then into an exhausted sigh. The royal yacht slowed in the water. A few minutes more and it would be at a dead stop.

Lynch returned to the top level and looked at Gault.

"They're not in here?" he asked, referring to the charges.

"Next door," Gault answered. "In the boiler room."

Lynch nodded. Then he turned and surveyed the door to the boiler room. His hand reached out for the handle.

"I think maybe—" Bonner interrupted, coming up behind him.

Lynch gladly took his hand away and stepped aside while Bonner leaned down to check the second door. Again it took him only a moment.

"It's clean . . ." he said. "On this side."

Lynch motioned him to step back.

"No," Bonner said. "There's something about this whole setup that's starting to bother me. Let me just check something else. . . ."

He turned the handle of the door slowly, careful not to disturb whatever might be waiting on the other side. When the lock clicked, he held the door shut for a moment. Then he opened it a fraction and peered inside. A minute ticked past with agonizing slowness.

"Oh, shit," he breathed.

"What is it?" Lynch asked.

"It's wired."

Everyone's eyes switched to Bonner.

"It's what I was afraid of," he added. "If there's nobody in here and this door is wired. It means . . ."

"We're too late," Lynch finished for him. "They reset the charges and got out before we got here. She's going to go . . ."

"Any minute, pal," Bonner muttered. "Any goddamned minute."

An aching silence yawned between them like a void. A void that each one of them knew was about to be filled by a sudden, searing death.

"So?" Bonner looked up at Lynch. "You want to keep going or you want to get topside and start swimming?"

"Can you . . . ?" Lynch began.

Something moved behind them on the bulkhead beside the engine room door. Lynch glimpsed it from the corner of one eye. John Gault had been covering the engine room door but had moved away when Bonner spoke and, like the rest of them, he had his back to the door. It was an ideal moment to be taken by surprise. Especially when they were wearing helmets. Lynch never doubted the usefulness of the helmets. They kept out gas, supplied essential information, and looked through fog and dark. They also cut peripheral vision and hearing to a minimum.

Lynch had no time to be polite. He shoved Gault out of the way and sprinted for the door. A sheet of metal slats detached itself from a section of engine casing and scythed through the air toward him. A man leapt from the space behind and lunged for the open doorway. He had a ten-foot lead on Lynch, and he almost made it. But almost wasn't good enough. Lynch swatted the spinning metal plate aside and dived. He hit the man behind the knees and brought him down hard, halfway through the door. Michael Kenney screamed as the rim of the high steel doorstep bit into his flesh.

"We've got to get out of here . . ." he sobbed through pain-tightened lips. "For God's sake . . . we've got to get out . . ."

Lynch hauled Kenney to his feet and shoved him against the bulkhead. The others crowded around.

"Where are they?" Lynch shouted. "How much time have we got . . . ?"

"I don't know . . ." Kenney sobbed. "I didn't set them. Eddie Doyle . . ."

Lynch slammed him back against the bulkhead. This time he did it with such force he wondered that his fist didn't go right through Kenney's chest. The IRA man screamed again, a shrill, almost feminine sound.

"I don't know," he groaned. "I swear to God . . . I don't . . ."

John Gault stepped forward, snatched a grenade from Kenney's belt, and brandished it in his face. It was a gas grenade.

"You guys love this stuff, don't you?" he said.

Kenney whimpered but said nothing.

"John . . . ?" Lynch began, a cautionary note in his voice.

"We're out of time," Gault cut him short.

He pulled the pin on the grenade and flicked it away. Kenney's eyes widened. Then Gault stepped over to the washroom, threw in the grenade, and shut the door. There was a loud report and then a few milky coils of gas began to creep through the crevices around the door.

"Summary execution, sunshine," Gault said. "Death in the gas chamber . . . but it won't be quick."

He grabbed hold of the IRA man and pulled him up. Lynch held on but only for a second. Then he let go. Kenney screamed and flailed wildly as Gault dragged him over to the washroom. The escaping gas had started to thicken. Kenney caught a trace and reeled backward, his face contorted by a rictus of pain. Gault's hand grasped the handle on the washroom door. Kenney's body spasmed involuntarily as a second, stronger gust reached down his throat, burned his gullet, and tried to turn his stomach inside out. Lynch held his breath. It wasn't working. Another second and the man wouldn't be able to talk if he wanted to.

"Nine charges . . ." Kenney screamed through a mouthful of rising bile. "Both hulls . . . under the boiler . . ."

"How long have we got?" Gault yelled in his face.

"Thirty . . . thirty-minute timers . . ." Kenney babbled. "I set them when the bridge went up. Doyle told me . . . he said he'd kill me . . ."

"When, you stupid bastard?" Lynch shouted. "When did you set them?"

Gault dragged Kenney back along the gantry, away from the probing tendrils of gas. He shoved the Irishman back against the bulkhead as Lynch had. This time it nearly ripped every muscle in Kenney's abdomen.

"Five after . . . ten after . . . I don't know. . . ."

Lynch looked at his watch. It was almost four-thirty. If the IRA man was telling the truth, they had five, maybe ten minutes to disarm the charges. He turned to Bonner. The Texan was already on his knees at the boiler room door, one arm through the narrow opening. A moment later he emerged with a fuse in his hand the size of a pencil stub. It was followed by a wad of Play-Doh the size of a small apple.

"It's Demex all right," he said, getting back to his feet. "Stuck to the bulkhead. The firing cap was wired to the handle. Open the door and . . . boom."

He pushed the door open with theatrical relish, and it swung teasingly in front of them.

"This one was easy," he said. "Now let's see if that little prick is telling the truth."

Bonner led the way. He barely glanced at the tangled nest of wires that spilled uselessly from the ceiling. He took the gangway down to the bottom level of the boiler room followed closely by Lynch, then Gault, dragging the wretched Kenney behind him. When they reached the bottom, Gault let the IRA man fall. He dropped to the deck like a sack of grain and emptied the contents of his stomach over himself. Then he contracted into the fetal position and moaned pitiably as the sickness coursed through him. The two remaining SBS men positioned themselves on the upper levels, one at the boiler room door, the other at the engine room door. Silently both of them began to pray.

Tom Bonner found the first six charges quickly. Three attached to each side of the hull, just as Kenney had said. None of them were booby-trapped. There hadn't been time. He took the fuses out of each one, broke off the blasting caps, and crushed them beneath his heel. Then he came to the charges under the boiler. He switched on his helmet light, got down on both knees, and peered into the space between the deck and the bottom of the boiler. It was dark and dirty. Surprisingly dirty compared to what he'd seen of the rest of the yacht. But Kenney was right. The charges were there. All three of them molded onto the boiler mounts, fuses intact, timers ticking.

But there was something else. Something strange. There seemed to be something wrong with the deck. It looked as though it was buckled, which should have been impossible for plates this thick. Unless . . . He reached under the boiler and felt around with his fingertips as lightly and as delicately as any surgeon. Then he gave a grunt of recognition and got back to his feet.

"Have a look under there," Bonner told Lynch.

Lynch looked at his watch. It said 4:31. He took a deep breath, then got down on his knees and peered underneath.

"See anything unusual?" Bonner asked.

"I can see the charges," Lynch said.

"See anything wrong with the deck there?"

"It's dirty," Lynch answered. There was a pause. "There seems to be an extra plate."

"Yeah," Bonner said. "The rest of the deck is so clean, you could eat off it. But under there it's dirty. My guess is that Murphy over there put in that plate and tried to hide it in the dark with grease and dirt and shit. My bet is there's a real skinny sheet of plastique under that plate and a pressure switch. Somebody lies down on the plate, he squeezes the switch. That's okay as long as he's lyin' on it. The minute he gets up, the switch springs and the plastique goes. Boom. One dead bomb-disposal man. One dead boat."

"What do you want me to do?" Lynch asked, getting back to his feet.

"When I get on that plate," Bonner answered, "you put your foot on there with me . . . and keep it there till I tell you to move."

Lynch looked at him.

"You go, I go?" he asked. "Is that it?"

"Hey." Bonner shrugged. "What kind of career you gonna have without me anyway?"

The Texan unfastened his helmet and pulled it from his head. It was too big and awkward to fit in the narrow space beneath the boiler. He set it down on the deck with the flashlight beam trained under the boiler. Then he wiped away the sweat that streamed down his face and gratefully scratched at the itches on his scalp. Lynch watched him, then took off his helmet and laid it down beside Bonner's. Gault hesitated a moment. Then he walked over to join them and pulled off his gas mask.

"One way or the other," he said. "I don't suppose these will make much difference now."

"Not a helluva lot," Bonner agreed.

Then he got down on his back and prepared to slide under the boiler. Gault kneeled down at his side to watch and to help in any way he could.

"Just wait till I'm on it now," he reminded Lynch. "Then stick your foot on it after me, hold it down hard, and don't move a freakin' muscle.

"No problem," Lynch muttered.

"Of course," the big man added, "I could be wrong. It might not be a pressure switch at all. It might be a plain old-fashioned detonator just waiting for somebody to spark it by lyin' on it."

Lynch braced himself against the boiler casing and edged his boot underneath so the toecap was poised at the edge of the plate.

"Okay," Bonner grunted. "Let's find out what it's gonna be, huh? Heroes or hellfire?"

He pushed himself smoothly beneath the belly of the boiler and onto the steel plate. It moved so fractionally under his weight that it felt as though it hadn't moved at all. He held his breath and waited. Nothing happened.

"Okay," he called back. "Put your foot on the bottom and wedge it in nice and tight."

Lynch leaned as close in to the boiler casing as he could and clamped his toe tightly down on the plate.

"I might have to jiggle around a bit while I'm taking out these fuses," Bonner's muffled voice called back. "Whatever you do, don't move your foot or let me bump it off for you."

It was an awkward position, but Lynch eased his foot onto the plate as far as he could and pushed down. He glanced at his watch and swallowed.

04.37 hours.

They might have three minutes left . . . at most.

Bonner removed the fuses first. One at a time he handed them to Gault. Then he did the same with the timers.

"I can't see real clearly in here," he grunted as he passed them out. "Can't see what kind of a margin I've been working with."

Gault looked at the clock face on the last timer. It was seventeen seconds from ignition. He turned it and showed it to Lynch. Lynch rolled his eyes heavenward.

"You don't want to know," he mumbled back at Bonner.

It took Bonner several minutes more to pry the plastique away from the engine mounts. One by one he passed them out too. Gault laid them carefully on the deck. At last the big man was finished.

"Okay," he called out. "Now we come to the tricky part."

Slowly, carefully, he eased his way out. Lynch kept his boot jammed down hard on the steel plate. Sweat streamed from his scalp, soaked his hair, and traced shiny, itchy trails down his face. Bonner's knee hit his boot hard and almost shifted it. Both men froze. Then the big man started again. At last, one inch at a time, he was free. He got back up to his feet and looked first at Gault, then at Lynch.

"Stay here," he said, an odd gleam in his eye.

Lynch looked at Gault. The SAS man shook his head. Neither of them had any idea what Bonner planned to do next.

Bonner walked over to Kenney, grabbed hold of him, and dragged him back toward the boiler. Kenney moaned and dry-retched but put up no resistance. Then Bonner laid him on the floor and quickly rolled him under the boiler and onto the steel plate.

"No . . ." Kenney tried to protest, his voice a strangled croak.

"If I were you, Murphy, I'd lie real still under there," Bonner snapped back at him. "And if you behave yourself, somebody's gonna come back and get you in a little while. That is, if there's anything left of you to get."

He straightened up and looked at Lynch.

"You can take your foot off now," he said. "Then I recommend that we all get the fuck outta here."
"What if it goes up?" he asked.
"There ain't no other charges to set off," Bonner shrugged. "The worst that's gonna happen is that between the plate and the boiler, Murphy down there is gonna end up like a jelly roll."
Lynch hesitated a moment, then slowly pulled his foot free.
"All right," he sighed. "Let's get those bloody charges somewhere where they can't do any harm, shall we?"

The five of them approached the queen's drawing room cautiously. The two SBS men up front, Lynch, Gault, and Bonner behind, each of them carrying almost forty pounds of Demex. They had reason to be wary. They had encountered a couple of men from Comacchio at the top of the main staircase who warned them that the yacht was still not secure. At least one of the hijackers had elected to make a stand on the top deck. Then, as they crossed the royal anteroom, the sound of gunfire intensified over their heads.
"Goddamn," Bonner growled. "Whoever it is, he's puttin' up a helluva fight."
Lynch looked at Gault. There was only one man it could be. And both of them wanted a piece of him.
They heard voices from the drawing room. English voices.
"Commander Lynch coming in," the lead SBS man called out.
The voices stopped.
"Code word?" someone called back.
"Mitre."
"Come in slowly."
The five of them filed into the drawing room. For a moment they saw no one amid the wreckage.
"It's all right," said a voice behind a pile of ruined furniture. "It's Commander Lynch and his men."
One of the Comacchio men from *Triton Two* stood up. Another stepped out from the door behind them, an MP5 in his hand, just in case. There was a sudden moan from behind the makeshift barricade.

"Casualties?" Lynch asked.

"We've taken a few hits," the first Comacchio man confirmed. "Bastard conned SAS into thinking he was one of us. Got us shooting at each other."

"Jesus," Lynch muttered.

He set the slabs of Demex on the floor and stepped around the barricade. Three men lay on the blood-soiled carpet. Two were wounded, one was dead. One of the wounded was a Comacchio man. The other two were SAS. Another SAS trooper tended to the two wounded men as best he could. An SAS captain sat beside the fireplace with his back to the wall, a radio in his hand connecting him to the helicopters that hovered outside. The queen's drawing room had been turned into a temporary field hospital and command post while the battle continued over their heads. The officer got to his feet and approached Lynch. At that moment there was a renewed burst of automatic weapons fire over their heads.

"Jeffrey Roberts," the SAS captain introduced himself. "You got the charges all right?"

Lynch nodded.

"What's the story up top?" he asked.

"We've got one of the hijackers isolated on the top deck," Roberts answered. "Trouble is, we haven't been able to nail the bastard yet. It's like a maze up there, and he keeps moving. He's well armed and got a lot of grenades with him. We can't rush him without risking more casualties to our own people."

John Gault appeared suddenly behind Lynch.

"What about the queen . . . Prince Philip?" he asked urgently.

Roberts shook his head.

"Still on board, I'm afraid. There's no way we can bring the chopper in to take them off yet."

"God almighty . . ." Gault swore, and started toward the door.

"Where do you think you're going?" Lynch asked.

"Where do you bloody well think?" Gault snapped back.

Lynch stepped after him, grabbed him by the shoulder, and spun him around.

"You heard the man," Lynch said. "You go rushing up there, you're as likely to get hit by our people as you are by him."

“I want him off this ship,” Gault muttered, his eyes burning with the fury and frustration of a week under siege. “He’s like a monkey on my back. Like something from a nightmare that you can’t shake loose. I want him off this ship . . . I want him dead.”

Lynch turned to Captain Roberts.

“How many men have we got out there?”

“Twenty-three,” Roberts answered. “We’ve got him cornered, there’s no doubt about that. It’s just a question of how to finish him off. I don’t want to lose any more men to the bastard.”

“I’ll go up,” Gault offered.

“No.” Lynch shook his head. “You’ve had a week of this. You’re worn down.”

“So is he . . .” Gault argued.

Lynch smiled faintly.

“He’s our man,” he said. “Let us take care of him.”

Gault hesitated a moment, then nodded. He understood.

“Hey,” Bonner interjected from across the room. “What is this . . . some honor-of-the-corps bullshit?”

“Something like that,” Lynch murmured.

“They’ve got the army, the navy, and the fucking air force up there,” Bonner protested. “That guy is going nowhere. Leave it . . . you’ve done your bit.”

“I—” Lynch stopped and corrected himself. “We . . . can’t leave it. Every minute he’s up there the risk increases that something will go wrong. You know that. We have to take him now.”

“Sure, but—”

“Tom—” Lynch cut him short. “Shut the fuck up.”

Bonner muttered and looked away. Lynch was right. They were all right. He’d done his share. Maybe more than his share. It was their fight. It was time to shut up and let them finish it.

“Captain.” Lynch looked at Roberts. “Tell your men to give me a twenty-second covering fire. Then tell them to hold their fire until they hear from me.”

Roberts looked back at him for a moment, then put the radio to his mouth and spoke quietly and quickly. Lynch slapped a fresh clip into his MP5 and stepped across to the drawing room door on the port side of the yacht. A moment later he dropped his hand. Roberts barked the order into his radio. There was a brief pause, then a deafening and sustained roar of gunfire the length and breadth of the ship. Everyone in the drawing room counted down the seconds. Then the firing stopped. Lynch opened the door and slipped out onto the deck.

Bonner waited a few seconds, then remembered the slabs of Demex on the floor.

"Unless you guys have any objections," he said, "I think I might just park this shit someplace else."

Gault helped him carry the plastique outside, and together they dumped it into the water, where it immediately started to dissolve into a million harmless particles. Then, just as they both stepped back inside the drawing room, there was a loud and ominous explosion from somewhere deep inside the bowels of the ship. Roberts looked at Bonner. From the expression on his face, it was clear that he feared the worst.

"Don't worry about it," the American reassured him.

"What the hell was it?" Roberts asked.

"Murphy's law," Bonner said.

Outside on the main deck Lynch climbed onto the gunwale, hauled himself quickly up onto the upper deck, and lay still. Most of the *Britannia*'s small boats were arrayed along the upper deck. The royal launch had gone, but there were still the royal barge, the sea boat, a couple of skimmers, two dinghies, the duke's runabout, and a garage for the queen's Rolls-Royce which Her Majesty always took on tour for motorcades. The whole deck was a labyrinthine nightmare of light and shadow that offered dozens of places for a man to hide. It was a natural fortress for a man like Doyle, who had already proved that he could inflict horrendous casualties on the surrounding forces as they attempted to winkle him out.

Lynch got to his feet and crept silently past the dark blue hull of the royal barge now pitted and pockmarked with bullet holes. All the time his senses strained to penetrate the enveloping clamor of hovering helicopters and small boats that milled around in the water picking up the last floundering hostages.

Then he heard something. A hiss or a slight scrape. Someone

moving nearby. Lynch's finger tightened on the trigger. His eyes searched the shadows.

Come to me, a lone voice murmured inside his head. *Come to me.*

Something immensely powerful seized him from above and behind and lifted him off his feet. A searing pain lanced down through his spine. Doyle had been hiding inside the sea boat. Reflexively, Lynch dropped his gun, reached up with his hands, and tried to grab hold of his attacker before his neck snapped. He swung his legs up high so that he could reach the royal barge opposite and use his feet to walk up the hull. It gave him just the momentum he needed. With all his strength he kicked off the side of the barge and somersaulted up onto the boat so that he broke his attacker's grip and landed behind him. Then he grabbed hold of Doyle's head and used the same move to break his neck. Had Lynch been a second faster, he would have done it. But Doyle reacted just as fast as Lynch and launched himself over the side of the boat to break Lynch's grip so that they both tumbled to the deck in a tangled, thrashing heap.

Lynch was first onto his feet, propelled by a murderous fury. Doyle was on his way up, something silver glittering in his right hand. Lynch sidestepped the blade, lashed out with the heel of his boot, and kicked Doyle in the head with every ounce of strength in his body. He connected so hard that the shock shivered up to his knee. It was a kick that should have killed an ordinary man. But Doyle, fueled by a lifetime of accumulated rage, seemed anesthetized to ordinary pain. He grunted, staggered backward, and fell. The knife skittered away across the deck. But he was stunned for only a moment. Lynch went after him. Doyle rolled away and under the sea boat. Lynch lunged around the stern to intercept him. He was just in time to catch Doyle as he scrambled out from under the boat. Lynch took two rapid steps and launched himself into the air to deliver a double kick. He connected with both boot heels in Doyle's left side. There was a loud crack and Doyle screamed and staggered away. Lynch landed nimbly and kept after him.

In all his years of service in the special forces of his country, Lynch had no sure way of knowing how many men he had killed. Unlike some of his colleagues, he had never wanted to keep count. It was not his way. Killing was part of his job. His duty. It had never been something he had relished. Now it was different. Something dark and terrible had welled up inside him. Something primitive. He wanted to kill. More than that, he wanted the pleasure of killing. He wanted to tear Doyle apart, to shred his flesh, to feel the last breath of life go out of his body and then obliterate everything that was left. He wanted to remove every filthy trace of Doyle from the face of the earth. And he wanted to do it with his hands.

Doyle retreated backward along the deck. It was over. He was finished and he knew it. Suddenly, inexplicably, he felt something he had never felt before. He felt a chill stab of fear in his heart. He felt it when he looked into Lynch's eyes and realized that it was like seeing his own eyes looking back at him. And there was no mercy in there. No hope. No pity. He felt a wall at his back. He could retreat no farther. He had come up against the steel-framed garage that held the queen's car. The armored Rolls-Royce that went everywhere with the queen on land.

"What are you?" Doyle grunted, his breath coming in ragged bursts. "SAS?"

"No," Lynch said quietly. "Garbage removal."

"Ah." Doyle managed a faint grin of recognition. "The infamous humor of the squadron. Come to settle the score, have you?"

"Something like that," Lynch said, and closed on him.

Doyle sagged against the garage door.

"I don't suppose you'd accept an honorable surrender at this point?" he grimaced.

Lynch hesitated.

Doyle chuckled softly. Then his left hand came up in a blur and he fired. Lynch spun away, but the bullet hit him in the right side and hurled him to the deck. For a moment he almost lost consciousness. He fought it and rolled. The pain in his right side was unbearable. But the suit had held. Nothing was broken. Bullets hammered into the deck around him and howled off into the night. Lynch rolled around the corner of the garage and struggled to his feet. Doyle came after him. Lynch circled around the garage. He saw a small service door, opened it, and slipped inside.

Instantly he found himself in total darkness. The garage smelled of oil and polish. He felt his way through the darkness, his fingers feeling the smooth, curved surfaces of the queen's car, willing his eyes to adjust to the darkness. The door opened and Doyle came in after him.

For a few brief seconds they were equal, Lynch knew. Each hunting the other in the dark. Lynch dropped to the deck and rolled silently under the big car. Desperately, he felt around for the heavy chocks he knew must be holding the wheels in place. Slowly, silently, he began easing them loose. A minute passed, then another. Doyle remained absolutely still, listening, the roar of the swirling forces outside muted to a drone. Then he heard what he was waiting for. He fell to one knee and loosed off two fast shots under the car. The bullets hummed beneath the car and tore through the plywood walls, leaving two perfect holes. Light from outside streamed inside like miniature flashlight beams. Doyle moved slowly around to the front of the car, his eyes struggling to penetrate the gloom.

The garage filled suddenly with a brilliant white light. Doyle stopped, blinded by the glare from the headlights. Lynch prayed that the car had some fuel in it. He touched the ignition wires together and hot-wired the queen's Rolls-Royce. The engine sighed into life. In a single fluid motion Lynch punched the car into gear and stamped on the gas pedal. The car leapt forward before Doyle could react. There was a soft thud, and then he was gone. The three-ton automobile crashed through the garage wall with a rending screech of timber and metal and slewed wildly across the deck.

Lynch slammed the brake down and cut the engine. The car seemed to skid in slow motion across the smooth surface of the deck, carried by the momentum of its own great weight. It slammed into the sea boat, knocked it out of its derrick, and sent it tumbling down the side of the yacht and into the sea. And then the car stopped, its front wheels on the edge of the deck. Lynch leaned his sweating brow against the cold, leather-covered steering wheel and listened to the sound of his racing heart.

"Maybe you could get Madge to sponsor you on the Grand Prix circuit," Gault said.

Lynch shook his head, too tired and sore even to smile.

"I don't think so, John," he said. "I think Red might be right. It's time for me to quit while I'm still in one piece."

"Now you're talking sense," Bonner mumbled nearby.

The three of them sat at the edge of the funnel deck overlooking the stern and watching the spectacle of organized chaos that continued to unfold around them. Helicopters criss-crossed the night sky, radios crackled, searchlights blazed, the warships of Her Majesty's Royal Navy edged ever closer, and the sea boiled with small craft. Then, out of the buffeting wall of noise, the sound of one helicopter rose above the rest. Lynch looked up as the chopper that would carry the queen and Prince Philip to safety hovered down over the fantail. Immediately below him, on the royal deck, two dozen SAS men arranged themselves into a protective huddle. Then everyone waited for the sovereign to appear.

The helicopter hovered closer and closer. Then it bounced gently and settled on the afterdeck. There was a brief pause and then the door to the royal apartments opened for the first time in a week. Judy Stone appeared first, followed by two SAS men. An eerie lull settled over everyone who was gathered there to watch. Gault leaned forward, his gaze focused on Judy. Her face was bleached of all color under the glare of the searchlights, and even from where he sat, Gault could see how tired she was. She hurried toward the waiting helicopter. Behind her, sandwiched between the two SAS troopers, Lynch saw the tiny figure of the queen. Her head was covered by a scarf, and a raincoat had been draped over her shoulders, hiding the bulletproof vest that she wore.

Someone cheered, and it was as if it were the signal for a great, spontaneous release of all the bottled-up fears and emotions that had bedeviled all of them for the past week. The cheer spread and was taken up by the soldiers and sailors and hostages who watched from the surrounding vessels until it washed over the *Britannia* like a great drowning wave of relief. Then came the Duke of Edinburgh, tall and erect, dwarfing the two SAS troopers who flanked him.

"Hey," Bonner yelled to Lynch through the tumult. "You think I might get a knighthood out of all this?"

Lynch shrugged.

"Think what it could do for business . . ." Bonner added.

Lynch smiled and was about to answer, when he saw a sinister rush of movement on the deck behind Bonner. Everybody was watching the queen and Prince Philip. No one expected to see a dead man come back to life.

Doyle stumbled out of the shadows of the funnel deck, his face streaked with blood and doubled over with pain as he struggled to hold together his shattered chest.

Lynch remembered the grenades.

He opened his mouth to shout the alarm, but the words froze in his throat. There was no time for him to do anything but act.

He ignored the pain in his side, leapt to his feet, and sprinted past the startled faces of Gault and Bonner. At that moment Doyle approached the edge of the deck and hurled himself toward the densely packed crowd of soldiers on the deck below with the queen and Prince Philip in their midst. Lynch hit him in midair. He wrapped his arms tightly around Doyle and his momentum carried both of them over the rail. John Gault and Tom Bonner were the only ones who saw them fall. A slow, tumbling fall down the side of the royal yacht, locked together in a death grip. They hit the water with a terrific splash and the dark ocean swallowed them both.

Gault and Bonner scrambled to their feet and ran to the ship's rail. Their eyes raked the black, boiling water below. Others saw them running and sensed that something dreadful had happened. Then, all the grenades on Doyle's body exploded at once. They saw the vivid red flash below the surface, heard the dull thump of the explosion, and then a violent fountain of spray leapt up at them. The water seethed like a caldron of blood and foam. Then it settled and there was nothing.

"No . . ." Gault muttered faintly. "Please, God, no . . ."

Bonner's face had turned gray. His knuckles gleamed white as his fingers ground into the deck rail.

"Why . . . ?" he mumbled helplessly. "Why . . . ?"

Behind them the rotors of the royal helicopter rose into a crescendo. But neither of them heard it. The wash from the spinning rotors snatched at their clothes, but neither of them felt it. The cheering rose to a new pitch as the helicopter lifted gently into the air. Then it wheeled away from the ravaged royal yacht and thudded swiftly off into the night.

The British Crown was safe once more.

Epilogue

From a distance the house looked abandoned and incomplete. As though the builder had gone broke before he could finish it and it had become the haunt of bums and vandals. Tom Bonner had done his best to clean it up in the few days he had been there. He had swept out the cobwebs, the birds' nests, and the mouse droppings on the floor. He had fixed the door and the broken boards in the windows, where kids had forced their way in to light a fire in the grate and spend the night drinking. And he had cleaned out their empty beer cans and wine bottles. He had even cut back the weeds and the long grass that had taken over the small garden. It had angered him to see that the cottage had fallen into disrepair so quickly, and he wished he could do more. But there wasn't time. He had to be in London the next day to catch the evening flight to Miami. The chief executive of the fastest-growing maritime security firm in the United States couldn't afford to take too much time off in his first year of business. Though, he had to admit as he looked down the heather-clad mountainside to the shining surface of Loch Linnhe, it was tempting to stay longer. After three days he was beginning to understand what Lynch had seen in this place. The solitude, the freshness of the mornings, the ever-changing light on the mountainside, the seductive fragrance of new heather.

Bonner checked the knot in his tie, fidgeted with his shirt cuffs, and glanced at his watch again. It was a few minutes before eleven o'clock in the morning, and he felt ridiculous in his dark suit and highly polished shoes, standing alone on the mountainside in front of Lynch's empty cottage with only a rented Range Rover for company. He looked at the small mound of stones nearby and thought how simple and unassuming a monument it was. If it wasn't for the fact that the stones were cemented in place, it could easily have been mistaken for another marker on a hiking trail. There wasn't even a plaque to indicate who or what it memorialized. Only those who needed to know would understand its significance. Until a few days ago Bonner hadn't even known what a cairn was. He had since learned that it was the highland way of doing things. Of remembering someone important. It was modest, timeless, and in keeping with the spirit of the country. Lynch would have approved. Bonner was certain of that.

Almost a year had passed since the hijacking of the *Britannia*. Almost a year since the armed forces of the United Kingdom and the United States had carried out the most spectacular hostage rescue in history. Almost a year since Lynch had died for Queen and country. Much had happened since then. The United States had seen action in the third world again. There had been an uproar in Parliament about the cost of repairs to the royal yacht. The queen had offered to pay for them herself, but the Prime Minister had declared it would come out of the defense budget, as it always had, and now there was talk of a new move against him in Cabinet. And Tom Bonner had quit the navy to launch his new business, just as he intended, and its success had surprised even him. Though he still had to find the right man to run his London office.

The sound of approaching car engines drifted up the glen. Bonner turned to look down the track, and a moment later the first of three Navy Land Rovers bumped into view. He walked back across the hillside a few paces and waited. The Land Rovers grunted to a halt in front of the cottage and the Navy drivers switched off the engines. The doors of the lead vehicle opened and Sir Malcolm Porter got out. He was dressed formally, like Bonner, and accompanied by a Navy chaplain. The doors of the second Land Rover slammed and John Gault appeared with Judy Stone, the two of them also wearing civilian clothes. The third vehicle brought the men from Lynch's old squad who had also come to pay their respects at this small, private ceremony to honor their fallen comrade.

Bonner greeted them warmly. He had come to know all of them in the past year and it had been only a few days since he had renewed his acquaintanceship with them at the official awards ceremony at Buckingham Palace when the queen had presented decorations to those officers and men who had played a key role in Operation Scepter. Lynch had been awarded a posthumous Victoria Cross. It was the highest military honor his nation could bestow and the only Victoria Cross to come out of the entire operation. His parents and a younger brother had traveled down from Inverness to accept the medal, and then they had graciously turned it over to the SBS, where it would be enshrined in perpetual glory at the squadron's headquarters in Poole.

Bonner had also attended a memorial service at Westminster Abbey, held a few weeks after the operation, for all those who had died during the hijack of the *Britannia.* But for those who were closest to Lynch, it wasn't enough. They had wanted to do something more. Something fitting. This memorial, on the beautiful Scottish hillside where Lynch had been happiest, was their personal tribute.

When everyone was ready, they gathered silently around the cairn to pay their last respects. Like the monument itself and the man it memorialized, the service was a dignified, no-nonsense affair. At the end Porter spoke for all of them when he paid homage to those qualities of honor and duty that Lynch embodied for all of them. Then they stood for a moment of silence and the only sound was the gentle rush of the wind in the heather. To Bonner it sounded eerily like the murmur of the sea. He was glad when it was over and everyone turned to go.

No one spoke until they were ready to get back into their cars. Then Judy Stone looked at Gault and Porter and Bonner and asked quietly: "What will happen to this place?"

Porter shrugged.

"Commander Lynch's will is in the hands of the Navy's legal department," he said. "I imagine this property will go to his family eventually. Either that or it will go to auction and they will receive the proceeds."

Judy nodded.

"Probably get picked up by some property developer for a song," she said.

"No," Bonner decided abruptly.

The three of them looked at him, puzzled.

"I talked to him about this place a few days before he was killed," the big man added. "There's no way I'm going to let it fall into the hands of some asshole who plans to build condos all over it. I'll talk to the family. We'll work something out to keep this place the way it is. Let everybody enjoy it. That's what he would want."

Judy smiled, leaned forward and kissed him on the cheek. Then Gault stepped forward and shook Bonner's hand. Then Porter.

"Superb idea," he said.

Bonner allowed himself a small smile. It *was* a superb idea. Lynch would have been amused at the irony, of course. But he would have approved. Bonner knew he would have approved.

"We thought we might stop off in town for a drink on the way back," Gault added. "Sort of a wake. Are you coming?"

"Sure," Bonner agreed. "I'll be along in a minute. You guys go ahead. There's just one last thing I want to do here."

Gault nodded. All three of them understood. Or thought they did. They turned and climbed back into the cars. A few moments later the three Land Rovers bumped back down the steep track the way they had come in. Bonner waited until the last vehicle had disappeared from view. Then he walked back to the lonely cairn. He stood and stared at it for a long time. Then he reached into his jacket pocket and pulled out a royal-blue velvet case about the size of a fat wallet. He opened the case and looked at the golden medal with its blue and white ribbon that nestled inside on a blue satin cushion.

"They don't hand out too many of these to Americans, pal," he said quietly. "A president, a general . . . and now me. For services to the British Crown, no less."

He snapped the case shut and held it lightly in the palm of his hand. Then he smiled.

"I can't tell you how good this would look on my desk," he added. "And I can't begin to tell you the kind of good it would do my business."

His smile broadened. The stones on top of the cairn were still loose. He had asked the builder to leave them like that till the next day. He removed the topmost stone and put the case in the small, secret hollow underneath. Then he replaced the stone.

At last he was done. He stepped back and gave the snappiest, sharpest salute he had given in years. It would be the last time he saluted anybody in this lifetime, he knew.

It was a salute only fitting for a knight of the realm.

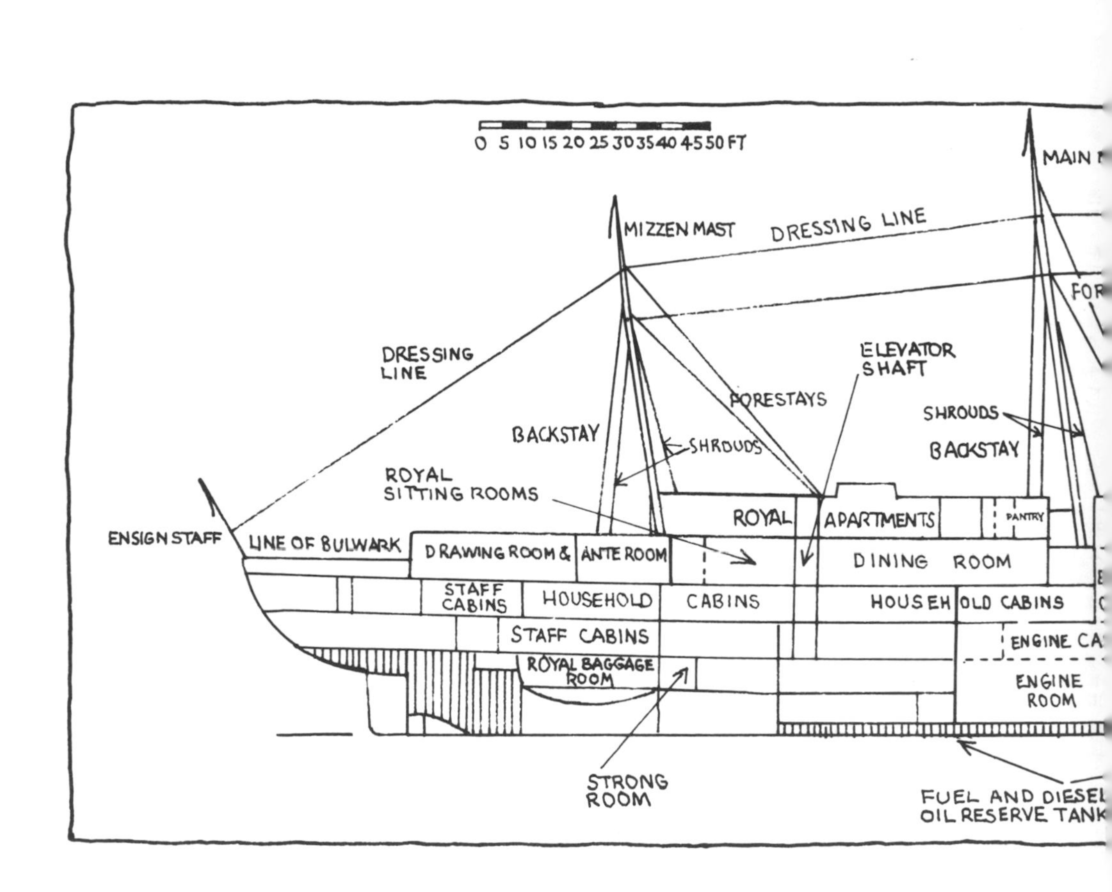
0 5 10 15 20 25 30 35 40 45 50 FT
MIZZEN MAST
DRESSING LINE
DRESSING LINE
ELEVATOR SHAFT
FORESTAYS
SHROUDS
BACKSTAY
BACKSTAY
SHROUDS
ROYAL SITTING ROOMS
ENSIGN STAFF
LINE OF BULWARK
DRAWING ROOM & ANTE ROOM
ROYAL APARTMENTS
PANTRY
DINING ROOM
STAFF CABINS
HOUSEHOLD CABINS
HOUSEHOLD CABINS
STAFF CABINS
ROYAL BAGGAGE ROOM
ENGINE ROOM
STRONG ROOM